"An epic thriller, captivating from beginning to end. Pope Annalisa compels readers to contemplate their own notions of spirituality, good and evil, power and justice, in the manner of the best literary fiction."

—Adam Marsh, editor, former literary agent of Reece Halsey North

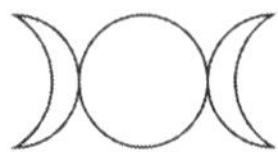

"I could not put this book down! Not only is the plot a real page-turner, but the book carries deeper messages about the mystery of why people are so psychically and physically fragmented. More importantly, it posits a way through our human dilemma to embrace our wholeness and our power."

— Dr. Kathi J Kemper, Wake Forest University School of Medicine, author of *The Holistic Pediatrician.*

POPE
Annalisa

a novel by Peter Canova

BOOK ONE OF THE FIRST SOULS TRILOGY

Trimountaine Publishing

Palm Beach, Florida

ISBN: 978-0-9821813-0-0 (hardcover)
ISBN: 978-0-9821813-1-7 (paperback)

Please send any inquiries to:
Trimountaine Publishing
P.O. Box 2320
Palm Beach, FL 33480
E-mail: trimountpub@comcast.net
Website: trimountpub.com; popeannalisa.com

Design and production by Deborah Lash, Lashomatic Design
Photography by Matt McKee
Model Sheena Williams provided by Exxcel Model and Talent Agency
Makeup by Coco Grace
Bishop's robe provided by The Costume Company
Contributive cover concept by Jahim Baskerville
Editorial services by Maggie Deslaurier

Interior images reproduced by permission of:
Title page: The Popess from the Medieval Scapini Deck reproduced by permission of U.S. Games Systems, Inc., Stamford, CT 06902 USA. Copyright (c)1995 by U.S. Games Systems, Inc. Further reproduction prohibited.

Image Credits:

p. 126: image courtesy of Florida Center for Instructional Technology, College of Education, U. Of Southern Florida

p. 156: School of Nuremberg; Solar King and Lunar Queen. (Scenes below: Achilles in battle, Alexander before Babylon, Alexander and Diogenes). Illuminated page from Splendor Solis: 7 Treatises on the Philosopher's Stone, ca. 1531-1532. Parchment. Inv. 78 D 3. Photo: Jörg P. Anders.
Location: Kupferstichkabinett, Staatliche Museen zu Berlin, Berlin, Germany
Photo Credit : Bildarchiv Preussischer Kulturbesitz / Art Resource, NY

p. 273: Detail of *The opposing fleets of the Turks and the Holy League at Lepanto*, Vasari, Giorgio (1511-1574) Location: Sala Regia, Vatican Palace, Vatican State; Photo Credit : Scala / Art Resource, NY

DEDICATIONS

To Professor Elaine Pagels and Dr. Stephan Hoeller, two people who helped resurrect invaluable ancient wisdom and made it intelligible to the modern world.

To Peter, James, and Michael — father, brother, and cousin who should have been here but couldn't make it.

BOOK ONE OF THE FIRST SOULS TRILOGY

Visit POPEANNALISA.COM

for background information on the book and
The First Souls Trilogy. Learn what Pope Annalisa has
in common with quantum physics, molecular biology,
and Jungian depth psychology.

ACKNOWLEDGEMENTS

The author wishes to acknowledge the following people, each of whom helped in their own way in their own time:

The female trinity—Kathleen O'Keefe, Ursula Martens, and Petronelle Cook, without whose help and support this would have been a far more impoverished work.

Adam Marsh, former agent turned editor, who edited this book. He saw something in the pile that caught his eye and then his imagination.

Peter, Sophia, and Nicholas—I hope their uncle's book can inspire them some day just like they inspire their uncle in their own way.

All the people in the book clubs who gave me helpful feedback.

The unseen force that inspired me to pay attention to the matters that counted, and gave me the ability to share my experience in words.

TABLE OF CONTENTS

POPE *Annalisa*

a novel by Peter Canova

BOOK ONE OF THE FIRST SOULS TRILOGY

DE REGNVM ANNALISA AFRICANA
PONTIFEX MAXIMVS ECCLESIASTVM ROMANVM

MAP OF KEY EVENTS

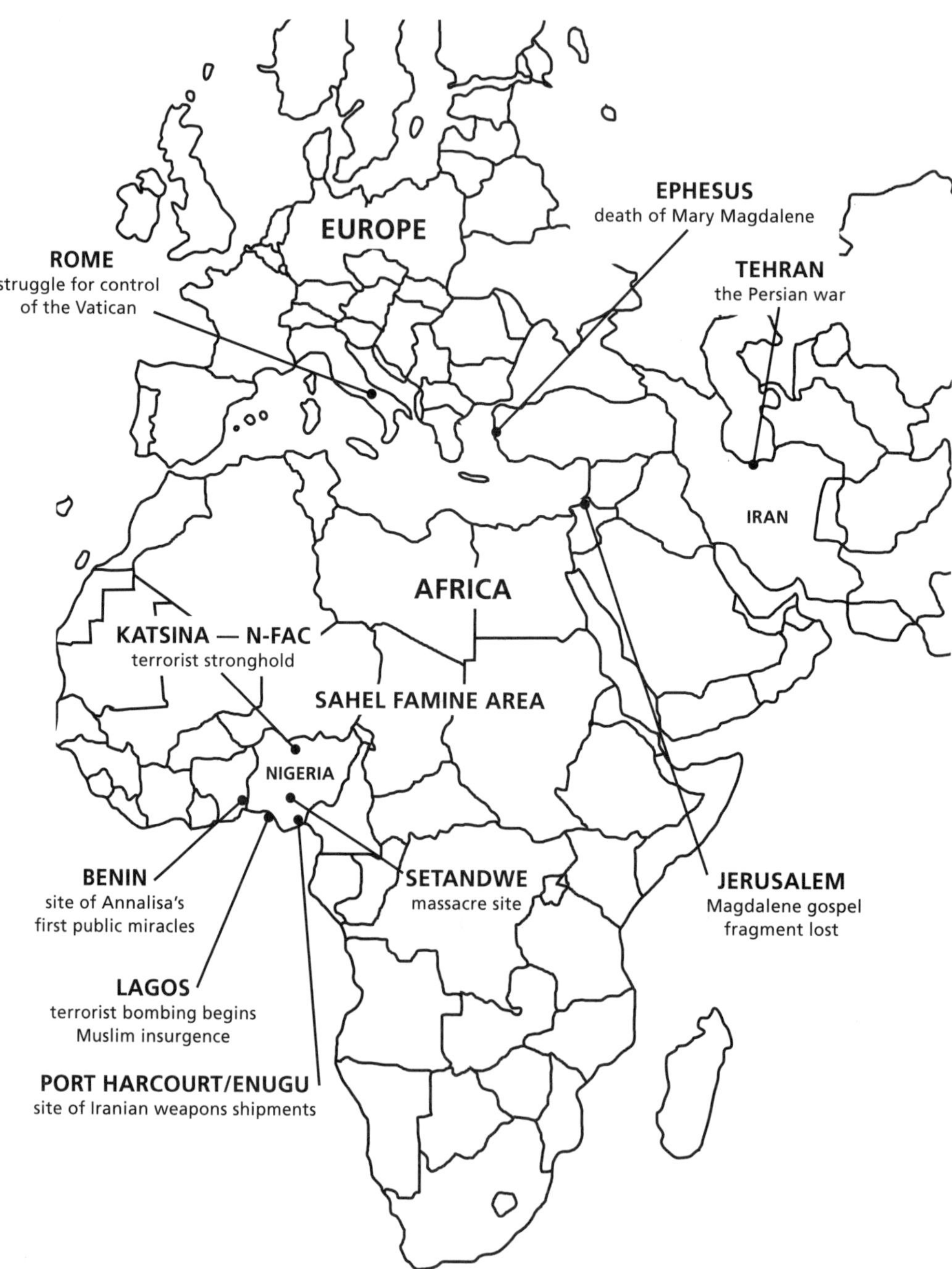

DRAMATIS PERSONAE

THE VATICAN

Robert Avernis American CIA liaison to the Vatican

Cardinal Giacomo Berletti prominent conservative cardinal who comes to support Annalisa

Pope Clement XV embattled Church leader prior to the Persian War

Cardinal Reynald De Faissy supporter of Annalisa and Roncalli

Ubaldo Deci cousin of Robert Avernis and lawyer for Mafia chief Ippolito Maniati

Cardinal Aldo DeGolia one of the seven primary opposition cardinals, he is the most phlegmatic of the group but a clever orator

Bishop Alvaro Maria Delgado leader of the fanatic Milites Domini order

Leo Dusayne Robert Avernis' superior at the CIA Rome station

Teresa Ferentinos British television reporter and religious scholar

Cardinal Gianmarco LoPresti one of the seven primary opposition cardinals, he is the most vigilant against the advent of the Great Heretic

Cardinal Heinrich Mannheim leader of the seven primary opposition cardinals against Annalisa. He wants to replace Clement as pope

Monsignor Desmond O'Keefe prefect of the Vatican Library, he is a friend of Roncalli and supporter of Annalisa

Cardinal Peter "Pietro" Roncalli Secretary to Pope Clement XV and supporter of Clement and Annalisa against Mannheim and the seven primary opposition cardinals, though he vacillates on Annalisa's true nature

Cardinal Francisco Tormada head of the Congregation for the Doctrine of the Faith, the Vatican doctrinal police, and one of the seven primary opposition cardinals

Cardinal Silvestro Trevi one of the seven primary opposition cardinals and Mannheim's most trusted associate

Cardinal Jut Van Kluysen in charge of Vatican finances and one of the seven primary opposition cardinals

Cardinal Henri Villendot one of the seven primary opposition cardinals, he vies for prominence with Mannheim

Colonel Roald Zugli commander of the Swiss Guards and Vatican security

NIGERIA

Alhaji Kadir al Kadu head of the Nigerian N-FAC terrorist network

Annalisa Basanjo Mercyite nun under investigation by the Church for alleged miracles she performed

Hakim Annalisa's uncle, a brigand and N-FAC terrorist

Bishop Ogunsanya bishop of Lagos who vehemently opposes Annalisa

Jill Tierney colleague of Teresa Ferentinos at UNN News

TEHRAN

Ayatollah Reza Gorbani a junior member of the Iranian Ruling Council and lover of Fatilah Jahani

Grand Ayatollah Ali Havenei supreme religious and political leader of Iran

Fatilah Celine Marchand Jahani French/Iranian woman running weapons for the Iranians

WASHINGTON, D.C.

John Davidson president of the United States

Virginia Davidson First Lady

Rachel Worth National Security Advisor to the president

JERUSALEM

Gallie Herron Israeli religious scholar and anthropologist

GLOSSARY OF ECCLESIASTICAL TERMS

Aeon(s) a spiritual being or entity, a projection of God's substance (see **Emanation** below). They may be thought of as angels or godlike beings. They were always paired as masculine and feminine forces. Thus, the Christ Spirit and the Holy Spirit were a masculine and feminine pairing. Aeons were aspects of God's essence projected downward into dimensions of increasing density, the lowest of which is the human soul in a material body.

Canons, canon law laws and regulations made and adopted by Church authorities

Cardinal highest dignitary of the Roman Catholic Church and counselor of the pope

Colleges, the College of Cardinals colleges are groupings within the Church having common purposes. The College of Cardinals consists of all Catholic cardinals as a collective body

Congregations different departments assisting in the running of Church affairs

Consistory an assembly of cardinals to advise the pope on matters of importance

Consubstantiality "of the same substance." In orthodox theology it refers to Jesus being of the same substance as God. In an expanded (heretical) sense it refers to all human souls as being derived from God's essence as opposed to being separate creations from nothing. (See **Emanation** below)

Curia or Roman curia the collection of departments, congregations, or councils that assist the pope in the governing of the Church or Holy See

Defrock to strip someone of his priesthood or holy orders

Diocese jurisdictions or districts of the Church governed by a bishop or cardinal

Ecclesiastical of or relating to a church, especially as an organized institution

Emanation(s) projections of God's substance as opposed to separate creations out of nothing (*ex nihilo*). Emanantionism typically holds that these projections or spiritual beings (called *Aeons*) occur in pairs representing the masculine/femine, yin/yang duality experienced in the material world. Each Aeon emanates another Aeon like descending rungs of a ladder. With each emanation, however, some of God's original light or awareness is lost. This is because God is the Whole or the Source. Since each successive Aeon is projected further from God, the degree of shadow or ignorance it contains increases with each emanation. Restated, the further the emanated being is *from* God, the more it experiences ignorance *of* God and a greater sense of separateness. The human soul is the lowest manifestation of this emanated spiritual force or process because it is mixed with the material world in the form of a fleshly human. The belief in emanation, though once held by many Jews and early Christians, is considered heresy by the Church

Ecumenical Council a gathering of the highest ruling powers of the Catholic Church to decide Church doctrine

Gnosis/Gnostics *gnosis* is the Greek word for "knowledge." It is not theoretical or intellectual knowledge, but rather knowledge gained from direct experience. Gnostics were among the first Christians. They believe Jesus imparted specific knowledge that would enable people to have a direct experience of the divine rather than believing in God's existence through abstract faith.

Holy See the diocese of the bishop of Rome (the pope). The authority, jurisdiction, and governing functions of the papacy as distinguished from the Vatican City State, which is a geopolitical entity

Papal infallibility a controversial Catholic doctrine holding that when a pope speaks on matters of faith and morals *ex cathedra* (in his official capacity as head of the Church), his judgments are free from error

Pontiff another name for the pope

Prefect a chief administrative official of a Vatican congregation or department

Prelate generally, a high Church official such as a cardinal or bishop

Synod a council or gathering, usually of bishops, to discuss and determine matters affecting the entire Church, narrower in scope than ecumenical councils

Vatican City the world's smallest sovereign political state

Vatican City government the bureaucracy that the oversees various political and economic functions of the Vatican City as distinguished from the Holy See, which governs Church religious matters of the Catholic Church

Ephesus, Roman Asia Province

And how is it thane of wymmen that we blameth tham so
In songs and in rymes; and in bokes eke thereto
To segge that they be false and vuele to leove, ffykel and . . . untrue?
More mildness and goodness is not many creature on Earth
as we may see by Mary Maudelyn.
— *Christine de Pisan,* The Book of the City of Ladies, *1364–1420*

AD 68

"Mary known as Magdalene, of Judea province," the soldier said, reading out the death proclamation following a hand signal from Lucius Mannemius, "you are guilty of sedition against the emperor and people of Rome. For your activities with the sect known as Christians, you are sentenced to die in the arena this day."

The wind moaned as it blew into the arena, then passed with a faint whine through the stone arches at either end. The stadium of Ephesus was built into the southern slope of Mount Pion. Once used only for competitive games, it now served other purposes under the Roman Empire. Mannemius had ordered the citizens of Ephesus to the stadium to witness the extermination of the Christians at the eastern end of the arena.

Ephesus was dominated by one of the seven wonders of the ancient world, the Temple of Artemis, and the goddess' following was strong. Artemis had watched over the city for ages; who were these arrogant Christian upstarts to deny all gods save their own? Even the emperors, who claimed to be deities themselves, allowed worship of the old gods.

For the past week, Lucius Mannemius had filled the stadium's seats with the curious, the idle, or those who shared his resentment of the new Christian cult. Today was a new day, and they were anxious to see more Christians mauled, burned, and tortured. The latest victims were tied to posts in the stadium grounds.

A canopy had been erected over the seats on the north side for the man who was conducting the spectacles. Lucius Ennericus Mannemius sat five feet above the dirt floor of the arena with the Praetorian captain Marcus Trocanus. Two other Praetorian guards stood on either side of them, and four others stood below them inside the arena. The crowd buzzed with anticipation.

But the games had stopped and the mob was silenced when three people had marched into the stadium. They had halted between the soldiers standing on either side of the dusty arena floor beneath Mannemius' seat. One of the women stepped forward. It was Mary Magdalene. She had come to publicly surrender herself. Mannemius could barely contain himself. His plan had worked. He finally had her, and he had wasted no time in her sentencing.

"Mary Magdalene," he said with his eyes closed, her name oozing out between his gritted teeth like a slow release of erotic pleasure. He peered down at the woman possessed of lustrous red-gold hair. She looked oddly Grecian in nature for a Jew; her features were like those of a sculpted goddess. With startling effectiveness, the serenity of her unlined face concealed her age of more than sixty years along with any fear she might be feeling.

Seeing her standing with one leg thrust forward, head held high, long hair and flowing robes cascading in the wind, Mannemius realized that he had never felt such power and authority radiate from any woman before. Her comportment was that of a Roman general with some unseen legion poised at her back. "Long have I hunted you around the world, and now we come to the end," Mannemius said. "You have heard your sentence."

"Lucius Mannemius." The woman's voice rang out loud and firm even for the superb acoustics of the stadium. **"You have stated before all Ephesus that if I surrendered myself to the authorities you would stop persecuting the innocent. I am here, and I submit myself. Will you make good on your word, or show yourself a liar to all?"**

Mannemius rose from his chair and walked down the steps into the arena until he stood a few feet from Magdalene and the two companions flanking her. He looked at Magdalene. His gaze then left her and he surveyed her companions.

The man with light brown hair and well-defined muscles displayed a steady gaze that indicated no fear. The young woman's countenance was almost ethereal, like she was somewhere other than this arena of death. Her luminous olive-skinned beauty stood in stark contrast to the matted dustiness of the arena grounds.

"You I do not know," he said, referring to Tezrah, Magdalene's young companion. "But you," Mannemius said, looking at the man, "you I know. I heard you died in Parthia, Averna."

"Sorry to disappoint you," Averna replied. "You look old, Germanicus."

Mannemius flinched. That derogatory reference to his resemblance to the hated German barbarians had followed him throughout his life, but his pale blue eyes soon rekindled with flame. "That's what comes from exile and forced retirement." Mannemius replied. "But I'm regaining my youth today, and you will wish you had died in the East before this day is over."

Hearing that, Magdalene knew that the mob was the only means she had to save her friends. She spoke again in a voice for all to hear. **"You promised if I surrendered that all others would be pardoned. That includes my two companions."**

The crowd grumbled, but this time in support of Magdalene. Trocanus leaned toward Mannemius and whispered, "They may want to see Christians killed, but they appreciate bravery, particularly from a woman. Keep your promise, Mannemius, or we'll lose the mob."

Mannemius bit his lower lip. The corners of his eyes creased in hatred at Averna, but the mob roared its support for the same woman whom they would cheer to see executed in a few minutes. He cursed under his breath, then shouted to the spectators, "Know that I am a man of my word, people of Ephesus. Magdalene has submitted herself to my authority. I will release all other prisoners as promised."

The crowd registered their vocal approval. They might be annoyed at being cheated out of some sport, but seeing such a brave woman die would make up for the ones the Romans were sparing, and women's deaths always aroused the crowds to a near sexual frenzy.

Mannemius gave a signal. The Praetorians began to untie the prisoners in the center of the arena. Some of them had been severely tortured, and Magdalene walked toward them. A Praetorian guard moved to intercept her, but he stepped back when the curious Mannemius gave a slight jerk of his head. The guard let her pass.

One woman crawled on her elbows in the dirt with bone shards protruding through the flesh of her broken legs. Magdalene bent down to hold her. She cradled and kissed the woman's head for a minute, then placed her hand on the woman's legs. She prayed in hushed tones inaudible to the buzzing crowd. Then, in a strong, clear voice for all to hear, she said, **"Stand and walk to your freedom, daughter of God, for the light of Christ and Sophia has healed you!"**

The woman tried standing, wobbly at first on fawn-like legs, but she took one step, then another and another and . . . she walked! The crowd rose to its feet as one. They emitted a collective gasp, then went deathly silent. The Praetorians stepped back in shock as the woman walked by them.

"Brothers and sisters," Magdalene shouted, **"be not infected by the**

sickness of the authorities. Humans do not revel in the torture and sacrifice of others to pacify the fear, rage, and anger in our own hearts. This is not the real world, but a sick dream from which you must awaken, and the message I bring is an awakening, a cure to the sickness and fear in your own souls."

"What manner of woman is this?" the startled Trocanus said to Mannemius.

Mannemius looked at the faces around the arena. He knew he had to do something quickly. "Sorcery, witchcraft!" he yelled. "Yes, they heal their own, but they curse you."

As Mannemius spoke, Mary continued making her rounds of the prisoners. She laid hands on one man with angry, oozing chest burns, blackened and blistered by the merciless prodding of hot irons. In minutes, the burns faded and vanished. On seeing this, the mob broke loose in pandemonium.

"This is the real world," Magdalene shouted, pointing to the healed man. **"Go *inside* of yourselves to go *outside* of the world, where goodness, healing, and mercy are the rule of being."**

Mannemius pointed to Magdalene. "Seize her!" he screamed to the guards standing beside him at the arena's edge. They hesitated, still startled by what they had seen. "Order them to bind that witch before she turns this crowd on us," Mannemius said to Trocanus.

"Seize her now," Trocanus commanded. "Clear the other prisoners out of the arena." The Praetorians jumped at the sound of his voice.

"She is too dangerous," Mannemius muttered to himself, resolving that Magdalene must be dispatched quickly. He ordered her tied between two posts in the center arena, then commanded that she be scourged as he and Trocanus approached her.

While they were binding her, she called to the crowd, **"I came here to die today though I have committed no crime. I die today because I demanded the freedom to seek God. I resisted the power of the authorities who tried to turn my face from God and heaven. You saw with your own eyes the people who were healed. That is what God does through those of us who wake to His presence; that is why they are murdering us."**

At a hand signal from Mannemius, one of the Praetorians slapped Magdalene hard across the face. The young soldier withdrew his hand quickly with a grimace on his face, as if the blow had hurt him as well. Averna surged forward to defend Mary, but the guards restrained him.

"LET HER SPEAK!" the crowd roared.

Mannemius knew her miracles and her bravery were winning them over, but fearing the capriciousness of the mob, he allowed her to remain ungagged.

"All are equal before God," Magdalene cried. **"The slave has as much right to live as the master, the wife as much right to be heard as the husband. These realizations shall heal you!"**

The crowd was silent. That meant they were listening, a fact not lost on Mannemius. "Honeyed words," he interjected, appealing to the mob. "These Christians are devious. They conduct secret rites where they devour flesh and blood. They refuse to serve in the army, and they practice witchcraft as you just saw. Rome is protecting you from them!"

Before Magdalene could respond, Mannemius signaled for the flagellation to begin. The first crack of the whip against her back cut her words in mid-speech. The Roman flagellum contained barbs that shredded the flesh, and Magdalene's skin was no exception. Twenty times the whip descended, and strips of bloody tissue hung from her body like flowing red ribbons.

Mannemius cast a wary gaze over the arena mob. Despite his words and the usual bloodlust of the spectators, the crowd remained silent. No roars of approval, no egging on the torturers. Magdalene was quiet after the first gasp of shock at the flagellum contacting her body. Mannemius could actually see many people in the crowd wincing with each bite of the whip. This was not good. "The lions, quickly," he commanded the Praetorians.

They knew what to do; they had had considerable practice on many before her. After a few minutes, a dozen men wheeled in a covered wagon. The roars from underneath the covering made known to all what lay beneath. The cart stopped near a metal spike affixed in the ground with a heavy iron ring. They uncovered the cart, and the mane of a large male lion came into view. The beast had a collar around its neck, and the attached chain extended beneath the bars of the cage.

A man carefully measured out the chain to the twelfth link and affixed it to the spiked ring. The cart then moved forward, and as the animal's chain started to draw tight, the man unlatched the door to the cage. He then ran toward the front of the wagon. As the wagon drove out of the stadium, the lion was pulled back and out of its cage.

It made a ferocious noise as it became aware of its relative freedom, and for a minute it bellowed at the crowd. It clawed the dirt and began a slow walk to orient itself. Everyone could see this was not meant to be a quick death, but a torture. The chain was not long enough to allow the beast full access to Mary, whose spread-eagled arms were tied with enough slack to let her kneel. But, the lion was still close enough that its claws, and perhaps a bit of its jaw, could just reach her.

The lion seemed in no hurry. After its circumferential exploration, it walked slowly in Mary's direction. It paused, sniffed at the air in front of her, and extended a paw. The animal took a few innocuous swipes, almost like a kitten at play, then reared back its shoulder and struck a vicious blow. The crowd gasped. Tezrah fell to her knees. The lion's claws had removed a portion of Mary's scalp and the side of her face.

"Mary!" Averna bellowed. A Praetorian grabbed his arm, but he butted his head into the man's face and broke loose. He ran toward the lion as if to plow into it like a human spear, but two other soldiers intercepted and restrained him, clubbing him with sword hilts. He staggered forward, dropped to his knees, and then toppled into the dirt.

Men now came in and distracted the lion away from Mary as Mannemius had ordered. Mannemius shouted, "Admit your crimes and the crimes of the Christians to all present, woman, and I might spare you."

Magdalene knew Mannemius lied. He believed she would die. He was merely trying to incite the mob against Christians. This man had hunted her for years, and he was responsible for the deaths of so many whom she had known and loved. He was the incarnation of every evil that had shaped her life, of everything that had tried to dominate and suppress her, and now he stood there with the smug look of triumph on his face.

Her mouth moved, but the mutilation by the lion rendered her speech difficult. Trocanus motioned to Tezrah. The young woman ran forward. She vomited twice at the sight of her friend's face hanging down in a skull-like half grin of exposed teeth. Regaining control of herself, she put her ear to Mary's mangled lips and relayed her words to the crowd. "She says that being prey for lions is preferable to being devoured by animals pretending to be human." She put her ear to Mary's mouth again. "She forgives you, Mannemius, and all the others, and she thanks you for helping demonstrate God's power. She blesses all here and asks them to think about what they see today." Again, she placed an ear near to her friend. "Truly, all are equal before God. Let her death show a woman's heart and courage are equal to a man's, that women and others deemed lowly are worthy of life."

With a violent motion of his hand, Mannemius cut short any further talk. "The power of your God, you say? If your God is so powerful, let him save you now." Mannemius ordered the men who had been distracting the lion to leave. The beast now had its full attention on Magdalene. It emitted a fearsome roar as it walked toward her, but then something strange happened. Magdalene moved her leg in the lion's direction, and it licked at her calf like it was grooming one of its own cubs.

Gasps and murmurs issued from thousands of voices. People stood and pointed to a spectacle they could hardly believe. The lion, which had mauled her so severely minutes before, had become tame immediately after Mannemius challenged the Christian God. For many minutes, the entire stadium was frozen in a living fresco.

When Magdalene finally tried to speak, Tezrah did not look for permission to relay her next words. "She says God has given you the choice, Mannemius. If you want her dead, you must slay her yourself."

Mannemius' lips pulled inward. "Slay her then! Do it now!" he ordered the soldiers.

The crowd roared like a thousand lions. "SPARE HER! SPARE HER!"

"Remember what you have seen here, people of Ephesus," Tezrah cried. "The authorities have no power over you except what you give them through fear and ignorance. Do not let them determine your fates. Turn your lives to God and seize your own destinies!"

Trocanus and the Praetorians looked around in wonder at what had transpired.

"Come with me, Trocanus," Mannemius said. As they neared Magdalene, he commanded a Praetorian, "Run her through."

The man hesitated.

"Trocanus?" Mannemius said.

"Leave her, Mannemius," the Praetorian captain replied. "Look at those wounds. She will die anyway."

"Are you actually afraid of this mob?" Mannemius said.

Trocanus' hand clutched into a tight fist, and drops of sweat gathered along the creases of his forehead. "She does not deserve to die," the Praetorian replied.

"What? Who are you to decide that?" Mannemius shouted. "I order you to kill her!"

Trocanus shook his head and darted his eyes toward each of the surrounding soldiers. Following his silent command, not one of them moved.

"You think to disobey me, is that it?" Mannemius said. He drew his short sword and walked toward Mary. As he raised his weapon overhead to deliver the blow, the cry from the mob obscured Mannemius' shriek, but his bellow was not one of triumph. It was, rather, a death growl because Trocanus' sword had run him through the midsection.

"Enough, you bloody old bastard!" Mannemius, eyes opened wide in amazement, heard Trocanus' words through his shock. Gushing blood flowed through the fingers clutched to his stomach. Six other guards cast their fates with their leader's decision and ran Mannemius through with their swords as he stood transfixed on Trocanus' blade.

The Praetorians simultaneously withdrew their swords, and Mannemius crumpled to the dust. The stadium was shocked into silence, as if their hatred had died with Mannemius.

Trocanus ordered the lion removed, and he shouted to the crowd, "The games are done in Ephesus. Go to your homes!" He quickly ordered the Praetorians into formation, and they marched toward the southwestern gate. On his way past Averna he said, "See to her," pointing to Magdalene. "I think she cannot survive long."

"Why are you doing this?" Averna asked.

Trocanus' eyes darted to the ground. "I am a soldier of Rome," he said, and he gestured back toward Magdalene. "But she was commanded by . . . by something greater than an emperor." With that, he turned and joined ranks with his men, and they marched off. The crowd emptied their seats and slowly gathered around the body of the nearly dead woman.

Magdalene clutched at Tezrah's robe and pulled her close, whispering to her. *"The way shown by the Messiah has been corrupted. The false god of this world still rules and clouds their vision. They have not understood, even those who walked with Jesus. I was given the message of truth for them. They were not ready to receive; perhaps it was not yet destined for me to give. Now I am silenced in death, but the truth must be heard. I shall return. I . . ."* Her words faded to a faint rasp only Tezrah could hear. And when Magdalene gave up her life, every person gathered there would bear witness in later years to their children and grandchildren that in their skin and bones and on the hairs of their flesh they had felt a tangible force withdrawing from the arena.

"A great soul has departed," Tezrah said, "and hers was no small death. We dwell in darkness, and she tried to light our way home, for God dwelled within her."

The throng pressed around Tezrah. "What did she tell you?" This from people who minutes before had cried for her blood.

Tezrah's voice cracked as she choked out the words. **"She shall come again, black of skin with the three alphas of God in her name . . ."** but these were strange words, and the people departed, their minds unable to define the feelings that lingered in their hearts.

So it was that the events of this day and the fate of that woman faded from memory, though it was rumored that the dead woman had committed mysteries to writing, explaining the ways of her God. Yet those who sought her writings for answers in the days after her death searched in vain. Those books were altered beyond recognition or burned, not by Romans this time, but by others who called themselves Christians. This was true . . . for as Magdalene often said, something about this life is not quite real, and nothing in this world is as it seems.

BOOK ONE

A Wind In Africa

PROLOGUE

Idugri, Nigeria 1985

There was no bright star overhead when the baby girl was born, nor did anyone come bearing gifts of frankincense and myrrh, but a wise man did pay a visit to praise the infant that lay in swaddling cloth on the dirt floor of the hut with the grass-thatched roof.

Drumbeats sounded in deep, rhythmic vibrations and fire licked at the black night sky of the African bush country. The baby had come into the world on a festive evening, arriving to the haunting sound of sonorous chants and the shuffling of a hundred bare feet around a roaring bonfire.

The wise man—the shaman some called him—smiled by the flickering firelight of an old kerosene lantern. He held out his arms. The nun holding the baby looked at the mother and father, both of whom lay exhausted on cloths that had been bundled up to form rude bedding on the ground.

"Ogun," the mother said, using the native word for "shaman" as she addressed the man. Her voice was weary but firm. "Sister Annaliese saved my child, saved my life too. I name my daughter Annalisa in her honor, and I have promised my husband our child will be a Christian though I follow Islam." She exhaled a resigned sigh. "Allah is powerful . . . and merciful in the strangest ways."

Still, the wise man smiled.

The mother looked directly into the pale blue eyes of Sister Annaliese. "Hear me: Christian though she will be, we will raise our baby to remember our African ways." She then nodded her head at the nun and fell back, spent.

The sister laid the infant gently into the wise man's open arms with no change of expression in her tender eyes and soft countenance. The *ogun* turned and carried the child into the hot night, out to the rough clearing carved from the dense trees and vines that was his village. As he came near the bonfire, the shimmering glow of reddish-yellow flames danced across his coal-black skin.

He stopped and held the baby high over his head. She did not cry; she did not make a single sound. The drums, the chanting, and the dancing stopped. The *ogun* spoke in a sonorous voice.

"See this child. See the child born in our village." He rotated his body for all to view the baby. "I tell you the hand is upon her; she is the wisdom, she has the power. She will be the one, and she will belong to the whole earth, my children; in its darkest hour the whole earth will know her touch."

The villagers gazed raptly at the tiny body held high in the air. Through the inverted triangle formed by the *ogun*'s upraised arms, they could see, in the distance, the small, robed figure of Sister Annaliese, waiting impassively to receive the baby back into her embrace.

When the old *ogun* had finished speaking, he lowered his arms and brought the baby close to his body. He shuffled slowly back to the hut where the nun waited, hands outstretched, to reclaim the infant. As he gave the child over, both of their hands touched the baby. For a moment, they stood facing each other in the fiery shadows with the small, kicking form suspended between them, between hands light and dark, male and female, Christian and pagan.

Then the *ogun*'s mouth formed a broad smile of beautifully white, fire-glazed teeth. He let go, and so the infant passed hands into a new world.

CHAPTER I

. . . but in me was he contained that I might recover the strength of the female. —The Gospel of Bartholomew

Jerusalem, 2025

Father James McPherson knew he was being followed, and under no circumstances could he let himself be caught. What he carried was too valuable to fall into the wrong hands. McPherson was trapped in a section of Jerusalem's old city between the Church of the Redeemer and Mount Moriah just north of the Wailing Wall, the Jewish holy site.

Moriah rose above him directly to the east with the Golden Dome of the Rock and the Al Aqsa mosque above. The Mount of Olives, dotted with gnarly fir trees, sat one hundred meters farther east, rising above the site of the ancient Temple Mount on Moriah. Ten minutes before, McPherson had met with a Palestinian Arab in the old city. The meeting was set up by none other than Hieronymus, the Latin Patriarch of Jerusalem.

The patriarch was also of Palestinian ancestry, and he had many contacts in the West Bank and Arab quarters of Jerusalem. Two weeks ago, an Arab had come to him purporting to have a fragment of a certain ancient document. He refused to say where he had obtained it, and he refused to show the document unless he was paid a large sum of money.

All he told Hieronymus was two words: a person's name, written in Greek, at the head of the purported text. It was enough. Hieronymus quietly passed the news along to the Keeper of the Texts in Rome. The Keeper had dispatched Father McPherson, with the money, to rendezvous with the man and make the exchange.

McPherson was dressed like an Arab, his kaffiyeh headpiece wrapped around to conceal his face; so sensitive was this meeting, so great the need for caution. The Arab had handed him the document, a single page that would alter history in the right hands. McPherson recalled his shock at seeing the first two words of the text written in Greek—Μαρια Μαγδαληνη—Mary Magdalene. Excerpts from the letter flashed across his mind—*Mary Magdalene . . . by my hand is this written . . . the two shall become one again . . . the hidden shall be revealed . . . the secret Church shall become visible . . . I shall return . . . the three*

Alphas of God in my name . . . The First Souls . . . and the god of this world shall be overthrown . . .

The Keeper had told him what to look for, and by those phrases McPherson knew the text was genuine without needing to have it analyzed or dated. He handed the Arab a small fortune then sealed the parchment in a tube which he placed in his briefcase. The Keeper had warned him to be vigilant and he was, pausing periodically to peer around corners, eyes darting from side to side as he made his way to the main street.

That was how he noticed the two men following him. Both were dressed in Western clothes, definitely not Arabs. McPherson could not be caught with the document. That would unravel everything. The streets in this part of the city were narrow so taxis were seldom seen. He had hoped to make it to the main boulevard to find a cab and head straight for the Tel Aviv airport. He needed to reach Rome, but his pursuers had blocked his passage to the west. He realized they were now looking him straight in the eye.

That was bad. They were not just following him any more; they were readying to capture him. McPherson was in his forties and still able to run. He retreated back toward the old city in a quick trot trying to use the narrow, winding streets to lose the men. He had no idea where he was going, but he dodged in and out of alleys and side streets.

Still hearing their running footsteps behind him, he redoubled his efforts. He came upon a merchant bazaar of street stalls and slowed his pace. Rows of cheap antique vase replicas lined the area in front of the stalls. No one was in the immediate area so he took the tube out of his briefcase, slipped it into a vase depicting Jesus at the Last Supper, and marked its position in his mind. He glanced at the sign on the storefront behind the open stall. It said *Ali Wafa.* McPherson resumed running, tossing his briefcase into an alley along the way.

Darkness was falling and he hoped the shadows would help him, but to his dismay he rounded a corner to face a wide open area. He saw Mount Zion to his right, so that meant southwest. He must be at the southern edge of the old city, probably heading straight for the Dung Gate. There were no buildings ahead for cover, just an open expanse with crumbled ruins along the ancient Herodian street at the southern base of the Temple Mount.

His pursuers were coming at him from the north. The south and west posed more open space where they could run him down. He had one chance. If he made a sharp turn to the east, he might be able to gain the stone ramparts beneath the Al Aqsa mosque where the lower wall of the old city bisected the higher wall of the Temple Mount plateau above.

He had a chance if he could reach the mosque. He was dressed as an Arab while his pursuers looked like Westerners or Israelis, and the locals wouldn't take kindly to Israelis chasing one of their own. McPherson put on an extra burst of speed. He looked back as he ran, and the two men were still keeping pace with him. After fifteen minutes of running uphill, he was spent. He managed to reach the surviving wall of an ancient stone building in the flats below the high ramparts of the intersecting city and Temple Mount walls.

He had to rest. He was temporarily out of view of his hunters. Multiple nooks and crannies overgrown with grass pockmarked the high walls. He spotted a deep, arch-shaped niche carved into the stone edifice. Whatever purpose it served originally, it was now a storage area for barrels and crates. Heavy iron bars covered the opening but luck was with him. The rusty grille stood open and he barely squeezed through. He closed the gate so it would appear locked, and he hid behind some barrels. If they searched inside he was trapped, but he had to rest. Hopefully his trackers would run past his location.

Seconds later he heard footsteps, and they paused close enough for him to hear the men talking. "Over that way," a voice said in Spanish. Thank God, it appeared they had passed him by. He waited for what seemed an eternity, then slowly crept forward and peered through the heavy metal grating. The way looked clear. While he had time, he pulled a pen and paper from his pocket and scribbled a short note. He placed the paper back in his pocket then pushed against the iron gate as slowly and quietly as he could, opening it just enough to wiggle back outside.

Which way to go? It was a dicey decision. Backtracking would be the quickest route to the city, but his pursuers might catch him out in the open again. He looked around. About a hundred feet away and six feet above the level where he stood, a metal stairway led to a landing between the end of the encircling old city wall and the face of the Temple Mount wall. The parapet of the Mount wall stood about twenty feet above the landing, normally an insurmountable barrier, but once again fortune was with him.

Temporary scaffolding covered the face of the wall connecting the landing to the parapet. Thank God the walls were in need of constant maintenance. If he gained the parapet, he would be on the lower Temple Mount plateau less than fifty yards from the mosque. He could then cut across the great square by the Dome of the Rock and descend down the western slope of Moriah.

He ran toward the stairs but momentarily froze when he heard a shout behind him. The men had emerged from the cover of a half-crumbled column some distance to the east. They must have been waiting to flush him out. The old stone blocks that formed the lower base of the stairs made perfect stepping stones so McPherson scrambled up, jumped the metal railing, then turned east and ran up the rampart leading to the landing. His pursuers were younger and faster, however. He could hear their footsteps gaining ground on him.

He was gasping for air as he reached the landing, and was only halfway up the scaffolding when the men arrived. McPherson climbed for his life, not pausing to look down, for a moment's lapse would be fatal. Things started coming to him now in slow motion. Arm slid over arm to grasp the metal bars with the languid reach of a swimmer doing the front crawl against the resistance of water. He clawed his way upward for an eternity.

His vision and his awareness of all things around him collapsed and focused on the crenellated openings of the parapet above. He rose ever so slowly until suddenly a new world came into view. His head was at eye level with the concrete plaza on the plateau above. He could see people walking in the distance, people and safety from the danger in the abyss below him. He was going to make it, going to complete his mission, he —

Then he felt it, felt a hand grasp his ankle. He was vaguely aware of kicking to get free. He looked down to see one man's hand on his ankle and the second man reaching to grab his other leg. The downward drag grew heavier. His eyes tracked back to the plateau. He clutched the parapet, inches from a plane of existence that meant freedom and life.

He glanced to the nearby southwest corner of the Temple Mount, the very place where Jesus was said to have rejected Satan after being offered the world. He looked one more time at the safe and unaware people in the short distance beyond, and he remembered the words of the Keeper—"Nothing in this world is as it seems." And reminding himself of that, he realized his safety did not lie on that Mount or in those people. His safety lay in something beyond. With both hands, McPherson thrust his body backward off the parapet.

As he fell, he thanked God that he dispelled himself of his illusions and did not carry them with him in the hour of his death. He let out one final scream of God's name in Arabic before he hit the rocks below in a crunching crack of oblivion.

"You fool, you pulled too hard," one of the assailants said to the other.

"No, the bastard pushed off. He killed himself!" the other replied.

They descended, then examined McPherson's body. They were searching for his briefcase or large documents, so they overlooked the small note in his pocket. Soon the onlookers above, drawn over by McPherson's scream, started shouting at them in angry voices. They fled. Now they were scared: not of the crowd, but of going back to Rome empty-handed.

CHAPTER II

O fruitless tree full of fire from
Death— The Acts of John

Setandwe, Central Nigeria

"See the people you are about to kill," the commander said to the men massed in the bush on the perimeter of the village. "Any second thoughts? Now is your chance to leave."

The dense vines crisscrossing the trees overhead made day seem like dusk, and the damp jungle gloom pressed down on Hakim. He looked around and saw one trembling man stand up from a crouch. The man was not one of the irregulars but another brigand like himself. The commander pointed toward the jungle, indicating the man could go. As soon as he turned to leave, the commander signaled two subordinates. One ran over to block the man's path, the other positioned himself behind the man, brandishing a machete.

When he saw his path was blocked, the deserter turned around to face the commander, and his life ended in that instant. The machete stroke was bad. It missed his neck but caught him above the jaw through the side of his mouth, causing teeth to fly and the top of his head to flop over in a grotesque parody of a human face. Annoyed by the bad knife work, the commander hissed, and the two men finished him off with several butchering strokes.

"Now then, those Christians are the enemies of Islam," the commander said, pointing to the village, "African tools used by the Western powers to control our country and destroy the true religion of Allah. Remember that and do your work. No survivors. Now go!"

Hakim advanced slowly with the rest of the men. The commander had positioned them so that his militiamen could keep an eye on the brigand recruits and make sure they performed, but when the killing started, order gave way and the chaos of blood lust took hold of them all. The men and the elderly were killed outright. The women were raped first then killed, but it was the children that were hardest for some. Hakim saw a heavy woman moving between two huts in a waddling sprint. She was clutching a baby to her breast. One of the raiders took aim. The shot stopped her on the run. She sank to her knees then collapsed on top of the baby. Hakim approached the dead woman to see if the baby underneath her lived, but then he heard a cry behind him. Some of the village men had regrouped and were charging at him with machetes.

He shouted for help. Some militiamen came to his aid, but they were still outnumbered. A fierce fight ensued. Hakim dropped his rifle; it was no help at close range. He emptied his pistol as he felt the machete cuts and prayed they wouldn't sever anything vital. A villager wrestled him to the ground and Hakim knew he would die. The cuts on his arms were causing them to buckle, and the man's knife drew near to his throat.

Just before his strength gave away, Hakim heard a dull crack and his face was showered with blood and brains as the villager's head blew apart. The body collapsed to his side with gouts of blood spewing from the glistening red crater in his cranium. Hakim lay there and a militiaman came over to inspect him.

Hakim's injuries weakened him, but he forced himself to get up. If he didn't rise on his own, the militiaman would kill him. He knew they had no doctors in the immediate area and they were in hostile territory. They would not leave anyone to be captured and interrogated, especially the brigands. Hakim was growing light-headed. He looked at the bush surrounding the edge of the village. He had to make it in there; it was his only chance. He could hide, maybe lose the militia then get some help if he could survive the bleeding.

He staggered along as fast as he could with his remaining strength until he made the edge of the vine-covered vegetation. He forced himself to walk upright, pretending to be unhurt. He moved with the main body until he found some other non-militia fighters. They banded together, and as they walked, they slowly receded from the main group. These men had no interest in killing him. They were carrying valuables plundered from the village, the real reason they followed the militia into the attack. Hakim carried nothing. He was too injured for any of that. His only goal was to survive, and survival was all he thought about as he made his way north through the jungle.

Hakim bound his wounds with strips of his own clothing. No arteries were severed but he had deep cuts and the bleeding was steady. He needed to clean his wounds and find medicine. Infection was a real danger in the jungle. They traveled for several difficult miles, finally stopping to rest. Hakim propped himself between the gnarled, exposed roots of a giant banyan tree. As he rested, he reflected on his life.

Since being exiled from his village for impregnating a young niece, he had been a man on the run. Nigeria was in chaos, a living hell. Bandits roamed, famine was depopulating many areas, and friction between Muslims and Christians bordered on civil war.

Hakim had made bad decisions in his life but he was not stupid. It was all about survival. Banditry did not make one rich; it just helped one survive, but was it the best way? His "comrades" would kill one other as quickly as the villagers they attacked, and they were always on the run from Muslims and Christians alike. Today he had seen the militiamen in action close up. They were disciplined; they acted as a unit. Their numbers were still small—they had to recruit bandits to attack such a large village—but growing. Hakim had increasingly seen their presence in the northern Muslim provinces.

They had the power of religion behind them. They were well fed and had more personal security than any brigand, and maybe they were right. Maybe the country would be better off under Muslim rule. Maybe the Christians really were tools the West used to keep the country divided. If he made it back north, he'd start looking into that, but right now—

He heard men yelling. His eyes shot open. "Run!" one man cried. "They've tracked us!"

"Who?" Hakim asked.

"Must be Christians from the surrounding villages. Run!"

Hakim stood to flee, but knife- and club-wielding men crashed through the bush on his right. It was going to be a standing fight for their lives, and Hakim could barely stand.

CHAPTER III

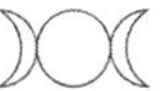

This is the judgment of the blasphemer— Pistis Sophia

Lagos, Nigeria

Evil roams this land," Cardinal Onomoh said, speaking from a raised dais. He looked to Bishop Ogunsanya seated on his right, then to the two monsignors on his left. "Be mindful of this as we inquire into the matter of the nun, Annalisa Basanjo, and the extraordinary events that occurred on November 14th, 2025, in the village of Toueme in eastern Benin."

Below and in front of the clerics, two nuns sat at a long table in an unadorned, wood-floored room of the Lagos archdiocese. One of the women was African, one European. "We have heard from Bishop Ogunsanya and Father Adokaly," the cardinal said. "Sister Dominique, will you now recount what transpired that day in Benin?"

The French nun's fingers fidgeted on the table. She took a deep breath and started to speak. "I remember the drums beating that day. The villagers were singing and chanting, praising the healings and pressing against the door of our small, mud-walled building when Bishop Ogunsanya and Father Timothy Adokaly arrived."

Sister Dominique closed her eyes as she spoke. It helped transport her back to that day that had shocked her to the core of her soul. She had witnessed a different world, and it caused her to question the one she had always known. She then gave her testimony:

"Sister Annalisa had always displayed unusual abilities before, but nothing like what happened in the village that day. Lines of people pushed at the door—women with sick children, men wasted with illnesses, and people with numerous deformities, including one unfortunate with a face so disfigured and a spine so hideously bent, he resembled a mule more than a man as he shuffled about on his hands and feet. Annalisa had been working with Reti, the crippled girl, for over an hour. This time, minutes after taking the girl's head between her hands, the child's body jackknifed in a violent thrust. Reti clamped onto the sides of the table with a slapping sound and squirmed as if something were hurting her. Her face contorted. She let out a piercing scream and I bolted to her side in alarm.

"But minutes later Reti stood. She not only stood but she walked! I followed her as she bounded out the door and down the stairs. Then she jumped into the arms of the nearest man. The villagers were beside themselves.

"One of them, whom I later learned had known the paralyzed girl all her life, cried out, 'She healed Reti, the lame girl! God be praised, the nun from Idugri healed a crippled girl!' He broke from the horde of people surrounding the building and ran to the opposite end of the hamlet announcing the miraculous event.

"Shortly thereafter, the bishop and Father Timothy arrived. The bishop's eyes narrowed as he surveyed the crowd. 'Muslims,' he hissed. 'Look how many of them are here. She is treating Muslims!' I heard him say. Ogunsanya inquired about the rumors of fantastic healings, including what he called, 'This alleged healing of a lame girl.'

"Oh, no, Your Excellency" I said. "Not alleged. It was real; I saw it happen. The girl left, walked out on her own two legs.

"'Calm yourself and come to your senses, Sister Dominique.'

"I'm sorry, Your Excellency, but what she did was—

"'Sister,' the bishop's voice was impatient as he interrupted me.

"Excuse me, Your Excellency," I replied, my enthusiasm quelled.

"'Good, now, tell me what you can.'

"But then a voice said, 'I am Sister Annalisa, Your Excellency. I think it is me you are looking for, yes?' We turned and saw her—Annalisa. I was exhausted, but her features looked smooth as cream, like the start of the day, and so collected and energetic!

"Father Timothy later remarked to me that she looked far younger than her forty years, and asked me if she were a Fulani because of her fine features. But mostly I remember him saying she could expose a man's essence with her gaze, illuminating the scurrying rodents in the caverns of one's soul. An unusual comment, but I understood what he meant. From the beginning, Father Timothy seemed at ease in her presence, but the bishop was sweating. It was like he was struggling to appear in control.

"Annalisa's smile was a complete contrast to the bishop's seriousness. 'These people carry many burdens,' she said, 'and pain brings compassion in its wake, you see? They have come for healing, not for fighting.'

"'You proclaim yourself a healer then, do you?' the bishop asked.

"Annalisa gave a vigorous shake of her head. 'I heal no one. Only God heals,' she said.

"'And He has given you the authority to act for Him?' the bishop asked.

"'Why, Your Excellency,'" Annalisa replied, 'perhaps you should see for yourself, then judge. Today we have more people than time. Would you care to watch while I work? Perhaps then your questions and answers will fall into place.'

"Bishop Ogunsanya's eyes darted around. 'Perhaps . . .' the words stumbled hesitantly out of his mouth. 'Yes, very well. Proceed,' he said, and we let people enter again from the lines outside.

"We saw a few people with minor ailments, and Annalisa told them how to cure themselves with certain herbs, but then a blind girl entered the room led by her weeping mother. The eight-year-old child had received a severe blow to the head as an infant, resulting in near total blindness.

"Annalisa seated the child in a chair, stood behind her, and placed her hands over the girl's eyes. She rotated her fingers in a light circular motion, whispering in the child's ear, periodically kissing the back of her head. Annalisa's body swayed back and forth. From time to time, the girl's eyelids fluttered rapidly, and her upper body moved as if unseen hands were rotating her shoulders from side to side.

"Hours passed, and darkness fell. Annalisa had been enveloping the child in her arms and caressing her constantly. The girl's forehead wrinkled as if something had startled her, and she started shaking. The bishop made a move to stop the proceeding but at that moment, in a commanding tone, Annalisa's voice boomed, 'The love of God upon you!'

"Annalisa collapsed to the floor. Father Timothy rushed to assist her while Bishop Ogunsanya went to the girl. She seemed to be looking around in confusion, then I think it struck all of us—*the blind don't look around!*

"The bishop lifted his pectoral cross in one hand. It had grown dark outside, so he pulled out a small pocket light to augment the firelight in the room. He shined the light on the cross. He held the backlit cross about two feet from the child and asked her to follow the motion of his hands. He saw her eyes move up and down then left to right, following the movement!

"'You can see? You can really see?' he asked in disbelief. 'Show me the shape of the object I hold.'

"I could almost feel the hairs rise on the bishop's forearm as a slow smile ignited on the girl's face. In a scene I will remember the remainder of my days, *she traced the sign of the cross in the air with her fingers!* As he moved the cross even closer, her small fingers circled the round shape of the red ruby in the center, and she gasped. For the first time in her life of shadows, she had seen a color!

"The girl's mother fell sobbing at Annalisa's feet. Annalisa quickly pulled her up and said, 'When anyone asks you, tell them God healed your child, not Annalisa. Think of Him at some time each day; learn to see how and when He appears in your lives.'

"After they observed what transpired, Bishop Ogunsanya and Father Timothy conferred with each other in low tones. The bishop's face creased in harsh, determined lines. When the mother and daughter had left, he said to Annalisa, 'No one should be able to do this. It is not natural, not right.' "And Annalisa said, 'Would you care to tell the child that, Your Excellency?'

"The bishop studied Annalisa's face in the shadowy light. Her question momentarily silenced him. Then he said with finality, 'What is the real source of the powers you display? Is it God or—you will stop whatever you are doing until the Church is satisfied.'

"And that is my testimony, Your Eminence," Dominique said. "That is all I have to say."

Cardinal Onomoh then addressed the African nun. "Sister Annalisa, you have heard all the testimony. Unexplainable miracles have occurred by your hands. How is this so?"

Annalisa rose and looked the cardinal in the eye. She stood no more than 5′2″ but her steady gaze and comportment negated the air of authority the cardinal enjoyed looking down on her from the dais. "God wants me to bring something to this world, yet you speak as if I have committed evil."

"And perhaps you have," the cardinal said, looking at the petite nun with contempt. "God speaks to no one anymore. The Church speaks for Him. You had best remember that."

"The Church did not heal the girl," Annalisa replied.

Bishop Ogunsanya's lips curled inward at her comment. His jaw clenched and his mouth seemed poised to spit venom, but he waited for Cardinal Onomoh's comment.

Onomoh's disgust was evident. "By your defiance you conceal something."

Annalisa stepped toward him. "No, you are condemning me for my certainty."

"Your certainty?" Onomoh repeated. "What do you mean by that?"

"I am certain of God's existence from the healing that flows through my hands while the Church merely takes His existence on faith."

Onomoh's fist slammed down and he bit his lower lip so hard as to almost draw blood. "You, a nun, presume to put yourself above the Church in such a matters?" he shouted. "Do you think that you—" he stopped in midsentence, suddenly looking disoriented. His eyes rolled back into this head. He swayed for a few seconds then collapsed into his chair with a choking sound. Ogunsanya and the others came to his aid.

After ministering to him for several minutes, Ogunsanya turned to Annalisa and said, "He . . . he has no pulse. Cardinal Onomoh is dead. I do not understand what is happening here, but I will find out. The Church will find out. I will see to that." His eyes bored in on Annalisa. "It was you. You must have . . . leave here! Leave immediately and cease your activities, but be sure that I will speak with you again. As sure as the sun sets, we will get to the bottom of this."

After they left the room, a trembling Sister Dominique said, "That was no hearing; it was an Inquisition. The bishop practically accused you of killing Cardinal Onomoh. They want to burn you at the stake. What have you done to anger the Church?"

When Annalisa did not respond, Dominique asked, "What will you do now?"

"Tell the superior I leave tomorrow for the north to help the famine victims," Annalisa said. "I will then be out of the bishop's jurisdiction."

"But the bishop told you to stop," Dominique said. "Defy him, and they'll discipline you severely, perhaps even confine you permanently to the convent. You will have to leave the Church to continue your work. That is the only way you can escape their control, but even then their reach is long."

Annalisa dismissed that thought with a vigorous shake of her head. "The Church cannot do what must be done, but what I do must be done within the Church."

"The north is very dangerous. Annalisa, please reconsider. You're setting yourself on a collision course with the Church."

Annalisa sighed. "No, Dominique," she said in a low voice. "It is not me who is setting the course." Then she turned and walked into the night.

CHAPTER IV

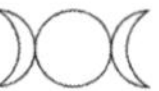

Faustus we are come from hell in person to shew thee some pastime: sit downe and thou shalt behold the seven deadly sinnes appeare to thee in their owne proper shapes and likenesse.
— *Christopher Marlowe,* Dr. Faustus

The Vatican City

For the sake of the Church, His Holiness must step down and allow for election of a new pope," Heinrich Cardinal Mannheim declared. His words would trigger a historic confrontation and they echoed off the room's ornately painted ceiling and gilded walls. No pope had abdicated in six hundred years, and no one had forced an abdication in a thousand. Mannheim's cold, pale eyes fixed on Pope Clement for his response.

Clement sat opposite and above Mannheim and the other six cardinals on a raised marble dais with Cardinal Roncalli, the papal secretary, seated below him and to his right. Clement made no response, not even with his sad brown eyes, but Roncalli's voice broke the heavy silence. "Explain yourself, Cardinal! Do you realize what you're saying?"

"Do you realize what is happening to the Church?" Mannheim shot back. Not one of the men had blinked at Roncalli's challenge. These seven men were the real power in the Vatican, and no accident brought them to their positions. Decades of conservative popes starting from John Paul II had filled the College of Cardinals and the Vatican bureaucracy with men who looked backward into history for their vision of the modern Church.

"And now," Mannheim said, "as if to confirm our fears, we find the dark time of the prophecies may be upon us." He gave a curt nod to Cardinal LoPresti.

The obese cardinal with the notoriously pious attitude held up a dossier. "Reports have reached us from Nigeria. They speak of a nun who performs great miracles of healing."

"What *miracles*?" Cardinal Roncalli asked.

"Healing cripples, restoring sight to the blind," LoPresti replied.

Roncalli's eyes narrowed. "Come, Cardinal LoPresti, we receive reports like that all the time from Third World countries. They never amount to anything."

LoPresti shook his head. "This report is from a bishop who says he witnessed the nun restore a girl's sight. No such thing has been done since our Lord walked the earth." The room went silent. "The girl's blindness was documented," LoPresti said. "Read the report. Even Muslims are converting because of her healings."

"You're saying she is the *Great Heretic?*" Roncalli asked.

"The prophecies say the Great Heretic will destroy the Church this very decade," LoPresti replied. "He, or *she*, will arise from the Third World, perform miracles, and come during turbulent times. Islamic terrorists are bombing American and European cities and wreaking havoc on our economies. Nations are nearing war. You add it up."

"There's more," Mannheim said. "At my request, Cardinal Onomoh held an inquiry to question the nun. He collapsed and died in the middle of the questioning just as she was refuting his judgment."

The gasps around the room were audible.

"This is terrible news about Onomoh, but His Holiness is not here for a lecture on dire prophecies and global geopolitics," Roncalli said. "Is using all this turmoil how you justify asking a reigning pope to abdicate?"

"This morning an entire Christian village was wiped out by Muslim militia in Nigeria," Mannheim said, "Annihilated in the very area walked by this 'miracle woman.'"

The room grew deathly silent at this second shock. Mannheim had not informed his colleagues so as to create a dramatic effect. The event took on more importance because Pope Clement himself would be in Nigeria in just six days, but Roncalli was prepared.

"We know of this event. I leave for Nigeria in a few hours to investigate," Roncalli said.

"But do you not see the pattern?" Mannheim said. "Yesterday the archdiocese in Mexico City was firebombed, the Poor Nation's Coalition kidnapped yet another bishop, and more clergymen were attacked in Argentina. The Muslims are rising in a modern clash of civilizations. An Irish priest died recently under mysterious circumstances right before the main Arab mosque in Jerusalem—new events, but the same pattern. The Church has been under systematic attack from within and without. I tell you, forces beyond mere history are behind this."

"Quite so," Cardinal DeGolia agreed. The sophisticated DeGolia was phlegmatic and quirky but one of the most eloquent speakers among the cardinals. "We're all aware of the long-standing rumors about a 'Hidden Church.' We believe there are heretics, even here in the Vatican, who are making ready for their leader to rise, and now this nun . . ."

"We'll root all this out with decisive actions," Francisco Cardinal Tormada chimed in. Tormada's irascible personality seemed perpetually peevish and on edge. He headed the Congregation for the Doctrine of the Faith. This department was the Church's dogmatic police force, called in previous times by another name—The Inquisition.

"What actions?" Roncalli asked.

"First," Mannheim said, "we must put our own house in order. We can start by bringing the liberal American bishops in line or defrock all of them."

The pope remained silent, but Roncalli responded. "Strip them of their priesthood? You can't be serious," he said.

"But we are," Cardinal Villendot replied.

Roncalli eyed the French cardinal, a would-be leader who was envious of Mannheim.

Mannheim spoke quickly to prevent Villendot from preempting the conversation. "America, the strongest Western country, has just elected a president with clear vision," Mannheim said. "The churches must rally the people to support men like him."

Newly elected President John Davidson had vowed to reverse the policies established by successive liberal administrations, policies that had allowed Iran to become a power. During that time, Iranian foreign policy had grown steadily more aggressive and the Western world had experienced an exponential increase in terrorism.

"You call for politicization of the Church?" Roncalli asked. "The West struggled for centuries to prove that separation of church and state was the only prudent course for society. It's ironic you think so little of the American Church and so much of the American government, Cardinal Mannheim."

"It's ironic that the Church's passivity encourages those who would destroy Western civilization, Cardinal Roncalli. A showdown with the Islamic world has been building for decades. We have the means to defeat them but not the will. They have been the aggressors and we the victims but that *will* change."

"Cardinal Mannheim," Roncalli said, "you're calling for a repeat of the Crusades. The Church must not promote war—governments are adept enough at that. That is not how we practice Christianity in this day and age."

"The governments and the Church have betrayed our civilization!" Mannheim said, raising his voice. He picked up a Bible from the table and held it high for all to see. "This is not a pacifist book. It is replete with examples of people fighting to keep their faith alive. I tell you that to love as a Christian means to preserve our families and all who want to live in peace by standing up to those who would destroy us." His comment met with murmurs of lock-step agreement.

"You are here to serve the pope, not make policy," Roncalli replied.

"Many different forces are tearing at us, and His Holiness has struggled with poor health," Mannheim said. "This is of great concern to the College of Cardinals during a time when we must take controversial actions to preserve the Church's future as an institution."

Roncalli's fingers curled into a fist. He leaned over and whispered to the pope, but Clement made a motion with his hand as if telling Roncalli to hold his tongue.

"It is the consensus of the cardinals and the curia that His Holiness must step down for his own health and the sake of the Church," Mannheim said.

Roncalli bolted upright. "Who are you to make that decision?"

"And if I choose not to abdicate?" Finally hearing Clement's soft voice caught them all off guard. There was a long silence.

Roncalli looked around at the seven men. Van Kluysen, the prefect for economic affairs, the man who ran the Vatican Bank. The greedy Belgian would lease out the Sistine Chapel for weddings and debutante parties if he could. Trevi, the bright young womanizer whom Mannheim saved from a scandal with a pregnant girl; Tormada and the others—despite their faults, they were determined in their views.

"The cardinals and the curia would bring the Church's functions to a halt until the matter is resolved," Mannheim replied to the pope's question.

"You threaten His Holiness?" Roncalli shot back in a loud voice that rang throughout the chamber. "He could remove the entire curia and replace all of you if necessary."

"Yes," Mannheim said, "but not so easily. Your Holiness," he said, ignoring Roncalli and addressing Clement directly, "your burdens are heavy. With an honorable retirement you would still be a venerated father of the Church. There is no disgrace attached to this."

Clement held up a hand. "I am preparing for an important trip. I will not be distracted from that duty. There will be no further discussion on this matter until my return. Cardinal Roncalli will personally question this nun who concerns you. That is all for now."

"Of course, Your Holiness," Mannheim said, seeming satisfied that Clement had not rejected their proposal outright. Roncalli picked up on that fact too.

After the others left, Roncalli studied Clement. The pope moved lethargically, and his hands trembled. He clutched a nearby curtain, probably to steady himself from another dizzy spell. Though the piazza below him teemed with life, Pope Clement gazed out onto a St. Peter's Square that now seemed empty and lonely, and the wavering rays of the late afternoon sun cast light and shadows across his weary face.

The Church Roncalli knew was slipping away. Mannheim would soon be pope, and then the Church would lose its soul, fully consumed by the drums of war. *What need for a Great Deceiver?* Roncalli thought. *We're going to hell anyway.*

CHAPTER V

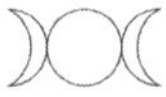

. . . before me was a pale horse! Its rider was named Death, and Hades was following close behind him. They were given power over a fourth of the Earth to kill by sword, famine and plague, and by the wild beasts of the Earth.
—Revelations 6:7-9

Setandwe, Nigeria

Teresa Ferentinos was finally ready to go on camera after throwing up twice. The smoky charnel house stench of human cinders floating up to heaven filled the morning sky with a ghastly pall. This had been an unexpected event for Teresa's first major assignment. She was supposed to be covering the forthcoming papal visit to Lagos when news of the Setandwe massacre broke and UNN rerouted her to central Nigeria.

The village of rude wood buildings and grass thatched roofs had lain in a clearing with dense surrounding jungle. The once verdant landscape now looked charred and surreal, stained ochre by the blood of its tortured victims, but it was the smell of burnt flesh that really got to her. Nigeria was not equipped for swift identification and burials. The threat of disease outweighed the formalities the living owed the dead, so the government decided to burn the bodies immediately.

The raven-haired reporter composed herself, looked into the camera, and spoke on cue. "This is Teresa Ferentinos reporting for UNN in central Nigeria. I'm standing in what once was the village of Setandwe, where five hundred people were victimized in one of the worst mass killings in modern times. I warn you that some of the footage is graphic and could be upsetting to younger or more sensitive viewers."

The camera panned the village at a sufficient scale to convey the death but not the grim details of the violence. "The government has ordered swift mass burnings of the corpses to prevent the outbreak of disease," Teresa explained to her global audience, "but there may be political motives involved too. The victims were Christians and the perpetrators thought to be Muslim irregular militia. The country is a political and religious tinderbox. By removing the remains so swiftly, the government may be seeking to minimize emotions and the desire for retribution they may bring, but the knowledge of what happened here may be impossible to eradicate." Teresa gestured across the breadth of the dead village as she made her point.

On the other side of the village in the direction to which Teresa was pointing, a nun knelt over a dying man easing his passage with words to guide him in the afterlife. She had been on her way to the north, but something had called her here. Now she knew why. She left the now still body and continued wading through the field of corpses.

She happened upon a woman's body lying facedown and spied a tiny foot protruding from underneath bloodstained robes. She kneeled down, grasped the dead woman's arm and shoulder, then lifted with a strength belying her diminutive size. The large body flopped over and revealed a child. Annalisa put her fingers to the infant's chest and nostrils. No hint of breath. In her effort to shield the baby, the mother had suffocated the child as she died.

The nun placed her hands across the baby's chest and drew a deep breath. "Ah," she sighed, "this is not your time, not your time." She caressed the infant's forehead then placed one hand on its temple and one on its heart. After a time a tingling shiver rose across her body and built to a visible tremor. Ecstasy seized her and she almost cried out in rapture. Just then a sucking sound issued from the infant, followed by a whimper.

The nun smiled and cradled the child until a voice came to her—*They come. It is not yet time.* The nun stood, looked around, and saw a provincial aid worker twenty yards away staring at her, his mouth agape. She had preferred no one had seen, but if that was the way it was to be . . . she walked over to the man, handed him the baby, and said, "Care well for this child. It is the hope and memory of this village." With that she left and vanished into the bush at the village's edge.

"Muslims, no doubt," Robert Avernis said to Cardinal Roncalli and Roald Zugli after examining the village for several hours. Zugli was Chief of Vatican Security and Avernis was the American CIA liason with the Holy See. "You can tell from clothing and items found on the dead attackers," Avernis pointed out, "but the villagers fought back. It seems the attackers didn't make much effort to remove their own dead. Peculiar."

"What's peculiar?" Zugli asked.

"They stage an attack to wipe out five hundred people but don't carry off their own dead," Avernis replied. "Most militias remove their dead when they have time. This seems more like the work of bandits. There's plenty of them around the country."

"So was it militia or brigands?" Zugli asked.

Avernis rapped his knuckles against his cheek. "I don't know. Maybe both. Maybe the guerillas needed bodies to carry out such a large-scale raid and they weren't too choosy about screening recruits."

Zugli nodded his head in disgust. He had high regard for Avernis' opinions. The young CIA operative had once been stationed in Nigeria and he had a handle on local affairs. He was also extremely bright. He had an IQ of one hundred fifty-four —so Avernis' boss Leo Dusayne had told Zugli—yet Dusayne did not seem too keen on Avernis. Still, Dusayne and Zugli were old friends, and Zugli knew Leo would only give him the best he had. When the Vatican and Washington agreed to establish a full-time intelligence liaison, it was Avernis whom Dusayne installed in the position.

Cardinal Roncalli was several yards away preparing to say a short mass for the souls of the departed. "How's the cardinal taking it?" Avernis asked Zugli. Roncalli's cassock was smeared with blood. He had just administered last rites to a woman who had bled out when her breast had been cut off.

"I suspect he's taking it like the man he is," Zugli replied. "Heartbroken but ready to minister to the living as well as the dead. What else can any man do in the face of this?"

Avernis nodded in silence. Just as Roncalli was about to begin the mass, another churchman came flying up the dirt path toward them, looking awkward and out of place running in his black simar. Avernis recognized him. It was Bishop Ogunsanya from Lagos.

"She's here, Your Eminence, she's here!" the bishop exclaimed through his dog-like panting as he neared them.

"Calm down," Roncalli said. "Who is here?"

"The nun, Annalisa Basanjo, the one in my report," Ogunsanya gasped, "the one you came to investigate. She was seen on the other side of the village in direct contradiction of my orders to cease her activities. You must come and talk to the man who saw her. Perhaps she is still here."

"I will go after I say mass," Roncalli replied.

"But she may be gone by then," Ogunsanya said, "and she was performing miraculous acts, unnatural things. We could catch her in the act. We—"

Roncalli held up a hand. "After mass, Your Excellency. We owe it to the blood of our departed. I will see her sooner or later."

Ogunsanya was biting his tongue but he nodded his compliance.

After the mass Roncalli said, "Now we'll see about the nun," and Ogunsanya led the cardinal, Zugli, and Avernis to the other side of the village.

They saw a man holding a baby as they approached. "Good man, you waited here as I told you," Ogunsanya said. "Tell the cardinal what you saw."

The man shook his head as if trying to shake cobwebs from his brain. "I was going through the village looking for any that might still be alive. I saw a solitary Mercyite nun. I could tell by her dress."

"Was she African or European?" Roncalli asked

"African," the man replied. "She pulled this child from under the body of a dead woman. I tell you, the child was still as a stone. For many minutes it did not move. It seemed like she was praying over the child and then it heaved. I could hear it suck in air from where I stood."

"What are you saying?" Ogunsanya prompted the man.

"I—I believe the child was dead. Come, see here," and he led them to the mother's corpse. "See how large this woman is? The baby was completely underneath her. That alone would have suffocated it, and who knows how many hours they lay here?"

Ogunsanya turned to Roncalli with a self-satisfied look.

"A number of things could explain this," Roncalli said. "Perhaps the child was positioned in a way to escape suffocation and had just come out of shock."

The man shook his head. He was sure of what he had seen.

"Then again," Roncalli said to the bishop, "how can you be sure it was the same nun we are investigating? Is she still here?"

Ogunsanya responded in a quick voice. "The nun was African, a Mercyite, and this man described her unique facial features to me. I have learned she was on her way to the north in disobedience of my orders. She may have just left the village, but there is no question it was her."

Just then Roncalli put a hand to his head and looked wobbly. At the same moment, Avernis staggered and bumped shoulders with Zugli. Adding to this odd scene and out of nowhere, an attractive young woman wandered into their midst, looking dazed. Roncalli, Avernis, and the young woman all seemed to be suffering some malaise. Zugli stepped toward her. "Who are you and what are you doing here?" he asked.

The woman looked confused, her forehead wrinkled in concentration. She was looking at something behind him. Zugli turned and found Roncalli and

Avernis staring straight at her in the same bewildered manner. They seemed to be in a hypnotic daze. Zugli felt the air turn electric with energy, and the hair on his forearms rose. He saw Bishop Ogunsanya and the field worker shudder in unison, but the baby was calm and quiet. Zugli stepped in front of the woman, breaking her eye contact with Roncalli and Avernis.

"What are you doing here?" he asked the woman again.

"I . . . I'm Teresa Ferentinos," she eventually replied in an English accent. "I'm with UNN news from London, here to cover the massacre. I was at the other side of the village doing my job—I don't even remember walking over here. Who are all of you?"

Avernis then stepped forward. He walked unusually close to her. "Ma'am we're all with the Vatican. This is Cardinal Roncalli from Rome. He's ministering to the victims, and we would appreciate no cameras."

"My cameras are back across the village," she said. "*You're* with the Vatican, Mr. . . ."

"Avernis, ma'am. Robert Avernis."

"You're a Yank and not a priest, so what do you do for the Vatican, Mr. Avernis?"

"It's Teresa, right? Well listen, Teresa, not now. The cardinal has been administering extreme unction to the dying. Please show respect; let him be about his work."

She pondered for a few seconds then nodded and walked away, but not before peering over her shoulder at Avernis as if to make sure he was not an apparition.

Zugli moved his head as if shaking off a dream. "What was that all about?" he asked.

It was Bishop Ogunsanya who answered him. "Is it not obvious? This place has been bewitched by that nun. That is what we are all feeling — the passing of evil."

Cardinal Roncalli gave the bishop a skeptical look but that was his intellect acting. He had felt something . . . *possess* him. That fact confused him, rendered him unable to refute or reply, and so the bishop's last words hung in the air untouched. *The passing of evil.*

CHAPTER VI

Disturbances in society are never more fearful than when those who are stirring up the trouble can use the pretext of religion to mask their true designs. —Denis Diderot

Lagos, Nigeria

Shortly after Robert Avernis arrived in Lagos from the massacre site, he received encrypted orders from Leo Dusayne in Rome diverting him to Enugu, a Nigerian provincial capital in the east: **WEAPONS SHIPMENT UNCOVERED IN PORT HARCOURT. IRANIANS SUSPECTED. MEET OUR INFORMANT IN ENUGU PER ENCLOSED INSTRUCTIONS.**

Avernis went to the Lagos airport at dawn hoping to make Enugu by evening. Roads were too dangerous to travel so the competition for airline seats was fierce. Avernis paid a tout to secure a ticket, paid the tout's brother for the boarding pass, and paid the airline for the ticket itself—all costs of doing business. It was an arduous process but Avernis knew the drill.

Under his previous cover in Nigeria as foreign regional manager for the Jersey Ship and Trading Company, he actually closed a few deals here and there selling imported Uncle Ben's Rice, which was probably more valuable to the local economy than oil, that black veneer of prosperity which lacquered over the country's underlying poverty.

"*No, I pay ten thousand Naira, no more,*" he would hear from the "Cash Madames," the bandana-headed women waving wads of bills around the waterfront to make their purchases. They controlled nearly all foreign trade around the bustling Port of Lagos. A Cash Madame could talk the pants off a preacher, and many of the home-grown entrepreneurs were millionaires. It had been a colorful way to contribute to helping America's balance of trade.

America now needed him for more serious matters, and the bump of airplane wheels touching down on the runway refocused him on the business at hand. He arrived in Port Harcourt at five-thirty. His destination, Enugu, was about seventy miles north and inland. He pre-negotiated a price with a cab driver and made him write the figure on a piece of paper. This way he avoided the all-too-common "misunderstandings" that resulted in fares fifty to one hundred percent higher than verbally agreed.

The road cut through dense jungle broken every so often by clearings displaying small collections of stick huts with thatched roofs. The children shouted, "*Oiboe Peppe*" as he drove by — man like white pepper — reminding him that here he was different, here he stood out. Enugu City was merely a larger collection of huts similar to those he had seen en route. The jungle appeared to press in on all sides of the city so that the townspeople seemed like intruders in a tenuous outpost the lurking bush was waiting to reclaim.

Avernis went straight to the home of the Company's informant, General N'Diki Azu. Azu was actually an ex-general who had been in an ex-army. An Ibo tribesman, he had fought in the rebel army of Biafra before being reintegrated into the Nigerian Federal Forces. He was pro-Western, a devout Catholic, and a well-educated man. He was also amazingly spry for his eighty-four years. He lived in a pleasant home outside of Enugu. A breeze rustled the palms as he offered Avernis a drink. As the two men sat on the stone patio of his expansive backyard, Azu began talking.

The story was that Nigerian longshoremen had discovered false bottoms in a shipment of mixed light and heavy equipment while trying to pilfer some of the goods, but tools of a different sort were found underneath. "My man got these," Azu said, and he pulled some pictures out of his breast pocket. Avernis recognized them—Chinese AK assault weapons.

In any other port in the world where goods clear through customs, sending contraband in this manner would be the stupid work of rank amateurs. Not so in Nigeria. Port customs in Nigeria were not just lax but extremely corrupt, and the corruption was an institution. Customs officials were bribed so the goods would receive cursory inspection and be assessed lower duties. The dock-workers often clipped a portion for themselves and resold them on the black market. The exporting companies built a fifteen percent pilferage factor into their prices, the importing companies got a credit for proportionately lighter shipments, but everybody was happy. It was the Nigerian method of peacefully redistributing wealth, and it kept the economy rolling.

"Are the arms still in the harbor?" Avernis asked.

"In a guarded warehouse," Azu replied.

"Can you get me in there?"

Azu lit up a French cigarette and answered on the exhale. "Difficult, but we will try. As a boy, I fought in the civil war. Terrible suffering, terrible," the general said as if working to distance his mind from those days. "There has always been an element among the Muslims in the north, particularly among the Hausa and Fulani, which has resented Christians and the Western presence in this part of Africa. I suspect these arms are headed for them."

"Possibly," Avernis said. "Judging by the Setandwe massacre they're getting more active . . . and violent."

The general then called in one of his men to guide Avernis to the harbor warehouse. "Nice to have met you, Mr. Avernis," the general said in parting, "and if it turns out you are preventing war in my country, I'll do the next job gratis." He paused and shook his head. "Something bad is coming. I feel it."

Avernis changed into black field clothes, waited until darkness fell, and drove to the docks with Azu's man. Fortunately, the warehouse backed into a fairly deserted area which they accessed by cutting the lock on the chain-link security fence. Azu's man was familiar with the building's layout and they had worked out an entry plan. There was a maintenance ladder leading to the roof that went past a circulation vent on the back wall. Avernis unscrewed the vent and shimmied inside onto a catwalk.

The inside was dimly lit and stacked with rows of crates. He scanned the room with night-vision goggles that were part of the tools the general had supplied. Azu's man had told him the warehouse guards were typical security, that is, it wasn't uncommon for them to sleep on the job. They also carried no arms. Still, he wasn't taking chances, so when he made it to the ground level he located a rear door and unlocked it for a quick escape route.

He crept around for a half an hour quietly prying open crates, but the work was difficult. He could not break the sides of the crates to alert the guards that an intruder had seen their shipment. The crates were securely nailed and most were stacked high so he was limited to inspecting isolated pallets that he could access from the tops of the crates. He did find a shipping label taped on one crate that read, **MAIDUGRI TRADING CO. KATSINA, NIGERIA,** so now he had a possible destination—Hausa country in the Muslim north.

Most of the crates contained Chinese assault rifles just as Azu had indicated, but then he hit on a large rectangular crate containing shoulder rockets. He saw Chinese guidance components but casting pieces stamped in Farsi, meaning they were assembled in Iran. This confirmed it — the Iranians were now extending their reach into Africa's most strategic country.

Avernis decided he had obtained enough information. It was time to clear out before anyone decided to patrol the back of the warehouse. His final task was to affix a homing transponder to the shipment; but as he bent to grope for a spot under one of the crate bottoms, he heard a hollow *punhh* sound and a wooden shard from one of the crates hit him in the face. Avernis recognized the sound from his training at the CIA Farm in Virginia. Someone had fired a silenced weapon at him and just missed.

He dove into a corridor created by two opposing stacks of crates, away from the direction where he sensed the shot originated. He flipped on his night goggles and began crawling, finding other corridors and peeking through cracks to try and locate his assailant. Avernis was not armed, but the shooter didn't know that. Hopefully whoever it was wouldn't be rushing down to get him. Finally, he spotted his man. The guy was perched twelve feet up on a temporary wooden platform erected for storing smaller boxes. Thankfully, the crates were stacked high enough to cover Avernis, even from the shooter's higher vantage point. The bad news was that his silenced pistol had Avernis cut off from his back door escape route.

Avernis began searching for a way out when he noticed that the platform on which the man stood was propped up by some 4x4 wooden beams. The beams rested in rubber devices resembling suction cups, one end supporting the beams, the other affixing them to the platform. The platform seemed hastily erected, probably meant to be removed after the warehouse was cleared, so the makeshift fastenings gave him a chance. He saw two beams about six feet apart and calculated that if he could take them out, the weight of the man and the boxes around him should bring the section down.

He crawled to where he was at an oblique angle to the beams, well to the side of the shooter's position. He found some pieces of scrap wood, picked one up, and tossed it across the room. The shooter turned to face the sound. Avernis grabbed another thick piece of wood, braced it to his chest, and charged into the first beam. Thank God he had been right—the beam gave away at the rubber support, and the platform buckled enough to jar the man off his feet. This gave Avernis enough time to strike into the second beam and roll away as the whole section collapsed.

The shooter toppled off, landing on the corner of a crate with a nasty blow to the ribs. He was writhing in pain when Avernis ran over and delivered a sharp kick to his temple. Avernis heard other voices and footsteps coming from the front of the building so he ran out the rear door and bounded into the waiting car. "Go! Go!" he shouted to Azu's man.

On the way back to town, Azu's man reiterated that the warehouse guards never carried guns. "Then that was no common warehouse guard," Avernis said. "Not with a gun and silencer too." They stopped on the outskirts of Enugu town, and Avernis changed into his regular clothes in the back of the car. The man then drove him to his hotel.

As Avernis exited the car, he knocked on the driver's window. When the man rolled it down, Avernis said, "By the way, tell General Azu he was right. I think your country is headed for trouble."

CHAPTER VII

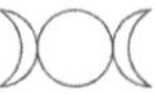

Appearances often are deceiving. —Aesop

Enugu, Nigeria

Avernis arrived at the hotel at half past nine. The building was a pock-marked stucco remnant from British colonial days. He was bitterly disappointed that he hadn't had time to place a satellite homing device on one of the crates, and now they would ship the arms out quickly, maybe even tonight. He could do nothing more but go back to Lagos tomorrow.

Avernis checked into his room and flipped on a switch. *Good, the lights work.* Bugs scurried across the floor in the dim light. He patiently stalked and stomped them but did not examine the room more closely for fear of other unwanted surprises. He succumbed to fatigue and flopped on the bed, clothes still on, and fell asleep. At some point, he woke up to a haunting, rhythmic beat playing in his head: *Da-Da-Dee-Dum-Dum, Da-Dee-Da-Da-Dum.* He followed the music outside to the small balcony attached to his room facing the grounds to the rear of the hotel.

In his tired vision, a dreamlike scene played out below him. He saw a stone courtyard enclosed on all sides by dense jungle trees and broadleaf plants. A string of tiny lights snaked through the vines and tree limbs, bathing the terrace in a soft, shimmering glow against the deep, deep black of the encroaching thicket. Africans and Europeans danced gracefully on the terrace as the musicians, off to one side, played the exotic music that had woken him. *Good opportunity,* he thought. He pulled out his low-lumen camera. *Maybe a player will show up on film, you never know.*

He snapped a series of pictures panning the entire courtyard and then, on maximum zoom, he saw her, a beautiful young woman talking to two African men. He spruced himself up and went downstairs. As he entered the courtyard, she stood talking to the men, who were dressed in flowing, native garb. She had green eyes, brown hair, and tawny skin. Avernis smiled at her, and her face lit up. She smiled back, extending her arm in the air with her wrist bent downward, beckoning him to come over.

Now this is too good to be true, he told himself. "Hi," he said. "My name is Robert, and it must be my lucky night to see a vision like you in the middle of the jungle."

"Robairr," she repeated in a French accent. "I am Celine."

"Ah, est-vous Francaise?" he asked.

"Mais oui," she said. *"Tu parle Francais?"*

"Okay, I'll admit you've heard the extent of my French, but I can dance. Would you care?"

She smiled and nodded. They took leave of the two Africans as he took her by the hand and led her onto the terrace. As they glided to the slow music, Avernis inhaled the sweet fragrance of Celine's skin. It was an intoxicating contrast to the damp, earthy smell of wood and leaf from the jungle. Her body felt wonderful against his hands. Shocks of energy coursed through him and concentrated in his groin.

"Thank you," he said when the music ended.

"De rien," she replied in French, "you are welcome."

"Celine, whatever brings you to this place?" he asked as they stood to the side of the dance floor.

"Oui, I know, it can be quite suffocating," she said, glancing at her African associates. "I work for an—how you say—an aeronautics company. We sell parts for small private aircraft. And you?"

"Foreign Manager for a trading company," Avernis said. "We sell food staples mostly."

They chatted for half an hour as the music played, small talk mostly, and Avernis was surprised she did not ask the typical probing questions women usually do in first encounters. They had a few drinks, and then she said, "This place is boring," while resting a casual hand on his knee.

The hand was not so casual for Avernis though. He felt it as if someone had touched him with a low-level stun gun.

"Do you come here often?" he asked to cover his flustered feelings.

"Fortunately no," she said, laughing. She glanced over her shoulder in the direction of her two African associates. "Robert, I have had enough of this. Would you care to join me in my room for a drink?"

She was too good to be true. And then it hit him—maybe she was. She kept looking at the two Africans. They were Muslims, judging by their clothing. Not that that was unusual anywhere in Nigeria, but there were not too many of them present in Enugu from what hc had seen. She had told him she was unaccompanied by any European colleagues. That made her a single woman doing business with two African Muslim men. Impossible? No, but it was unlikely since the northern twelve states of Nigeria had adopted the strict customs of Sharia, Islamic law, two decades ago. Most Muslim men still had problems considering women as equals.

"That's a tempting offer," Avernis said, trying to buy time and sort out his thoughts.

She smiled, patted his hand, and said, "Wait here a minute." Then she walked over to the Africans and started talking. They looked annoyed.

Is this job-related paranoia? Avernis asked himself while Celine conversed with the men. Any number of plausible reasons could explain her presence here with two Muslim businessmen. *Are you going to blow a chance at spending the night with her by spinning some conspiracy fantasy?* Then he reminded himself he was on assignment. One-night stands worked in James Bond movies, but in the real world his F.O.F.U alarm was ringing.

F.O.F.U was the motivating acronym modern CIA trainees and operatives used to be vigilant against breaching agency rules. It stood for Fear Of Fucking Up, and it particularly referred to breaking basic protocol. In this business, it was the small, dumb mistakes that got you compromised or killed, especially when women were involved. It went against every hormone in his body, but he was going to give her some lame excuse for not accepting her offer.

The annoyance the two Africans were showing spilled over into heated bickering. After a few minutes of arguing, Celine turned her back on them and walked toward Avernis.

"Come with me," she said, and she took his arm in hers.

The party was beginning to disperse as the couple walked through a deserted arched tunnel leading to the front of the hotel. "Your friends seemed agitated," Avernis remarked.

"Ah, they are associates, not friends," Celine said. "We have been disagreeing all day on the scope of a job we are to perform. Listen, Robert, I am sorry. I have to go back and work this out with them. I won't be able to have that drink."

Avernis nodded. His fortune was his misfortune, as fate would have it. His calm assurances of no hard feelings seemed to impress her. She pressed him back against a wall, wrapped her arms around him, and crushed her body against his with a full kiss on the mouth. She clutched his collar and nipped at his neck like a wild feline. After a long minute, she pulled off.

"I have to go," she said, pushing him away.

"I don't think we'll see each other again," he said.

"Maybe, maybe not," she laughed, and just like that, she strolled back down the tunnel from the direction they had come, leaving him to wobble like a drunkard back to his room.

CHAPTER VIII

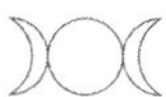

Bad circumstances make for strange bedfellows or good friendships—and sometimes, both.—Anonymous

Lagos

Teresa Ferentinos had been on a long, grueling trip around the world covering the pope's tour, then the grisly interruption of the massacre, and now she was wondering why it could not have ended in a better place than Lagos. Nigeria's major port was vital, bustling, overcrowded, and ripe with various odors, most of which were not refreshing. The tropical air was so dense with humidity that it felt like a giant sponge pressing stale moisture down on her head, giving her an incipient sinus headache.

Teresa and an American colleague, Irving Hirsch, were sitting in the Pan African Hotel bar together with the rest of the UNN news crew. Teresa's coverage of the pope's world tour had brought the network unexpectedly high ratings and earned her accolades from fellow journalists. Lagos was the final stop for the pope and then she could go home.

"A nine-stop papal trip could have been a real yawner. Teresa, you made it interesting and intelligible to the viewers," Hirsch said.

"Thanks, Irv," Teresa said. "You Yanks are always so liberal with your praise compared to the Brits. But really, the situation is inherently dramatic."

"I'll say," Sheila Cassin, the crew coordinator, chimed in. "First time ever a pope was audibly booed at most of his stops. He spouts forward-sounding platitudes but moves backward."

"Granted, it seems that way," Teresa said, "but we have to be careful in our analysis because it will affect the slant on our coverage. I don't get the sense that Clement is a knee-jerk reactionary."

Paul Ford, the production manager, shook his head in disagreement. "The Church's actions seem to belie your observations."

"Perhaps," said Teresa, "but isn't it more a case of inaction than action?"

Ford leaned back in his chair and clasped both hands behind his head. "How do you mean?"

"Well, it's not like Clement has done anything reactionary; actually, it's not like he's done anything at all. Most of the unpopular Church policies were instituted by his predecessors."

"So, what's the story here, Teresa?" asked Jill Tierney, the crew's camerawoman. "What are you saying?"

Teresa held up a piece of paper on which she had been doodling. It was an outline of St. Peter's domed basilica surrounded by bands of tightening concentric rings. "I think the Church is treading water, caught between a rock and a hard place," she replied. "They won't respond to pressing issues like celibacy and female clergy. They're afraid of weakening the central authority of the Church and the pope in these uncertain times. After all, it's that authority that has held them together for two thousand years."

"And a two-thousand-year-old habit is hard to break, eh?" said Irving Hirsch, who was the executive in charge of the tour coverage. "I like it — Clement, the juggling pope of a tottering Church caught in the throes of a modern world crisis. It makes sense and has sound reasoning behind it. Okay, that's a go, folks. I think Teresa gave us a great summary story for our last leg of this trip."

"Right," said Paul Ford. "Now, do you think we can find any decent food in this place?"

"Well, they have a large glump of stuff that looks like pizza dough," Sheila said. "I saw people eating it in the restaurant. It's called *gari.*"

"Nothing like glumpy dough for dinner," Ford snickered. "Shall we?"

The group left, but Teresa and Jill decided to remain in the bar for a while before having an unappetizing-sounding meal.

"You have a quite a knack for religious reporting," Jill said to Teresa as they conversed. "Are you a churchgoer?"

"Not really," Teresa said. "I guess there's a desire in all of us to feel a part of something, a larger whole, whether it's a women's club or a terrorist group. Religion, at least, offers membership in a body that looks for the higher truth and instills grander aspirations."

"Ooh, lofty," Jill chided her.

Teresa laughed. "I'm a witness to great events. Bringing clarity and insight to those events, that's my job, that's what I love. Really, though, I see a great drama here. The Church is the one institution in the world capable of lifting the consciousness of a huge portion of humanity—will it ever fulfill that potential or will it slide back into obscurity? Even worse, will it drag the world down with it?"

"Clement must be asking the same question," Jill said. "The old boy looks like he could use all the help he could get about now."

✠

Robert Avernis arrived in Lagos from Port Harcourt late in the afternoon. After a long nap, he came down from his hotel room for a drink and a bite of dinner. Besides the change of scenery, he liked to talk to his old pal Eddie, the bartender. Eddie was a Yoruba and a wealth of local lore and information. It was Eddie who had explained the meaning of the Yoruba tribe's facial scars to Avernis, told him about the sexual practices of the females from different tribes, and given him insights on topics ranging from tribal relations to the common man's perspective on government and business in the country.

Tonight Eddie was on his favorite topic of sex again. "If I ever get a chance at your girlfriend, man, she never go back to a white guy no more," he proclaimed with a snicker.

"Moot point, Eddie," Avernis said. "Haven't had a girlfriend in quite a while." Avernis then noticed Teresa, the reporter from the massacre site, sitting across the room. The first time he saw her he had been under that mysterious malaise, but now he could appreciate her charms. She was stunning. Just his luck she was a reporter. She had questioned his position at the Vatican, and he needed no such scrutiny. Leo Dusayne was on his ass enough without getting his cover blown by some overzealous snoop. He kept glancing at her, though. No harm in looking. "Eddie, you know them?" he asked, pointing to Teresa and Jill.

Eddie glanced over. "No. Just came in today." He sized up Avernis and said, "Hey man, you lookin' hungry. Why you back here again anyway? Only married women here. You a young, good lookin' guy. Should be in London or Paris. Why you come back down here?"

Avernis sighed. "Thought I understood at one time, Eddie, but now I'm losing track."

While the two men bantered, Teresa and Jill sat drinking at their corner table in the back of the room. There were about thirty people in the lounge, perhaps a half dozen of them European. The room lighting was on the dark side; the ambiance looked like a European decorator's conception of African décor, complete with mahogany elephants' heads and simulated ivory tusks hanging on the wall.

As they drank and chatted about home and living the single life, Jill said, "Check it out. There's a really cute guy at the bar with his eye on you."

Teresa looked up and saw a young, athletic-looking man with light brown hair staring at her with no attempt at subtlety. She almost spit her drink back into the glass. Teresa and Jill both burst out laughing, then settled into girlish giggling.

"Wait, I think I know him," Teresa said. "Yes, I do. He was in Setandwe with some Vatican people. And you're right. He really is cute."

"Yeah. Probably horny as hell too, judging from the looks of this place," Jill said. "What would he be doing here?"

"This is rather the Death Valley of the social world isn't it?" Teresa said. "It is curious though. I mean, what brings different people to this corner of the world?"

"Corporate greed, I'd imagine."

"Jill, you're a cynic, but I'm curious about him. Come on, let's ask him to the table."

"Why not let him come to us?" Jill asked.

"There's something about him . . . anyway, it's the modern age, and I'm impatient," Teresa said with a wink. She started to rise off her seat to approach Avernis, but then—

A deafening roar, like the sonic boom of a jet plane, concussed the bar, and the building shook as if hit by an earthquake. A powerful blast fragmented the wall behind the bar, causing bottles, barstools, and splintered wood to fly inward.

The force of the explosion threw Teresa and Jill back against the wall behind them. Seconds before the blast, Avernis had dropped his room key. He stooped to pick it up just as the room exploded, and ended up with the remnants of the bar on top of him. That action saved his life. It protected him from the fragments of concrete, glass, and wood blown out from the bar wall.

He did not know how long he was buried under the rubble. Dazed and wobbly, he eventually managed to push and kick himself clear of the refuse. His first instinct was to run his hands over his body to see if all his parts were still there. Amazingly, nothing was missing, but he felt warm blood running from his nose. He stood in complete darkness. He sniffed the air. No trace of gas, but mixed in with the dust he detected the familiar residue of plastic explosives he had once smelled during his training exercises in Virginia.

He heard moaning all around him, and he called out, "Anybody, anybody who has matches or a cigarette lighter on them, light them up. We need light."

Suddenly he realized he had his small flashlight in his breast pocket, the one he used for reading during the frequent power outages; he prayed that it was still there. Eventually, his fingers made contact with the thin metal tube. He gave the head a half-turn, and the light ignited to reveal a kaleidoscope of fragments. Ghostlike clouds of dust particles haunted the black edges of the circular beam.

His eyes were adjusting to the shadowy lighting, and he noticed movement on the floor. Rubble was rising as people kicked the debris off themselves. Some people were not stirring at all. Avernis tried to orient himself. He found the bar under which he had lain, and he was able to discern the direction of the wall behind the bar, only the wall no longer seemed to be there. Instead, sharp teeth of ragged concrete framed a gaping space like the snarling maw of a predatory beast. The gash trailed off into grim darkness.

He ran things through his mind. There had been an explosion, probably a bomb. The blast had come from the lobby area that was directly behind the bar. The wall had been blown inward, and he was looking outward toward the lobby.

"Whoever is able to walk, come toward my light," he called out.

From out of the murk, a number of figures approached Avernis, shuffling eerie and zombie-like amidst the debris. He cast the light around in a semi-circle. He counted eight people, but then he heard more movement in the distance. The two women he had been watching just before the blast came into view.

"All right, people," he said, "first we're going to see if we can create any other sources of light. They don't use gas here, so if anyone has matches or lighters, we can make torches with cloth from our clothes or pieces of wood. We'll check this room out, and if we find anyone injured, we'll try and get them out to the street. Okay, let's move quickly; we don't know how badly the building has been compromised."

In this manner, the survivors found five more people who were hurt or unconscious, but alive. There were some whose wounds were too grave to be moved and others who lay dead, including Eddie, whose body Avernis found partially protruding from under a pile of mortar and glass. Poor Eddie, he would never get to make good on his boasting. His head clung to his neck by a few shreds of flesh; one of the glass shelves had propelled off the wall of the bar and nearly decapitated him. Avernis blanched. *Oh, God, is this what my father looked like when they killed him?*

But he had no time to relive bad memories. He helped the survivors grope their way through the remains of the lobby by the faint illumination of the makeshift lighting. First they circumvented the black pitfall of a large hole in the floor and then a collapsed portion of ceiling until they could see lights which they followed like beacons to the open air. The lights were from a group of taxis normally stationed around the rotary in front of the hotel entrance. The drivers were milling around in confusion.

Avernis called out to them. "Has anyone gone to notify the authorities?"

He was told they had.

"Okay," he said. "There are still people in the hotel. I want you to bring your taxis as close to the building as possible and train your high beams into the lobby so they can find their way out."

He directed the cabs to the optimum locations where they would throw light into all angles of the lobby. After they got into position, he shouted, "Does anyone have a torch?" remembering that the Nigerians used the British term for a flashlight.

One of the drivers produced a light that Avernis took. He then started to walk back into the building. As he ascended the shard-strewn steps, a hand grasped his forearm, arresting his momentum and spinning him around. He found himself face-to-face with Teresa. His last recollection was of staring at her in the bar. Her beauty suddenly anchored him against the madness surrounding them as it caused him to rewind his life a few frames back, before the blast had changed everything.

"Where are you going?" she asked.

"Back inside," he said. "There may be more people who need help."

"And you're going in by yourself?"

"Look, there may be more bombs in there or the structure may start to collapse. I can't be asking people to go back in with me."

"Well, *I'm* going with you. I've got friends in there," she said.

"You've got blood on your neck, turn around," he said. She did as he asked. "There's a bad cut on the back of your head. You should get to a hospital."

She looked at him with wild determination in her eyes, as if charging back into the wreck of the bombed-out hotel was her sole ambition in life. "Listen, Mr. Avernis, I don't know you, I don't know whether you're incredibly brave or plain stupid, but I'm a reporter with UNN." She held up her press ID in one hand. "Aside from my friends, going back in there is my job," and the finger of her outstretched arm pointed directly into the smoking blackness.

"I know you're with UNN," Avernis said, turning his head to the side to spit out a bloody wad of saliva.

"My colleague is on her way to retrieve a camera from our truck, but I don't suggest we wait for her, you agree?" Teresa said.

Avernis was worried about appearing on camera, but he knew he could not stop her. "Okay," he said in resignation. "We'll get you another flashlight, but keep that camera out of my face while I'm working."

"Camera-shy, are you?" she asked, but he did not answer.

They entered the building. The upper levels were apparently intact, because hotel guests were making their way down and out between piles of fallen rubble. The lobby was hit hard. Avernis saw corpses and parts of bodies, but no living people. He glanced at Teresa. She put her hand to her mouth but kept following him. He had to admire her spirit; she was tough.

They made their way to the left where the bar and restaurant were located, but a pile of collapsed ceiling stopped them. "This is where the restaurant was," Avernis said.

"Oh, dear God," Teresa moaned. "My friends are in there! We've got to do something!"

Avernis held her arm. "Look, the floors and ceilings are concrete. The restaurant is buried. It will take a crew and heavy equipment to dig it out. I'm really sorry . . ."

"Oh, Jesus, please," she whimpered.

"I'm really sorry, but there is nothing we can do. I've got to go where I can help, okay?"

"I'll stay here; I'll dig with you," she pleaded.

"Why don't you go back and meet your colleague, do your report from outside?" Avernis said.

Teresa gave a dazed, mechanical nod and started to walk toward the light at the entrance. Avernis left the opposite way into the darkness. Teresa was almost at the entrance when she stopped, turned, and looked back. *I can't leave my friends.* And with that resolve she walked back into the smoke and gloom on unsteady legs. She came to the point where the restaurant had collapsed and started pulling at pieces of concrete. She thought she saw Jill approaching, but then she started to swoon.

Avernis had been working farther inside when he heard a woman's scream. He had been able to retrieve three injured people, and he directed the newly arrived crews to others too hurt to be moved. He then took off in the direction of the noise. He worked his way to the corner around recently collapsed material. There, on the ground, he saw Teresa's limp body, and as Jill Tierney was shouting for help, her video camera rolled on amidst the wreckage of the night.

CHAPTER IX

God has mercy on whom he wants to have mercy,
and he hardens whom he wants to harden—Romans 9:18

Central Nigeria

The long-winged bird glided over the rolling, verdant hills of bush and trees and corpses. The terrain was a parterre checkerboard of thatch-roofed hamlets separated by clumps of jungle. The roads were carved out of a type of ocher-tinted clay found only in Africa, and they formed ribbons around the small hamlets creating random patterns across the vast landscape. A lone figure walked along the main road.

The white-robed nun was leading a donkey that dragged a makeshift litter behind it. As she crested the top of a hill, she came upon the grisly scene described by people in the village a few miles back. A dozen mutilated bodies lay in the low scrub by the side of the road.

She cupped her nose and mouth against the smell and drew close enough to see the death agony stamped across the face of one of the men. She was unable to tell on which body his decapitated head belonged. Several of the heads were intact, but all of the bodies were missing appendages and bore the hideous, hacking marks of the machete.

Then she heard a thrashing in the bush to her right followed by the breathy grunting of something tired or desperate. In a sudden burst, the reedy scrub parted violently and a figure exploded from the thatch, rushing down on her like a snarling animal, a sickle in his hand raised to strike. His eyes seemed intent with a feral desire to slice her apart, but the nun stood calmly, making no move to protect herself. A mere three feet away from her, his body torqued to deliver a gutting blow, but then his head exploded and he spun around as pieces of brain and bone spiraled out of his ruptured skull. He landed in a crumpled heap on the road, looking like a dying, rabid dog as the gunshot's sound dissipated into the air.

Six men emerged from the roadside a short ways behind her. The leader walked over to her, a piece of straw rolling between his lips. He stopped and looked at her with curiosity as he motioned to the others to examine the dead man. "I think this is the last of them," one of the men replied as he poked his gun barrel into the corpse's skull cavity.

The leader turned to the nun. "Unusual, what fate or fortune protects you?" he said. "Nearly impossible to make a head shot on the run. He knew we were on his heels yet he stops to attack you, a nun? Why would he do that, do you know?" But the nun was unresponsive.

"I think you *do* know." The man studied her intently. "What do you carry within that death stalks you? And death *was* upon you, but you did not flinch. You know what this land is, don't you?" Still no word from her. He leaned close and spoke into her ear. "This is hell and we are trapped animals condemned to live in it. What worse fate than being born? That brigand," the man said, pointing to the dead body, "he understood, and it drove him so mad he would stop to sacrifice you even as he ran in death's shadow. They don't understand," he said, pointing to his men. "We were all insane to be born into this, but you know that or you would not roam here alone. Go on to your destination; I think no harm will come to one such as you, for you understand hell, don't you?"

"And you know your prison," she said, "but not your jailer. If you knew that, your torment might end."

He pulled back from her, eyes narrowed and fixing on her for a long moment. Then he motioned to his men to follow him. As they walked away he kept turning to stare at her until they disappeared over the road's downward slope.

A short time later, as she moved on, she heard a faint groan emerge from inside the thicket. She turned and stepped toward the bush. As if swimming through a lake of dense flora, she thrust her hands into the vines, then pushed them aside with both arms and plunged in. After several minutes, she located the source of the moans.

The man had deep cuts in several places. He had lost a lot of blood and was naked from the waist up, his shirt used to make tourniquets for his viciously chopped arms. He must have crawled off, unnoticed in the heat of the night ambush, and so eluded death. But he was dying now, and she knew she needed to muster all her strength to haul him out to the road.

She brushed the flies off the man's open wounds, but when she got a clear look at his unmarked face, she put her hand over her mouth and staggered backward. Her legs weakened and she sank to the ground. Shaking, she knelt in a prayer-like posture, face hidden in her hands. She stayed frozen in that position until a loud groan made her jump.

Trembling, she looked at the dying man and then toward the road, an easy walk back if she remained unburdened. The man moaned again. If she didn't act immediately he would die. She made her decision. She clenched her fists and stood with a firm, upward thrust of her legs. She unwound the rope sashed about her waist, placed it underneath the arms of the slack body, and began to draw him slowly through the web of vegetation.

✠

Dr. Ondogwu was intrigued when the nurses called him to look out the window. A nun was leading a donkey onto the hospital grounds. The animal was dragging a litter bearing an injured person. Dr. Ondogwu ran down three flights of stairs to greet the travelers. He was in charge of emergencies, but he was curious besides.

"What have we here?" the doctor asked.

"A badly injured man," the nun replied, pointing to the figure strapped to the litter.

The doctor's curiosity was growing. The nun was a young woman with smooth, coffee-and-cream-colored skin, delicate, high-arched brows, and limpid eyes. Her nose was short and straight, her features fine, and her lips were well formed. A beautiful face, yes — she had the look of the Fulani — but what most intrigued him was a certain glow about her that belied her bloody, soiled clothes and the trudging journey she must have made to get here.

"From where have you come, Sister?" the doctor asked.

"From the south," she said. "I found this man between Setandwe and Madugra."

"That is at least fifteen miles away," Ondogwu said as he knelt and examined the man on the litter. "This man should be dead. How did you keep him alive with such wounds?"

The woman smiled and waved her hand in the air. "Oh," she said with a soft laugh that somehow did not seem out of place, "perhaps God has a plan for this one, you see?"

Before Dr. Ondogwu could respond, a man wearing glasses and dressed in a khaki-colored safari-style suit walked up to them. "Doctor, what is this all about?" the man asked.

"Mr. Ibrahim," the doctor said, "this is Sister . . . I am sorry, I did not ask your name."

"Annalisa."

"Yes, Sister Annalisa." Ondogwu introduced her to Mr. Ibrahim, the hospital administrator. "Sister Annalisa has brought a man here, one of the brigands who were caught this morning," the doctor said to Ibrahim.

Ibrahim's eyes went wide. "The ones who massacred Setandwe? That means this man is a murderer and a thief, Sister, don't you know that?"

"That is what I have heard," the nun said.

"Sister, many have died in our hospital because of this man and his gang," Ibrahim said, then spat on the ground. "The neighboring Christian villagers caught them and gave them what they deserved. These men give Islam a bad name. We will not waste our scarce resources on such as him, even if he could pay . . . and he obviously cannot."

Annalisa reached into a pouch strapped over the donkey and pulled something out. She opened her fist and there was money in her hand. "This is all I have."

Ibrahim, shook his head, said, "No, no, no," then stalked away.

Dr. Ondogwu turned to Sister Annalisa.

"Dr. Ondogwu, you are an Ibo, yes?" she asked.

"Yes, I am an Ibo and a Catholic," he replied.

"You are a long way from your tribal land. What brought you here?"

"My work," he said.

The nun smiled. "So, you are an Ibo and a Catholic, but most importantly you are a doctor, and your purpose is to heal the sick, not judge them. Judging is the work of God, healing is the work of God through man."

"Ibrahim thinks differently," Ondogwu said. "He is a Muslim, tired of people killing in the name of his religion. He's a good man."

"Then I say in the name of Allah, it is still the will of God. Only the name changes, not the spirit," she said, and when she clasped his hand, electrified gooseflesh formed on Ondogwu's forearm.

He should not cross Ibrahim, but he could not shake the image of the lone woman dragging an injured stranger miles through the countryside. She held on to him until he said, "Very well, Sister. We will help him, and I will persuade Mr. Ibrahim." Ondogwu winked at her. "I am the head of emergency here, and there is no one to replace me for many miles around. I am sure Mr. Ibrahim will not want to lose me."

Annalisa thanked the doctor then went to the wounded man's side. Ondogwu saw her hand tremble as she touched his shoulder. The man's eyes flickered open for a few seconds. Seeing the nun, his eyes went wide, as if the angel of death hovered over him. His mouth quivered, trying to form words. She nodded to him, but he passed out again.

Does he know her? Ondogwu asked himself. *Strange, that robber looked like he had seen the devil. Well, criminal or not, I will save him.* In that instant, he surprised himself—why this sudden determination? Ondogwu's eyes tracked Annalisa's every step as she led her donkey away. He felt a pang of . . . what? Loss? A sudden emptiness, perhaps, like something he needed had been given to him then suddenly taken away.

She had said she was going to the Sahel famine area. He had tried to dissuade her—the place was evil, infested with thieves and murderers. But his pleas were to no avail. As she grew smaller in the distance, the doctor stared until he caught his last glimpse of her, his mind tense with worry, and he asked himself, *if God had watched over that brigand, surely He would watch over the nun—would He not?*

CHAPTER X

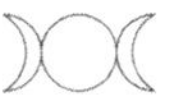

But before all these, they shall lay
their hands on you . . .
Luke 21:12

Niger, Africa
The Fringe of the Sahel Desert

The three men hiding in the bush smacked their lips as they eyed the four nuns walking the narrow trail. The nuns walked the jungle path between the two main roads that diverged at the village of Desan. They were probably on a mission to help what was left of the starving populace on the fringe of the Sahel. Three of them were young, two African, one European. The last one was also African, but she was older. They would kill her quickly.

The women probably had no money and they carried no food, but they had other uses. The starvation and mass exodus from the drought had broken down all local systems, including the police and judiciary. All that remained were these human vultures who haunted the jungles lying just south of the desert's border, preying on passers-by, scavenging off the misery of the dying land. The pickings were slim but easy, particularly the women, whom they culled from the fleeing refugees with the ease of lions cutting baby antelope from the herd.

These predators liked to take souvenirs after they finished with the women. In his backpack, the leader carried a few desiccated ears, several fingers, and some even choicer parts from his victims. It had been at least a month since they'd had any females. How exciting it would be to have celibate, Westernized women kicking and screaming as they took them, and the white one would be their first European.

The nuns froze as the first of the trio rustled out from the bush to block their path, gun in hand and machete slung over his shoulder.

"Where are you going?" he demanded.

"Yes, and why do you trespass on our land?" The second voice came from behind the women.

They turned and saw another man with a large skinning knife. He held up a leaf and grinned as he sliced through it like butter. The nuns cringed, holding shaking hands to their lips in prayer, all except the pretty African one, who seemed to be in a daze. No doubt she was frozen with fear and unable to react. Good — all the easier to do what they wanted.

Sounds of thrashing and grunting issued from the bush to the left. "The bad man is over there," one man said. "You hear him? He will hurt you. Follow us. We will keep him away."

At gunpoint, they led the nuns off into the jungle. The women held hands and quietly prayed. After a short trek, they came to a clearing where the third man waited. "What do we have here?" he said, rubbing his crotch and savoring the fear on the women's faces. "Oh yes, I am the bad man, and no one will help you. Now, let us not waste time."

He went straight for the European woman. The young African nun seemed to snap out of her trance, and she stepped in front of him, shielding the woman's body with her own.

"No! Get back and leave now. I beg you, leave us now."

The man shoved the palm of his hand in her face and pushed her hard to the ground. "You beg me? Wait your turn and you will beg me, but not to go away."

He turned toward the European woman and pounced. She screamed as he began to tear at her habit. The older nun tried to intervene but one of the other men grabbed the back of her hair and punched her in the face. Blood flew in all directions as she collapsed to the dirt, whimpering. The first man had the European nun on the ground, slapping her face in between grabs at her exposed breasts.

"OMASA FIDEKE ENTEMBALE! INTAKANE FENINSALA! SA! SA!"

The sibilant voice cut through the jungle in a reptilian hiss and froze everyone in their places. They all looked at the younger African nun who shouted out while still lying on the ground. Then, in their native tongue, one of the men said, "Did you hear her? She speaks in the old language, the secret language!"

The terrible voice continued to emanate from the nun on the ground, in a language only the men understood. *"I know your cult, your gods, the things you worship: an ancient blight on the land. Fools, you think they are the power under the sun? Far greater exists that you cannot comprehend. Listen to what I tell you and leave; leave or you shall perish as your ancestors perished at ancient Entembale. Leave, and never return here or be cursed by the fire and venom. SA! SA!"*

Two of the men men dropped their weapons and shrank back. "What are you? Witch! You know the tongue of the old path. What are you?" They turned and fled into the jungle. The remaining brigand stood, gun pointed at the nun, hand shaking and finger trembling on the trigger. Suddenly, his eyelids drew back wide. "Ohhh," his voice quivered. The gun dropped from his hands like a lead weight. His body went limp as his muscles melted, and with arms slack to his side, he fell face-first into the dust.

The nun continued to scream, then fell silent as her body heaved several times with a writhing, whip-like snap. The other nuns pulled themselves together seeing that no one was seriously injured beyond shock, a split lip, and some nasty bruises. They went to the fallen brigand, placing fingers on his wrist and carotid artery.

"He's dead," Sister Elizabeth said.

Renweg, the European nun, slowly gathered up the tattered ends of her habit and looked at Annalisa. "What did you do to those men, and what was that awful language you spoke?" She recoiled, thinking of the cobra-like sound of the words and the alien voice.

"I do not know," Annalisa replied. She looked at the incredulous faces of the other nuns. "I was shouting at them, that much I recall, but I do not know what language of theirs I would speak. Yoruba, Fulfulde, or German? I speak some French and Hausa."

The other three nuns shook their heads in unison. "No," Sister Adea said. "Between the three of us we would have recognized those languages. This was a strange tongue, and your voice, it sounded like . . . like it came from an animal."

"All I remember is praying," Annalisa said. "I knew those men had done great evil here."

The nuns were silent as each of them tried to digest the shocking events. Eventually, Sister Elizabeth, the eldest of them, spoke from between swollen, painful lips. "It was a miracle; the gift of tongues was visited on Sister Annalisa to save us."

The women then proceeded toward the village under the twilight's fading glimmer.

"When will I see you . . . find wisdom and you will find yourself . . . where does wisdom lie?"

Elizabeth heard Annalisa whispering to herself but could not make out the words "What's wrong?" she asked.

"Something is coming, I feel it," Annalisa replied.

"Is it those men?" Sister Elizabeth asked, fear gripping her spine and jerking her body upright.

Annalisa shook her head. "No, they are gone. Something else is closing in on us."

"What is it?" the older nun asked in alarm.

"We have gone where we were needed in this corner of the world, to the sickness, to the violence, to the death . . ."

"Yes?" Mary Elizabeth asked, trying to draw her out.

Annalisa looked at her and their eyes met. "That world of great and terrible things—*now, it will be coming to us.*"

And Sister Elizabeth could only wonder at the certainty of her words.

CHAPTER XI

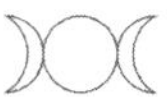

Nigeria will be a prime battleground where the crescent will rise against the cross in the new millennium. —From a letter by Milites Domini leadership to its functionaries circa 2018

Lagos

Cardinal Roncalli turned in for the night in his bedroom in the Lagos archdiocese compound. The pope would arrive the day after tomorrow from Buenos Aires, and Roncalli would have a full day making advance preparations for the pontiff's visit. He would also meet the controversial nun, Annalisa Basanjo, in the morning. Bishop Ogunsanya's men had tracked her up north and promptly brought her back to Lagos.

Before retiring, he said a prayer for the pope, who had been looking pale and frequently complained of fatigue after his public appearances. The people were holding him accountable for the Church's inaction, and they were not holding back their anger. Clement was feeling the pressure.

At some point after falling asleep, a loud knocking awakened him.

"Eminenza!" It was the voice of Roald Zugli, the head of Vatican security. "Eminenza, I'm sorry but we have a problem."

Roncalli looked at the red numbers on the bedside clock. It was four in the morning.

"Give me a few minutes, Roald; I will see you downstairs."

When Roncalli entered the conference room, Zugli and Bishop Ogunsanya stood waiting for him. Zugli's prominent, pointy nose was a common characteristic of the Swiss-German cantons from which the Guards derived, as was the attention to detail that he displayed in his work. Colonel Virgile Ossore of the Italian counter-terrorism unit was also present. With groups like the Poor Nations Coalition so frequently attacking Church targets, the Italian government had assigned Ossore to augment protection for the pope during his tour.

Zugli spoke first. "Eminenza, I'm sorry to disturb you, but last night it appears a bomb exploded in the Pan African Hotel."

"A bomb? Was anyone injured?" Roncalli asked.

"Many killed and injured," Ogunsanya said. "Incidentally, we have located the nun, Sister Annalisa, in the north. We're flying her down tomorrow for you to question her."

"Very well, Your Excellency," Roncalli said. He noted Ogunsanya's tone of voice. It was clear where the bishop stood concerning the nun. No matter. He would meet the woman soon enough and form his own opinion, but more urgent issues now demanded his attention.

"I was at the American embassy two hours ago," Zugli said. "I met with my old CIA friend, Leo Dusayne, Avernis' boss. He flew in on a special flight. Robert was in the hotel but escaped unharmed. He was at the meeting too."

Since the bombing happened so close to the pope's visit, the three men had examined possible connections. They identified only two groups likely to take action against the pope. One was the PNC, the Poor Nations Coalition; the others were Nigerian Islamic terrorists.

"The PNC are the ones who kidnapped and ransomed some of our bishops in Latin America and Southeast Asia," Roncalli said.

"Yes, but it's doubtful they were responsible here," Zugli said. "They've only operated in Western or Christian nations and assassination isn't their style. They fancy themselves as Robin Hoods. They might try kidnapping a pope for the ransom money, but this bombing and the circumstances here don't fit their MO."

"And the Muslims?" Roncalli asked. "What about them?"

"Could have been any number of groups," Zugli replied. "No one has claimed credit yet."

Ossore frowned. "So, is this bombing connected to the pope's visit?"

"Very possible," Zugli said. "The fanatical Muslims aren't happy about his visit but they know security will be extraordinarily tight after he arrives."

"Does the fact they targeted the Pan African Hotel tell us anything?" Ossore asked.

"The Pan African is the international hotel where most Westerners stay and conduct business," Zugli said. "That fact, coupled with the pope's visit, may be the Islamic terrorists' way of telling the West their presence is not wanted here."

"So it may be an anti-Western protest," Ossore said. "But we cannot preclude the possibility they *will* attack the pope."

"Of course we can't," Zugli replied. "The Nigerian army is providing security. We've done background checks on the soldiers guarding the archdiocese compound. They're all Christians."

Roncalli stood and walked the length of the conference table. "I'm puzzled by one thing. Why would the Muslims take action here in the south? You'd think they'd be busy establishing an independent state up north where they've already invoked Islamic law."

"That would mean civil war with the other tribes, Eminenza, and they aren't ready yet for a repeat of that," Zugli explained. "The different tribes here exist in a working balance since the last civil war. The Muslims may want to play on Nigerian nationalism against the West for the time being rather than secede."

"Roncalli stopped pacing and looked at Zugli. "But what is their goal in all this?"

"It's always about power, Eminenza, and power here means oil," Zugli said. He stood and walked over to a wall map of Nigeria. "See where the Yorubas and the Christian tribes are concentrated here in the southern tier of the country bordering the ocean. "Now see where the oil is." Zugli pointed to the offshore coastal waters. "The Muslim extremists are in the north but the oil is in the south. It's not an independent state they want; they need control of the entire country for the oil production."

"That makes sense," Ossore said. "Oil, and water for that matter, is becoming scarce in the Middle East. Under Iranian leadership, the Muslim oil-producing states are pooling their resources to sign deals with Asian nations and cut remaining oil supplies to the West. Tehran would love to stop the flow of Nigerian oil as part of their strategy."

"Currently, the Yorubas dominate the government," Zugli said, "and governments here dole out positions of influence to the tribes in equal measure to keep the peace. The Yorubas have continued that practice, but more of them are converting to Christianity. The Muslims see this as a Western plot to Christianize the south and gain control of the oil."

"And there lies the connection to pope's visit. It must seem like one big validation of their paranoia," Roncalli said. "The age-old struggle repeats itself."

After the briefing, Zugli remained a few minutes to talk. "Tell me, Roald," Roncalli asked, "this Iranian oil embargo — how seriously are the Americans taking it?"

Zugli sighed and shook his head. "It's extremely serious, Eminenza. You can take America's pulse by listening to President Davidson. America pulled back from the Mid-East when they had Iran surrounded; Iran has been a threat ever since. Some, like Davidson, have said the Muslim oil pacts are tantamount to war. He's calling for an end to the appeasement-and-containment policy of the past two decades. His support is growing in the American senate. The man has charisma and a clear direction."

Roncalli shook his head. "I always thought of the Church's problems as being isolated, these attacks on us by different groups, but what I heard today tells me it is part of a pattern—we are being swept into a global shadow war."

Zugli considered his statement. "It could indeed become a hot war. It's been my unfortunate experience, Eminenza, that when a relentless adversary treats you like a combatant, you had better become a combatant or perish."

The Church caught up in a war? Roncalli thought. How could it ever defend itself? Had Mannheim been right all along? God forbid.

CHAPTER XII

. . . a prophet has no honor in his own country.
—John 4:44

Lagos

Priests and nuns alike froze in the corridors of the Lagos archdiocese. They were all aware of the woman in the bishop's office who was the target of Ogunsanya's vehement shouting.

"How dare you disobey my orders?" Ogunsanya yelled. "Do you admit you did so?"

"I saw people in need and tried to help," Annalisa replied. "I believe that is what we are here to do."

Ogunsanya slammed his palm on the table that separated him from the nun sitting opposite him. "What you are here to do is obey the Church. You went north, to the *Muslim* north. Reports of your so-called healings are spreading like a plague up there. I don't yet fathom the nature of your works, but you are rebellious, and that speaks ill of you. What have you to say for yourself?"

Annalisa said nothing, but she did not look down, or to the side, or anywhere else but straight at the bishop. She was not trying to taunt him, but to let him know there was no shame attached to her actions despite his protests. The bishop seemed unnerved, however.

He did not scream at her this time, but his anger seeped out in measured words. "You will now go to the east wing to meet Cardinal Roncalli. Yes, that's right; the pope's secretary himself will judge you. That is the measure of the trouble you have caused. You profess to love the Church? Well, you'll soon find yourself condemned by it." Ogunsanya then turned his back to Annalisa and looked out a window. After a minute of icy silence, he flung his hand out to his side and said, "Go."

As she traversed the corridor, all eyes followed her. The bishop's efforts had not been entirely in vain—their faces showed the fear he had wanted to see in her.

Roncalli had come with the authority to put a quick end to the nun's calling and all the miracle rumors, but his first encounter with her was nothing he could have expected. The thought came to him that an unspoken language passes between human beings, that people *feel* one another before speaking. Most people would dismiss these impressions in the instant they occur, and so they lose the opportunity to sense the truth of a person at a very profound level. When first words are spoken, barriers of language and ego, of rational mind and guarded thought gain ascendance and obscure people's real essence, leaving them to deal with imperfect reflections of one other.

It was not so with *this* woman. She emanated an undiluted force that traversed space and time. Her essence imprinted itself on him so totally that it adhered to him like honey, coating his senses like a sweet balm. Still, he was uneasy. Tradition said the Great Heretic was charismatic, insidious, seemingly good, and not even aware if its own evil. Not initially, at least.

Rays of late-afternoon sun cast a soft glow in the room and revealed a physical beauty to match the aura she radiated. Her skin was the color of coffee and cream, smooth and calm. Her features were striking—the full lips of her African ancestry sculpted in defined, statuary lines; the fine, straight nose, almost European in appearance; and the high, arching brows, delicate and reminiscent of a Japanese geisha—it was as if the most beautiful features from every race had been taken from God's palette and painted upon her visage. Roncalli, who stood over six feet tall, towered above the petite nun. She was slender, not more than five foot two, but neither his height nor his authority affected the steady look in her eye.

Roncalli began to question her. He told her that her healings were stirring up Muslim extremists in the north who might retaliate against the Church, to which she replied, "I have met many Muslims, but none who harbor desires such as these. I never seek to proselytize. God heals any who accept His healing, Christian or Muslim alike. Any who have changed faiths did so of their own choice. You want no conflict, Your Eminence, but refusing to heal Muslims helps the very ones who promote divisions between people."

Roncalli then delved into her background and was shocked to learn that a nun based in her village back then, Annaliese Steurer, was the daughter of a famous conservative German theologian who was a major influence on Cardinal Mannheim.

"She believed women were entitled to roles in Church life equal to men," Annalisa said.

"Sister Annaliese wanted to be the first female priest. Since that was not possible, she told me I had to grow up and become the first woman pope to make up for it. Hah! Imagine that!"

Roncalli then asked her about the old village shaman who taught her.

Annalisa smiled. She told him the old man could make snakes slither back into the jungle and beckon birds down from the trees to alight on his shoulder. He knew when people were good or bad, when they were sick, and where the sickness was rooted. He taught her of the "still place" where he would travel to seek answers.

She's describing a contemplative state. Roncalli nodded to indicate that he understood.

"I spent so much time in the still place, people began to feel I was . . . not right. When I would walk by, they would point their fingers to their temples in little circling motions and shake their heads from side to side."

"That must have been difficult," Roncalli said. "But tell me about your early life in as much detail as you can."

She inhaled deeply and closed her eyes. "I can think back," she said in a wistful voice, "I do remember certain things . . . " and so she began her story:

Annalisa's father was a Yoruba, a Catholic whose people were predominantly animists, but he was a chief who bore the facial scars of his tribe. He took a wife from the Fulani, unusual in that she was from a northern tribe and a Muslim too, and she bore him a daughter.

The truth was that as long as Annalisa could remember, nobody liked her—they feared or adored her, but nobody just *liked* her. Her presence inspired and unsettled, comforted and challenged, and there was just nothing as simple as "liking" involved concerning her. Even so, the bolder villagers, or the ones who thought themselves wise, admonished her: "You think your ways and arts to be good? Be warned, evil stands behind that which appears pure. You are being seduced."

One day when she was still a young girl in her village, some men barged into her father's home. "Annalisa has been bitten by a lethal snake. She will be dead in minutes!" they declared. The chief and his distraught wife sent for the *ogun* then ran to find their nine-year-old daughter, hoping she was still alive. They found her on the ground with the snake, holding it by the throat and talking to it.

The *ogun* sauntered up with a smile on his face. Annalisa looked around at the circled villagers. She released the reptile. The villagers gasped as it writhed away into the bush. Annalisa not only lived; she did not even look sick.

"So, I see the snake has bitten you," the *ogun* said.

Annalisa looked up at him, smiled, and said, "Yes, but that was before he knew me."

Word about that got around, and the incident did nothing to lessen the unease about her in the village. *Different, apart.* There was a woman in the village whose daughter played with Annalisa from time to time. In deference to the chief, the wary woman did not discourage her daughter, but she always kept the two of them in sight to thwart any mischief.

The woman had lost a bracelet some days before and happened to inquire of her daughter if she knew the bracelet's whereabouts. "No," said the daughter, who was playing jump rope with Annalisa, "but ask her, she knows things."

"Annalisa?" the mother replied in disdain. "She never speaks," and she looked into the large doe eyes of the silent, peculiar girl. "How can she help?"

Annalisa held the woman's gaze. An image quickly formed in the mother's mind—it was of the bracelet falling from her wrist in the field where she had been extracting cassava root. Compelled, she scurried back, rummaged through the dirt, and found the trinket.

Incidents like these could get one killed in the superstitious bush country, but none dared harm a chief's daughter, and everyone remembered the old *ogun's* prediction about her. Yet, even the girl's mother was concerned about her daughter's "strangeness."

A large East Indian community existed throughout Africa, and one day a man from Delhi wandered into the village. He was roaming the world as an itinerant spiritual pilgrim. He would work for food, and indeed, he labored a few days for the chief. On hearing Annalisa's mother express concern about the girl, the man took Annalisa's hands in his for several minutes as the puzzled woman looked on.

"Burnt seeds," he muttered as a look of awe overtook his face.

"What?" the mother asked.

"My God! A most ancient soul, she . . . she . . ." the man's trembling voice trailed off into a whimper and he went to his knees. He stumbled over his next words, muttering about atonement and Great Sin.

"What do you say? Speak up!" Annalisa's mother said.

The Indian snapped to it. "After this lifetime she will be done with this world," he said, "done with the wheel of karma if she answers the call. No actions she takes in this life will create new karma, so they are like burnt seeds producing no earthly fruit. She spends much time in the other world. The events of this world are like reflections in a mirror to her, yet she will come to a balance before her ascension. She must!"

Annalisa's mother was a Muslim, and all this talk was alien to her. Taking no comfort in his words, she had him thrown out.

Different, apart. Annalisa remembered walking outside her village when a commotion near a hut attracted her. A boy was screaming in agony. He had stepped on a piece of broken glass that pierced clear through his foot, and people had gathered around him.

"Get it out!" the mother shouted at the father.

"How can I without making it worse?" the father snapped back.

Annalisa flowed between the frantic people with trancelike calmness, and the crowd fell silent. Annalisa knelt, cupped her hands over the boy's foot, then withdrew her hands. The glass was out; the boy had not so much as whimpered. The mother's eyes glazed over. Then she focused on Annalisa for a split second . . . and slapped her hard across the face.

Annalisa withdrew into the solitude of the jungle and cried. It was not the slap that hurt her—it was the isolation, the terrible strangeness of it all. Annalisa never looked at people; she looked through them. On the skin, on the surface, was where their cruelty and evil lay like so much dirt, yet inside dwelt the shining golden center that was each of them, that part of them that was Oneness. And Annalisa pondered how evil could arise from good, but the people were not aware of any of these things. They were like sleepwalkers stumbling around in a fearful amnesiac fog. The chilling realization that haunted her was that in the Creation, something had gone horribly wrong.

Don't they see that? They all must be dreaming, she concluded. *Am I the only one awake?* It made her conscious of being two people in two worlds, and it shouldn't be that way. She rested in the still place until hands touched her shoulder and a voice said, "What have you been doing, child? You have been gone three days!"

Coming out of her trance, her eyes focused. She saw her Uncle Hakim. Hakim did not yell at her or scold her as most of the elders would. He gathered his embroidered robe in at the waist and sat next to her. Annalisa's face was parallel to his but she did not look directly at him. She moved her eyes to the far corners and took in his form from the periphery.

Hakim brushed a lock of hair from her forehead then stroked her temple. "Are you injured?" he asked, running his hands up and down her body, but Annalisa shook her head.

"Good." His hand came to rest on her leg, drawing circles on the tender flesh of her thigh. Annalisa winced and jerked her body to the side, breaking contact with his hand. "Well then," her uncle said, "We should get back. Your parents are worried . . . "

✠

Roncalli felt Annalisa's pain by the end of her story. Her saving grace was Sister Annaliese, who told her that all the things that happened in the still place were of God, and Jesus too had dwelt in the still place where he healed the sick and even raised the dead.

For the first time, her composure broke and the serenity left her face. "I sought Jesus . . . at times I think I feel him . . . but something of him has eluded me. I don't know why."

She's being honest, but she says Christ eludes her. Roncalli made a mental note of that. *She exists in a split world.* "Now, Sister," Roncalli said, "Claims have been made about your healing powers. Some are very serious, involving disturbing stories of life and death. Let's get to that matter now."

CHAPTER XIII

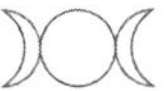

A good tree cannot bring forth evil fruit, neither can a corrupt tree bring forth good fruit—Matthew 7:18

Lagos

"Most astonishing of the allegations comes from an eyewitness I met in Setandwe who claims you actually brought a dead child back to life. Is this true?" Roncalli asked.

Annalisa's lips moved ever so slightly. "The eye is a good viewer but a poor interpreter of reality. No *human* has such power."

"Is that a yes or no?" Roncalli asked.

"I held a living child," Annalisa said, "and you are testing your own faith, yes." It was a statement, not a question.

Roncalli did not respond. Instead, he asked about her other healings, including that of the blind girl witnessed by Bishop Ogunsanya. "People believe what they want, but I heal no one," Annalisa said. "I am just a channel; the power of God within each person heals them."

"The abilities you channel, how do you know they come from God?" Roncalli asked.

"Do you remember," she said, "how the Bible declared one recognizes the tree by the fruit it bears? Man judges man by actions, but God judges man by intent. If the intent is pure, then the tree will bear the sweet fruit of righteous fulfillment."

"But Satan may still deceive in the guise of purity," the cardinal said.

"Everything is subject to the will of God, and even evil must, in the end, be turned to God's purpose," she replied.

"That view could be used to justify evil actions," the cardinal responded.

Annalisa shook her head. "God does not cut himself off from people, but people do cut themselves off from God when they commit intentional evil. Evil punishes itself; people have a way of punishing themselves."

"How would you know that?" he asked.

"I have seen it," she said. "Not with my eyes but"—she patted her chest above the heart—"I can see all the illnesses, how they begin in the attitudes and emotions. We live by God's power. Evil is simply error, our misuse of God's energy.

It is like a current passing through a faulty conduit. It produces sparks, then fire, and eventually the person burns out."

"Are you familiar with the Book of Revelations?"

"Oh, yes," Annalisa said.

"Revelations and other prophecies have foretold tribulations for the Church," Roncalli said, "prophecies involving"—he almost said *false prophets,* but he caught himself—"prophecies involving miracle workers."

His direct approach elicited no reaction from her. She continued to listen with a polite smile on her face. "I see," was her only response.

"Some are also concerned that a hidden church has existed over the ages, a church that will rise to destroy the true church. Have you heard of such things?"

She smiled. "The only hidden church I know lies in the heart of each human being. It is their sleeping aspirations to realize God's grace."

As they spoke, odd images kept flashing across Roncalli's mind—a woman with reddish-gold tresses and an older man with coarse, graying hair that hung below his ears. He sensed a tension between them, but as they approached each other, they merged, silhouetted against a flaming sun wherein Christ stood with outstretched arms. All three figures were then blissfully consumed in the fiery globe. The peculiar thing was that he thought the woman was Annalisa and the man was him! And why was Christ enfolding them in the sun?

"You feel plagued by doubt," she said, her voice cutting through his day-dream. "This holds you back from things you must do." The accuracy of that comment from out of nowhere startled Roncalli. It exposed his personal need more than he would have revealed to anybody other than his confessor. She continued, despite the surprise registered on his face.

"You seek to become resolute to meet your challenges. Your life need not be paralyzed by the pattern of your parents, your mother, for we all have the power within to change our course, but you have important choices to make, and they will soon be upon you. These choices will impact lives far beyond your own, do you see? You need to see God's hand."

Roncalli was taken aback. She had dredged up suppressed memories from his subconscious . . . and she was accurate! "Why are you saying these things? What do you know of my family, of my mother?" he asked.

Annalisa still held on to his hand. "She died in an accident after drinking."

Roncalli had *never* told that story to anyone. In minutes, she had cut to the core trauma of his life in a way that enabled him to link it with his present timidity and inaction over the Church he loved crumbling around him. He needed to see God's hand in the world to reassure him. Was this nun that hand of God or was she, as many thought, the claw of Satan?

"How could you know these things you have told me?" Roncalli asked the nun. "Where do you get such information?"

Annalisa pursed her lips, looked down at the floor, and kept silent.

"Why did you come to the Church?" Roncalli asked. "Would you obey the Church?"

"I could *only* work within the Church. What does the Church require of me?"

"I'm not sure . . . not yet," Roncalli replied.

A cloud then seemed to pass over her face. "Your Eminence, I must tell you something," she said, "and I hope you will not find it . . . improper."

"Yes?"

"It has to do with the Church, or at least it begins with the Church," she said. "I saw men, men of the Church grinding their teeth in outrage and anger that seemed to flow outward and encompass the world. I saw great turmoil on earth, and I sensed loss, as if something of great importance had been lost."

Roncalli's mind jumped to a possible assassination attempt on Clement in Nigeria.

"The tribulation you spoke of—it will begin, soon, but at the end may lie salvation."

Roncalli's veins constricted, but he resolved not to speak any more on this subject right now. "Sister, thank you for sharing your concerns with me," he said. "I will heed your statements. I would like to talk with you again before I leave, but now I must prepare for the Holy Father's arrival tomorrow."

The cloud passed from Annalisa's face, replaced by an innocent smile. "May I personally greet the Holy Father, Your Eminence? He may never be back here again."

Roncalli thought for a minute. From this meeting, he could not say with certainty that she was harmless. If he were to trust his senses, this nun was good, and yet there were still many questions. A second opinion would help, and who better to provide one than the Holy Father? "Sister, come by here tomorrow night after the day's ceremonies, perhaps around eight o'clock. I cannot promise you anything, but I will ask the pope if he can give you some time."

Her hands clapped together in glee. "Oh, thank you, Your Eminence, thank you."

When Annalisa left Roncalli he was dwelling on her omen of a coming tribulation. It had hit a nerve. A confluence of events was pushing the

Church through a perilous channel like the Odyssey's ancient Scylla and Charybdis — the beast that devours on one side and the depthless whirlpool on the other. The Islamic world was rising in a global war that was sucking in the Church, a Church being slowly eaten away, abandoned, even attacked by its own people in anger and frustration, a Church required to make penance for the damage caused by its outmoded practices.

On the dim shore ahead, lurking in the shadows, was the Great Heretic, the one who would destroy the Church from within, the one who was prophesied in the Breverarium book kept in the Vatican's vaults.

Roncalli went about his preparations for the pope's arrival, but his mind kept straying back to the nun. Who was she? Most importantly, would she play a role for good or evil during these days of dark tidings?

CHAPTER XIV

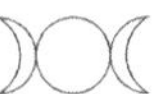

Of the three and five mysteries—Pistis Sophia

Lagos

Teresa Ferentinos saw Robert Avernis escorting a nun through the ring of soldiers guarding the archdiocese compound. She had been lingering outside with other members of the press awaiting an official statement from the Church about the bombing.

"Mr. Avernis, wait up!" she called as she ran toward them. "It's Teresa Ferentinos and Jill Tierney—from the hotel, remember? I never had a chance to thank you for getting me out of the building. I fainted from a concussion. The hospital just released me."

Avernis looked at her. "No thanks needed. Glad they let you out so soon."

"Only after she threatened them," Jill said.

"Just doing my job," Teresa exclaimed. "We're with UNN covering the pope's trip to West Africa. Mr. Avernis, can you tell us about any reactions inside the compound to the bombing? Can we interview you about that night?"

Avernis gave a firm shake of his head. "Teresa, I can't give interviews or comment on Vatican business. Cardinal Roncalli asked me to see Sister Annalisa out, and we need to go now."

"Cardinal Roncalli is having you escorted?" she asked the nun, while Avernis looked chagrined at having mentioned names. "You must have some high standing in the Church."

"Hardly, and you must be very persistent as a reporter," Annalisa said.

"So I've been told," Teresa replied. "Sister, why were you seeing Cardinal Roncalli?"

"When two people have a meeting, it is not polite to discuss it without the permission of the other person," Annalisa told Teresa with a smile.

Rebuffed, Teresa suddenly grew wobbly and unsure on her feet. Jill held her arm. Teresa said to Avernis, "I've seen you three times now, and three times I've felt . . . not myself."

"It must be your concussion," Jill said.

Avernis held a hand to his temple. "It's not just her. I'm feeling weird again myself. It's in me but seems to come from outside me. I don't know how else to describe it."

"It's to be expected," Annalisa said, and she took their hands in each of hers. Flashes of heat lightning had started to punctuate a sky that had been turning dusky, but then a booming roll of thunder cracked, and everyone looked up. Jill Tierney cried out as a bright burst of light seized the heavens, and she fell to the ground. In an instant, it was all over.

"This need not happen again," Annalisa muttered. "Thank you, Mr. Avernis. I will let myself out from here," she said, and she walked away.

Teresa shook off her sluggishness. "What just happened?" she asked Jill, helping her up

"You . . . you didn't see that?" the pale and frightened Jill asked.

"See what?" Teresa asked, her face wincing in bewilderment.

"Above you, the three of you. I saw . . ."

"Saw what?" Avernis asked, looking to the sky.

Jill made a brisk movement of her head as if trying to shake the images out. "In the lightening flash . . . three elongated figures above each of you like holograms, grave, majestic images but ghostly looking."

"Oh, Jill, come on," Teresa said. "It was only a trick of the light."

Jill shook her head. "I saw something. And what did that nun mean about *it's to be expected?* How do both of *you* feel?"

Both Teresa and Avernis no longer felt their malaise; they agreed that the excitement had probably startled it out of them.

"Who is that nun?" Teresa asked. "Very curious."

Avernis knew Annalisa was a controversial figure with the Church, but he wasn't about to make any more comments, so he just shrugged.

Teresa may not have seen any visions, but her radar was up. There was more to that nun than met the eye. There was a story there, and she was going to find it before she left Africa.

CHAPTER XV

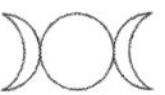

And some fell among thorns; and the thorns sprung up, and choked them. —*Matthew 13:7*

The Vatican City

Cardinal Mannheim looked at his fellow prelates through bleary eyes. Disturbing dreams had invaded his sleep last night. They were vague, just a hint of dream-vision, but they had to do with that Nigerian nun in the report. Events were moving at a rapid pace. That should be good—the more turmoil to shake up the Church, the better his chances of replacing Clement. The bombing in Lagos would work in his favor, rattling Clement and showing everyone the seriousness of the threats they faced.

But his dream, the nun . . . not now. He snapped himself to attention. He had other things on his mind. He dismissed his night musings and spoke to the fourteen assembled men.

"We are going to change the direction of the Church," Mannheim said. "You all hold key positions in the curia or the Vatican City government. You are in a position to play important roles in this new Church we will make."

Six of the fourteen cardinals present were Mannheim's closest associates, men he had gotten appointed, the same ones who confronted Clement last week. The others were conservative heads of important congregations or held key curial and Vatican City positions. It was time to get them indoctrinated to the new order.

"What do you mean by 'new Church'?" Cardinal Mendez asked.

"I mean a Church that will alter the course of history, not one that will be swept away by it," Mannheim answered. He nodded to Cardinal Van Kluysen.

"We have set aside reserves to aid Christians in Africa under attack by Muslims," he said.

"Aid?" Cardinal Diencsiwicz said. "But the Church is short on money, and that is the role of governments or international agencies."

"Governments and agencies are slow to act and as likely to help Muslim states as Christians with their misguided liberalism," Mannheim said. "Besides, we propose a different form of aid."

"What do you mean?" Dienesiwicz asked.

"Weapons," Cardinal Tormada replied.

That set off a round of loud exclamations. "This has never been done," Cardinal McLaughton said. "It will be highly controversial, the Church's engagement in wars."

"We will do it through channels that will not be traced back to the Vatican," Cardinal Trevi said.

"And as for war," Mannheim said, "Christians around the world are under attack in every sense—politically, spiritually, and physically. Our religion is tired. This leaves us vulnerable to the fanatical vigor of Islam, an aggression borne of malice and ignorance. Christianity is apathetic, eaten away by centuries of godless secularism. We need to show everyone that our people and our faith are worth fighting for. We must show that we can protect our own."

Mannheim then outlined his plan of using local parishes as rallying points to help organize Christian defense militias along with the provision of arms by untraceable sources. Nigeria and the Sudan would be the first proving grounds as frontline Muslim-Christian flash points. "We will insure there are no more Setandwe massacres again," he concluded.

"Well spoken," Mendez said. "I for one believe the time is well past for us to take a stand. Have you enlisted Milites Domini's support, and has the Holy Father approved this?"

Mannheim tapped his fingertips together, then said, "We are considering ways to approach Milites Domini. That Alvaro is a tough bastard, and he has no illusions about the threats we face. He should support us. As for the Holy Father, when something needed doing, when have I ever gone to him? Leave him to me. The final decision will not be his."

The men nodded, none of them really surprised at Mannheim's certainty . . . after all, they knew which way the wind was blowing.

✠

Cardinal Van Kluysen returned to his office after the meeting with Mannheim. Van Kluysen was the prefect for economic affairs, the man who ran the Vatican Bank and one of Mannheim's inner circle. Mannheim looked down on him as a bean counter, and that annoyed him. Van Kluysen had his own ambitions—not to be pope, there was no money in that—but that was why the phone call he just received seemed so intriguiging.

"This is Bishop Alvaro Maria Delgado, Eminence. Do you know who I am?" The man's voice was low and serious-sounding, as if he were concerned someone could overhear him.

Bishop Alvaro, the leader of Milites Domini? Speak of the devil! Why is he calling my private line? Van Kluysen indeed knew of Alvaro and his order. Milites Domini held an almost mythic position in Church circles. They were unique in Catholicism as a lay order constituting a personal prelature. That meant their bishop, currently Alvaro, had no geographic diocese. His only superior was the pope, and him in name only, for everyone deferred to Milites Domini. They were wealthy, powerful, and possessed a certain sinister reputation.

"Bishop Alvaro, yes, I know of you," Van Kluysen replied.

"Good," Alvaro said, sounding matter-of-fact. "You know then that we have been quite successful over the years in matters of finance, a field of endeavor close to your heart."

Since they were technically a nonreligious order, Milites Domini was permitted by the Church to engage in commercial ventures. Their membership included prominent businessmen and politicians in numerous countries around the world. Milites was reputed to be sitting on a fortune, but the circumstances under which they acquired their wealth were shrouded in scandals, scandals that never seemed to reach any conclusion or affect the core of Milites' operations.

Van Kluysen asked, "Are you seeking to make a financial contribution to the Church, Bishop Alvaro?"

"We have much to contribute to the Church," Alvaro replied, "and also to you, Your Eminence."

There was a moment of silence, then Van Kluysen said, "Continue."

"We are men of like vision, and we both know the Church faces great problems," Alvaro said. "I have a way to solve those problems, a way that will be of personal benefit to you. This is a delicate matter best discussed in person."

"I see," Van Kluysen said. "Why don't you visit me in the Vatican then?"

"No, no, Your Eminence." Van Kluysen was surprised at Alvaro's vehement tone, but the Spanish bishop softened his next words. "You see, Your Eminence, the success of what we propose hinges on the utmost secrecy. It would be better in all respects if we were not seen together, and there are too many eyes in the Vatican. I suggest you come to Toledo."

The leader of Milites Domini asking a cardinal to come to him? *He must be up to something quite extraordinary,* Van Kluysen thought. Only Alvaro would dare make such a cryptic call to the Vatican's prefect for economic affairs, but Van Kluysen was hooked, if not by the mystery of it then by the allure of some benefit from Milites' fabulous wealth.

"I may be able to come within the next two weeks," Van Kluysen said, trying not to sound too obliging.

"That will be . . . satisfactory," Alvaro replied.

When the call ended, Van Kluysen reflected on the conversation. He was under no illusions — something nefarious was in the making, but then Vatican history often favored men of boldness and secrecy, and Heinrich Mannheim was not the only Vatican cardinal with big ambitions.

CHAPTER XVI

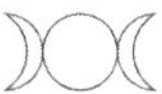

I knew it was a beginning, but I never imagined where it would lead.
—Robert Avernis, The Plot Against the Pope, *Cambridge Press, 2036*

Rome/Lagos

Well, well, looky what we've got here," the voice of Leo Dusayne said over the scrambled satellite link to Robert Avernis at the archdiocese compound in Lagos. Avernis looked at the series of pictures on his laptop, the same pictures he had taken at the hotel in Enugu. A red circle began to electronically wind its way around a woman's face.

"I know her!" Avernis exclaimed. "Her name is Celine. I made contact with her my first night in Enugu."

"Celine? Bob, that's Fatilah Jahani," Dusayne said. "Iranian father, French mother. Our computer database identified her. She runs errands for several extremist groups based in Tehran."

Dusayne was speaking from the CIA's Rome station. He was with Tom Stanton, Deputy Regional Director for West African Intelligence, collating information on the Port Harcourt-Katsina gun shipment uncovered by General Azu.

"She's a terrorist?" Avernis asked, tugging his collar to loosen his necktie.

"She helps the flow of weapons and intelligence to terrorists," Dusayne said. "She uses her Western upbringing to move around unnoticed, but she's in thick with some of the ayatollahs in Qom. Just how did you meet her, Bob?" Dusayne's tone of voice sounded accusatory to Avernis' ear.

Avernis' palms grew clammy. "I made contact with her in Enugu. She said she worked for a company that sold parts for private airplanes. She was with those two Africans in the picture."

"What was the exact nature of your contact?" Stanton asked.

"Purely social," Avernis replied. "She spoke French-accented English. She, uh, she put a move on me."

Dusayne's eyebrow cocked at Stanton. "She what?"

Avernis was glad Dusayne could not see his facial expressions. "She, you know, well, she asked me up to her room."

"Were you making a play for her?" Dusayne asked.

Avernis denied any such thing. Dusayne gave Stanton a skeptical look.

"So, this seems to clinch it," Stanton said, staying focused. "The Iranians are in Africa stirring the pot as we suspected. They must be arming the Muslim radicals who want to take over the country. Nigeria is the last piece of the puzzle to choke off our oil supply."

Avernis knew they were referring to a coalescing strategy in the Islamic world, spearheaded by Iran. The Islamic hardliners were on the verge of establishing an oil cartel under radical Muslim control, and that cartel was in the process of concluding an exclusive agreement with China. That country's rapacious economic growth needed endless supplies of energy to keep moving, and with a population that size, China's leaders had become like sharks, having to keep constantly in motion or die.

America, on the other hand, was an overly ripe economy that had failed to shake its oil dependence. The West had handed its radical Islamic opponents a perfect means to strangle them. After all, choking the West by having sovereign nations sign exclusive agreements with China, North Korea, and other Asian countries was only free trade in action. Most countries friendly to the West had exhausted their supplies. Nigeria was now America's only remaining oil source of any significance.

"Fucking ragheads," Dusayne said. "How long till we stomp their asses? I thought that's why Davidson got elected. If the Muslims gain control of the Nigerian government, we're cooked. Okay, Avernis, that's all for now. I'll be speaking with you *very* soon."

"Stupid SOB," Dusayne spat out as soon as the link with Avernis was closed. "He should know you can't take anything at face value. Things aren't what they seem in this business. Almost fucks up an assignment looking to get laid."

"We don't know that, Leo," Stanton said. "You've always been hard on him, ever since Virginia. As I recall, you didn't recommend him. Why? What's in his psych-prof?"

Dusayne's eyes rolled recalling Avernis' psychological profile. "He's brilliant and eager—has a hundred and fifty-four IQ. His father was killed visiting the ancestral home in Sicily. Poor guy sat next to the table of a Mafia-targeted judge in a Palermo café. When the bomb went off, it killed the judge and the father. Purely an innocent bystander, bad luck. That was the biggest event in the kid's life."

Stanton tapped his pipe on the table. "So why did he join the Company? Surely not revenge?"

Dusayne shook his head. "Revenge? Better if it were that concrete. No, this kid is an idealist. Justice, maybe. He's got all kinds of naïve, romantic notions about things like justice swimming in his head, and this ain't a romantic business. Patriotism is good, but crusaders we don't need. We play shadow games. We're not lone rangers bringing the black hats to jail. Justice isn't that tangible in our world."

Stanton smiled. "He's different, but who knows, maybe that difference will be an asset some day."

"Yeah, maybe," said Dusayne sounding unconvinced and fanning the "Celine" picture in the air, "But no surprise to me he got a hard-on for some broad and nearly fucked things up. I'm going to give him a basic refresher on Security 101."

Stanton let out the last puff from his sputtering pipe. "I'm sure you will, Leo, I'm sure you will."

CHAPTER XVII

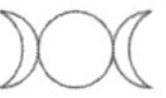

. . . omens have combined to give me a dark feeling. —*Margaret Fuller*

Lagos

Less than an hour after speaking to the nun, Cardinal Roncalli received a call from Rome at the Lagos Archdiocese.

"Pietro, Heinrich here."

Mannheim? What does he want?

"I was curious to know, have you met with the nun?"

Roncalli remembered Mannheim had wanted to send Trevi to interview her. It probably galled him to have to place this call. "Yes, I have met with her," Roncalli replied.

"And?"

"And what?" Roncalli said. Mannheim always had his own agenda, and Roncalli was not about to accommodate him with anything but minimal information, regardless the topic.

Mannheim emitted an impatient sigh. "Have you censured her, made her refrain from her activities?"

He's fixated on the nun, Roncalli thought, hearing frantic anxiety in the man's voice. He had to be careful. He did not want to lie about his thoughts, but he was not about to let Mannheim railroad him into a decision. "It's too early to draw conclusions," he said.

"What conclusions? She is destabilizing our relations with the Muslims at a minimum."

"She is an exceptional woman," Roncalli said, "of that there is no doubt. If she is a genuine healer, and she may be, we would be wrong to suppress her ministry. We could relocate her to a less sensitive area."

"Don't you understand?" Mannheim said. "No one else has performed such miracles in ages. Her miracles are meant to seduce, to cover her true intentions. What will you do then?"

"Let the pope decide," Roncalli replied. "I'll leave the decision to Clement."

"Bring her to the pope? I don't think that's wise."

"Why not?" Roncalli retorted. "He is the head of the Church, though perhaps not in *your* eyes."

"I can make this decision myself," Mannheim said.

"Only if the pope doesn't want to deal with it," Roncalli reminded him.

There was silence on the other end of the line, followed by a "Good day," and a click.

Mannheim seemed determined to stop the nun regardless of facts. *Does he know something I don't?* Roncalli wondered.

✠

Cardinal Mannheim had been troubled since his dream last night. The overriding sense of his vision was that he had forgotten something important, something that would come back to haunt him, and he was fanatical about covering all his bases.

The nun was the center of his dream. He had never met her; he did not even know what she looked like, but in a dream, one knows who is who. She was a force, a large, looming presence that he *felt* more than the faceless figure that he *saw*, but he knew it was her. She was inimical to everything he stood for. If she had her way, she would destroy all he held sacred. Her ominous words in the dream echoed in his mind:

My message will be heard, Mannemius, another God will be revealed . . . be revealed . . .

"I stopped you once; I will stop you again," he vaguely remembered shouting. He had no idea what he had meant by that. The dream had concerned him enough that he called LoPresti and had another talk with him about the prophecies.

Mannheim considered himself an eminently rational man, but at the end of the discussion he drew on a feeling from somewhere deep inside his being. He was concerned about attacks by Muslims, but Cardinal Mannheim's worry was the destruction of Christendom and his beloved Church from a cancer within.

CHAPTER XVIII

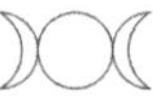

If absolute power corrupts absolutely,
does absolute powerlessness make you pure?
—Harry Shearer

Lagos

It was another hot, humid day when the pope arrived in Lagos. The trip through Latin America had been hard on Clement. Crushing poverty from overpopulation had led many on that continent to support militant populist groups, and the people had greeted their pope with jeers and hisses. Clement was profoundly shaken, and Roncalli felt his pain acutely.

The cardinals had chosen Clement for his mild manner following the overbearing reign of Pius XIII, but his gentleness was ill-suited for the problems they faced. Roncalli had studied history. The Church was similar to the old Weimar Republic of Germany between the two World Wars: a weak government, major internal and external crises, and dangerous polarization. Those circumstances had produced Hitler; what would the Church produce?

Though large segments of Catholics worldwide cried for Church reform in the face of the new millennium, the conservatives greatly outnumbered the liberals within the Church's upper echelons, and the Vatican hierarchy was deeply suspicious of grassroot movements. They equated reform with anarchy and populism with neo-Marxism. They were chomping at the bit to squash any liberal aspirations and show the world the Church would enforce its ancient ways with the authority of its imperial Roman heritage.

Only the thin veil of Clement's papacy stood between the clashing of these two worlds. Poor Clement. That veil could be torn away at any time, and what would Clement do?

But for now, the pope seemed to be buoyed by the sizeable crowd that greeted him at the airport in Lagos. He smiled and waved at the people, who were overjoyed at the first papal visit to their country. Responding to the enthusiastic throng, Clement walked the length of the security barriers, touching outstretched hands amid cries of "Papa, Papa!"

Roald Zugli was nervous. He stuck to the pope like glue, along with other members of the Swiss Guard and Colonel Ossore's counterterrorism unit, but no trouble materialized. After the brief ceremony at the airport, the pope left in a specially reinforced car surrounded by a convoy. His destination was the archdiocese compound, where he would rest until he delivered his main address at the national soccer stadium two hours later.

Teresa and Jill followed the papal entourage in a UNN news vehicle that was part of the media caravan trailing the pope. The new replacement crew from Cairo was now with them. Derek Foote, a Brit from the Cairo news desk, was the new exec replacing Irving Hirsch. Sandrine Terremont, a Frenchwoman, and Ismela Ghali, an Egyptian, provided the second camera and technical setup functions. They seemed like good people, but they reminded Teresa of her murdered friends.

The pope and Cardinal Roncalli retired to a private room after the pontiff had greeted the bishop and all the members of the archdiocese staff. Roncalli could tell that Clement was anxious to talk.

They sat in the sparsely furnished room. The pope looked at Roncalli for a time without talking, as if unsure what to say. Roncalli wondered if something was wrong with him.

"Do you know why our problem is so complex, Pietro?" the pope asked as his hands cradled the jeweled pectoral cross about his neck. He fixed his gaze downward on the cross, which he held a few inches outward from his body.

"Your Holiness?"

Clement let the cross rest once more against his chest. "The Church lives in two worlds, the spiritual and temporal. Those worlds are often at odds, and we dwell between them."

"It has always been that way," Roncalli said.

Clement continued talking as if Roncalli were not in the room. "When a business goes bankrupt, financial problems are all they face. We face something far worse."

The restless pope stood up and paced as he continued speaking. "If we bow to pressures and abandon the age-old practices of the Church, what happens then?"

Roncalli could not tell if the pope was really asking him or posing rhetorical questions.

"Either way, the result is the same," Clement continued. "People will turn to cults or violent aberrations of established religions. We are facing a moral and spiritual bankruptcy that can lead to corruption and dissolution, to error, and even to a form of neo-barbarism."

Roncalli was surprised. The emotional pitch of the normally stoic Clement was rising as he spoke. Clement's face grew paler the more he carried on.

"Can you imagine a world without the Church as its guiding light? A world where Islamic fundamentalism is the most dynamic religious impulse? Can men ever be trusted to maintain their own moral order without the grace of God's wisdom, without the conscience of the Church?"

Roncalli suddenly realized what was happening. Clement, poor Clement. His face, usually so kind and gentle in expression, was now as hard-set as weathered old granite. He looked tired and drawn by the pressures of the world chiseling their designs on his soul. One blow too many had cut into the surface of his being, exposing its soft core; his insides had become dried and hardened like cured leather. Clement had retreated inside himself and made his decision.

"Papa, I have failed you," Roncalli said to Clement.

"Failed me? In what way?" the pope asked him.

"I have failed you," Roncalli repeated. "I did not speak my mind to advise you when you needed help. It wasn't that I lacked faith; I was afraid."

"I don't understand," Clement said. He took a seat opposite Roncalli. "Afraid of what?"

Roncalli cupped his hands over his face and let out a deep sigh. "Papa, I came from a broken home. When father lost his business, he had us move to New York from Chicago to get work. Mother did not want to leave."

The pope listened without interrupting.

"Mother was very unhappy. Things deteriorated between my parents, and my father had an affair with a woman he met." Roncalli's facial muscles now tightened perceptibly. "My mother became very depressed and took me back to Chicago after a fight with my father. She started drinking. One night while drunk, she fell down the stairs; her neck was broken. She was hospitalized but died shortly after."

Clement now remained quiet as Roncalli tried to cope with the emotions he had rekindled. After a time, Roncalli lifted his head and looked at the pope.

"You see, Papa, the Church is my new home, but now it too is a house divided. I have seen how life's pressures can crush people who are set in their ways, like my parents were. I saw conflict and instability tear my old home apart; I do not want to see it happen to my new home."

Clement remained silent, letting Roncalli speak his heart. "We are at a crossroads. When faced with change, we can adapt or resist. I did not see the Church willing to adapt, so I advised you to make no choices. I was paralyzed with concern and indecision, just the way it was with my parents. I could not help them, and I did not help you."

Clement placed a hand on Roncalli's shoulder. "Do not blame yourself for that, Pietro, any more than you should blame yourself about your parents."

Roncalli hands squeezed together. "Forces are pushing on us, and they demand answers. Something *must* be done, so this is what I advise: at least allow priests to marry and let women assist in the celebration of mass—nothing more. Nothing more, because the Vatican hierarchy will stand nothing more, nothing less because the people need some sign of change to have hope things will be different."

"People have always strayed from the word of God, like the Hebrews did during Exodus," Clement said. "We should not part with our traditions because of the misguided."

"Papa, those things I ask you to change are traditions of the Church, not commandments passed down from the Revealed Word," Roncalli said.

"Those traditions are the collective wisdom of the Church fathers preserved through the ages," Clement said, shaking his head in disagreement, "and I will not be the first of my line to gainsay that wisdom. Pietro, do you forget that after the Lord departed it was the Church that succeeded Him in authority?"

Clement had made up his mind. Pushed and criticized, he would not go down in history as the pope who surrendered to the new world. It was safer to stand by a two-thousand-year-old tradition than to reform it, even if that meant sacrificing relevancy in the modern age.

Roncalli's mind was spinning: *Am I so different from Clement, or even from Mannheim? Am I not just as afraid of reforms? Revolutions bring chaos. What is this Church over which we anguish? What truths does it really embody and preserve?* "Where is the truth?"

"What did you say?" Clement asked.

"I feel compromised and impotent from inability to see a better way," Roncalli said.

"We *have* a way, Pietro," the pope said. "The way that preserved us through adversity for two thousand years."

Roncalli nodded his head and turned away from Clement. "Of course," he said in resignation. He stared a long time at the wall until he was aware that Clement had not spoken for a while. He turned toward him. "Papa, I'm sorry I . . . " Roncalli froze. The pope was splayed across his seat at an awkward angle, his body rigid and his face pale. Clement's face was contorted, and saliva flowed down his chin.

"Papa!" Roncalli cried, rushing to his side. Clement was breathing in shallow, tiny gasps. Roncalli felt for a pulse and had difficulty locating it. He ran to the door, flung it open, and shouted. "Roald! Roald, I need help. The pope is dying!"

CHAPTER XIX

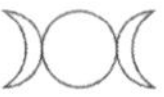

... Even things that seem evil turn to the purpose of God.
— Frequent saying attributed to Annalisa

Lagos

They cordoned off the entire west wing of St. John's hospital in Lagos as a crisis center for treating the pope. They informed the press that the pontiff had suffered a "mild stroke." Armed soldiers and anti-personnel equipment surrounded the hospital itself to keep reporters and the public away. Speculations flew in the tense atmosphere.

Cardinal Roncalli sat in a makeshift conference room with Roald Zugli, Robert Avernis, and Colonel Ossore. The men were awaiting news from the physicians treating the pontiff.

After several hours, a team of Nigerian doctors entered the room to address them. Their spokesman was a Dr. Olufeme. "The pope has suffered a severe stroke," the doctor told them. "He was critical last night, but currently he has stabilized. As with many strokes, the damage to the body occurred primarily on one side, in this case the right side. He has lost feeling in the right arm and leg, and his speech is greatly impaired."

They bombarded the doctor with questions. After he calmed the men down, Dr. Olufeme summarized the prognosis. "It is hard to predict the extent of recovery from a stroke. I must not downplay the fact that this was a serious stroke, and the chances of the pope recovering complete mobility so he can walk unassisted are slim. The chance of recovering full, unimpeded speech is also unlikely."

"Can we expect *any* improvement in his condition?" asked Zugli.

"Maybe," the doctor replied, "but it will take a year, maybe more, to tell to what extent."

"Doctor, we appreciate the work you have done," Zugli said. "Now that we have an idea what we are dealing with, we would like to fly a team of specialists in from Rome. Do you have any objections?"

"Not at all," said the doctor. "We anticipated that in this case."

"Doctor, how is he now?" Roncalli asked. "Is he awake and cognizant?"

"He is in and out, mostly out. Rest is what he really needs right now. You might be able to see him early this evening."

The doctors did allow Roncalli a brief visit that night. Clement had looked frail without his papal regalia. Absent the trappings of his office, it was easier to see him as just another human being, one who had paid a heavy price for the burdens he carried. He could not move. His mouth could only form a little O when Roncalli told him millions were praying for him and people were keeping a candlelight vigil outside the hospital.

Roncalli was resting on a sofa in a waiting room after visiting the pope when Bishop Ogunsanya pushed through a swinging door. "Cardinal Roncalli, I'm sorry to disturb you at a time like this, but I have a situation," he said.

"What situation?" Roncalli asked, rubbing his eyes.

"Concerning the nun, you know, that Sister Annalisa." Ogunsanya replied.

"What about her?"

"She is outside raving about how she has to see the pope. I told her the pope was in no condition to be seen by anyone, let alone her. She was insistent. She said if I did not help her, she would force her way in to see you or be dragged off by soldiers in front of the press."

Roncalli sensed the bishop was not as put out by the "situation" as he let on. Perhaps he was hoping the foot of some higher authority would descend upon her annoying little neck.

"Where is she now?" he asked Ogunsanya.

"Outside haranguing the soldiers. She claims she must see the pope before it is too late."

"Too late for what?"

"I certainly do not know," the bishop said, "but there are international news cameras out there, and I am afraid of her making an embarrassing scene."

"Bring her here to me."

"Of course, Your Eminence," the bishop said, trying to contain a satisfied smirk.

Teresa Ferentinos and other reporters had been pleading with one of the soldiers to see Bishop Ogunsanya or Cardinal Roncalli. Teresa was most persistent but the soldier grew more annoyed and obdurate. He had prohibited them from directing their camera toward the hospital grounds and told them to step back a hundred feet from the perimeter. Just as Teresa and Jill were walking away, they noticed a nun arguing with another soldier.

Jill tugged at Teresa's blouse. "Isn't that her, the nun from the other day?"

"Yes," Teresa said. "And what on bloody earth is *she* doing here?"

The nun and the soldier continued arguing.

"Sister, why are you here?" Teresa shouted, but the nun could not hear her.

Bishop Ogunsanya then appeared. He conferred with the soldier and the nun. To Teresa and Jill's surprise, Ogunsanya then yanked the nun by the hand and led her back toward the hospital.

"Something's up, and we definitely need to find out who that woman is," Teresa said.

✠

Ogunsanya's lip curled. "I hope you have something important to tell the Cardinal."

"The pope, tell me, what have they told him?" The words shot out of Annalisa's mouth as soon as she saw Roncalli in the waiting room. "Have they filled him full of nonsense about paralysis? About wheelchairs and convalescence?"

Ogunsanya stared at her. "Sister Annalisa! You forget your place. You—"

"Bishop, please, I will handle this," Roncalli said. "I'd like to speak to the sister alone."

The bishop stiffened, but the tone of his voice was compliant as he said, "Of course, Your Eminence." Ogunsanya knew he was speaking to a man who might influence his prospects for the vacant seat created by Cardinal Onomoh's death. So, without further words, he promptly departed the room.

"Now, Annalisa, what is this all about?" Roncalli asked the excited nun.

"Your Eminence, what happened to the pope . . . it is the beginning of the tribulation, that vision I had, but his affliction is providential."

"Providential? The pope taken ill and you say this is providence?"

At that comment, Annalisa pulled back from him. She had to make him understand or she would never get to see the pope. She slowed the pace of her words, took a step forward, and looked at him directly, as if assuring him that she was in full possession of her faculties.

"I know the pope cannot talk or move easily, particularly on his right side."

Roncalli seized her hand and spoke in a low voice. "How can you know that? Everyone was told it was a mild stroke. Only a handful of people know about his paralysis and speech difficulties, and not one of them would make those details public."

"I saw it," she said. "I felt what happened. The pope can be healed; God has further plans for him. The Holy Father must stay on the throne of St. Peter."

"Must stay? Must stay or what?"

"Must stay, or the world may not survive the challenges it will face."

Roncalli studied her face. She did not appear hysterical or irrational in any way, but . . . "Annalisa," he said, "do you realize how fantastic this sounds? You are implying you've had a vision commanding you to heal the pope, is that correct?"

She nodded her head. "It must be done quickly, and I must see him alone, before a pattern of illness locks in his mind, before the doctors tell him things and he sees people react to him as an invalid."

"Annalisa, you don't understand. The pope's life has been in danger, even before now. Security is very nervous; they will never allow you to be alone with the pope."

"They will if you vouch for me," she shot back without hesitation.

"You have healed people before with others present, have you not?" he asked her.

"This time I was told to be alone with him, I do not know why."

Roncalli remembered someone saying that nothing intimidated her. He barely knew her, many suspected her alleged abilities, and she insisted on being alone with the helpless pontiff.

Seeing the hesitancy in his face, she said, "Yes. Either I am insane, or you accept that God works through human beings to unfold His plan."

Roncalli tried to reason things through. She had abilities, if one believed the reports, and she did have an extraordinary effect on people around her — one way or the other. He himself had felt something from her, and it had been a good feeling. He did not think she would try to harm the pope, but others feared she was the Great Heretic.

If he allowed her access to the pope and the pope should . . . God forbid! How would he explain to Mannheim, or even Zugli, that he had allowed someone suspected of being a prophesied evildoer access to the pope's sickbed? Yet he *had* been praying for help and for guidance. *What if this is the answer and I do not listen?*

Her soft voice cut through his thoughts. "Listen to your heart for once instead of your mind, Your Eminence. If we try and he is not healed, what is there to lose? But if the voice speaks truly and he can be helped, think what we all lose by ignoring God's will."

She had virtually repeated his last thoughts back to him. If the pope died, the way to the papacy was finally cleared for the likes of Mannheim. That would be the end of the Church as Roncalli knew it. Could the Great Heretic do any worse? He let his instincts decide. "Wait here," he told her. "I will ask the pope if he will see you."

She clasped his hand. "Thank you. That is all I ask."

"All right then," he said. "If the pope agrees, I will speak to the security people. And Annalisa, please call me Pietro from now on."

Clement's eyes were open when Roncalli entered the room and approached his bedside. "Papa, there is somebody here to see you. Do you remember the nun we spoke about in the Vatican? Her name is Annalisa, do you remember?"

The pope's eyes widened slightly as he looked at Roncalli. He tapped twice against the sheets with his left index finger, a sign indicating "yes" according to the communication system the doctors had taught him.

"Papa, I have met with her, spoken to her at length. She is an exceptional woman. I do feel a presence about her, a good presence; I feel that she walks in the light of the Lord. I think she can help. Will you agree to see her?" He had no idea how Clement was reacting to this; there were no body movements or facial expressions by which to gauge. For a long minute, Roncalli waited for a reply.

A bead of sweat dripped from Roncalli's temple. He watched the pope's hand, and just before Roncalli spoke to ask if he had understood, the pope's left index finger tapped once . . . then once again against the bedsheets.

The relief he felt was enormous. Roncalli let out a captive breath, as if his life had depended on the answer. Whether or not she performed miracles, Annalisa was adept at stirring people's emotions. With the most nebulous of reasons, she had swayed him to emotionally advocate her case to the critically ill pope.

It was a humid evening in late November of the year 2025 that Pope Clement XV and Sister Annalisa Basanjo met face-to-face—or, more precisely, eye-to-eye, for that was about all Clement could move—in a dingy hospital room in Lagos, Nigeria. Her first action was to hold Clement's dead right hand, and Clement took notice. His eyebrows rose and his mouth moved as if to speak.

Pietro Roncalli observed them through the narrow strip of glass embedded in the door of the pope's room. He saw the nun raising one of Clement's hands between hers. She lifted the hand to her lips, kissed it gently, and then slowly lowered it to rest upon the pope's chest. For a long time she gently stroked his arms, his forehead, and his hair, appearing to speak intermittently.

When she placed both hands on the pope's temples, Roncalli, though drawn to the scene, turned away, feeling that he was intruding on something private, solemn, and inviolable. He asked Zugli to keep watch in his place.

Even if he were in the room, he would scarcely have heard the nun's voice except, perhaps, when she said: "You know, you have a big heart, Papa, and healing comes from the heart, where God dwells. Let the Lord now come forth from his dwelling . . ."

Outside the pope's room, the heaviness of the day's events pressed like a weight between Roncalli's eyes. The implications of the pope remaining incapacitated . . . he didn't have the energy to think about it. Praying for Clement was his final act before sleep overtook him.

Eventually, Roncalli awoke on the sofa that had served as his makeshift bed. He yawned and looked at his watch. It was past midnight. He walked down the hall and asked one of the guards if Annalisa was still in the pope's room.

"No, sir, gone now, but she was with him three hours," the soldier said. "She told us not to wake you, that you were very tired."

Roncalli entered the pope's room. Clement appeared to be sleeping normally. Roncalli looked at the slack, distorted mouth and the position of the stiff right arm. Nothing had really changed, except that the pope had a bit more color in his face, probably from resting.

Roncalli returned to his makeshift sofa bed in the hospital waiting room. He collapsed upon it, trying to sleep away the sinking feeling in his heart. He had hoped against hope that Annalisa's visit might really do something, but this was a stroke with very real damage, not a type of illness susceptible to suggestion or imagination as the basis for a cure. The last thought he had before fatigue forced slumber on him was the question, why don't real miracles ever happen anymore?

CHAPTER XX

. . . their scheme of the universe all cut and dried . . .
—Henry David Thoreau

The Vatican City

Seven cardinals gathered in Mannheim's office after receiving news from Africa of the pope's illness. Mannheim surveyed them from his own high-backed, ornately carved rosewood chair. People around the Apostolic Palace euphemistically referred to it as "the throne," but never, of course, in front of Mannheim. As usual, the men were bickering amongst themselves. DeGolia was using his sarcastic wit to taunt the volatile Tormada when Mannheim rapped on his mahogany desk.

"Eminences, please listen. As you know, we received word the Holy Father has been felled by a stroke. Let us take a moment to pray for him." They bowed their heads. After the prayer, Mannheim spoke again. "The pope's condition is grave. Specialists are en route to Nigeria to treat him."

By prearrangement with Mannheim, Silvestro Cardinal Trevi spoke next. "Brothers, we've discussed this before, but today we must make detailed plans for a succession."

"Is Clement in danger of dying?" LoPresti asked.

"That is unclear," Trevi replied. "However, he is substantially paralyzed."

"Clement is finished," Mannheim said. "Even if he lives he will willingly pass the ring to another." Mannheim surveyed the room, taking mental notes of any potential opposition. Trevi would back him without question, because Mannheim knew his secret—he had fathered a child with a woman in Rome and was supporting her for her silence. He had admitted this to Mannheim outside the confessional because he needed assistance. Mannheim quashed the scandal, and he now had an influential cardinal beholden to him.

The rest of his tally was by process of elimination. Tormada was too volatile, DeGolia lax and unreliable. LoPresti was too sanctimonious and he was inextricably tied to the memory of Clement's unpopular predecessor, Pius, who had become an insufferable autocrat upon assuming his office. That left Van Kluysen and Villendot.

Van Kluysen was the son of a prominent Flemish business family. He was greedy, and there were persistent rumors of him taking kickbacks on Vatican investments. He was clever, but he was a bean counter at heart, not material for a pope in anyone's mind.

Villendot was a potential problem. The French cardinal was jealous of Mannheim's intellect and force of personality. Villendot's grand conceptions of himself exceeded the reality of his natural endowments. He was bright, but not as bright as he thought himself to be. He was subtle, but under pressure, he became obvious. He had vision, but often it was clouded by his petty envies. Mannheim decided that none of the men in the room would challenge him. His real competition was Berletti, a popular conservative cardinal.

"Brothers," Trevi said, "we've long known Cardinal Mannheim is the best choice for our next pontiff. He is diligent in his work, and composed in his relations"—clever allusions to remind them of the weaknesses of Tormada, DeGolia, and LoPresti. "He will never bend to forces seeking to change the Holy Mother Church."

After a few minutes of exchanging comments, they all agreed, even the reluctant, outvoted Villendot. Whether a new pope was elected, or the College of Cardinals ruled in the interim, Mannheim would lead their group, just as their group would lead the Church.

"One question," DeGolia said. "Will Alvaro support your candidacy?"

Mannheim looked down and tapped on his desk. "Who knows what Milites Domini will do? They always have their own agenda, but Alvaro has recently given me helpful information, disturbing information, and now is a good time to share it with you."

The other six looked at one another, prompted by Mannheim's cryptic tone.

"Last week," Mannheim said, "Milites functionaries in Ireland got wind of something to do with a priest named McPherson. They were suspicious of him for a while—you know they have their spies everywhere—and they searched his apartment. They found a letter. It instructed him to go to Jerusalem to meet with a contact and obtain a document of incalculable value, *'one that would make visible that which has been hidden.*'"

Tormada leaned forward in his chair. "My God, that has always been code for revelation of the Hidden Church and the Great Heretic!"

"Yes," Mannheim replied. "The letter instructed McPherson to make delivery in Rome."

"Rome?" Trevi exclaimed with incredulity. "Dear God, that means the leaders of this conspiracy are right here, perhaps even in the Vatican! What happened to McPherson?"

"The Milites people are clever. They left the letter undisturbed," Mannheim said. "Two of their functionaries followed McPherson to Jerusalem. It appears he collected something — information or instructions — at a drop point. Next thing he's in East Jerusalem dressed like an Arab going into a Palestinian commercial building where the Milites men can't follow — they stood out too much — and he emerges forty minutes later.

"McPherson starts to head back toward the Israeli sector, so they assume he's made his pickup, and they move to intercept him but he notices them. They chase him all the way up to the base of the Al Aqsa Mosque on the Temple Mount, but he falls off the ramparts and dies. Actually, he more likely *jumped* off the ramparts, killing himself."

Tormada shook his head. "So this McPherson was the priest we heard about who died in Jerusalem? But what of the document?"

Mannheim shrugged. "They searched the body, nothing on him, but he had been carrying a briefcase. He must have ditched it along the way. The scene attracted attention and the Milites men had to run. It was impossible to backtrack and find the briefcase, so a very important clue to the conspiracy lies lost somewhere in Jerusalem."

"Damn it all!" Tormada exclaimed. "But at least we have proof a conspiracy exists, and now this nun in Africa . . . seems too coincidental. Do you think she really—"

"She is dangerous at least," Mannheim said. "At worst . . . she may be the One of the prophecies. Something evil is afoot here. Taking care of her will be a priority."

CHAPTER XXI

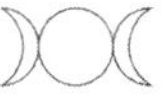

A miracle is an event which creates faith.
That is the purpose and nature of miracles.
— George Bernard Shaw

Lagos

Cardinal Roncalli drifted in an uneasy twilight state somewhere between dreaming and consciousness. It was unfair for the pope to shoulder all the blame. After all, he had advised Clement. He was pained by the criticism heaped on the pope for avoiding the hard questions, but what else could he do? The Church was too divided to give answers. The conservatives were pressuring to retain the status quo. Roncalli was hoping to buy time for Clement and the progressive minority to find solutions that would not tear the Church apart. They needed time to develop workable responses to the staggering problems they were facing.

Roncalli's body tossed as the thought hit him: *Clement is the wrong pope to deal with the Church's problems.* These were radical times, and only two radically different paths were open. The conservatives would rely on an unyielding, authoritarian papacy with rigid adherence to dogma. They would accept a smaller, pared-down Church of hard-core believers to face down future challenges. On the other side, the progressives would let the dice fly into uncharted territory. They would unleash reforms that risked undermining the foundation of St. Peter's Church in the very effort to revitalize it. Only a miracle worker could craft a middle ground. Clement was incapable of doing this.

Suddenly, Roncalli felt someone tap on his shoulder. "Your Eminence, come quickly, the Holy Father!"

Roncalli's eyes barely focused in time to see Robert Avernis running back toward the pope's room. His heart jumped, and he struggled to rise from the sofa, causing a wave of dizziness. In those few seconds his organs seemed to drop to the bottom of his feet. *Please, Lord, help me . . .* but he got himself up and rushed down the corridor, tensing again as he burst into the room to see what had happened to the stricken pope.

He froze in the doorway, feeling as though his blood had drained from his body. Clement was sitting straight up in bed! He was smiling and soothing an elderly nun who knelt by him as she clutched his hands and wept uncontrollably.

"My God, Cardinal, my God." He looked to his right and saw Roald Zugli. The colonel's eyes were red and glistening. Roncalli suddenly became aware that several Italian soldiers were in the room, some of them on their knees crossing themselves.

"Sister N'Reta went to check on him a few minutes ago and found him like this, singing to himself," Zugli said. "It is a miracle; truly what we are seeing must be a miracle!"

"Jesus, Mary, and Joseph," Avernis whispered.

The pope then saw Roncalli. "Pietro, good, good you are here, come," *and he motioned with both arms while he spoke!* He had some trouble with the right arm, but still it moved.

Roncalli approached the pope, who reached out and greeted him like a long-lost friend. Clement clasped Roncalli's hands so firmly that a shockwave bolted up the cardinal's spine, and he knew without doubt something extraordinary had occurred in this room.

"Papa, Papa, I thought . . ." Roncalli choked the words out then lapsed into silence, overcome with emotion.

"I know, I know, Pietro," the pope said. Then, in a voice clear and strong, Clement addressed the other people. "My children, thank you for the outpouring of your love. I must speak alone with Cardinal Roncalli, but as you go about your lives from this day on, I want you to remember that God spoke this day. His act of love was spoken to *all* of you, to all of your hopes and dreams, and not just to those of the old man who lies in this bed."

The people cleared the room, crossing themselves as they departed. Roncalli and the pope still held each other's hands, both with eyes closed. In reverent silence, they reflected on the event that had answered their quiet desperation like a thunderclap. For a time they prayed in muted thanks, then the pope began to tell the story of his journey from perdition:

"I was encased as in ice or concrete. Every part of me felt hardened and contracted until I heard Annalisa's voice. Gradually, warmth grew inside me. Slowly, my mind's eye cleared like winter frost melting off a cottage window in the afternoon sun. It seemed I was looking through hazy glass and seeing the blurry whiteness of snow beyond.

"That whiteness grew ever brighter, like an all-encompassing radiance. I focused on it, was absorbed by it, and then I was able to feel it, connect with it. I felt the hardness around me suddenly break up and dissolve like crusts of paint might wash off an old brush to reach the pliant softness underneath. I felt the veneer of pride, anger, and fear scraped off my soul by an awesome power with a feather's touch."

A peaceful smile drew across the pope's face as he spoke his next words. "I think at that time I might have felt my body move, my leg, my hand perhaps, and I recall my voice uttering just a noise—*ahm, ahm*—and I knew I could talk then, but words were not enough to praise the presence I felt. Those simple sounds I hummed seemed the most—no, seemed the *only*—appropriate expression to glorify that presence. Nothing more, nothing less would do."

The color in Clement's face was rising to a rich pink hue as he spoke. "I felt as if a veil were torn from my eyes so I could see. I felt my heart redeemed so I could feel, and my spirit renewed so I could live. Of all men, Pietro, I was blessed with baptism *and* resurrection all at once. In error, I had allowed my petty anger to rule my actions, but I was renewed in *God's* will by the waters of the Holy Spirit. In error I walked a path that was killing me inside, and I was called back from the dead."

The pope released Roncalli's hands and drew his own palms inward to lie across his chest, where he rested them firmly as if to protect the memory of his experience from escaping his heart.

"A man must be true to himself; I know that now. I know what I am to do, Pietro. I know my part in God's plan. I am the bridge from the old to the new, and here is how I will start building it: when I return to Rome, I will call for bishop's synods to be held on all continents to discuss reforms as they see the issues."

Roncalli's eyes widened.

"Birth control, celibacy, the pedophilia problems, the roots of poverty—let them tell us their views on these matters," the pope declared. "Once the issues have had sufficient discussion, I will convene an ecumenical council of the entire Church. We will determine a collective response to these problems and to all global issues facing us."

The pope paused momentarily in his rapture, and Roncalli reflected on the extraordinary things he just heard. That Clement had experienced a profound revelation was indisputable. Faced with the inexplicable fact of his recovery, Roncalli could only conclude that God was truly at work here. He had witnessed a miracle as a palpable experience.

Clement's eyes looked through Roncalli, seeming fixed on some unseen point beyond. "Other things came to me, Pietro," he said, placing his right hand on

Roncalli's shoulder. "There is one who will cross this bridge I will make, a leader, that much I saw, but like Moses was unable to enter the Promised Land, I will not be there at the crossing. As for the nun, Annalisa, she will have a great part, I think, in the redemption of the Church, just as she played a role in my redemption."

Visions, Roncalli thought. First Annalisa, and now the pope. Was this business of visions contagious?

"Pietro, I have decided that Annalisa must come to Rome, and there beside us she will fulfill whatever destiny awaits her. I will make Annalisa the new cardinal of West Africa."

It took Roncalli a few moments to absorb the implications of the pope's statement. He was not merely admitting a woman to the priesthood; he was elevating a woman to the highest position in the Church next to the pontiff himself.

"Do I have your support in this, Pietro?" the pope asked.

"Yes, Papa," Roncalli replied without hesitation. "You have my support in this as in all of your plans, but the Church will never accept her."

"Why not?" the pope asked. "What is it we fear? Our doctrines? Our customs? I will get theologians to support the case for doctrinal changes to allow her to take holy orders. As pope, I am able to influence these matters."

"No," Roncalli answered. "It's not doctrine or custom. It's the repudiation of our past, of everything we ever proclaimed in God's name as His will."

"The Church will not admit its fallibility in religious matters, is that what you mean?" asked Clement.

"Yes," said Roncalli.

"Then why will *you* support me, my dear friend?" asked the pope.

"Nowhere in scripture is there a prohibition against women in the ministry," Roncalli noted. "We've resisted change too long, and the effort has exhausted us."

"Is it that simple?" Clement asked. "Come now, Pietro, No theological objections?"

"Oh, theological objections will be raised for sure," Roncalli said, "but by others, not me. God sent Christ to overturn the customs of the past and proclaim a new covenant. If God now speaks through the Church, through you, Your Holiness, should we not assume he *still* guides us to new understandings as he has done before? You see, Papa, I never believed the Holy Spirit died on Calvary those two thousand years past. He proved that to us today."

The two men embraced each other, and Roncalli felt a great weight lift from his soul. Oh, there would be severe trials ahead, of that he had no doubt.

The radical actions Clement spoke of would trigger a war within the Church as they finally confronted long-smoldering issues, but now he and the pope were united around a vision. The Church was the reflection of a world edging toward conflict. Roncalli now realized it was unavoidable, and oddly, that was a liberating thought.

CHAPTER XXII

But when you come home at night with only the
shattered pieces of your hopes and dreams . . .
—Alan Beck

The Vatican City

No one at Vatican Communications suspected how much the incoming message would alter the plans of their boss, Cardinal Mannheim. Father Borghietti was feverishly copying a radio message from Roald Zugli coming in via relay from North Africa. As the content of the message became apparent, there was clapping, and many in the room crossed themselves.

Immediately upon finishing his transcription, Borghietti took off at a trot through the streets and courtyards that led southward to the second floor of the Apostolic Palace. He headed for the offices housing the Vatican secretariat of state. Father Borghietti wanted to be the first to deliver the good news to Cardinal Mannheim.

He was panting as he told the staffer in the reception area he had urgent news for the cardinal about the Holy Father. A minute later, he was ushered into Mannheim's office. Mannheim sat on his purple-lined velvet chair. He lorded over an expansive, Brazilian mahogany table, the legs of which were intricately carved with gryphons and scrolls.

The office walls were cut Circassian walnut inlaid with burled walnut panels and topped with friezes of smooth-grained leather. Above the grand fireplace of yellow sienna marble, two carved, ebony cherubs reached upward to pluck hanging grapes and enjoy the pleasures of food and drink for the first time. Gilt-edged portraits of former popes adorned the walls.

Mannheim's office was so vividly opulent that if one were to shut one's eyes, the images would still penetrate the lids and register on the brain. Father Borghietti knew the rooms were built to convey a sense of power and authority, but any room with Mannheim presiding over it was imperious enough to connote royalty without any props.

The cardinal indeed looked imperious today behind his desk in the black cassock and scarlet zucchetto of his office, and Borghietti knew one's career in the Vatican depended on the good graces of this man.

Mannheim inquired of the priest, "You have some news of the pope, Father . . .?"

"Borghietti, Your Eminence, Father Borghietti from Communications. Yes, I have wonderful news, but you may read it yourself."

Mannheim snatched the note from him. His eyes passed quickly over the text then angled upward under their pale brows. He looked at the priest who was still leaning over his desk. "That will be all, Father," he said.

Borghietti had wanted to see Mannheim's reaction, he wanted to bask in the reflected warmth of the good news, and Mannheim was unceremoniously dismissing him!

Germans — no simpatico whatsoever. If not for the black simar lending some contrast, you could not even see the expression on the man's bland, pale face. Oh well, at least he had been the bearer of good tidings. Maybe the cardinal would remember him in the future.

Indeed, Mannheim would remember the priest who brought him the note, but not exactly for the reasons Borghietti hoped. As he read, the cardinal's mouth twisted off to one side and his teeth grated almost audibly. The letter said:

Pontiff made miraculous recovery from a massive stroke during the night. Has regained most faculties including speech and walking. Expect him to complete tour and arrive back home this week. Details forthcoming. Per instructions the Pope/Roncalli, for public consumption: the stroke was mild, all hospital activity here for precautionary purposes only.

Roald Zugli

Piece by piece, Mannheim shredded the paper in his hands, reducing it to confetti. He flung the pieces of his ruined ambition into a wastebasket, watching them float downward and disappear like delicate crystals of snow melting into the hard, indifferent earth.

CHAPTER XXIII

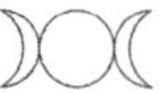

Ask me no more, thy fate and mine are sealed.
—Alfred Lord Tennyson

Lagos

Cardinal Roncalli looked out a window and saw Teresa Ferentinos among the press corps waiting for news of the pope just as Annalisa entered St. John's hospital. It was a fateful day. No doubt Teresa would give her right arm to witness his meeting with the nun. It started with a faint tap on the door of the hospital waiting room.

"Come in," Roncalli said.

The door opened and Annalisa entered.

"Roncalli stood and positioned a chair in her direction. "Annalisa, please, sit."

"Pietro, you wanted to see me. I assume it is about the Holy Father. Is he doing well?"

"That is an understatement. He is doing *so well* that every specialist who arrived this morning from Rome is baffled. They wondered at first whether he actually had a stroke. He drags his right leg slightly, otherwise he is fine, speech completely restored, mind alert, and spirits better than I have seen in years."

"Ah, good, good!" Annalisa blurted out like a child who had received a promised gift.

"Annalisa, I am at a loss for words to describe my feelings about this. It is almost too much to absorb the implications of the pope's sudden healing—not just the healing itself, but his new attitude and how that will help the Church at this crucial time."

Roncalli noted that the news of the pope's epiphany did not seem to surprise her. "Annalisa, can you tell me how—?"

She raised a hand and halted him in midsentence. "Pietro, please, I know it is common for people to ask questions, especially people with good, rational minds, but for me to sit here and dissect God's actions would be counter to His way. If you find it wondrous, accept it as such. Wonder grows to belief, and belief to the certainty of knowing; that is the meaning of this, not just for the pope, but for all who witnessed."

As usual, this unassuming woman shot an arrow directly into the inner ring of his thoughts and feelings. It *was* time to stop the analysis, to stop the running commentary of his rational mind. The pope was well, and a new direction was on the horizon.

And then it hit him— *God had spoken. He spoke to us in our deepest darkness!* It was a miracle! He had tried to keep the possibility of miracles alive in the warmness of his searching heart, but before today he had banished it to the coldness of his skeptical mind. He took a few steps toward Annalisa, then kneeled in front of her. He gathered her hands into his and kissed them. "Thank you, Annalisa. Thank God for what He has shown me through you today."

She closed her eyes and her head swayed gently in calm repose. When he saw teardrops flow down her smooth skin, he asked, "Why do you cry?"

She replied, "I cry in wonder at the beauty that flows from God's fountain. You have many trials ahead, Pietro, but now you will be ready to face them."

He felt a purpose and a resolve grow in him; he knew she spoke the truth. He realized the future would not bare its secrets on a silver platter; there would always be gaps and shadows of the unknown. Yet, for the first time since he was a child with a child's faith and acceptance, he now knew that Someone must be watching over them.

Roncalli delivered the pope's message with joy and excitement, yet it caused the first crack he had seen in Annalisa's composure.

"No, Pietro, no, no. I cannot possibly be a cardinal."

"Why do you say that?" he asked her. Roncalli thought it was not modesty; there was a strong sense of trepidation in her words.

"The world of a cardinal, the Vatican, is not my world," she replied. "Here, I am needed. What would I do in Rome?"

"Annalisa, I cannot answer that question, but the Holy Father had a vision that you have an important role to play, and that role was somehow connected with coming to Rome. Beyond that, think of the service you could do for the Church and the world as a cardinal. It is a position of great influence and, to a large degree, it will be what you make of it."

"The Holy Father saw this in a vision, you say?"

"Yes," he said. "He was quite definite about it."

She placed her thumb and forefinger at the upper corners of her eyes by the bridge of her nose and began rotating them as if to ease some tension. After a minute, she said, "May I find a place I can be alone for a while?"

"Of course." *How odd,* he thought. *She would be a cardinal of the Church, yet she acts as if it were a death sentence.*

It was almost eleven p.m. before Roncalli returned to Clement's room. The pope was in bed looking over some papers. He peered at Roncalli above the rims of his glasses.

"Not quite what I expected, Papa," Roncalli announced.

"She declined?" Clement asked with concern in his voice.

"No, she accepted—finally."

"So she was reluctant?" Clement asked.

"She refused at first," Roncalli said.

"That surprised you?" the pope said.

Roncalli pursed his lips, trying to articulate his answer. "What surprised me was not so much that she declined but more the way she reacted. She anguished over the whole issue, and I have yet to see that woman falter over anything."

"Yet this is perhaps the biggest event, the biggest change in her life," Clement said. "Is her reaction really so hard to understand?"

Roncalli shrugged. "I had the impression she was prepared for anything that might happen. She seems to have an inner balance that can cope with any circumstance no matter how unexpected."

"What changed her mind?"

"I'm not sure," Roncalli said. "She disappeared for hours then came back and said, 'I accept,' with no further explanation. She seemed tense, not happy, but I did not feel it appropriate to pose intrusive questions in light of her obvious difficulty; I was just glad she agreed. Perhaps someday I will ask about her change of heart."

"I think you acted wisely," Clement said, and he patted the bed twice in satisfaction. "Excellent, excellent, Pietro."

"Papa," Roncalli said, "there are details we must discuss concerning her ascension to the cardinalate. She must be ordained first as priest and bishop. We must declare what this action means for Church policy on ordination of women, and we must be prepared to deal with the reaction of the College of Cardinals."

"Of course, Pietro," said the pope. "You are correct to give these matters forethought, but I mean to have this done regardless of how the cardinals react."

"How will you approach them?"

"By ordinary consistory," the pope replied.

Roncalli was surprised. Consistories were an ancient tradition. They were conferences between the pope and the College of Cardinals with the cardinals acting in an advisory capacity on specific issues. They had fallen out of use for centuries before being resurrected by John Paul II in 1979, but popes like Pius XIII had seen little use for them.

"Papa, why would you do that?" Roncalli asked. "You are not bound by the cardinals' opinions. Why give them a forum where it appears you are seeking their approval?"

Clement smiled as if he had already predicted and answered the question. "Two reasons, Pietro. This action is without precedent; the College should be allowed to express its thoughts."

"And the other reason?"

"The other reason," Clement said, "is that I want to know which cardinals object the most and on what grounds. I want to know how they line up during this time of self-examination which I will initiate, and Annalisa's appointment will be a barometer."

"May I suggest a refinement to your plans?" Roncalli asked.

"Of course, Pietro, what is it?"

"Create her as a cardinal now, *in petto.*" Roncalli referred to an old, outmoded procedure whereby the pope would announce the creation of a new cardinal but withhold the cardinal's name until a future date.

"*In petto?* That has not been done in a long time," Clement said. "I don't understand."

"Remember," Roncalli said, "there were several expectant candidates, particularly Ogunsanya. Your decision will be a shock, and these men need time to be informed privately out of courtesy and respect." As he spoke, Roncalli could picture Bishop Ogunsanya falling out of his chair at the news. "The people here expect to have a new leader, but you do not want to telegraph Annalisa's selection before returning to Rome and conferring with the cardinals. Announcing a choice now but revealing the name later would solve that dilemma."

The pope listened carefully then said, "I value your help, Pietro. My eyes have been fixed on another world since my" — the pope paused to grope for the right word — "experience," was all that he could find.

"There is another reason for secrecy," Roncalli said. "Creation of a cardinal *in petto* was often done when naming the person outright might put the life of the candidate in immediate danger."

"You believe her life is in danger?" Clement asked.

"Possibly," Roncalli replied. "Remember, Papa, there has been a bombing here in Lagos. Intelligence suspects Islamic fringe groups. We know certain elements in the Muslim community resent Annalisa because some people abandoned Islam on her account. If you now announce her as the new cardinal of West Africa, how might those extremists react?"

"I understand, Pietro," Clement said. "In fact, I see wisdom in all your comments.

It is done then; she will be created cardinal *in petto.* As for the consistory: get input from the theologians to support this decision—you know the ones to approach. Make it clear they are to keep their work in strict confidence. As soon as they produce a proper document, schedule the consistory. Now, Pietro, we are going to see of what substance the Church is made."

As Roncalli recounted the incredible events of the past few days in his mind, the wind, which had been still since the pope's arrival in Lagos, suddenly blasted through the room's open window, breaking cups, scattering papers, and throwing trays down on the floor. Roncalli rushed to the window but had difficulty closing it against the powerful draft.

As the wind beat against his face, the trees outside bent in its wake. The metaphor was not lost on Roncalli. Miraculous events had occurred here, and now a wind from Africa was making its force felt in their lives too. He picked up the broken debris from the floor, thinking how that wind would rearrange the Holy Church itself . . . and he tried his best to put the pieces back in place.

BOOK TWO

Cardinal Signs

CHAPTER XXIV

We must no longer be children, tossed to and fro and blown about by every wind of doctrine, by people's trickery, by their craftiness in deceitful scheming. — Ephesians 4:14

Qom, Iran

Grand Ayatollah Ali Havenei looked over the lectern at the new generation of religious leaders with the same arch-browed, unyielding eyes so reminiscent of Ruhollah Khomeini, father of the religious revolution. They sat in rows of chairs resting on intricately arranged mosaic tiles. The domed room was defined by a wall punctuated with numerous arches framed by the spiral columns so common in Islamic architecture.

"Make no mistake about it," he told the bearded young Islamic scholars at Howzeh-ye Elmieh Religious University, "we are at war with the West. No, this is not a new war, this is no new declaration of war," he intoned as he surveyed the room for those select steely sets of eyes that would one day join him on the Ruling Council. "This is the continuation of a two-thousand-year-old struggle."

Howzeh-ye Elmieh University in Qom was the real center of power in Iran, not Tehran, the capital. That was because the Grand Ayatollah Khomeini had graduated there and the mullahs had ruled Iran ever since. Khomeini had not only instituted religious rule over Iran, but with his doctrine of *Vilayat-i Faqih* he had gathered all power into the hands of a single ayatollah, the first time that was ever done. Ali Havenei was the direct religious and political descendant of Khomeini and heir to the throne of the Shi'ite Islamic theocracy.

"Once Islam was strong, the preeminent power in the world," Havenei reminded the young students, "but it was not quite strong enough. We conquered Eastern Rome, took the Balkans but were stopped in Italy and Vienna. From that time on the West became ascendant, the tides turned, and the Islamic states became vassals to the West."

Reza Gorbani had once been an eager acolyte like these young men. He sat and listened, seated immediately to the right of the ayatollah. That Havenei had honored him with such proximity was a clear indication that Gorbani was soon to be inducted into the Ruling Council.

"Allah," Havenei said, "decreed in His infinite wisdom, that we were not ready to bring Islam to the entire world. The suffering and servitude we endured under centuries of Western imperialism was the penance we had to pay to stand where we are now—on the verge of an Islamic resurgence. We honor past heroes such as Saladin, the Sultan Mohammed, and Bin Ladin, but today it is Iran, *Shi'ite* Iran that leads Islam. And now in closing, I present a former graduate, Reza Gorbani, to summarize our goals."

Gorbani smiled. Indeed, this day would propel his career. He prided himself on being a realist. Though he had graduated from this very university, he knew religion for what it was—a means to power and domination. That critical perspective was needed with all the religious fanaticism around him. He had to walk a fine line, presenting his views without affronting the religious sensibilities of Havenei or the young scholars gathered today.

Gorbani took the dais and spoke slowly. "Allah," Gorbani said, "has clearly indicated on whom He shall bestow His blessing in the struggle between Islam and the West. Look at recent history. Two decades ago, America had our necks in a noose, but they lacked the will to pull the rope. They faltered," he said as he clutched a hand to his throat, "and now we hold the noose around *their* necks." As he said that, he slid his hand upward in a symbolic choking action. "*We* will not falter . . . Allah and history shall honor the decisive."

Applause. Gorbani knew the situation had less to do with Allah and more to do with America losing its political will in Iraq two decades ago under pressure from socialist Europe and its own liberal elements at home, but he had no problem crediting Allah for historical events if it instilled a sense of inevitability in the faithful.

"Dictators of the past—the Hitlers, Stalins, Maos, and Saddams—all used nation-states as a base of power, and all ultimately failed when confronted by stronger nation-states. Bin Ladin used Islamic fervor and transnational terror, but lacked the resources of a nation. We, however, work on all fronts. As a nation we have become a dominant regional power. But we quietly support the Arab freedom fighters who attack and demoralize American and European cities. In global geopolitics we are close to forming a pact with China to cut oil supplies to the West. We *are* the Islamic resurgence. Under Ayatollah Havenei and the Ruling Council, we will bring Islam to preeminence in the world and Iran to the leadership of Islam!"

Thunderous applause. Havenei was happy, the young scholars were frothing at the mouth, and Gorbani knew his little speech had sealed himself a seat on the council.

When Gorbani returned to his apartment, the best part of a perfect day awaited him — Fatilah Jahani. Fatilah was proof of his great fortune. The beautiful young woman was a favorite of the ayatollahs but she was of like mind with Gorbani. She was worldly, practical, and she understood power. She kept religion in perspective as a means to an end. In short, she was sophisticated, a very refreshing oasis in the often provincial desert of Iran.

"How did it go, Reza?" she asked, casting her seductive green eyes upon him.

"It was as perfect as you, my love," and he put his hands on her waist then under her shirt, moving them up to clasp her breasts.

"Wonderful," she said. "You'll be an ayatollah any day now."

"None too soon," he said as he kneaded her nipples to hardness with his fingers. "The council is euphoric with their own successes and think our victory is pre-ordained. They forget that America is still a formidable power. The new president, Davidson, seems determined to halt America's slide. These are dangerous times and we need perspective."

"Exactly, Reza," Fatilah said as she undulated her body against his. "The worst thing is a heavy hand. Move slowly and cautiously, and we can win without provoking the West."

"Havenei is old," Gorbani said. "Once he's gone, I can grow to dominate the others and steer Islam's ship in the right direction. And you, my love — why, you will be the new *shabanoo.*"

She laughed. "There are no more empresses in our Islamic state. We don't need titles, Reza, we just need control . . . just get control."

CHAPTER XXV

A woman's asking for equality in the Church would be comparable to a black person's demanding equality in the Ku Klux Klan. — Mary Daly, theologian

The Vatican City

Today, the pope would create the first female cardinal in two thousand years — but none of the gathered cardinals knew that yet. Only Mannheim knew something was coming. Yesterday, Roncalli informed him that Clement was rejecting any notion of abdication. Furthermore, the pope would dismiss anyone who tried to impede his authority or the operations of the Holy See, even if it meant dissolving the entire College of Cardinals. The stunned Mannheim was trying to figure out what to do next.

The walls and ceilings of the somber, sumptuous room wherein the cardinals were meeting depicted painted figures from bygone eras. The portraits cast their ethereal eyes upon the assembly of scarlet-robed men. Those figures from myth and history had watched many ceremonies over the centuries, and if paintings truly capture the souls of their subjects, then a distinguished audience indeed would watch the creation of Annalisa as Cardinal Basanjo of West Africa. What would old Pope Leo say about female priests? Would Apollo really care about the affairs of Christians? Would those cherubs holding the hem of God's robe pay attention and honor the woman before them?

The cardinals seated themselves in crescent rows of ascending seats that invoked images of the old Roman Senate. That was natural since Imperial Rome was the model for the Church's organizational structure and hierarchy. That same imperial Rome had tried to stamp out Christianity but ended up marrying it instead, and like most married couples, Rome and the Church adopted aspects of each other's personalities . . . and personas.

The College of Cardinals functioned like a senate — though it officially dropped that name in 1983 — advising a pope-emperor who wielded nearly absolute authority. This is why the pope sat on a slightly raised dais to the front and center of his advisors, forty-eight of the world's one hundred and forty cardinals. The princes of the Church listened in restless confusion while Clement spoke at length about Annalisa's life and service in the work of God and about his experience of her healing gift. Roncalli knew what they were thinking: why was this woman, believed by some to be the Great Heretic of the prophecies, the topic of a papal consistory? The pontiff was just now speaking the words that would throw many of the dour-faced cardinals into fits:

"And so, my brothers in Christ, we have decided to create as cardinal the nun Annalisa Basanjo. *Quid vobis videtur?*"

The pope had asked in Latin, "how does that sit with you?" The question was a formality. The pope had already announced that he had created an African cardinal, but he had withheld the name until now to protect Annalisa from potential attack by Muslim extremists in Africa. The old rhetorical question announcing her name was a matter of form, part of a ritual where the cardinals would nod their heads or lay down their biretta skullcaps to indicate their agreement. In two millennia, there had *never* been a dissent on record—until now.

A voice behind Roncalli roared, "*Hoc omnino male videtur et ego hanc abominationem protesto!* " (It does not sit with me at all, and I protest this abomination!)."What evil are you bringing into our midst?"

Roncalli turned to identify the speaker. It was Tormada, the grand inquisitor himself, prefect of the Congregation for the Doctrine of the Faith.

Clement's announcements about synods and ecumenical councils had shaken the College, but a female cardinal! The men were in shock. Yet despite their consternation, Tormada's open expression of anger against the pope was unheard of. His outburst took them aback, sending an audible ripple of unease throughout the assembly. Mannheim and Villendot, who sat on either side of Tormada, restrained the outraged cardinal, grabbing his arms and literally hauling him back into his seat. Mannheim quickly stood and spoke.

"Holy Father, forgive our brother for speaking in anger. We are only human, and when beliefs we hold dear are radically challenged, sometimes we lose our equilibrium. Surely Your Holiness could have achieved his ends without calling this consistory. Please tell us then, what purpose may we serve here?"

The tension in the room subsided, though Villendot kept a restraining hand on Tormada's arm and whispered furiously in his ear. Clement, whose facial expression had remained remarkably calm, even during Tormada's outburst, said, "We understand the feelings here are a result of our unprecedented actions. Accordingly, we forgive the nature of the response. As to the purpose for this meeting: we would hear your thoughts, not only on this cardinal's appointment, but also on the larger question of women's role in the ministry."

"That is impossible," Villendot declared. "This is a doctrinal issue with grave implications. It requires theological interpretation that would take years."

"On the contrary," Clement replied with a firm voice. "What is required is information and decisions. The documents on your desks provide the opinions of theologians in relation to my decision."

"Then I take it we are to break up in the customary language groups to discuss this subject?" Mannheim asked.

"No," Clement replied, sitting tall in his chair, dressed in the full regalia of his office, his staff with the image of the crucified Christ held firmly in his hand. "We will hold a general discussion here and now. However, please take a few moments to confer with one another in this room to gather your thoughts before the dialogue begins."

Mannheim kept a grip on Tormada's robe as he sensed the Spaniard priming for another tirade. "Very well," the German replied to Clement. "We had best begin."

By keeping all the cardinals in one room, Clement and Roncalli were able to observe which ones clustered with one another in conference. The largest group, gathered around Mannheim, included such powerful figures as Villendot, Trevi, the orator DeGolia, and Tormada, in whose ear Mannheim whispered intently.

"Don't be a fool, Francisco," Mannheim warned Tormada. "No matter what you think of Clement or his actions, he is the pope and now he's acting like one. Roncalli warned us not to oppose him. Another outburst and he may decide to fire all of us — then where would we be? We can't fight against this evil from the streets of Rome."

"But this can't be done!" the irate Spaniard insisted. "A doctrinal reinterpretation cannot be made with a wave of the hand, and to foist this witch upon us . . ."

"*Anything* can be done by a determined pope," Mannheim replied. "I know my theology as well as my Church history. He quietly got theologians to support his position, and now he is forcing it on us."

LoPresti was shaking his head in stunned disbelief. "Clement is weak. He was ready to abdicate. Now he's directly challenging us as if he wants a war. She's the one we were warned of, I tell you! They're under her spell, the pope and Roncalli. They've become the enemy."

Mannheim nodded. "The shadow's hand is in this but we can not argue prophecies, not now. What they've done is devilishly clever. They have opened their attack on a broad front, and for now we must defeat them politically."

"How?" Tormada asked.

Mannheim squinted as he thought matters through. "The nun is like a Chinese puzzle, a box within a larger box. The Ecumenical Council is a bigger, more immediate threat than a single female priest. A council takes time, time we can use to rally our forces. We can't stop this business about the nun today. We must fight on battlegrounds we can win."

"At the least then," LoPresti said, "let us make our best arguments then try to settle for her ordination as a special papal exception and not open to all females. Agreed?"

With their strategy set, the cardinals took their places and a general meeting was called to order. For nine straight hours, they debated with the majority of cardinals cleaving to one negative line of opinion while the pope, Roncalli, and three other cardinals weighed in with opposing sentiments. They discussed the precedents and the nuances of the pope's decision as well as the mechanics of how one becomes priest, bishop, and cardinal simultaneously.

Counterarguments were made on theological points, and articles of canon law were cited as to why a woman could not become a bishop. If Annalisa could not be a bishop they pointed out, neither could she be created a cardinal. The pope told them he would amend that canon law or simply remove the requirement for a cardinal to be a bishop, a rule that Pope John XXIII had imposed. The cardinals reluctantly preferred the amendment. They were afraid of lowering the entry requirements for the College of Cardinals.

Some cardinals said Annalisa could not become a priest because four years of education in the seminary were required. The pope replied that he was granting a dispensation for that requirement. Besides, Sister Annaliese Steurer, the daughter of the eminent theologian Freiherr Steurer, had grounded Annalisa well in theology. Annalisa also had hands-on pastoral experience the likes of which seminarians could only imagine. Mannheim slapped the table in surprise upon hearing the connection between his idol, Steurer, and the nun.

Finally, Cardinal LoPresti, who was prefect for the Congregation of the Sacred Sacraments, said, "The issue of women in the priesthood was decided by Pope John Paul II's infallible pronouncement in the apostolic letter *Ordinatio Sacerdotalis*. It stated that a woman may not become a priest, hence she cannot be a bishop or cardinal."

The conservatives knew this was their last and best chance to counter Clement, for popes were reluctant to overrule former popes. Yet Roncalli had foreseen the danger of this argument and had prepared Clement with a bold counter.

"It was *not* John Paul who claimed the infallibility of that statement in the nineteen-eighties," Clement replied. "It was rather the Congregation for the Doctrine of the Faith that declared his statement infallible. John Paul's own pronouncement was not made *ex cathedra,* and so the Congregation was in error by acting outside of its authority in declaring the infallible status of the pope's statement."

That explanation earned a look of contempt from Tormada. It was his Congregation, also called the Holy Office, which Clement had just slapped on the wrist for trying to set John Paul's opinion in stone.

Clement continued his rebuttal. "The Holy Office's decision was also based on the premise that because Christ was male, people have grown accustomed to male clergy. This reasoning was based on debatable opinion and not on grounds of faith or morals." The pope paused to let them absorb his point.

"The previous decision by the Holy Office," said Clement, "may now be superseded by a newer and higher understanding. The Holy Office may correct itself, or I will issue my own *ex cathedra* pronouncement, if necessary."

Roncalli saw a number of backs visibly stiffen. The pope was threatening to override the Holy Office with an infallible decision of his own!

"Please remember," Clement continued, "in 1976, a pontifical commission found no underlying basis in scripture or in canon law to bar women from the ministry."

As Roncalli had expected, there was no rejoinder on this point because it was factually accurate. Clement paused a minute before issuing his inevitable conclusion. "We believe the Holy Office, in light of this new age, will see fit to correct its prior decision with no need for action on our part. This may be done without concern of inconsistency, as the matter is not theological in substance. We are correcting something that was in error to begin with."

There it was. Roncalli knew they would buckle. The pope had given them two choices: save face by changing their own policy, or be forced to do so publicly by a papal override. Clement had just forcibly reminded them who led the Church.

Yet Clement did not wish to alienate them totally; he wanted their support for his planned Ecumenical Council. He agreed to their proposed compromise by telling them that Annalisa Basanjo's cardinalship would occur as a unique act by the pope and not a general policy change allowing women into the ministry. The decision about women in the priesthood would not be made before full discussion occurred in front of the Ecumenical Council. The cardinals knew that process would take several years, so they left mollified in some measure.

Clement had exerted papal authority in a manner not seen for centuries. He had rammed Annalisa down the throat of the Church to redress the entrenched bias against women, but it would make her a hated target. Roncalli silently resolved to protect her in any manner he could.

Mannheim walked up to Roncalli silently and said, "An eventful day, Cardinal."

"Quite," Roncalli replied.

"Tell me, Pietro, we were ready to censure this nun yet now she is making history. What really happened down there with her and the pope?" Mannheim questioned him in a manner more solicitous than Roncalli could ever remember coming from the German.

"It was just as you were told," Roncalli said. "The pope had severe, visible damage from a stroke until she treated him. The doctors are all puzzling over his recovery. Of course, we are not telling the whole story to the world, but she is a remarkable woman, a woman of God, and I am sure she will bring a new dimension to the Church."

"A miracle worker raised by shamans, coinciding with events indicating the time of the prophecies is upon us and this does not concern you? You are so sure of her purity you would vouch for her then?" Mannheim asked.

Roncalli shrugged. "Me vouch for her? The pope spent significant time with her and has set a historic role for her to fill. What could be a better endorsement, my dear Cardinal?"

Mannheim wanted to say something about delirious choices during serious illness but thought better of it. He was wasting his breath on the pope's lap dog. "Of course, of course," was all he said to Roncalli as he hurriedly excused himself.

"Lots of little intrigues to hatch today?" Roncalli inquired under his breath as the German departed, but Cardinal Mannheim was covering ground faster than Roncalli's faint voice could carry.

CHAPTER XXVI

But the relationship of morality and power is a very subtle one.
—James Baldwin

London

Teresa Ferentinos was prepared when the first hazy reports about a female cardinal trickled in from the wire services less than a week after she returned from Nigeria. Teresa had felt Annalisa's presence with Robert Avernis that day in front of the archdiocese compound. She also observed Annalisa going in and out of the compound on several occasions, including just before and after the pope's astonishing recovery.

Teresa stayed on a few more days in Nigeria to investigate the mysterious nun, and what she learned was remarkable, so much so that UNN authorized her to do a segment on her findings. When the news hit about Annalisa's ordination to the cardinalate, Teresa was quickly able to adjust the material, and so she broke the scoop of the century with this global video broadcast:

"This is a special UNN news report: a new female cardinal for the Catholic Church. In this thirty-minute segment, we discuss the historic appointment of the first female cardinal in history." A still picture of Annalisa Basanjo then flashed onscreen while the story title rose dramatically from the bottom of the frame:

PRINCESS OF THE CHURCH
FROM AFRICA TO THE VATICAN

"This is Teresa Ferentino in Lagos, Nigeria, where a remarkable nun, Annalisa Basanjo, first came to our attention."

The news report went on to show video clips of Annalisa going in and out of the heavily restricted archdiocese compound in Lagos. The next segment showed Bishop Ogunsanya leading the nun through a barricade of vigilant Nigerian soldiers into the hospital where the stricken pope was being treated. The reporter then said:

"We know that shortly after the nun's visit to the hospital, the pope, who was said by insiders to be in grave condition from a stroke, seemed to make an astonishing recovery. Was there a connection between the sister's presence and the change in the pope's physical condition? We traveled to her home village of Idugri in western Nigeria to learn more about this extraordinary woman."

In the next segment, Teresa interviewed people from Annalisa's village. They spoke of strange and miraculous occurrences surrounding the child Annalisa. They told of the shaman and the German nun. Teresa gave other details of Annalisa's biography then summarized the news piece:

"Some are afraid of her and what they see as her supernatural powers; to others she is a saintly figure roaming the countryside helping all in need. We heard reports of numerous, and in some cases incredible, acts of healing. One interesting and perhaps significant item of note: we are not the first to visit this village to inquire about Cardinal Basanjo. The Catholic Church itself sent a bishop here to investigate her history and activities.

"No one from the Church, including Bishop Ogunsanya, will speak on the subject. Was miraculous healing involved in the pope's recovery? Is any of this connected to the sister's historic creation as a cardinal? The Vatican is one of the most secretive places in the world and it may be a long time, if ever, before these questions are answered."

The video then showed some stock footage of assembled cardinals to juxtapose Teresa's next point:

"The Vatican was emphatic in asserting that admitting a woman to the priesthood was a special action by the pope and the general opening of ordination to women will be a question to be taken up at a new Ecumenical Council.

"The announcement of the new Ecumenical Council, Vatican III, was overshadowed by the proclamation of the new cardinal, but it represents a significant shift for the Church, which has been accused of burying its head in the sand in dealing with the pressing issues of the twenty-first century. . . . "

And so went the beginning of a new career for Teresa Ferentinos as UNN's new Vatican Correspondent. It was a coup for a religious reporter, which would normally be a dead-end research job. Now her face would be in front of a camera far more frequently, and a beautiful face it was—luxurious jet-black hair, clear gray-blue eyes, prominent cheekbones, and a narrow, high-bridged nose she had inherited from her Greek ancestry.

Teresa had won a couple of local beauty contests in her native Britain and she enjoyed being in the limelight. She had a typically Greek figure of voluptuous proportions, not heavy but curvy, and she dieted now and then to keep her svelte look. The result was a narrow-waisted figure, generous in the hip and bust, and much in demand with the male population of London.

She was also strong-willed. When she was nineteen, Teresa's parents, Greek immigrants to the U.K., had pushed her to marry the handsome son of a wealthy Greek shipping magnate. The man was crazy about her. Her parents thought he was a Greek god, but Teresa thought he was just a goddamned Greek.

"He's conceited, overbearing, and he'll cheat on me within three months because that's the way those arrogant bastards are," she had said. "They think they own the world, those men. They're filthy rich, party-circuit playboys whose fathers made all the money. Their ambition in life is to see how many women they can shag on their private yachts off southern France or Ibiza."

It was not that she didn't want money and the jet-set life—she wouldn't have minded that—but she didn't plan to get it by becoming the trophy wife of a wenching, overbearing, Greek tycoon of a husband. She was smart, motivated, and good-looking, and she was going to make it on her own. A husband and family could come later—much later.

And now she was moving to a new career opportunity in Rome. She had a few friends there but more importantly she had a couple of "ins" at the Vatican. She knew Monsignor O'Keefe, prefect of the Vatican Library, from several religious conferences over the past few years. She also knew—well, sort of knew—Robert Avernis with Vatican security. Now *that* was a relationship she looked forward to cultivating, and not just for professional reasons. *Who knows?* She enticed herself with a few flights of fancy.

But today was not just about girlish fantasies or the heady feeling of newfound fortune. Teresa had to make a difficult decision. She had not been completely truthful with her UNN bosses. There was a piece of information she had withheld, information that would give bombshell ratings to her network, but also have far-reaching consequences for the world's first female cardinal.

Several people in Idugri had told her that at the age of fifteen, Annalisa Basanjo had to leave their village for a while. The reason? *She was pregnant.* Teresa was not able to corroborate the story beyond hearsay from several unrelated sources, but that would have been enough for UNN. Teresa doubted the Vatican had knowledge of this. It would be a terrible embarrassment to both the Church and the new cardinal. It could also affect Pope Clement's tottering papacy.

Did she have the right to cause all that damage? Her instincts told her there was far more to this story than met the eye and she should not muddy the waters. Besides, she was not about to destroy the first female Catholic priest in two thousand years with a hint of scandal, and so her personal instincts prevailed over her professional requirements. UNN would not be happy if they knew, but damn it if she'd be the one to break that story.

CHAPTER XXVII

Great fear seized the whole church
and all who heard about these events. —*Acts 5:10*

The Vatican City

What is this abomination?" Cardinal LoPresti hissed, pointing at the figurine hanging in the hallway in front of the papal apartments.

Mannheim and Roncalli studied the object along with Roald Zugli and Robert Avernis. The figure had the head of a rooster, the legs of a serpent, and bore a shield and whip.

"A demonic symbol here in the Vatican. How can this be?" LoPresti asked, looking at Roncalli as if he should know the answer.

"I'll show this to Monsignor O'Keefe," Roncalli said. "Maybe he can identify it."

"Yes, O'Keefe, not you, should identify it," Mannheim said. Then he addressed Zugli. "Roald, you must investigate who could have placed this outside of the pope's bedchambers."

"Yes, Eminenza," Zugli replied.

Mannheim and LoPresti then stormed off down the corridor and into Mannheim's office.

"Did you see that UNN reporter's newscast about the nun this morning?" the somber LoPresti asked. "The woman Clement has just made a *bishop* is a witch raised by shamans. Now this demonic object shows up at the pope's doorstep. Can my case be clearer? My God, we are in the times of the Great Heretic. We have brought the evil into our midst."

Mannheim nodded. "Yes. I'll have Trevi find a reliable party in Africa to start checking the nun's background, something Clement and Roncalli never thought to do. We need something incriminating to use against her. She's the lever that could bring Clement down, but the danger is that she could bring the Church down too."

LoPresti shook his head. "Demonic symbols in the Vatican! We have just seen the tip of the iceberg with this woman. I don't want her around long enough for us to see what lies beneath."

The Vatican City

"She's coming to Rome, my friends. She arrives today," Pietro Roncalli told a group of his closest confidants. "I backed the pope's vision and made this all possible. I acted on instinct rather than reason and brought this woman of miraculous powers into the Church despite the prophecies and the trouble it will cause. Now we've found a demonic object here in the Vatican just as she comes. What does it mean? Have I committed a grave error? I'm the first to admit I don't understand where it's all heading," Roncalli declared to the group. "I can use all of your thoughts and counsel. Tell me what the prophecies say."

For more than a millennium, prophecies of saints and mystics had lain stored in the Vatican. Pius XIII, Clement's predecessor, had secretly ordered Vatican scholars to compile and cross-reference all prophecies concerning the twenty-first century. The predictions covered the Church, the papacy, and worldwide events. The compilation, *Breverarium Prophetium Humanae Vitae* (Compendium of the Prophecies of Human Life), lay sealed in the Vatican archives available for scrutiny only by popes and high-ranking Church officials. Collectively, they had proven astonishingly accurate in predicting the future and in describing the reigns of individual popes over the centuries, right up to the present time.

Five men sat around the table in a small reading room in the Vatican library. They were discussing ancient prophecies contained in the Breverarium, a three-inch thick, wine-red, leather-bound book. Monsignor O'Keefe had made sure they would not be disturbed. Joining O'Keefe and Roncalli were Umberto Segri, the patriarch of Venice, Archbishop Maccario of Ostia, and Cardinal De Faissy of France. Their small number was symbolic of the isolation they experienced because of their progressive views in direct opposition to the Vatican majority.

Archbishop Maccario spoke first. "Let's start with one fact: a cross-referencing of numerous sources all point to one disturbing event. During this very decade of 2020 the line of popes is to end, and the Church meets its demise."

Annalisa's own premonition about the Church and a tribulation seemed to reinforce that prophecy, Roncalli thought, but he did not share that information.

Cardinal De Faissy then said, "The prophecies speak of a Great Deceiver who will be instrumental in unleashing the forces of destruction. You sat on the secret pontifical commission that compiled this collection of prophecies and issued commentaries on them, Desmond. Can you tell us anything about this being?"

"The Great Deceiver," Monsignor O'Keefe said, "is also called the Great Heretic in some of the prophecies. I'll use the male gender for sake of convenience, though the Great Heretic is an enigmatic figure whose sex in not named. He—or she—is a miracle worker who gains great influence over the masses, and it's implied he fools even the elect. This is usually interpreted as meaning the Church, so the Great Deceiver could, potentially, rise from within the Church."

"But what would be the nature of such a being?" Roncalli asked. "Would he be human or supernatural, and how would his evil manifest?"

O'Keefe closed his eyes to aid his memory. "The prophecies and commentaries are not precise on that point. The inference, however, is that he is incarnated as a human with supernatural powers, and possessed of evil. It is entirely possible that this being may not be born conscious of his destiny, but that his powers and evil will grow over time. From his perspective, he may be doing good. Such a person might be deceiving himself, at least to a point, and that is what is so insidious about this figure, what makes him so hard to identify.

"The unfortunate reality," O'Keefe continued, "is that prophecy becomes truth only after the fact. Clement's illness, his recovery, the new direction the Church is taking, and a woman becoming the Church's first female prelate—it is difficult to decipher these events at this time. But the powers of evil will work through time and history as well as supernaturally."

Umberto Segri now spoke. His patriarchate of Venice seemed to produce a series of farsighted men who wanted to bring the Church in line with the modern age. Pope John XXIII had once been the Venetian patriarch, as had the tragic John Paul I. Segri was cut from the same cloth.

"I can only speak to the accuracy of the Breverarium prophecies by example of the first John Paul," he said. "John Paul was a humble, intelligent man. He was the last hope for Church reform in the twentieth century. Sadly, his life was expunged before his reforms could begin. I personally believe he was poisoned because, among other things, he had been determined to reform the scandal-ridden Vatican Bank back in the late 1970s.

"The astounding part of the John Paul mystery is found in a thousand-year-old prophecy by Malachi of Armaugh concerning the popes. Astonishingly, he identified the brief reign of one modern pope, the 'white light,' whose shining lamp would be extinguished by poisoning. John Paul's birth name was Albino Luciani, which literally translates from Italian as *the white light.*"

A chilled silence hung in the room. "I know where you're headed, Umberto." It was O'Keefe again. "There is another pope mentioned in Malachi's prophecies as living during our era—*De Gloria Olivae*, the second-to-last pope, the inference being that he is somehow tied to the Great Heretic."

"The Glory of Olives, yes," said Segri. "An enigmatic figure, not a bad man, but something he does hastens the downfall of the Church. Has he come and gone or is Clement *De Gloria Olivae*?"

"This title, *De Gloria Olivae*, is puzzling," said Archbishop Maccario. "The only thing I can think of is the Mount of Olives. Is Clement planning on making any pilgrimages to the Holy Land, Pietro?"

"No, Nello, not in the foreseeable future," Roncalli answered. "He just returned from a long trip, and he has many preparations to make prior to the Ecumenical Council."

Segri, the patriarch, suddenly made a series of sharp knocks on the table and said, "Yes, yes," in a whispery voice. "The Glory of Olives. I only thought about it now. Clement—his family is from Campania, my home province."

The men stared at Segri, puzzled by what he was trying to say.

"Campania is Italy's prime area for *olive* production," Segri explained. "*The Glory of Olives*. Clement's family is the largest producer of olives in Campania. His parents were quoted in the newspapers saying that he was the *glory* of their family when he became pope."

The small room was stone quiet. De Faissy then repeated a segment of the Gloria Olivae prophesy, "*And he will do something to hasten the downfall of the Church.*"

Those words cut Roncalli's heart like a knife. Clement's two most important actions were calling for the Ecumenical Council to discuss reforms and elevating Annalisa. If he were *De Gloria Olivae* of the prophecies, did that mean his actions would unravel the Church? He thought of Mannheim's warnings that reforms would destroy the Church's ancient authority.

Roncalli, at age fifty, was the youngest man present. He had risen in the Church under three conservative popes because he was brilliant, articulate, and he had decided early on the only way to achieve Church reform was to move quietly and wait for the right moment. The right moment had been a very long time coming, and now it came borne on foreboding winds.

O'Keefe saw the expression on his friend's face. Before the others could speculate any further, he said, "All this is food for thought, but interpreting ancient prophecies through current events is a tricky task. Just stay alert and keep evaluating things as they happen."

"I agree, Desmond," Roncalli said. "Let's adjourn now and contemplate these matters."

The men shuffled out the door. After the others had left, O'Keefe pulled Roncalli back.

"What is it, Pietro?" O'Keefe asked as soon as they were alone. "You'd be a terrible poker player with those expressions of yours."

"That business of *De Gloria Olivae* doing something to undermine the Church," Roncalli said. "If Clement is *De Gloria Olivae* then his Ecumenical Council, his appointing a female cardinal—it calls into question how much reshaping the Church can take before it is no longer the Church. Are these reforms the precursor of the downfall, and is Annalisa the Great Deceiver?"

O'Keefe held up a hand and said, "Whoa, there now, Pietro, aren't you jumping the gun? We have *no* reforms now, and this process of synods and ecumenical councils will last three to five years. I'll be lucky to see any change in my lifetime. As for Annalisa, you trusted your heart concerning her, and she healed the pope. Be vigilant, but give her a chance until proven wrong. You'll be the first to call her out if her intentions are evil."

Roncalli smiled. "Desmond, you're right as usual. You're about to warn me not to stare at the future and trip over the present."

"No, Pietro," the monsignor replied, "I'm warning you to watch your feet and not fall over the precipice. I don't need prophecies to tell me we're in for a fight, but the Church is dying. We need more than change; we need a complete renewal. As for Annalisa and the council, I'll consider them changes for the better until proven otherwise."

"Rumblings of conflict, war, and destruction all around us," Roncalli said. "It's like a rollercoaster—a scary plunge down and, if we survive it, a long climb up."

"You know," the Irishman said, "it's times like this I wish I were a rabbi. They don't have all this theological mumbo jumbo, and I think they make more money."

The attempt to lighten the atmosphere went right over Roncalli's head. He was staring blankly and tapping his fingers on the table.

"Maybe we are in for a plunge," O'Keefe said, acknowledging his friend's seriousness, "but remember, Pietro, if you never take a plunge, you never really live."

CHAPTER XXVIII

The whole visible universe is but a storehouse of images and signs to which the imagination will give referative place and value; it is sort of a pasture which the imagination must digest and transform. — Baudelaire

The Vatican City

Annalisa looked out the airplane window and thought the whole world must revolve around Rome. Her eyes widened, trying to take in the length and breadth of the city. This was her first plane trip, and the perspective of the Eternal City from on high was breathtaking. She saw the Coliseum as the plane circled before landing. She then caught a brief glimpse of a key-shaped outline—the massive Bernini colonnades leading to the dome of St. Peter's, the Vatican, her new home.

The two priests assigned to meet Annalisa at the Fiumicino airport had no trouble picking her out of the crowd. She was African and a nun—that narrowed the field considerably. They waved to her and she saw the placard with her name on it.

"Your Eminence, welcome to Rome. I am Father DeFeo and this is Father Ferragamo. We are here to escort you to the Vatican."

Your Eminence, how odd sounding. Yet that was her new title, and it reminded her that her life would be different from now on.

Rome, like Lagos, was a bustling collection of humanity, but Rome had an entirely different feel. The sounds of people and traffic were familiar, but the sights and the smells were very different.

Where Lagos was simply slapped together, Rome was intricately composed like fine, flaky layers of a delicate pastry. Each layer was a segment of history that passed through the view of Annalisa's mind. The power, the wealth, the artistry, and the skill that had lived and worked its craft on this city were monumental

They skirted an open-air market where the vendors sold meats, produce, clothing, and sundry items. "May we stop for a minute?" Annalisa asked. "This market reminds me of Africa." She wanted to mix among the people. That was the best way to feel the pulse of a city.

"Sorry, Your Eminence," Father Ferragamo said. "Cardinal Roncalli will be receiving you at the Vatican shortly. This is the Trastevere area. If you care to return another time, someone will be happy to bring you."

She smiled, and nodded her understanding. She was gaining an education just from driving through the clogged streets of Rome, so she was content. Today she had learned something important too: the Italians were even worse drivers than the Nigerians.

Roncalli greeted Annalisa as he walked across the courtyard. "Welcome to Rome, Your Eminence." He embraced her and kissed her on both cheeks.

"Oh, please, Pietro. That title still flusters me. It is very good to see you again," and she kissed the ring on his hand. With their difference in height, she did not have to bend very far to do it.

Roncalli stretched his arm out to point to the area around him, and the shoulder cape of his simar hung over Annalisa like an enfolding, protective wing. "Come with me. We will talk as I show you around a small portion of the papal palaces today. I have reserved some time to spend with you."

Fathers DeFeo and Ferragamo, who had accompanied her to the cardinal, now took their leave. Roncalli walked Annalisa through courtyards and porticos, through chapels and offices. He told her of the history and the people who created the Vatican—of Bramante who did the original design of the buildings but died before their completion, and then of Michelangelo, who succeeded him and left so many memorable artifacts. Michelangelo had been older when he started, and so he too had passed on before his works were done.

Annalisa gazed in awe at the brilliant paintings, tiles, and frescoes. She marveled at the elaborately detailed carvings and statuary. "I have heard the history behind the building of the Vatican is notorious," she said. "But these artists and craftsmen were truly inspired by a belief in God no matter the failings of the people who commissioned them."

She had never seen such concentrated extravagance in her life. Vivid colors and opulent materials registered on her visual senses the way a rich meal might affect someone on a diet—it was pleasing but hard to digest.

"You must be tired from your trip," Roncalli said. "We have temporary quarters for you until you select an apartment."

"Does the Vatican have apartments in the Trastevere?" she asked. "It looked good to me."

Roncalli smiled. "You want to live there? Interesting. Well, yes, we can arrange that."

The temporary efficiency apartment was utilitarian. Modern by Vatican standards, it was built sometime during the 1970s to house visiting foreign prelates. Though Italians would consider it modest, Annalisa felt spoiled, having spent most of her adult life roaming the backcountry of West Africa and taking shelter where available. It had a refrigerator, a stove, running water, and a latrine. At night, from this time on, she would be able to read by a steady supply of electricity, not by the flickering light of a candle. That was a luxury beyond price.

"Tomorrow we discuss your future, but today your time is free. Would you like to rest?" Roncalli inquired.

Annalisa smiled and clapped her hands together. "Pietro, all my life I have walked from place to place and that is what I want to do now. I will take a shower then walk around Rome. I saw interesting places on the way that I want to visit."

"Rome is a big city, and it's easy to get lost," Roncalli said. "If you care to wait, I can arrange for a guide to accompany you."

"No, thank you," she replied, "I'll go by myself. I'll learn more by getting lost."

Roncalli was learning to understand her quirks. He smiled and said, "Fine, but at least let me find you a map."

✠

Annalisa's apartment was on the south side of St. Peter's Basilica. South was the direction of Africa, as good a way to go as any, so off she went. She only used the map to identify points of interest, not to navigate. She felt wherever she would arrive would be exactly where she should be, and that was all she needed for walking.

She meandered past the Stazione Vaticana to the Porta Cavalleggeri then down the Viale Delle Mura Aurelie. For a long time, she strolled along beneath the Janiculum Hill until she came to an area of converging roads. There she saw a gigantic statue of a man astride a horse with the name *Garibaldi* inscribed on it. A large park-like area rose up the hill to the north behind the statue.

She walked east, and the landscape became crowded with residential buildings as she traveled downhill. The pattern of Rome was both alien and familiar to her mind. Large green areas with no buildings alternated with pockets of human habitat. This was similar to the way clumps of jungle separated the neighboring villages of her homeland, but the places where the people lived — they were so different! The crowds, the mazes of streets, the aromas in the air, and the sheer variety of structures would make her head swim if she thought about it. She concentrated on one building at a time to keep her equilibrium.

Eventually she came to an open-air market in a large plaza where the signs read PIAZZA SAN COSIMATO. Here was the life she was looking for, loud and boisterous, just like the marketplaces of her homeland. People were bargaining with facial and hand expressions as well as with words, just like in Africa. They seemed friendly and happy, judging from their faces and the way they treated their children. Annalisa liked that.

She was dressed in plain clothes and her Africanness did not seem to attract any attention. She bought some fruit, trying to communicate with the vendor in English. Finally, she just exhibited the money in her hand and he counted it out for her. She took the bag and started walking away but then heard his voice calling, "Signorina, signorina." When she turned, he stood jangling change in his palm. She thanked him as she retrieved the coins, and he smiled and tipped his cap to her.

She happened to wander into the Trastevere, the area she had chosen to live. It was not one of the city's best neighborhoods, but one in which the people were known as "true Romans." She strolled down lanes where grass grew in the cracks of the thick-walled buildings, candles lit small shrines to roadside Madonnas, and old men rolled balls on long, grassy surfaces, playing some kind of game.

She traversed a small alleyway off the main street, lured by the smell of freshly baked bread. She came upon an old woman sitting on the narrow pavement, propped up against the wall of a building. The woman's knees were tucked close to her chest, and her long black dress draped between her legs. As Annalisa approached, the woman held out her hand.

Annalisa knelt to the woman's level and extended her palm, which still contained the change from the fruit vendor. Up close, the woman was not as old as she had first appeared to be. Her dark eyes looked younger than her face, which seemed prematurely wrinkled. Missing teeth gave her mouth the concave appearance of an older person. She clasped Annalisa's hand in hers but did not take the money. Instead, she spoke words Annalisa did not understand.

"Non, non accetto elemosine. Lavoro per mantenermi."

Then the woman gave a slight start but continued to clutch Annalisa's hand.

"Oh, una persona religiosa, non, una persona spirituale. Cosa posso dirti che tu non sappia gia'?"

She drew Annalisa's hand in and kissed it. *"Forse Dio mi ha dato questa opportunita' di parlarti,"* and she reached in the folds of her dress to withdraw a deck of cards. She fanned the cards out in front of Annalisa, indicating that she should take one.

Annalisa pulled a single card, facedown, from the deck. The woman motioned Annalisa to turn the card over. It was a picture of a female in a blue robe and gold- trimmed blue cape holding a book. On her head was a golden, mitered crown encrusted with jewels. The caption below read *La Papesse.* The woman pressed Annalisa's hands together over the card.

"Possa Dio farmi essere il primo a dirtelo, Mamma." She kissed Annalisa's hand once more, took the coins that the nun had placed on the ground, and then stood up. She made a slight bowing gesture and said, *"Il mio regalo per te,"* and walked away.

Annalisa watched her amble down the alley and around a corner. She closed her eyes and leaned against the rough stone wall. In an instant, she was in the still place by the familiar riverbank looking across to the other side. *What does it mean*? she asked.

It is the beginning, the invisible voice replied. *The message must be heard.*

When will I know, when will I see you? she asked.

When you find wisdom. Find wisdom and find yourself.

Annalisa's eyes opened to see the rosy gold dusk of a setting sun emblazoning the buildings. It was time to return. She found a taxi and handed the driver the written directions Pietro had given her to return to the Vatican.

Annalisa pressed her cheek to the window as the cab whisked along the street. She had always walked lightly through this world, but today seemed exceptionally dreamlike. Most pointedly, she felt a sense of motion carrying her somewhere—and that motion was not from the taxi taking her back to the Vatican.

CHAPTER XXIX

. . . malice to conceal, couch'd with revenge . . .
—John Milton

The Vatican City

The next morning Annalisa decided to tour the Vatican before she met with Cardinal Roncalli. The Vatican was geographically part of Rome, spoke the same Italian language, and mostly used Italian employees, but the attitude of the people in the Vatican was singularly distinctive.

The difference was readily apparent on their faces. Unlike the population of Trastevere, people in the Vatican seemed unhappy — more than that — they seemed disgruntled. Annalisa was still in plain clothes and she was garnering strange, sometimes furtive looks. These were not inquisitive glances that asked, *Who are you? I have never seen you before;* these were judgmental stares that proclaimed, *You do not belong here.*

She tried to enter an area manned by the Swiss Guard. They refused her entry. "I'm sorry, ma'am, only prelates are allowed here."

Annalisa smiled. "I see. Well, does a cardinal qualify?"

"Of course, ma'am."

"Then I suppose I qualify," she said.

The guard's hands began to twist around the wooden shaft of his ceremonial halberd poelaxe. "I uh, I'm sorry, ma'am. You have not completed the formal ceremony yet."

Annalisa took pause for a moment. "May I ask, are you refusing me on your own authority?"

"Oh, no, ma'am. We have our orders."

"Someone ordered you to not admit me here?"

"Only prelates allowed, sorry, ma'am." The guard was sweating.

"I have a pass from Cardinal Roncalli," Annalisa said, and she proffered the paper.

The guard bit his lip, and his fingers fidgeted as he glanced at the paper. "Uh, ma'am, I'm sorry, our orders supersede your pass."

"Supersede a pass from the pope's secretary?"

"Ma'am, I'm sorry but we have a job to do."

Annalisa saw the man's distress. She decided not to press the issue or ask who gave him his orders. The ceremony formalizing her position was in little over three hours. If someone had gone to such pains to risk confronting Cardinal Roncalli, whoever bore her such animosity would make himself known in time.

✠

At 1:00 p.m. sharp, Annalisa presented herself at Cardinal Roncalli's office. Like many areas of the Apostolic Palace, the dimensions of the cardinal's office were immense, but the prelate's friendly countenance brought things back to human scale.

The cardinal greeted her, and he ordered two espressos. "Helps to keep me going at this time of day," he explained. Like most Vatican prelates, his day started at 5:00 a.m. with the celebration of mass, usually at the pope's private chapel.

Roncalli inquired after her well-being. Annalisa did not mention the incident with the guard. "Your ordination and investiture will happen in a few hours," Roncalli said. "Afterward we can discuss your duties and functions, but now let's get you ready for the big moment."

And Cardinal Roncalli prepared her well. Two hours later, Annalisa was ordained as a priest and consecrated as a bishop. Finally, she underwent the ceremony of the "opening and closing of the mouth" that created her as the first princess of the church. Now she wore the dress of a cardinal — the caped, scarlet simar trimmed in watered lace, the fascia sashed about her waist, and the zucchetto crowning her head. It was a safe bet that in all of Church history, hers was probably the most hair ever to protrude beneath a cardinal's skullcap.

At the solemn conclusion of the ceremony, something toward the corner of the room tugged at Annalisa's awareness. She turned slightly, and seven pairs of eyes drew her attention, all locked on her. Seven cardinals stood together in a corner with their hands folded piously at their chests. Their faces were impassive, but she could read their thoughts, particularly those of the cardinal with the pale blue eyes. Those eyes ignited smoldering memories in her heart like revenant embers of a fire that had once burned something inside her soul.

When she turned her head back to receive the pope's kiss on her cheek, the seven cardinals simultaneously turned their faces to the opposite wall. Only one of them spoke, and then so softly that only his companions heard.

"See how long she lasts," Tormada hissed. "Just see how long she lasts."

CHAPTER XXX

. . . the spectator brings the work in contact with the external world by deciphering and interpreting its inner qualifications and thus adds his contribution . . .
— Marcel Duchamp

The Vatican City

Come in," Monsignor O'Keefe replied to the knock on his office door. Robert Avernis entered. "Ah, Robert, good afternoon."

"Afternoon, Monsignor," Avernis replied. "Do you have any information on that demonic symbol we found last week?"

"Yes, in fact your timing is amazing," O'Keefe said. "I was just discussing that with a young lady who has identified the symbol."

"Good," Avernis said, "maybe this lady can explain what it means."

"I'd be happy to," a female voice answered.

To Avernis' surprise, the head and shoulders of a woman appeared from around the the old high-backed chair facing O'Keefe's desk. The backrest was so tall and wide she had not been visible from his vantage point.

Avernis' head snapped back. "Teresa? Teresa Ferentinos? What are you doing here?"

O'Keefe responded. "Teresa is a friend and fellow scholar, Robert. She's moved to Rome. UNN has assigned her as a reporter to the Vatican."

"Really?" Avernis said. "Well, I guess that figures. You scooped the media world with your story on Cardinal Basanjo, but you deciphered the meaning of the figure? How's that?"

O'Keefe replied again. "My personnel available for research is limited. Teresa has a graduate degree in comparative religions and theology. She also has UNN's resources apart from our library. When she came to tell me she was moving to Rome, I asked for her assistance, and I think she's done a fine job."

"I see," Avernis said, sounding dubious. "And what did you find?"

Teresa looked at O'Keefe. The monsignor nodded. Teresa pulled out a picture of an engraving. It was identical to the figurine.

"This figure is *Abraxas*," she said. "It may or may not be demonic as you mentioned. Originally it was used by Gnostic Christians to symbolize the supreme Deity. He carries a whip and shield, called wisdom and power respectively. Abraxas is occasionally depicted driving a chariot drawn by four horses, which represent the four elements."

"Gnostics? What are they?" Avernis asked.

"An early Christian sect," Teresa replied. "They were branded as heretics and banished by the Church in the fourth century."

"For what?" Avernis asked.

"For claiming to possess secret teachings of Jesus, the knowledge he revealed about the truth of this world and the real origin of human beings."

Avernis cupped his hand to his chin. "That's quite a claim. But you said the figure may be demonic?"

"Amulets and seals bearing the figure of Abraxas were common in the second century," Teresa said. "They were used as recently as the thirteenth century in the seals of the Knights Templar. By medieval times, Abraxas was relegated to the ranks of demons."

"Why?" O'Keefe asked.

"It's not certain," Teresa said. "My guess is that it was part of the suppression of the Gnostics by the orthodox Catholic Church. The Church destroyed the Templars and Cathars in France, both considered Gnostic heresies, and declared their symbols to be demonic."

"That tells us *what* the symbol is. But *who* placed it and why?" Avernis asked.

"That's for you and Roald to figure out," O'Keefe said.

"Right," Avernis said. "Good work, Teresa. Thank you. Mind if I speak with the monsignor privately?"

"Sure, I was leaving anyway. Nice seeing you again, Robert. Do you realize this is the first time we've been in the same place without something weird happening?"

Avernis' brows knitted together. "Come to think of it, you're right."

"Maybe I'll see you again," she said. "I'm living in Rome now."

"I heard. Great. I hope to see you soon."

Once they were alone, Avernis said, "Monsignor, isn't it a little unusual for you to involve an outsider—a reporter no less—in internal Vatican security matters?"

O'Keefe shrugged. "Well, she didn't know it was a security matter, at least until you walked in. I just asked her to identify the object as a matter of curiosity. She's a good friend and trustworthy. She would say nothing if I asked her. Not to be combative, but why are *you* handling this matter? Aren't you technically an outsider too?"

"The Swiss Guards are adept at security," Avernis said, "but I have more investigative training. Commander Zugli asked me to help out."

"Exactly," O'Keefe declared. "Your situation with Zugli is like mine with Teresa. We lack certain resources here, particularly with the cutbacks, and we need outside support."

"Okay," Avernis nodded. "I have no say in this, but I suggest you don't let Cardinal Mannheim know about her. I don't think he'd like the idea."

"Astute observation," O'Keefe snickered.

"Monsignor," Avernis said, "these Gnostics Teresa spoke of—it sounds like the Church really had it in for them. What did they actually do?"

O'Keefe sighed. "Here's an honest answer, not the Church's party line, so don't repeat this, okay? You see, Gnostics claimed that *human beings* are actually *God beings* in human form. We are direct extensions of God's essence into the material world, and we can all attain the Christ spirit. They also believed, however, that certain evil forces work on this plane to keep us ignorant of our divine origins. So sin, to a Gnostic, was ignorance, forgetting what we really are."

"Well," Avernis said, "I already see one point of contention. The Church says there was only one Christ, one son of God. To say all humans are latent Christs is blasphemy. The evil force you mentioned is the devil I assume?"

"Not exactly," O'Keefe said. "It's actually scarier than that, but that's too long a digression. The point is that whenever a true revelation occurred, these forces would twist and distort it to obscure its truth. For this reason, a succession of redeemers from the divine realm appears throughout history to renew humanity with the correct knowledge, or *gnosis,* of our real nature."

"Like Jesus did?" Avernis asked.

"And Moses, Krishna, Buddha, Zoroaster, and Muhammad," O'Keefe said. "*Gnosis* in Greek means 'knowledge derived from direct experience.' Gnostics held that Jesus and the other redeemers handed down oral teachings and certain techniques to gain a direct enlightened experience of themselves as part of God. Such spiritually mature, sacred knowledge was difficult to dispense on a mass basis. Most people back then were, as they are now, too bogged down by mundane living to delve into such matters."

"So they let Churches and priests do their work for them, eh?" Avernis said.

"Cynical, but true," O'Keefe said. "Anyway, the Church was divided in its understanding of Jesus' message. The literal-minded majority fixated on Jesus' outer pronouncements. The Gnostics focused on the secret inner teachings. Gnostics might say the Church only recognizes the shell, but Gnostics eat of the almond inside. Of course, there is less need for priests and dogmas if each person can grow to experience his or her own enlightenment of the Kingdom within."

Avernis nodded. "Now I see the real Gnostic threat — the Church losing its power and control as the gatekeeper to heaven."

"More than that," O'Keefe said. "If the Gnostics truly derived their tradition from Jesus' most sacred, mystical teachings, they, not the orthodox Church, would be the original Christians, so to speak, the true hidden Church driven into exile. O'Keefe paused as Avernis contemplated his statements, then he said, "Not to change the subject, Robert, but what did Teresa mean earlier about seeing you for the first time without something weird happening?"

"That? Oh, it was peculiar. A couple of times in Nigeria we were all suddenly seized by a . . . a feeling, a force. It wasn't nausea but it was a kind of dizziness, almost like hyperventilating or being on some kind of drug high."

"You were by yourselves?" O'Keefe asked.

"No, the first time we were in a group — Cardinal Roncalli, Roald, and a Nigerian bishop were there."

"They were affected too?"

"No, only Teresa, myself, and Cardinal Roncalli."

"I see. And the other time?"

"At the archdiocese compound. It was Teresa, myself, and Cardinal — then Sister — Basanjo."

"Was Cardinal Basanjo affected?"

"No. She said something peculiar though. Something like, 'this won't happen again.'"

O'Keefe raised an eyebrow. Was Cardinal Basanjo at the first occurrence?"

"No. That was at the massacre site, but she had just left the area a short time before. Are you an MD too, Monsignor?"

"Oh, no," O'Keefe smiled. "It just seemed like such an unusual story. Anyway, I'm glad you came back with no tropical illnesses."

"Me too, because I have to travel again for a few days," Avernis said. "I hope we get a break on learning who's placing these symbols before I return."

"Going anywhere interesting?"

"Can't tell you" Avernis said with a wink. "Spy stuff, you see?" He pretended to be kidding, but O'Keefe knew he was quite serious.

CHAPTER XXXI

Politics at all times leads to bloody wars. . . .
— Friederich Durrenmatt

Tehran, Iran

Tehran — that was the destination that Robert Avernis could not divulge to Monsignor O'Keefe. The United States had broken diplomatic relations with Iran a year earlier to underscore the American contention that Iran was International Terror Central. President Davidson was concerned about the pending pact Iran was brokering between the Islamic oil-producing states and China.

Secretary of State Dennis Kanellos visited Cardinal Mannheim and requested that Vatican diplomats meet with the Iranians. The Vatican was in the best position to gather and convey information for the U.S. government. As a non-secular state, it was viewed more impartially than the Western governments. The Vatican also had a secret CIA liaison. Avernis could directly observe and report on the talks as part of the visiting delegation.

They were meeting Ayatollah Mualimi; Reza Gorbani, a junior cleric; and Fahrdad Qazai, a parliamentary diplomat. The Vatican contingent was led by Archbishop DeSerra, the papal nuncio. Also present were Betros Furanian, the Vatican Ambassador to Iran, and Roberto Nervi, aka Robert Avernis, secretary to the nuncio.

Qazai said, "We are pleased to receive you. Please, sit." He indicated some sofas by a coffee table. "We regret that Ayatollah Mualimi is very short on time today."

And without the clerical watchdog, they don't trust the government bureaucrat, Avernis thought. He noticed Gorbani translating for Mualimi, but he sensed the old buzzard probably understood more English than they were letting on. "We understand," DeSerra said, "and we need not take long in respect of the ayatollah's time. His Holiness, the pope, in his desire to see peace between all nations and faiths, expresses his concern about the oil pacts with China and the Southeast Asian cartel."

"But why should a commercial transaction between sovereign nations concern the Vatican?" Qazai asked.

"The world's oil supply is numbered," DeSerra replied. "America and the Western economies have been slow transitioning to alternative fuels. Their economies are already in deep recession, and this pact will have dramatic political and economic impacts."

Mualimi replied with Gorbani translating. "We are sorry for America's troubles but they always lecture the world about responsibility. We are not responsible for their oil addiction. True, their economy is in deep decline. China is now the world's dominant economy and they are willing to pay the highest prices for long-term contracts. America never allowed us such escalation clauses in their long-term agreements."

"If it is simply a matter of money, I'm sure the Western powers would be happy to negotiate," Furanian said.

"Ambassador," Mualimi said through Gorbani, "We have no special authority in this matter. Iran is just one member in a group of nations that have decided the deal with the Asians is in our best national interests. All we can do is pass on your concerns."

Bullshit, Avernis thought. Iran subverted the Shi'ite government in Iraq and had the heads of state in Egypt and Saudi Arabia assassinated by their terrorist allies. The Iranians brokered this deal by cajoling or intimidating the Islamic nations, and now they were playing dumb.

"In the interests of world security, I must tell you the Americans see the oil pact as a thinly disguised embargo," DeSerra said. "President Davidson believes it is an attempt to weaken and destabilize his country. The Americans already know about Iranian involvement in the wave of terror attacks in American and European cities. Can you not find a way to fairly allocate the remaining oil to avoid potential conflicts?"

"Is America threatening us?" Mualimi asked through Gorbani, to which DeSerra made a vigorous denial.

"Well then, we repeat, all we can do is pass on your concerns to our member states," Gorbani said, this time without any direction from Mualimi.

That confirmed to Avernis that Mualimi understood English. The junior cleric would not have spoken on his own without the older ayatollah's understanding and tacit consent.

"Before Ayatollah Mualimi leaves, Archbishop, we would like to register a concern of our own," Gorbani said. "You know the situation in Nigeria between Christians and Muslims is precarious at best. Local Muslim leaders have talked of a nun, a supposed miracle worker. This woman is charismatic and she has been seeking converts among the Islamic population. Now, Rome has made her the first woman priest, a cardinal, no less! This seems a true provocation, especially to the Nigerian Muslims."

Avernis had to keep from gagging—*the best defense is a good offence, I suppose.*

"Not at all," Ambassador Furanian said. "The Church investigated Cardinal Basanjo when she was a nun. She never sought converts. The converts were a result of her healing powers—she treated Christians, Muslims, and Animists alike."

"Come now, Ambassador. Do you expect us to believe these fantasies about healings?" Gorbani said. "This is a thinly disguised effort by the Church to tip the scales in Nigeria."

Like you shipping arms to the Hausas? Avernis wanted to ask.

"There was no conspiracy as you suggest, Mr. Gorbani," Archbishop DeSerra said. "But it is a moot point. By removing her from Africa, we have addressed your concern."

Avernis was impressed. *These Vatican guys are good.*

"Perhaps," Gorbani said, sounding tentative. "In any case, the ayatollah must leave now."

With that the meeting ended. Afterward, Furanian shook his head in futility.

"You both did well," Avernis said to the nuncio and the ambassador. "The problem is that our audience isn't listening. They're bold, determined, and they don't give a damn about consequences."

Tehran, Iran

"The Western powers use the Church like a hidden dagger," the gray-bearded Havenei had frequently lectured Gorbani. "Despite their protests today, the Church has opened up a religious front in Nigeria. Control of that nation is key to our plans. The Islamic militias can attack Christians, but to win we must neutralize the source of the problem."

So it was that Havenei and Gorbani met with some unusual guests immediately after the Vatican emissaries left Tehran. They sat opposite representatives of the Poor Nation's Coalition in Havenei's sparsely furnished, unadorned office. It had taken months to get the PNC to the table. The West applied the name "terrorist" to them the same as they did to Islamic groups, but the PNC was different.

They were from Christian countries albeit they had abandoned profession of that faith. Religion did not fuel their ideology like the Islamists. Religion, rather, in the form of the Catholic Church, was their frequent target. The Islamic freedom fighters were a religio-cultural phenomenon, whereas the PNC was multicultural and focused on the economic and political poverty of all Third World nations.

"You have made us and offer, and we are here to discuss it, "the PNC man called Renaldo said.

"Good," Havenei said. "Your group has correctly perceived that the Catholic Church is an arm of Western imperialism. We are not anti-Christian. We are anti-American, anti-imperialist, the same as you are, but the Church is a front for these activities that oppress our people as well as yours."

Renaldo and his colleague Franco looked unimpressed. "What does this have to do with us?" Renaldo asked.

"You have made your reputation and a good deal of money staging sensational operations," Havenei said. "I have three things to offer you—a sensational idea and spectacular publicity."

"You mentioned three things," Franco said. "What's the third?"

Havenei smiled. "More money than you ever dreamed of. That and the chance to take it from the institution you say is the arm of the rich to oppress the poor."

The PNC men glanced at each other askance as Havenei laid out his grand scheme. At the end of his speech, they looked a lot more impressed. "You see the strength of this plan," Havenei said. "It is a sleeper operation. You will have years to prepare for it. It also strikes a large institution at its most vulnerable moment—during a changing of the guard."

There was no need for Havenei to explain to them why his people could not carry out the operation directly. Iranians would stand out in the Vatican, and if discovered, the political fallout would be enormous. If he had sized up these men correctly, Havenei believed his offer would hold great appeal. Havenei's plan was bold; it would strike at the heart of their mutual enemy. The PNC had a streak of idealism, a Robin Hood mentality. Besides, they were always looking for money to buy off the poor or other allies in Latin America or the Philippines.

"How would this be done; what are the logistics?" Renaldo asked.

"We would fund you with two million dollars," Havenei said. "Call it a mobilization fee. It should be more than adequate to make preparations, particularly given the long lead time. However, this current pope has had health problems. Perhaps the wait will not be that long after all," Havenei snickered.

"And what of the money derived from the operation?"

"We are not greedy," Havenei said. "Our main interest is crippling the Church. We will split seventy-thirty in your favor. One strict rule though — we can never be associated with this operation."

Havenei could see from their faces that the generosity of his offer had startled them.

"A bold and interesting idea, just as you claimed," Franco said, "but what's to prevent us from doing it on our own or just taking your two million dollars?"

Havenei smiled. He had wondered when this topic would come up. "There are several answers to your question," he stated evenly. "That you will execute this idea is not a question — it suits your style and enormous money is at stake. You simply do not have adequate funds to stage this operation alone. Even if you did and you acted on your own, or whether you took our money and ran, the response is the same. You would become the enemies of all Islamic freedom fighters."

Havenei paused a moment for the statement to sink in. "Our reach is long. Do you want that kind of a war when we can profit at the expense of our mutual enemies?"

"We understand," Renaldo said as if expecting the answers Havenei gave. "We will be in contact with you after we talk to our people."

Havenei was satisfied after they left. "They will agree," he proclaimed to Gorbani with supreme confidence. "They stand to gain everything."

Gorbani pinched at his sallow cheeks in appreciation. He was impressed. Though he thought Havenei to be arrogant and often reckless, this move made sense. It would be difficult to trace the action back to Tehran using the PNC as proxies, and the benefits of striking a crippling blow to the Church were enormous.

"When this plan is completed," Havenei said, "the Church won't be sending any more 'miracle workers' to Muslims in Nigeria or anywhere else."

Gorbani nodded. He had little doubt it would put a halt to their missionary activities . . . for good.

CHAPTER XXXII

The events in our lives happen in a sequence in time, but in their significance to ourselves, they find their own order . . . the continuous thread of revelation. — *Eudora Welty*

The Vatican City

Annalisa's first contact with a large group of cardinals might have been the stuff of witch burnings. Annalisa had told Roncalli she wished to spend her first year as a cardinal studying Latin, Italian, Church history, theology, and canon law. "I must speak their languages and understand their rules," she told him, referring to her fellow cardinals.

So it was for the first six months that she was cloistered away in the library under the tutelage of Roncalli's old friend, Monsignor O'Keefe. This had earned her the derisive name of "Cardinal Apprentice" among her peers.

Today she was walking through the Vatican Gardens at lunchtime when she saw a large gathering of black- and crimson-robed cardinals. Some caught sight of her, then the others turned around as if linked by a chain. She could feel their contempt radiating ten feet ahead of them. They had been gathered around a tall tree, and as she approached, the crowd started to part with angry rumblings that seemed directed at her.

In front of the tree, at the head of the gauntlet formed by the parted cardinals, stood Mannheim, LoPresti, and Tormada. Mannheim motioned for Annalisa to step forward. The men backed aside a few steps to reveal the object that was causing all the commotion.

A horned, round-headed, human-like stick figure with a body in the shape of a cross and claw-like feet hung on a tree branch.

"What do you know about this?" LoPresti asked, pointing his ring finger at her.

The look in the men's eyes told Annalisa she had already been accused, judged, and found guilty. "I know nothing about it," she said.

LoPresti turned to the others and said in Latin, "Are we supposed to believe her? These demonic symbols appeared even as she came to the Vatican. Does she take us for fools?"

"No, I do not take you for fools, but I said I know nothing about this," she replied in perfect Latin to the amazement of the men. "I'm sorry for your disturbance. Good day." She walked away through the stares and the grumbling and more than a few vicious comments.

"Maybe we have underestimated the abilities of the Cardinal Apprentice," DeGolia said to his colleagues. "She learned quickly. A multilingual person has a tremendous advantage in our world."

"That is not the point," Mannheim snapped. "She needs to be out. Out!" Mannheim stopped as if he had become aware of himself ranting. The others expressed surprise to hear the normally self-composed German carrying on.

"It's . . . it's the prophecies," Mannheim said, now looking self-conscious about his loss of control. "She comes into our midst, and the Church falls in steady decline."

The others took their time nodding in acceptance of the statement. Mannheim knew they were puzzled, but he would not confide the real reason for his emotions to anyone—the fact that somehow the damned African woman had invaded his dreams and stayed there from the moment he had read the report about her mission in Africa.

It was always a similar theme. He was in a high-ceilinged hall that glowed with a bright light. A gallery of seats ringing the room was clasped together at one end by a throne on a dais. The seats looked empty, but he knew they were occupied. He could feel them, all countless numbers of them, *and the unseen occupants sat in judgment of him.*

Only on the throne could he see anyone; it was the nun. He stood before her as if he were her prisoner. "You will not lay hands on me again . . . Mannemius." It was always the same statement, but this time he remembered the name she called him: *Mannemius.* Who was he? Mannheim awoke in a cold sweat each time he experienced the vision. Each episode hardened him in the conviction that the woman would not only cause the downfall of the Church, but she would spell his personal doom as well.

It was always the same since she had come to the Vatican. Her detractors, hands cupped at the sides of their mouths, would spout some crude joke like, "Do you think the pope ever had a black woman before?" The common reply was, "I don't know, do you think the nun ever had a pope before?"

It was nothing she had done; it was just that she was there. It is not *who* she was, but *what* she was—an unwanted change foisted upon their well-structured world. The Church's problems, the crying pressure for reform and the deteriorating global condition, had caused the wagons to circle in the Vatican.

The energy of the cardinals was turning inward. The threat of a new ecumenical council and the world's restless yearning for change was driving many of them into the inner sanctum of resistance. The collective psyche of these men was wound tight and ready to uncoil at any moment. It would cut to pieces anything in the path of its whip-like release, and Annalisa knew she loomed large in their path; any misstep would trigger their reaction.

The daunting situation might have been too much for a simple, backcountry African nun, but Annalisa had a perfect defense. Her weapons were pictures, symbols, dreams, and synchronous occurrences that cried for her attention should she ever miss the point. They intertwined to form patterns in her mind, and the patterns told a tale.

They all wove together to write the unfolding story of her life. She knew she was in Rome for a purpose. That purpose was slowly revealing itself, and she had glimpses of her destiny that gave her a sense of reading the pages of a diary she had written at the beginning of time and was only now remembering. Each day illuminated a new entry in her life's journal, each new episode was coupled with a sense of remembrance, of recognition, as if she had lived it all before. It was by the river in the cool, quiet solitude of the still place these things came to her, that the voice came to her.

"When will I see you? Why do you elude me?" She implored.

The familiar, disembodied voice called to her from the opposite side. *"Find wisdom and find yourself."* It was always the same reply.

A vision of pain and fire drew closer to her now. She had done something, something she could not remember, yet she knew it was a Great Sin and it weighed upon her soul.

"Great light attracts great darkness," the voice warned. *"By measure must you reveal the truth, lest too soon your light be extinguished."*

He requires something of me, she told herself, *and he tries to preserve me until that thing is revealed. "What truth is mine to reveal? Tell me, why am I here? What is my true purpose?"*

And this time her answer came clearly: ***"YOU SHALL OPEN THE GATES OF HELL."***

CHAPTER XXXIII

So God created man in his own image . . .
male and female he created them. — *Genesis 1:27*

The Vatican City

"Those fuckin' mullahs are gonna get their asses kicked if they keep it up." That was Leo Dusayne's comment after Avernis returned to Rome to brief him and Tom Stanton, the Deputy Regional Director, about his meeting in Tehran.

Not the most sophisticated observation, but not without some accuracy, Avernis noted. Publicly, president Davidson was heating up the rhetoric. As a government insider, Avernis sensed the president was quietly preparing the country to break out of its two-decade-old lethargy in a prelude to increased counterterror or even military measures.

Avernis now focused his attention in his own backyard. Zugli had told him that a second disturbing symbol had been found in the Vatican. O'Keefe already had information on it. Avernis called O'Keefe and arranged a meeting. Teresa would also be present. Avernis still found it peculiar that the monsignor was utilizing a news reporter on a Vatican matter. On the other hand, he was powerfully attracted to her. She was gutsy — the night of the bombing showed him that — and clearly, she was smart.

He also sensed her attraction to him, but a personal relationship would be awkward. She was a reporter — a nosy one at that — and a *Vatican* reporter to boot. He was a CIA agent posing as Vatican security — tough mixture in a job where discretion was required, particularly with Leo Dusayne waiting in the wings to chop his head off. Now she was his neighbor in Rome, and that *really* complicated things. Just take things as they come, that was his advice to himself.

"Robert, good day," O'Keefe said when he entered the office.

"Hello, Robert," Teresa said.

Did he catch a tone and a glimmer in her eye when she greeted him? *No, don't flatter yourself, stud.*

"I hope your trip was fruitful," O'Keefe said.

"It was . . . interesting," Avernis replied. "So, what about that second symbol?"

O'Keefe put the poster of the image on the wall, and nodded at Teresa.

"This is a figure symbolizes the *Monad,* or God in an undivided state," she explained. "Some say it originated in the seventeenth century, but it's actually a combination of ancient astrological symbols. It's another Gnostic sign for the supreme deity: God."

"The Gnostics again?" Avernis said. "Is this symbol demonic too? Sure looks that way with those horns."

"You know, it's interesting," Teresa said. "Like the Abraxas symbol, the Monad was originally a symbol of the one True God but was later branded as evil or demonic by the Catholic Church. So, the answer to your question depends on your point view."

"Point of view?" Avernis said.

"Yes," Teresa replied. "Gnostic Christian or orthodox Catholic."

Avernis raised an eyebrow. "I thought the Gnostics were extinct. Could the Church be harboring heretics, Monsignor?

O'Keefe's forehead creased. He clasped his hands together and looked down at his desk. "Some are worried about a secret counter-Church, about the Great—about heretics," he said, reversing his direction in midsentence.

Avernis then posed new questions. "Let's say the two figures we found aren't demonic but do represent God in a positive sense. Why the repetition? Do they differ in any way that might tell us something?"

Teresa nodded. "Maybe so. In Abraxas, Gnostics perceived God as wisdom and power, the forces that organized creation. When the Monad symbol appeared I remembered that Gnostics were the first and last Christians to recognize both the male and female aspects of God. In Abraxas, power was believed to be a male characteristic while wisdom was female."

"The original feminists, eh?" Avernis said.

"In spades," Teresa replied. "Gnostics believed the Holy Spirit, also called Holy Wisdom, was the female aspect of the trinity. They had female leaders, even female priests. When the orthodox factions prevailed and expelled or exterminated the

Gnostics, the entire Church became male in character, and the Holy Spirit was neutered.

"Now, for the Monad symbol. I think those 'horns' you described might be a crescent moon superimposed over the sun. The sun and moon are classic, ancient symbols of the God and Goddess. Look at the lines projecting downward below the level of the sun and the crescent moon," she said "Break up the single combined image on the left and you can discern the separate male/female symbols, see?"

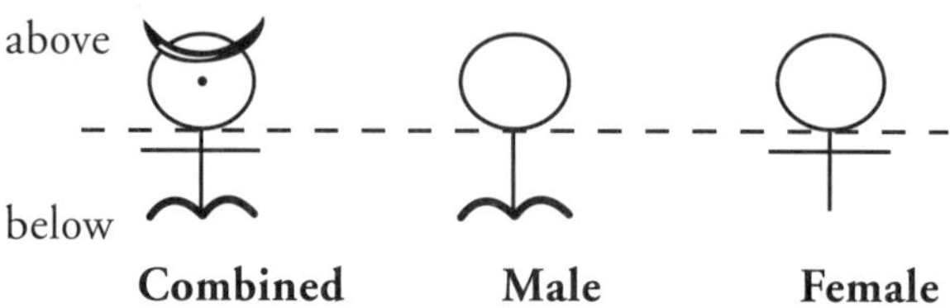

Avernis and O'Keefe readily recognized the common symbols for the sexes.

"Gnostics believed the undivided God divided Its substance into opposite polarities to generate the energy of creation," Teresa said. "'As above, so below,' the ancient adage says. Maybe the Monad means a Father-Mother God generated us as male and female to mirror Its own essence. But if I'm wrong, maybe it means humanity, men and women alike, are all damned and going to the devil, hence the horns. I'm not sure what it's saying."

"Whatever the message," Avernis said, "who's saying it and why are they doing this?"

"There must be an answer Robert," O'Keefe said. "Please find it. We need to know."

CHAPTER XXXIV

The smoothness of his manipulation was marvelous.
— Henry Brooks Adams

Toledo, Spain

"We are agreed then," Cardinal Van Kluysen said to Bishop Alvaro. Alvaro came as close to smiling as the heaviness of his dark, solemn features would allow. And why not? The plans he had woven for so many years were finally in motion.

"This is a very delicate matter," Van Kluysen said. "It took months to set this up. We must be extraordinarily careful, but we need strong leadership in the Church for these precarious times. I have no doubt we are doing God's work in this."

The twenty million dollars you'll get will eliminate your doubts, Alvaro thought. The Belgian's greed was phenomenal, but he had just committed to his role in a plan that would one day give Milites Domini control of the Vatican.

Hitler, Mussolini, Franco — that unholy trinity had shaped the world in which Milites Domini was born almost a century earlier. Milites was a throwback, an anachronistic parasite that had latched itself onto the spinal column of the Catholic Church like a malignant tumor.

The peculiar thing about this shady organization was that many of its hundred-thousand members were good people, but then again, so were many of the people in fascist Germany, Italy, and Spain who were slow to see the nature of the beast.

The order's founder, Father Oswaldo Ochavar de Falanca, or the Blessed Oswaldo as his acolytes referred to him, led a life that read like a Catholic version of *Mein Kampf.* Father Oswaldo was from a lower middle-class Spanish family, and he had gone to great lengths of deception to avoid being killed by anti-clerical Republican troops during the Spanish Civil War.

He was fearful, or more accurately, paranoid, about liberalism and communism. After the war, this common priest, much like the common man Hitler, had a vision, and much like Hitler, he proceeded to collect a small group of followers. They became the nucleus of something that grew to be large, powerful, and sinister.

The formula for the spectacular growth of Milites and the rise of the fascist parties of the 1930s was amazingly similar. They started with a vision and an enemy. In Father Oswaldo's case, the initial enemies were communism, socialism, modernism, liberals, and Islam. Eventually, like Nazism, the enemy was anyone who opposed Milites' goals and methods. His vision was a Western world united under Catholic dominance, which meant a Catholic Church united under Milites dominance.

Comparing the tactics and structure of Milites with that of the fascist parties showed they had cross-pollinated in the same ideological womb. Milites had successfully lobbied the Vatican, besieged at that time by hostile Italian communists, for changes in canon law that granted Milites a unique status as a secular institution. With papal sanction and an anti-communist credo, Milites promised average Catholics a way to achieve spiritual perfection without being full-time priests or monks in a religious order.

Milites invented a hierarchy of which even Hitler would have approved. First, an elite, fanatical inner core of priests and and celibate lay people called *functionaries* was created. This equivalent of Hitler's SS lived in special chapter houses where the levels of daily indoctrination were intense. For several hours a day, the functionaries wore the medieval cilicio, a ring of barbed wire, around their arms, legs, or other body parts. This had been the practice of the Blessed Founder. There were also associate members who were celibate but allowed to reside in their own homes, and, finally, *super-functionaries* who could even have a wife and family.

Milites snared new recruits by appealing to people's well-intentioned desire to bring God's light to those trapped in the darkness of liberal secularism and false religions. The recruitment methods they used demonstrated their close ideological links with fascist political parties and religious cults.

Once their powerful message hooked the idealistic acolytes into Milites' sphere, the real indoctrination started. Like any good cult, Milites was proficient at removing higher critical functions from the thought processes of its members. Just as the cilicio was an instrument for mortification of the flesh, Milites' brainwashing tactics mortified the mind. Functionaries swore oaths of obedience to the Milites hierarchy, renewed each year in a somber ceremony.

Members of all ranks were required to memorize the founder's maxims and to submit to the "humilities." The humilities involved a daily questioning of one's actions for consistency with the order's principles, followed by confession to a priest. Moreover, weekly examinations of personal failures or violations of principles were held in group settings — this ensured that guilt and peer pressure remained alive and well in Milites.

The Blessed Founder, Oswaldo, called Milites' rank-and-file his "lambs," but his brand of authoritarian clericalism would not allow Milites to pluck any old sheep from the pasture. Being top-down in its own internal structure, Milites recruited members from the highest levels of international society—technocrats, financiers, and politicians.

Logic would dictate that educated, powerful, and intelligent people should shun an organization like Milites Domini, but human beings are rarely logical. The Blessed Oswaldo had, after all, founded Milites on a revelation from God to combat the enemies of Christianity. Those enemies—communism, socialism, liberalism, and Islam—were also the perceived enemies of many powerful people in the West, and having common enemies makes for all manner of strange bedfellows. Milites provided a distinct service for these people; it sanctified the idea of hating one's adversaries, and after all, everyone wants God on his or her side.

The Blessed Founder's war on the enemy was a war of love for Christ, and he believed all was fair in love and war; any dirty trick was excusable in the life-and-death struggle to preserve Western culture under Church leadership. This philosophy led Milites into peculiar fields of combat. First, they went to Latin America in the early 1960s to take on the Jesuits, whose liberation theology sided with the hopes of that continent's poor.

When the smoke cleared, the Jesuits were routed. Bishops loyal to Milites' agenda were installed in many dioceses, and universities controlled by Milites were founded in four Latin countries. Milites' suppression of the Jesuits to become the preeminent force in Catholicism was comparable to the S.S.'s suppression of the S.A. to consolidate Hitler's power in the Nazi Party. Milites' victory in Latin America was also tantamount to Hitler's invasion of Czechoslovakia: the opening battle of a campaign for international dominance.

As the only recognized secular order in the Church, Milites was allowed to make money, and that worked nicely with their efforts to accumulate power. On the economic front, highly placed Milites members in European business, often using unwitting dupes, had engineered a number of fraudulent business transactions. They negotiated subsidies from various national governments to be paid to select companies engaged in international export and trade. After a time, these companies were collapsed. In the aftermath, hundreds of millions of subsidy dollars disappeared, but little was traced to Milites due to the tangle of foreign shell companies and confidential corporate shareholders.

Several people under investigation for the incidents died mysteriously, a shockingly common occurrence in the scandals with which Milites' name had been linked over the years. If an imaginary coroner had examined this chain of deaths, he would have found himself writing post mortem certificates with the term "acute myocardial infarction" (massive heart attack) on an inordinate amount of occasions. He would also have scratched his head at the absence of any previous heart problems in the victims' medical histories.

Shortly after the incidents of the vanished subsidy funds, Milites became a major player in world currency markets. It created a chain of international banks and trading operations in those areas where it conducted its religious missions. In this manner, the accumulation and movement of large blocks of offshore funds could be kept under a veil of secrecy.

Bishop Alvaro was proud to bear the title of Father of the Order, the fourth in that line. The founder was truly blessed to have created such an instrument of power as Milites Domini, and he would be proud of Alvaro as a successor, the man who would realize his dream of consolidating political and financial domination of the Vatican.

How mysteriously God provides the instruments to achieve one's ends, imperfect as those instruments may be, he thought as he eyed Van Kluysen with well-concealed contempt. But Alvaro was a master chess player, and he knew one did not capture the kingdom through a single avenue of assault. Chess pieces represented both religious and temporal power.

A bishop was not enough; he needed the strongest piece on the board for his gambit, and that could only come from the temporal world of politics.

"Rest assured, Eminenza," Alvaro said as Van Kluysen readied to depart, "you have done the right thing for the Church. We are pressed on all fronts. The Great Heretic is rising; the signs are all around. And when he, or *she,* declares openly, the Church must be in the right hands to withstand the onslaught."

After Van Kluysen left his office, Alvaro checked his watch. It would be the right time in America now. He picked up the phone to call a number he used on only rare and special occasions. If any of his acolytes could have seen him at that moment, they would have been surprised or frightened, for the dark bishop was smiling.

CHAPTER XXXV

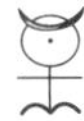

Good government cannot be found on the bargain-counter.
— Calvin Coolidge

Washington, D.C.

President John Davidson picked up the phone in the White House bedroom. It was a direct phone line about which few people knew and it was the most secure line in the world.

Davidson's family were converted Catholics from the American heartland of Kansas. A mutual acquaintance had introduced John's father, the now deceased General MacDonald Davidson, to Bishop Alvaro soon after the general's conversion. The two men found mutual cause in their militant defense of Western, Christian values in the face of unrelenting assaults by Muslims and insidious liberal politicians who weakened the will of the Western nations with their moral ambiguity and globalist illusions.

It is said that converts make the most fervent Catholics, and that was true for General Mack Davidson. He became a devout lay member of Milites Domini. Alvaro grew close to the family and participated with the general in grooming the exceptionally bright and articulate John Davidson for a political career.

"I fought in three Middle-Eastern wars just to see the spaghetti-spined politicians capitulate it all away, and look at the mess we're in now," the general told Alvaro. "My son will never be a soldier, never be a pawn like I was. He's smart and shrewd enough to go all the way in politics, and that's where the power is. Only America can save the West, and we need to save America. John will do that some day: that's my dream for him."

And Alvaro agreed. John was the fair-haired son of an Anglo-Saxon, albeit Catholic, family. Ivy-league educated but rooted with middle-American values, he was articulate, confidant, and charismatic. He was also focused. He could have been a partygoing lady's man in college, but he kept his nose to the books and graduated with honors, even after lettering in two sports.

John graduated law school and worked in a prestigious Washington, D.C. firm where he married a colleague. During this time, a network of advisors put together by Milites Domini associates coached John so that the young man became politically savvy even before he made his first run for a congressional seat. Cleverly disguised Milites money financed that successful campaign as well as his first senatorial campaign, which he won by narrowly defeating a longtime incumbent.

John made waves as a senator, criticizing the liberal administration of President Tom Winston, rallying the tired, frustrated, and demoralized people of America, the world's economically declining superpower. Now that Mack Davidson was dead, John looked to Alvaro not as a father figure—the Spaniard was too severe for that sort of warmth—but certainly as a mentor.

"John," Alvaro said, "it's good to hear your voice, my son."

"Yours too, Father." Davidson, like many other Milites Domini members, often referred to the order's leader as "Father."

"I am calling with great news," Alvaro said. "John, that dream we so often spoke of with your beloved father; its time is drawing near. It is in motion."

"Excellent," John replied. "I'm ready, but then you've known that for a while. The important thing is that with your help, I can make this country ready."

Such confidence, Alvaro beamed inwardly with pride. What a great act of providence that had brought these two men of vision together. John was a perfect family man, with a beautiful wife and two children, who moved in all the right circles, yet he had distinguished himself from the crowd. He had the image of being a maverick with magnetic appeal. People thought of him as an intelligent man who was forceful but measured.

Only Bishop Alvaro knew of the cold steel that lay underneath. Only he knew how far John would go in defense of Christian values. The masses would not understand, or they would misinterpret John if they really knew him, so like other bold men possessed of a vision, John kept his true intentions shrouded. "The people need to be led by you, not blinded," Alvaro told him. "Be cautious of revealing too much of yourself; you lose power that way. In secrecy there is power." And John had heeded his advice.

"Father, we'll have midterm elections here in eighteen months," Davidson said. "I need more like-minded politicians in office, men of courage and foresight to help me in what needs to be done. That will take a great deal of money. Can I count on the order?"

"That is exactly why I'm calling. I'm making sure you will have all the money you need. We can begin seeding money in now, but in twelve months we will be able to give massive support."

"Excellent," Davidson said, and the men spent time discussing the details of moving funds so as to legally circumvent U.S. campaign-finance laws. "You know, Father, sometimes my goals seem so grand and distant, like an abstraction or a dream. It takes discussions like these to bring it back to reality."

"What you are feeling is the effect of time, the gap between conceiving a vision and realizing it," Alvaro said. "That is the way of this world, and that is why the Lord gave us the virtue of patience. Patience prevents mistakes during these interim periods."

Alvaro had great respect for the concept of patience. Learning patience was the very reason the Blessed Founder had introduced the practice of wearing the cilicio, the barbed-wire bracelet worn on the wrists and legs. If one did not move slowly and methodically, the result was pain. Practicing patience had made him a chess master in life as well as in sport.

"Be patient, John," was Alvaro's final advice to the president. "Soon, the world will be aware of great and dramatic changes. It is all coming sooner than you think."

CHAPTER XXXVI

I am well acquainted with your manner of wrenching the true cause the false way. — William Shakespeare

The Vatican City

The face of the enemy, Cardinal Mannheim mused as he looked across his desk at Annalisa. *So small, so disarming. A weak man could break her in two.* Yet, by definition, the Great Deceiver would seem like that. What better front than a seemingly meek woman? But Mannheim's mind and his dreams told him this was no timid soul.

She had cleverly hid herself in the library for the past six months, but today was different. Today they would draw her out. He smiled, pleased with how the trap had been laid. Mannheim had persuaded Clement to prohibit Annalisa from performing her supposed miracles in public. He had argued that the Church was subject to criticism by the press and misunderstanding by the masses. At this time, they did not need more controversy. Clement agreed, at least until the notoriety surrounding the female cardinal subsided. Today, however, they would accompany a group of prominent cardinals on a visit to a hospital in Rome, and there were many needy people there. She would be hard pressed not to act.

"Cardinal Mannheim," Annalisa said, "you have been most kind to inquire about me. May I now ask you how you came to the Church?"

She gave no information and now she is probing me, Mannheim thought. He considered her for a moment and said, "In the last days of East Germany I was a young seminarian in Kaiserdorf when the communists arrested my mentor, Father Kaltenbrunner. He was our village priest, and they tried to shut down our church. That church meant everything to us, and I chained myself to its doors. When the soldiers came for me, the villagers barred their way. They used gas and clubs, broke up the crowd, and arrested me."

Annalisa's face showed genuine admiration.

"The communists fell a year later. The villagers stormed the prison and freed me before the guards could harm me out of spite. They remembered me. Eventually, I became the priest of that church. We were in economic shambles. Even West Germans despised us. I led that community out of poverty and despair with the

Church's moral discipline and authority. The people were shattered, but I would not let them give up."

Annalisa nodded her understanding. Annaliese Steurer had told her about the difficulties following the fall of East Germany. "You lifted their spirit?" she asked.

"Pah," Mannheim snorted. "I lifted their *pride*. I never allowed them to feel inferior to anyone. The Church was the only vestige of civilization left, the only source of power for us. I became a father to the village just as the Church had been a father to me. The Vatican took note, and here I am." Mannheim thought he saw the admiring look on her face eroding as he spoke. "Is there something wrong?" he asked.

Annalisa clasped her hands. "Wrong? No, you were very brave."

Mannheim leaned forward on his desk with one arm, and in the other hand he gripped his pectoral cross as if swearing an oath. "The Church has always been an island in this hellish world. I would do anything to defend her . . . *anything*." Mannheim searched her face for a reaction but she kept an even composure. A cat-and- mouse conversation, he concluded. "Well, shall we go? The bus should be here."

On the bus, Annalisa sat in a back seat. The other prelates were laughing and talking in Latin, so she understood smatterings of conversations. No jokes about her today, at least. The bus' squeaking brakes interrupted her reflections. They had arrived at the hospital, where an excited press entourage met the half-dozen cardinals. They had had scant opportunity to see the female cardinal the past six months, sometimes joking that she was a prisoner in the Vatican. Annalisa nodded an acknowledgement to Teresa Ferentinos, whom she recognized among the reporters.

The prelates started to make their rounds, blessing patients from ward to ward. At one point they walked by a room and an older woman came rushing into the corridor. She went straight to Annalisa and, weeping, she clasped her hands.

"You are the one who performs miracles, the cardinal from Africa. I live in Trastevere, your neighborhood. Eminenza, please, I beg you. My daughter, Stefania—she is a simple girl, an innocent. She has been in a coma for years. The doctors say there is no hope, they want to stop the life support. She does not deserve to die. She is all I have. Please help me, Eminenza, please!" The woman's pleadings gave way to anguished sobs as she fell down on her knees.

"Here, here," Cardinal Mannheim said as he came forward and lifted the woman from the floor. "Let us go in and see your daughter."

Once in the room, they gathered around the comatose girl's bed.

"She fell from a third story balcony," one of the doctors explained. "The poor girl was already retarded but the blow to her head, well . . . " he finished his prognosis with a negative gesture that the near-hysterical mother could not see.

"I don't care what they say," the mother cried, turning from her daughter's bedside and clutching at Annalisa's knees. "They say you healed the pope himself. Please, can you not help my poor girl? She suffered all her life, now she is neither dead nor alive. You are God's justice and mercy. I believe in you. She is all I have. Please, I beg of you."

The emotional tension in the room was reaching a crescendo, and trying to calm the mother, one of the doctors said, "Signora DeRosa, please."

"Can you help her?" Cardinal Mannheim interjected in a voice loud enough to be heard by the press in the rear of the circle ringing the bedside.

Annalisa looked at Mannheim. He pursed his lips in anticipation, and the corners of his mouth were turned upward in an odd smile. Annalisa lifted the woman from her knees and turned her to face a crucifix above Stefania's bed. She then dialogued with the woman.

"What do you see?" she asked the mother, pointing to the crucifix.

"A cross," the woman replied.

"Who is on the cross?"

"Christ," the woman answered.

"What does he represent to you?"

"God," the woman said. "He represents God to me."

"Yes," Annalisa said. "You have heard the story of Jesus and the Roman centurion who implored him to heal his son? Jesus himself said it was the centurion's faith that would heal the boy, and it did. Even so may God act through any person of faith."

Annalisa cupped the woman's chin in her hand and lifted her head to look her in the eyes. She held her gaze for a moment, and said, "*You* have such faith, Signora DeRosa." She turned to the gathered group and said, "Let the doctors do their work and let God do His through this woman of faith. For one week, I ask you to work with her before you take final action. Is that too much to ask?"

Annalisa saw the smirk vanish from Mannheim's face. If she had interceded directly to heal the girl, she would have violated the pope's orders. If she had refused the mother, they would label her a charlatan or claim she was cold and uncaring, and that would throw the premise behind her cardinalcy into question.

Nonetheless, she *had* interceded, but in a way that worked through the doctors and the power of prayer.

Of course, the doctors agreed to her request—what else could they do? And Signora DeRosa fervently declared her desire to pray and have Stefania healed.

"Well then," Mannheim said, "we must move along. God be with you, Signora."

✠

Annalisa knew what Mannheim had wanted and what the mother wanted, but tonight Annalisa would learn the most important thing—what the comatose girl wanted. In her still place Annalisa called Stefania, and she began her dialogue with the comatose girl:

Annalisa: *"Stefania, do you hear me?"* ***Stefania:*** *"Yes, I'm here. My body is tired. The pain. It's so painful in that body, so limiting."* ***Annalisa:*** *"You can leave or go back, the choice is yours, but first remember your purpose, why you chose that body with all its challenges. What did you need to learn?"* ***Stefania:*** *"It was . . . about accepting love. It was about learning to receive, learning to not always subordinate myself to others, letting my Self come first."* ***Annalisa:*** *"Have you completed your desire to express that in your body?"* ***Stefania:*** *"No."* ***Annalisa:*** *"Then I will help you move toward your body, but if the pain is too great, you may go into the light."* ***Stefania:*** *"I want to finish this now, in this body. Yes, help me."*

Four days after the hospital visit, Signora DeRosa clutched Annalisa's arm as Annalisa was picking through vegetables at the outdoor evening market in Trastevere. "Eminenza, oh, Eminenza," the woman cried, "my Stefania is out of her coma!"

"Yes, I heard the news," Annalisa replied. "That is wonderful, Signora DeRosa."

"Last night she came out," the woman said. "God heard my prayers; you kept my faith."

"Stefania will learn much from your love, Signora DeRosa. Of that I have no doubt."

"Oh, bless you, Eminenza, and bless Cardinal Trevi too. He encouraged me to seek you out."

Annalisa paused. "Ah, *Trevi.*" Trevi, Mannheim, and their cohorts would not be happy. The newspapers were not crediting Annalisa for the puzzling recovery. They said, rather, it was the doctors' last-ditch efforts and, just maybe, Signora DeRosa's prayers that were responsible.

"Eminenza, do you think Stefania knew, even in her coma, how much I wanted her back? She thinks she is a burden, but I don't mind her handicaps. Do you think she knows that?"

Annalisa smiled and clasped the widow's hands. She looked at her and said, "Signora, rest easy. Trust that Stefania has received your love. Perhaps in this life, Stefania's purpose was to understand love through the feelings you have given. I do not think she would have returned otherwise. And God, Signora DeRosa, works in mysterious ways. He blesses both those who give and those who receive."

CHAPTER XXXVII

To understand reality is . . . to perceive the essential nature of things.
— Dietrich Bonhoeffer

The Vatican City

It was the same dream that had plagued Cardinal Mannheim during the past year. He sat on a dais surrounded by soldiers. *Roman soldiers.* He knew he represented the might and authority of the empire. The torches flickered and cast their shadows on the beautiful woman with reddish-gold hair who stood before him.

She warned him, *"You shall not lay hands on me this time, Mannemius."*

And despite that any one of a hundred swords could dispatch her in an instant at his command, he was afraid. There was an unseen legion behind her, a force that caused him to know the pains of the damned in a fleeting instant of terror, and he woke up in a cold sweat.

He knew the African witch was behind it. The dreams had started the first time she appeared. Though the woman in his dreams looked nothing like her, he knew she was in her, possessing her, guiding her with unwavering purpose. She must be the one spoken of in the prophecies, coming in a time of such peril. The Church was withering, and nations were nearing conflict. Terror was on the rise and radical Islam was in resurgence, posing the greatest menace since the Middle Ages.

And she was clever. She had cloistered herself in the Vatican Library, growing in knowledge and power, giving Mannheim and his colleagues no target at which to aim. He had tried to convince Clement to assign her more duties so as to flush her out into a position of vulnerability, but Roncalli intervened. "First you want to silence her so as not to be an embarrassment then you want to thrust her into positions of responsibility. Why not leave her alone? She was disadvantaged from the beginning and she is taking the time to mature in our ways. Leave her alone." And Clement agreed.

Damn Roncalli, the enabler of this insidious evil! He brought her into the bosom of the Church, and now he was nurturing her. He was either deluded or a devil's pawn himself. Even though fighting the Ecumenical Council was absorbing most of his time, Mannheim vowed that he would find a way to excise her.

✠

When Annalisa arrived at the library, Roncalli was expressing his dismay to O'Keefe at the mired Ecumenical Council process. "It will take a decade at this rate," he exclaimed in frustration as Annalisa entered O'Keefe's office. Roncalli was so irate, he did not notice her. Roncalli flopped down in a chair while O'Keefe looked on in helpless concern.

After a minute of dejected silence a voice said, "Pietro?"

Roncalli turned. "Ah, Annalisa. Didn't see you there. Sorry you heard all this."

Annalisa smiled. "If you please, might I offer a suggestion?"

"A suggestion?"

"Yes, about the Ecumenical Council." She sat next to him and held her hand out, fingers splayed. "Try to pull my fingers apart. No, please, don't be impatient, just try."

Roncalli sighed but did as she asked, easily pulling her fingers farther apart. Annalisa now bunched her fingers into a fist. "Try again," she said.

Once more Roncalli tried, but this time he could not separate the bunched up digits. Annalisa smiled. "Ha! You see, that is the problem. Your friends are separated, scattered around the world like an opened hand," Annalisa said. "But your opponents are concentrated here in the Vatican." Again, she contracted her hand. "You outnumber them, but they are grouped together like a fist, where they can be most effective."

O'Keefe looked on, intrigued to see his pupil speaking up and taking initiative.

"Nothing in canon law prohibits bishop's synods from being held in Rome," Annalisa said, "so bring them all here. Stop conducting synods on all the continents. Hold them here where you can concentrate your strength against your opponents, day-by-day."

Roncalli looked at O'Keefe. O'Keefe sputtered, "That-that's—"

"Brilliant!" Roncalli exclaimed. "That's brilliant! I was so fixed on the traditional way. It's not customary, but it is not a violation of canon law either. Annalisa, you've been too quiet. You really need to express yourself more often."

"Hah," Annalisa laughed. "I do express myself, just in a different way, you see?"

Roncalli stood and smiled. "If anyone asks, I'm giving you all the credit for this idea. I'm going to start putting this in motion now," and he bounded out the door.

"You've given him a new lease on life," O'Keefe said. He studied Annalisa for a moment. "I've been meaning to ask you. Periodically, we have been finding mysterious symbols and pictures around the Vatican. They actually started about the time you arrived," and he showed her the symbols. "Do they have meaning to you?"

Now Annalisa looked at him. Her eyes roved up and down, encasing him in a circle of thought. "I suppose they could mean many things," she said.

O'Keefe persisted. "Most see them as evil. Do you believe good people can create unintentional evil? Can the good we do turn to evil in any manner without our conscious awareness?"

Annalisa tightened her concentration on him, and what she learned changed the way she would regard Desmond O'Keefe from that time on. *He knows me!* "Evil as compared to good," she said in a deliberate tone, "is merely a longer, rockier path to the same place."

O'Keefe cocked an eyebrow. "That view would upset most people, you realize that?" Annalisa closed her eyes and folded her hands. *I know*, her voice invaded his mind. *The question is, what do you know . . . know . . . know?* Her words echoed in his head and sent blood rushing to his brain. As she left him sitting in bewilderment, words from the Book of Luke kept coming to him, words of foreboding: *I am come to send fire on the Earth.*

CHAPTER XXXVIII

Both men and women are fallible. The difference is, women know it.
—Eleanor Bron

Rome

Robert Avernis finished his brandy in the bar of the Parco dei Principi Hotel. He needed it to drown the butterflies in his stomach. He smoothed his hair with his palms and tugged at his sport jacket. He was feeling increasing pressure from Washington to utilize the Vatican to produce intelligence on the Iranians. The Vatican, in turn, was getting obsessed about the security breaches and the meaning of the symbols being found on a monthly basis.

It was not so much his work that was tying his stomach in knots, however—Teresa Ferentinos was doing that. She had asked him to meet her for lunch in a restaurant outside the Vatican to discuss the latest symbol.

Avernis gave one more tug at his lapels and went to meet her in the lobby. When she stepped out of the elevator a few minutes later, every cell in his body thrilled. She was simply a knockout. She wore a modestly low-cut black dress and gold-filigreed Byzantine necklace. Her luxurious raven hair perfectly framed her pale complexion and classic Grecian features. He caught himself thinking of the meeting as a date. Was that what she intended? *I'm getting ahead of myself. Let's see what's up*, he thought.

"Hi, Teresa," he said, feeling like a high schooler greeting his prom date.

She returned the greeting with a sly, albeit warm, smile.

"About lunch—you left it up to me," he said. "You like good antipasto? I know a terrific casual little place just off the side of the Spanish Steps."

She smiled. "Do they have chargrilled octopus there?" she asked.

"You like octopus too? They've got the best."

And with a big smile she said, "Great, let's do it."

At the restaurant, Avernis slipped his friend Enzo, the maî tre d', enough euros to secure a private table off the busy main dining area. Built-in wine racks and festive paintings lined the room's walls. Table candles provided most of the lighting.

"So," Avernis said, "this is something of a surprise. Is there a reason you didn't want to meet in the monsignor's office?"

"Actually a couple of reasons," she said. "The monsignor was tied up all day and I have a new perspective on all this. I wanted to run it by someone. I also never had much chance to talk with you after you rescued me in the hotel a while back. I have to say I'm disappointed you couldn't ask me out to dinner in all this time," she said, giving a playful nudge to his arm. "It's not like I know a lot of people in town yet."

Suddenly, despite his attempts to keep things professional, he felt like an ass. "I'm sorry. A lot of it was my work and travel, but believe me, it wasn't for lack of interest."

She eyed him with mock suspicion then laughed. "Okay, that sounds better. Oh, and don't worry, I *have* made a few friends here."

I'll bet, he thought.

Now let's talk about the symbols," she said. "You remember the last one," and she took out a picture.

"This caused a huge uproar," Avernis remarked. "It was found in front of the high altar of St. Peter's. LoPresti nearly had a coronary. It's also the first one that looks medieval."

"It's called the Sacred Marriage, from a sixteenth-century alchemy manual full of Gnostic imagery," Teresa said. "The sun and moon are depicted again, like in the previous Monad symbol, to represent the Gnostic belief in a Father-Mother God. See the king and queen below? They represent the divine earthly incarnations of each aspect of the deity above."

Avernis looked puzzled. "I don't follow," he said. "What incarnations?"

"You're Catholic so you know that the Christ spirit was the Son of God in the flesh of Jesus of Nazareth," Teresa said. "Well, documents unearthed in the last century showed the Gnostics believed there was a divine female incarnation, a counterpart to the Christ."

Avernis cupped his chin in his hand. "I never heard such a thing. Who was this incarnation? Why is there no record of this?"

"There is . . . in a way. The spirit counterpart to the Christ was Sophia, the Holy Spirit, held in the most ancient annals to be feminine in nature before the Church neutered her. She had several fleshly incarnations, including Eve. Now, orthodox Christians might look at this picture and say the female queen is Mother Mary, but the Gnostics said otherwise."

"Who?" Avernis asked.

"Mary Magdalene," Teresa replied, "another reputed embodiment of Sophia."

"Mary Magdalene? The prostitute?" Avernis asked in astonishment.

"The Bible never said she was a prostitute," Teresa said. "That was a false interpretation. In the recovered Gnostic gospels, Mary was Jesus' most prominent disciple, but that's another story. Let's focus on the sum of what we've got. The Abraxas symbol — God using wisdom, a feminine quality, and power, a masculine quality, to create the universe. The Monad symbol — God having a masculine and feminine quality making the universe in His/Her image with masculine and feminine duality. Now this new image — God incarnating in the flesh, not in just a masculine body but in a feminine one too."

"So, whoever is planting these things may be making some feminist statement to the Church," Avernis said. "Why don't they just write a theological treatise?"

"This is heresy, Robert. An ancient heresy eradicated from Christianity two thousand years ago. How do you think Cardinal Tormada would receive a paper on this?"

"He's not taking it too well now," Avernis said, agreeing with her point. "Well, it has to be an insider. No one could sneak around the Vatican like this for months, and it has religious overtones too. I wonder if it's a disgruntled nun protesting the Church's policy toward women?"

"Or a female Vatican worker would be my guess," Teresa said, "except that it's very sophisticated and arcane. How many nuns or secretaries would be aware of such things right down to the subtle symbologies?" Teresa said.

"That's true," Avernis said. "I'll pass this on. Monsignor O'Keefe is the only one taking this in stride. Roncalli and Mannheim seem worried about it, and LoPresti froths at the mouth every time something is found. I mean, from a security standpoint I'm concerned someone is roaming around causing a fuss and we haven't caught them, but otherwise, what's the big deal unless . . . unless this is a prelude to some violent action."

Not wanting to burden the remainder of lunch with a new worry, Avernis switched subjects. The conversation turned to an exchange of personal histories, with Teresa asking most of the questions. Avernis was cautious but he told her about his life growing up in Boston and about his family. He spoke of his family's roots in Sicily and how they too traced their ancestry back to Greece long ago, the probable reason why his name ended in the letter *S* instead of a vowel. He had lost his father at the age of thirteen. The older Avernis was the victim of a bomb blast meant to kill a Sicilian judge.

Teresa instinctively reached over and held his hand. "Listening to you, I somehow sense your defining principle is tied to what happened to your father."

"What do you mean?" he asked.

"I have a theory," she said. "I believe everyone has a defining principle for their life. Most people aren't self-aware enough to be conscious of it, but the extent to which they identify that principle determines how rewarding their life is."

Avernis took a sip of Chianti then swirled the red fluid around in the glass. "Explain to me how that works in your own life."

"I'm a kind of scribe, a witness and translator of events," Teresa said. "I think there is meaning in history and the events of our lives. I want to capture the truth in those events to the best of my ability. That information affects people, hopefully even enlightens them. That's why I became a reporter; it's my way of making meaning out of life."

A wave of sadness swept over him. She was intelligent and perceptive. She had hit a mark that came close to home concerning his father, but if he spoke of it, it could open the door to questions about his work, his *real* work, and that would not do. If she got a foot inside that door, she would see too far into his life. She was that sharp.

"I guess," he said, fingering the rim of his wineglass, "I'm just one of those people who hasn't figured it out yet." He diverted her attention to the great food and romantic surroundings. It was not difficult to do. The couple loosened up, becoming lightheaded and dreamy over carafes of wine, growing cozier by the minute.

"Would you like to go for a walk in the Borghese Gardens?" Teresa asked.

That simple question electrified Avernis with anticipation. As they walked out of the restaurant arm-in-arm, Avernis' vid-phone rang. It was Dusayne.

"Bob, this is Leo. Get your ass over here pronto."

"What's going on?" Avernis asked. *Why the hell was Dusayne calling now?*

"We just got tipped off," Dusayne said. "Your girlfriend is in town."

"My what? Who do you mean?" Avernis mumbled as Teresa listened. "What's going on?" he asked.

"What's going on is Fatilah Jahani," Dusayne said. "You remember, your 'Celine' from Nigeria. Well, she slipped into Rome last night."

Avernis almost dropped the phone. He looked at Teresa, whose puzzled expression harbored questions he could not answer. "I'm sorry," he said casting his eyes down to the floor. "I have to go."

CHAPTER XXXIX

Our doubt is our passion and our passion is our task.
— William James

Rome

Avernis entered a cab, telling the driver his destination as Leo Dusayne related it to him. Dusayne further briefed him as the taxi drove along. Avernis struggled to put Teresa out of his mind. He was just getting close to her and then this interruption. He had given her some excuse about an emergency at the Vatican as he left. She was disappointed but gracious; more the reason he felt bad about lying. Women never look kindly on hit-and-run intimacy.

"Fatilah entered Rome by train last night from France," Dusayne explained. "She's traveling with a French passport under the name of Celine Marchand. The Italians identified her off a computerized database scan of her passport photo. We checked with every hotel in town and found where she's staying."

"Odd," Avernis mused. "Why would she risk passing through a customs point? She must know there are ways of spotting people like her."

"Yeah," Dusayne said, "but she's not wanted for anything. She's done nothing illegal, at least nothing overtly illegal the Italians could arrest her for."

Avernis almost threw his hands in the air. "What do you mean? She entered the country on an illegal passport."

"Actually, she didn't," Dusayne said. "Her full name is Fatilah Celine Marchand Jahani. Her parents were divorced. In France, she legally assumed her mother's maiden name and she uses her own middle name first. Her passport is legal. French Securité is aware of her, but again, nobody has pinned anything on her yet."

Avernis snorted in disgust. "We all know better but do nothing about it. The games we play. Still, she must be here for a reason, and she's making it easy to be found and observed. She didn't stay at a private residence but at a hotel where she had to register her passport. It's too sloppy. Doesn't make sense."

"Whatever," Dusayne said. "It doesn't matter because now she's under watch and get this — you're going to get reacquainted with her."

Avernis was too dumbfounded to speak.

Dusayne explained that as soon as the Italians spotted "Celine," a flurry of electronic exchanges ensued between Rome and Washington, including information of Avernis' prior contact with the Iranian errand girl. Soon the orders came in from Langley: Avernis was to make contact with the woman again.

"They want you to get close and plant a STAT on her," Dusayne said.

STAT stood for "satellite transponder/audio transmitter." A new technology developed back in 2021, the STAT was a small, round piece of silicon the width and size of a dime. It operated off the new generation of Omnigen satellites. The transponder portion was a locater that worked like a GPS guidance system. The audio component was a kind of "superbug." It transmitted sound to the satellite on the same electronic beam as the transponder. The satellite encrypted and amplified the sound waves then retransmitted them back to earth. Special decrypting devices at Langley decoded the transmissions and enabled them to be heard with only a few seconds lag from real time. After all that work, a special coating activated and dissolved the device within forty-eight hours so the subject would never learn they'd been bugged.

"You'll tail her," Dusayne instructed, "and at the first convenient moment, you'll 'bump into her.' Your story is that you're here on business, saw her by coincidence, and you'll be all excited and oozing charm. Shouldn't be too hard to do with a broad that looks like that, you lucky bastard."

Avernis snorted. "Yeah, said the spider to the fly. It'll be like charming a cobra with a flute, mesmerizing until you miss a note and get bitten. I don't know, Leo. You really think she'll buy this 'coincidence'?"

"Only if you change your attitude. The orders came from the director himself so get with the program," Dusayne said. "Ours is not to question why, ours is just to do and . . . well, if you get successful and do her, kid, you'd better be careful."

"Cut the James Bond crap, Leo. We'd better get the rules of contact straight here. And why the hell is the director involved in this?"

Dusayne shrugged. "Washington worries a lot these days. All right then, let's go over the rules of contact."

His briefing completed, Dusayne instructed Avernis to hook up with some agents at the site who were following Jahani, then make contact with her at an opportune moment. Time was of the essence since none of them knew how long Jahani would be in Rome.

He thought about how he'd run out on Teresa. "I'm disappointed but I'm glad we had some time together," she had said.

Though she gave him a departing kiss on the cheek, Avernis left the hotel trying to rationalize the less savory aspects of his job, such as having to leave Teresa and head for a rendezvous with the likes of Fatilah Jahani.

✠

Teresa's heart and mind were in turmoil, and she had to make a quick decision—should she follow Robert Avernis?

Teresa lived on her reporter's instincts. Avernis' peculiar behavior in Nigeria now surfaced from the back burners of her mind. In Nigeria, he had been unusually sensitive about being caught on camera though she wanted to make a hero out of him. He had been evasive and standoffish in the face of her obvious interest in him until recently.

Then there was the phone call. Several things raised Teresa's antennae. Avernis said his problem was a Vatican emergency, yet his first questions were, "My what? Who do you mean?" In Teresa's view, those questions had to do with a specific person. When he said good-bye, he could not look her in the eye, and the tone of his voice seemed uncertain. Finally, his body language was tight and nervous, similar to when he had refused to let her do a story on him in Lagos.

Her starvation for lack of a newsworthy story had heightened her senses. In truth, her Vatican assignment was not all it had promised to be. She had hoped to do pieces on Cardinal Basanjo and the changing Church, but they had the new cardinal cloistered away like she was still a nun, and the Church did not seem to be changing. Even the Ecumenical Council process was crawling.

Being a Vatican reporter, she found, was like being a pigeon. One did not have press conferences with the pope. Most of the news was doled out by *l'Ossevatore Romano*, the official Vatican newspaper, then those crumbs were regurgitated to the public like so many little news birds feeding their chicks. Her one possible story, the Gnostic symbols mystery, was out. She had sworn to O'Keefe as a friend and fellow scholar that she would not make that public.

As a result, she was focused on Avernis' story. She had to admit she also had a personal interest in him. Her intuition told her Robert was hiding something. Sure he was in Vatican security, but even there he seemed out of place. He had been her knight in shining armor, and what woman could resist that? She felt a vague concern about a wife or girlfriend being involved, but following the man around Rome was a tacky, untrusting thing to do, and certainly not a great way to start a relationship. Was a bruised ego making her decision? She admitted the personal element to her concerns, but it was an overriding flash of intuition that told her to follow him.

Through the restaurant window, Teresa observed him entering a taxi at a cab station across the street. She sprang outside and grabbed the next cab in line.

"You speak English?" she asked the driver.

"Yes, Signorina, sure," the man replied.

"Good. Follow that taxi that just left please, and don't get too close."

"Fausto's car? He do something to you?" the driver asked.

Teresa needed some excuse for involving the poor man in this exercise. What would make sense to an Italian cab driver? "No, I don't know Fausto. He's driving my husband and I . . ." she paused for dramatic effect, "I think my husband is having an affair."

"Ah." The driver made a series of sympathetic tongue clicks. "Your husband, he make a bad choice," the man said, looking at Teresa in the rearview mirror. "I'm sorry, Signora. You don't worry; traffic is slow today. We have no problem following Fausto."

They ended up at the Monti quarter in the central city, where Avernis' taxi left him on a sidewalk. Teresa thanked her driver for his good work and gave him a generous tip. Teresa kept her eye on Avernis in the distance. She had to be careful. He kept glancing around as if he thought someone was following him. He turned a corner and walked onto the Via Del Boschetto, an area replete with artisan and antiquary shops. Fortunately, the street was full of window shopping tourists so Teresa had ample cover to observe him.

Then something peculiar happened. Avernis opened the rear door of a parked car and stepped in. Teresa tucked her hair under a hat she had brought along and walked across the street to a kiosk. Pretending to read a magazine, she observed Avernis with what appeared to be two men. Fifteen minutes later, Avernis exited the car and walked across to her side of the street but farther down from her position. He entered a store. Teresa crossed to the opposite side of street and walked past the car, verifying there were two men inside. She then entered a shop diagonally opposite the store Avernis had entered and watched through a picture window. Twenty minutes later, he came out.

Teresa's hands clenched into fists and a gnawing sensation clutched her stomach. Now she understood the nature of Avernis' "emergency." He was walking out of that store arm-in-arm with an attractive brown-haired woman, looking like he couldn't wait to get her home.

CHAPTER XL

Doubt is an uneasy and dissatisfied state. . . .
— Charles Sanders Peirce

Rome

Robert Avernis had to keep reminding himself that Celine was a terrorist because she looked and acted like an average young European woman. Actually, she looked far better than average, wearing khaki shorts that showcased her slender, tawny legs and slim ankles. Her blouse was padded at the shoulders tapering in a V shape toward her narrow waist, and her low-buttoned neckline revealed remarkably ample curves for such a lean body.

Avernis was fixating on the shape of her delicate wrists, which he found curiously erotic. He forced himself to snap out of his mini-trance, reminding himself with whom he was sitting. *That's the problem*, he thought. *Too damn easy to fall into this . . .*

He had approached her in the art shop. "Celine?" he had said. "It is you, right? I don't believe it. It's Robert, remember? We met in Enugu a while back."

Seeing him, she almost dropped the expensive crystal she was holding. "It's you!" she said.

Curious. The way she said that sounded like she was expecting someone, but not him. *Did I stumble on a meeting and she thinks I'm her contact?* he wondered. The next few minutes would tell.

She asked him what he was doing in Rome. He told her he often came to Rome to ship goods for his import/export company, and the objets d'art on Via Boschetto sometimes made good filler items for excess cargo space.

A slow smile crept over her face. "We were interrupted in Africa," she said. "Fate has us meet again." She clasped his arm. "Take some time off work and join me for a drink."

"Absolutely," he said. This was happening more smoothly than he believed possible. Either she was somehow onto him and setting him up or she was the most lax terrorist he could imagine. Then again, she had been this way in Nigeria and nothing came of it. Maybe she was just adventurous with her spare time. But was she really buying this "coincidence?"

They walked along arm-in-arm, making small talk until they found a cozy café. The décor was set up like a home living room and the waiter seated them on a sofa in a quiet corner. After several drinks, their light banter turned more serious and suggestive as time passed. It would be easy to believe it was a real date or flirtation, and Avernis gave himself two reminders to keep his perspective.

First, this was an assignment, and Celine was the enemy. The second reminder was Teresa. Celine's charms were considerable, but Teresa was genuine; this woman was not. Teresa had nobility about her. She had made that obvious when she confided her belief in her purpose to him. No matter how attractive Celine was, she worked for killers, people who had done great harm to others, people bent on dominating others.

At one point, Celine gave him a kiss on the cheek. "Excuse me," she said. "I need to visit the ladies room." She pulled a small makeup purse out of the larger shoulder satchel she carried and walked away.

There it was, her satchel bag, no more than twelve inches from where he sat. It was too damn easy. He could not have hoped for a better place to plant the STAT. Chances were she would carry the bag around frequently. He slid over and spread the satchel apart. He made a quick search for a weapon or anything unusual, but found nothing. It was full of feminine paraphernalia, and had a number of inside zipper pockets. He planted the STAT in one of the inner pockets, making sure it was not one that contained change since the device resembled a coin.

He rearranged the bag as he had found it and slid back to his position. Mission completed, but Avernis could not shake the feeling that something was wrong. What woman, let alone one with something to hide, went to the restroom and left her handbag behind with a virtual stranger? All that remained now was to leave on terms that might allow future contact.

Celine returned. They picked up where they left off and Celine moved closer to him. Her body language was becoming more forward. She ran her fingers over his cheek, sizing him up with her green eyes. "I like you, Robert."

He smiled. "I'm making progress then, am I?"

She giggled. "You're doing okay. For an American."

The sky outside turned dusky. Celine placed a hand on his thigh beneath the table, putting her fingernails to expert use that had Avernis getting stiff. *Terrorist and cockteaser, what a combination*, Avernis thought.

"You know, I'd like to make love to you," she said.

"But?" he asked. She seemed to look at him with eyes both sad and tender. *Is that part of her act?* he wondered.

Celine glanced at her watch. "Yes, there are always buts in this life. I'm sorry to say I have appointments now, and I leave tonight. It was a surprise to see you again, and I enjoyed myself," she said.

If he didn't know better, he'd say she was a good woman carrying some deep sorrow that made her mysterious and alluring. But he did know better. "I understand," he replied. "After all, it was an unexpected meeting."

"Yes," she said, "very unexpected."

"Will I see you again?" he asked.

Celine put her hand to her chin, considering his question. "I have a difficult work and travel schedule, but if we met like this today, anything is possible."

"Here," Avernis said, reaching into his pocket. "I travel a lot too, but you can reach me any time through my company."

She took the card and looked at it. "I think, somehow, we will see each other again, hopefully when we have time to finish what we started," and she winked at him. "Now, walk me out and then I must say adieu."

As Avernis watched her walk away, he held a short imaginary conversation with his boss even though the STAT was out of range. "I hope you heard all that, Leo," he muttered, "because something about this whole thing smells."

CHAPTER XLI

He is always One and He exists in them all . . .
for He is the source from which all are emitted.
—Allogenes (The Foreigner), a Gnostic gospel

The Vatican City

Papa, we need your influence to accelerate the Ecumenical Council," Cardinal Roncalli told the pope. The alliance of Milites Domini, Vatican bureaucrats, and conservative bishops was still exerting its retardant effect.

"The Church must run its own course," the pontiff replied.

A very laissez-faire attitude for a pope, Roncalli thought, but Clement did give him the green light to enlist the aid of the Jesuits and progressive foreign prelates for his cause. Annalisa's idea of bringing the bishops to Rome had also helped cut months off the process.

Just then, Roncalli's vid-phone vibrated. When he saw the caller ID number, he excused himself and stepped into the hall. It was Desmond O'Keefe. The monsignor would not call on this line unless it was something important. He flipped the device open. O'Keefe's ruddy Irish face greeted him, looking more worried than spry today.

He held the phone a bent arm's length away on video mode. "Desmond?"

"Peter"—O'Keefe called him by his American name from time to time—"I'm sorry to bother you, but we might have a problem."

"What is it, Desmond?"

"It's Annalisa. Tormada has asked her to attend a meeting of his congregation. They're discussing some treatise by a controversial theologian. Now, why would Tormada ever request her presence at such a meeting? Something is up, and mark my words, lad, it spells no good."

Roncalli considered the situation. Tormada's congregation was The Doctrine of the Faith, the body that insured adherence to Catholic dogma. From time to time, they might invite a guest in for expert opinion, but to invite a novice cardinal was extremely unusual. Tormada's blatant antipathy toward Annalisa's appointment further underscored the validity of O'Keefe's concern.

"Tell her not to go," Roncalli said.

"No good," O'Keefe replied. "She was invited, and she insists on attending."

Roncalli frowned. "I'm finishing a meeting with the Holy Father. Go with her and help her until I get there."

O'Keefe accompanied her as instructed. When Tormada saw Annalisa and O'Keefe enter the room, he immediately approached them.

"Monsignor, what brings you here?" he asked O'Keefe.

The Irishman gestured toward Annalisa. "Cardinal Basanjo has never attended such a session before. She invited me here to help her so as not to interrupt your proceedings."

"That is so," Annalisa said.

Tormada gave them a dubious look. "How courteous," he said, not hiding his sarcasm.

"Uh, hmm," O'Keefe coughed, clearing his throat to help him with his next announcement. "Cardinal Roncalli asked me to tell you he too will be attending."

"What?" Tormada snapped. "Why is *he* coming?"

Thinking fast, O'Keefe ad-libbed. "I believe the Holy Father has an interest in the discussion, but Cardinal Roncalli will have to answer that question." O'Keefe could see the hot-tempered Spaniard was furious, but he had paved the way for Roncalli. Tormada did not dare affront the pope's secretary for carrying out the Holy Father's orders.

Tormada bit his lower lip and gave O'Keefe a withering look. "Very well," he mumbled. He then called the meeting to order.

For nearly an hour, the group heard summaries and debated points on the work of an Austrian theologian. The work was titled "On The Nature of the Soul." Roncalli stepped in about halfway through the discussion and quietly took a seat. It did not take him long to realize this hearing was going to be a condemnation of the Austrian's treatise.

At some point in the discussion, Cardinal LoPresti, who was another guest at the proceeding, posed a question to Annalisa. "This topic, the essence of the soul, is fascinating and quite fundamental. I would like to hear some fresh views on the subject. Cardinal Basanjo, what is your opinion on the origin of the body and the soul? Were they creations or emanations of the divine?"

With that question, everything became clear to Roncalli. Annalisa had received no formal training in theology. That had always been one of the vulnerabilities in elevating her so rapidly to the cardinalate. LoPresti was trying to trap her into making a statement they could use to have her removed. Since Annalisa and O'Keefe were not near him, Roncalli spoke out to forestall Annalisa from answering.

"If it please the Prefect, doctrine on this question is long settled. At the Fourth Lateran Council and the — "

"Cardinal Roncalli," Tormada said. "You are out of order. Cardinal LoPresti posed a question. I will be pleased to recognize you after Cardinal Basanjo responds."

Roncalli bunched his fist into a ball. Annalisa was on the edge of a theological precipice. Emanationism was the belief that the soul *flowed* from God's own substance as a projection of the divine with no separation. It opposed the Church view that the soul was *created* and separate. If she should endorse emanationism in any way, Tormada could use it to end her career. Before O'Keefe could even advise her, she smiled at Roncalli and began speaking.

"Church doctrine on the subject is clear," Annalisa said. "I refer to the dogma of *creatio ex nihilo* as defined at the Fourth Lateran Council and at the Council of the Vatican."

Roncalli's eyes were not the only ones in the room that went wide at that statement. He looked at O'Keefe as if to ask, *did you teach her that?* But the monsignor shrugged, looking just as surprised as everyone else.

"The latter council expressly condemned emanationism, and anathematizes anyone asserting that 'finite things, both corporeal and spiritual,' have emanated from the Divine substance."

The exact recitation of the dogma left LoPresti sputtering. "Uh, yes, but, uh — "

Annalisa spoke right over him. Roncalli tried signaling her to stop. She had already thwarted their trap. Anything more would be counterproductive.

"The topic does raise some interesting questions, though." She looked to her left, then to her right, making eye contact with each of the participants.

"We say the body perishes, and the soul is immortal, but we say both body and soul are *created*. How can we define these different classes of existence the same way? It seems the body should be created, the soul emanated. If the soul is immortal, something must eternally sustain it. If something eternally sustains it, the Sustainer and the soul must be connected, which implies they are forms of the same substance. God is the only infinite thing in the universe, so, hypothetically speaking, it could be argued the soul emanates from God."

The room was completely silent.

"These speculations," Annalisa said, "are all hypothetical, of course. I am sure finer minds than I possess have the answers."

The room breathed again. Amidst a loud buzz of murmuring, Tormada said, "I think we are done here for today." He then slammed his book shut and walked out of the room.

When the proceeding ended, Roncalli pulled Annalisa and O'Keefe off to the side as soon as he could reach them. "What were you doing in there?" he asked Annalisa. "You impressed everyone with your knowledge then you 'hypothetically' question the dogma as if rubbing your real opinion in their face. You did it in a way they could not condemn you, but Tormada's congregation evolved from the Inquisition, in case you were not aware. You were playing with fire. Why?"

"Hah!" Annalisa exclaimed. "I did not need to know about any Inquisition to realize I was on trial the minute they invited me. Pietro, I cannot hide from these men, and I cannot be a wooden mannequin sitting mute and still while they dress me up or down. I am what I am."

"Yes, but your profound ideas appeared designed to provoke," Roncalli said. "That did not seem like you in there, confronting them like that, I mean."

Annalisa shook her head. She took a step forward toward Roncalli and placed a hand on his left shoulder. "Turn around please, Pietro."

Roncalli looked puzzled but he rotated around and came to face a full-length mirror.

"Look in the mirror, Pietro. Tell me what you see?"

"I see my reflection," Roncalli replied in a flat tone.

Annalisa looked over his shoulder. "What if tomorrow you looked in this same mirror and saw someone else's reflection? Inside, you know yourself to be yourself, but the mirror says otherwise. How would you feel? Confused, disoriented, robbed of your identity, separated from yourself?"

Roncalli did not answer. He glanced at O'Keefe, who appeared as perplexed as he was.

Annalisa smiled, aware of their confusion. "'The Lord thy God is one.' This is the most profound statement in the Bible. The Kingdom of Heaven is within, not without. If we want to find God, we must look within to our underlying unity with the universe, not without to our superficial appearance of separation. This dogma of creation does the same thing to the human soul as looking in a mirror and seeing someone else. It makes us believe we are something other than what we are, something less. It turns us away from the essence of God that lies within us."

At that statement, Roncalli looked at O'Keefe, whose unbroken attention was on Annalisa.

"The idea that God has created souls like windup dolls and left them on their own to bounce off the walls of an earthly insane asylum is pernicious," Annalisa said. "We must have passion and a spiritual path in life, and everyone's path is different. I have my beliefs, and I am not upset with differing beliefs. However, when the Church promotes ideas that place obstacles and detours along the path, it is time to consider, or perhaps even reconsider, alternative visions."

Roncalli was silent for some time. Then he said, "Annalisa, what you have just said might be interpreted as heresy. If your opponents heard these things, they could twist them in such a way that would do damage to you and the pope. I want to meet with you and Monsignor O'Keefe to better understand your views. Desmond?"

"Oh, yes," O'Keefe said in an oddly eager voice. "We should talk, but in complete privacy."

The trio decided to meet outside the Vatican in Annalisa's apartment in the Trastevere. When they arrived, they found the door ajar. Roncalli entered first, looking around cautiously, listening for intruders. He saw the living room in shambles, but he blanched when he looked at the wall. He tried to block Annalisa's view, but she came up behind him and saw it anyway. It was a message, simple and direct:

NIGGER GO HOME!

CHAPTER XLII

The Church will suffer great ills; a torrent of evil will open a breach on her, but the first attack will be against her fortune and her riches.— From the Brevararium — Ravignan, a Jesuit Priest, 1847

The Vatican City

They woke Roncalli after midnight, and now he stepped into the room to meet the man who had disturbed his sleep. The chamberlain of the Church, Cardinal Torante, had his eyes cast to the floor. He sat next to Wolf Von Kessel, a Vatican financial advisor.

Von Kessel exhaled a dense cloud of smoke from his lungs. A narrow, hawkish nose overshadowed his sunken cheeks, and there were reddish-gray circles under his eyes. Roncalli recalled Von Kessel once proclaiming with pride that he had not smoked in five years. Now the thin German banker inhaled deeply one more time before stamping his cigarette into an ashtray and rising as the cardinal entered the room.

"Herr Von Kessel," said Roncalli. He shook the German's hand and gave an acknowledging smile to Cardinal Torante. "To what do we owe your visit tonight?"

"I am sorry to disturb you so late in the evening. I wish I were here under better circumstances, Your Eminence, but such is not the case," replied the financier stiffly.

"I see," Roncalli said, gesturing toward the chairs. "Why don't we be seated and talk."

And talk the banker did for well over an hour, an hour that Cardinal Roncalli wished he could have excised from his life like a cancerous growth.

Von Kessel's voice droned on and on, " . . . over a billion dollars lost counting funds from affiliates and other traders . . . "

Roncalli stopped listening. A wave of panic rolled across his mind. *Good Lord, they've lost a staggering sum of money. My God, the Church is on the brink!*

The devil must have timed this. Once the greatest institution in the West, the Church was already in a serious, steady decline. Churches were closing for lack of priests and parishioners, droves of young Catholics were drifting away, and donations had been dwindling sharply for years.

For a few seconds Roncalli allowed Von Kessel's voice to filter in again, " . . . the same Asian trading debacle that caused the demise of the English investment company . . . "

But Roncalli wanted to hear nothing more about investment companies. The German's words triggered a train of negative associations in the cardinal's worried mind.

" . . . fortunately, not all of the instruments were margined or it would have been worse . . . "

Roncalli pinched his eyes shut with his forefingers to ward off an impending headache. In an age where nations were bickering dangerously over vanishing resources, the Church needed all its strength, and now the Vatican coffers were near empty.

" . . . I'm so sorry, Your Eminence, I— "

Roncalli raised a palm toward the German. "Herr Von Kessel, I have heard enough to understand. I would like to have a word with Cardinal Torante and then he will return to discuss our options with you."

The now mute German nodded his head.

The two cardinals retired to the inner reception room. Roncalli closed the heavy wooden doors behind them then turned to address Torante.

"Matteo, you realize what a disaster this is? Where is Van Kluysen?" he asked referring to the Belgian cardinal in charge of overseeing the finances of the Vatican Bank.

"He just left for London, Pietro, trying to see if we can recoup anything," Torante said. "It makes one wonder if there is any connection—Van Kluysen I mean—to the rumors over the years of personal gain through his family's business and all that."

"There will be an investigation, without question," said Roncalli, "but we have more immediate concerns. Churches and seminaries are already closing in record numbers because parishioners no longer support their dioceses. These monies we lost stood as a reserve, not to mention their use in our missionary work and other activities."

"I spoke with Van Kluysen earlier," Torante said. "He assured me this was a severe wound, yes, but not a death blow."

"Van Kluysen is playing this down for obvious reasons," Roncalli said. "This can permanently cripple the Church."

"You mean financially, of course?" Torante asked.

"And spiritually, Matteo." Roncalli's brows drew together. His index finger tapped out his next words in staccato rhythm on a nearby table. "The Church is already being abandoned by the poor, who see it as part of their problem, not their hope; the affluent educated see it as hypocritical and irrelevant in the modern world, and now . . . "

Roncalli saw the stricken look on Torante's face and decided to end this monologue, which after all was helping no one. "I must prepare to talk to the Holy Father, Matteo. Go back to Von Kessel, and I'll speak with you later."

✠

Pope Clement XV stared out the window at the Eternal City after hearing Roncalli's grim report. "This is a grave setback," he told Roncalli. The pope sighed. "Dear God, where are we heading?"

"We had a direction," Roncalli said. "You made a promising start with Annalisa and the announcement of the Ecumenical Council, but the curia is fighting the process and—"

Clement raised his hand. "I am the initiator of the change, not the life of it. It must have its own life to be absorbed into the body of Christ."

Roncalli saw the pope was under strain so he did not argue the point. Still, he found Clement's position on the reforms inexplicable.

"I knew the risk involved by allowing the council," Clement said. "In light of this terrible news the risks have increased significantly."

Roncalli's mind flew back to the *Gloria Olivae* prophecy and the downfall of the Church. He mentally berated himself. He wanted to help Clement, but was torn between his desire for change and his fear of it. Finally, he said, "The Church as we know it is on a dire path. You are the pope, Christ's anointed through Peter, and you must make the decisions. I can only advise you to pray for guidance and watch for any answers as they come most deeply into your heart and mind."

The pope looked at Roncalli as if expecting him to say more. Roncalli avoided his eyes and gazed downward. The cardinal was rapping a punishing knuckle against his own cheek.

"Yes, I . . . I will pray for the strength to act as I am guided," Clement said with a hint of disappointment.

Roncalli almost spoke again, but remained silent, biting his lower lip. He looked up and studied Clement. The pope's face was a mixture of confusion and concern. He imagined the thoughts running through the pope's mind. Events now assaulted the vision Clement had had in Nigeria, and doubt must be casting darkness across his path. He had seen a glimpse of hope back then, when Annalisa had healed him, but who now was capable of healing the Church, indeed the whole troubled world?

Clement could not go back; his course was set for better or for worse. But if his thoughts in any way mirrored Roncalli's, he could not help feeling that he was facing a black hole, and hell waited on the other side. Believers no longer believed, and now the money to support the tottering Church façade had vanished. How long before the end, before the downfall of the Church during his papacy?

CHAPTER XLIII

The will to domination is a ravenous beast.
—Andrea Dworkin

Toledo, Spain

Cardinal Jut Van Kluysen, Vatican Prefect for Economic Affairs, did indeed visit London as Cardinal Torante had informed Roncalli. He stayed there exactly eight hours, a curiously short time to review Vatican options during the worst financial disaster in the Church's history. The next morning he rose before dawn, not really having slept to any extent. The bleary-eyed cardinal hurriedly packed and caught an 8:00 a.m. flight to Spain.

A few hours later, Van Kluysen stood in an office in Toledo facing a bizarre sight. Seated opposite him was a stocky, olive-skinned man. The man's thick, black eyebrows loomed over two black holes that appeared to absorb light wherever he gazed, and just now he was gazing at Van Kluysen. Even more unsettling were the two men standing behind him at either shoulder. They were actually wearing hooded black robes, part of the garb worn by their order on certain occasions. Van Kluysen figured they must be freshly arrived from one of their arcane rituals.

It wasn't so much the robes the men wore that bothered Van Kluysen; it was the slow flow of blood he saw dripping from their loose sleeves. He knew what that was. They wore barbed-wire bracelets, some nonsense about pain reminding them of duty and obedience. Despite their theatrics, he knew one could never take these people lightly.

"Bishop Alvaro," he said, addressing the seated man. "I came straight from London."

Alvaro nodded. He had not kissed the cardinal's ring hand. Indeed, sitting there, Van Kluysen felt Alvaro was the cardinal and he the subordinate given the man's comportment. The entire room bespoke the secrecy and quiet power of the order to which these men belonged. The dark, wood-paneled walls and dim lighting from candle sconces lent a shadowy quality to every move and spoken word. *Under the circumstances,* Van Kluysen mused, *that was a good thing.*

Alvaro lifted his head slightly, but still no light penetrated the black orbs beneath his brows. "Tell me what is happening at the Vatican," he said in a deep monotone voice.

Van Kluysen adjusted his glasses in a futile attempt to get a better fix on the man's eyes. He felt skittish talking to someone without being able to get a facial read. "There's panic as you would expect," Van Kluysen said. "Did you—"

Alvaro waved a hand. "Yes, yes. The money is in your Liechtenstein Anstalt."

"Untraceable, of course?" Van Kluysen asked as his fingers rolled furiously in his palms.

"Completely," Alvaro replied. "As we promised."

"And the British trader?"

"Ah yes, well, you heard he disappeared," Alvaro said. "Under the circumstances, I doubt he'll be coming back."

The dire implication in that statement was a source of both anxiety and relief for Van Kluysen. He was just a moneyman. Many activities these people engaged in were beyond the pale as he knew it, and he did not inquire further out of concern for his own health. Besides, he had never met the Britisher, and Von Kessel, the German, was merely a dupe whom he had steered toward placing the Vatican's money with the Singapore-based trader. It seemed they had covered all tracks properly so he changed subjects.

"When will you make your move on the Vatican?" he asked Alvaro.

The dark bishop was momentarily silent before replying. "Not too soon, I should imagine."

"What? Why not?" Van Kluysen asked with a panicky tinge to his voice.

Van Kluysen felt Alvaro's shade-enfolded eyes x-raying him from head to toe in the long silence. The Belgian cardinal knew he had made a mistake by blurting out his concern, and his palms went damp with anxiety.

Alvaro then spoke. "Do you play chess, Your Eminence?"

"No," Van Kluysen said.

"I thought not," Alvaro said. "Your . . . " Alvaro paused a second to choose his words, "your *desire* for money limits your vision to short-term goals, swift solutions."

Van Kluysen's teeth ground at that statement. How dare this common bishop lecture him! Then he remembered: Alvaro was no common bishop, and Van Kluysen was in the lion's den.

"Chess is the strategy of kings, developed in an era where power was attained by cunning as well as might. Chess teaches one to think forward, use all the pieces at your command to whittle away, isolate your target, and finally seize control."

Van Kluysen squirmed in his seat, grating at being a helpless audience.

He hoped there was a quick point coming from all this. Fortunately, Alvaro obliged him.

"Losing all that money is one thing but the time it takes to feel the pain of that loss is another. We will deal with Clement soon, when the desperation reaches a sufficient level."

Van Kluysen knew he was in no position to protest Alvaro's timetable. "I had merely hoped a swift change in power would squelch any inquiries," he said.

"There must be some degree of inquiry or that in itself would be suspicious," Alvaro replied. "Stay calm. We executed the plan as agreed. Nothing will be traced. Anyway, you are part of Mannheim's inner circle. He will protect you for his own reasons. Look to him. I must leave now; I have a meeting to attend."

Mannheim. It dawned on Van Kluysen that he would soon have to face the powerful German cardinal. Mannheim would be furious with him for losing the Vatican's money, but as long as he thought it was just bad judgment, he would probably cover for him. Mannheim had his own agenda and the lost funds would be a political liability for him. *Yes, stick with the plan.* Van Kluysen started to relax for the first time that day because of one comforting thought: *the magnitude of all this would motivate a lot of people to pretend like nothing ever happened*, and the Vatican was very good at doing that.

Toledo, Spain

The smell of incense permeated the dark room in a lingering smoky haze. "Sit," the dark-skinned man said after performing the invocation mass in Latin.

The twelve men pulled down the cowls of their robes and sat at a long, rectangular table. Bishop Alvaro Maria Delgado took his place at the head of the group. The bishop's heavy black eyebrows hung low over deep-set eyes and gave him a perpetual brooding appearance. It has been said, "never judge a book by its cover," but in Alvaro's case the man's dark countenance was an accurate reflection of his personality.

Alvaro gazed around the room, and wherever the sleeve of a loose, baggy monk's robe had rolled back, he saw a circle of small scabs around the man's wrist.

"Good, good," he muttered. It meant they were still practicing self-mortification with the cilicio despite their high rank in Milites Domini. Even now, Alvaro was wearing the barbed bracelet around his wrist. He had to move carefully to prevent the metal thorns from piercing his skin. It made one constantly think about one's actions—that was the genius of the founder's little device—and Alvaro, an expert chess player, doubly appreciated the deliberation it required.

"Brothers," Alvaro said to the group, "make no mistake, the West is in moral and spiritual decline, and the founder created our order to prevent that. The Blessed Founder formed Milites Domini nearly a century ago," Alvaro reminded the men. "His vision was that we should become the sentinels of Christianity, the sword arm to defend the Holy Mother Church against its enemies. With patience, we have grown strong, and the task for which we have prepared is now at hand."

The men smiled at his words but Alvaro cut their satisfaction short. "War with Islam is imminent," he growled in a gruff voice. "Islam has been on the terrorist offensive for two decades. Now the Persian fanatics are emboldened and seek to control the world's remaining oil supplies. Does anyone here believe we are fully prepared yet?"

It was all he could do to keep from clenching his fist and starting the blood flowing. *Patience, that is what the cilicio teaches, patience.* Alvaro relaxed with that thought. The black-robed men squirmed in their seats and shot sideward glances at one another but no one spoke or raised a hand before Alvaro answered his own question.

"We must not only prepare morally and spiritually but also politically. Father DeNavarre is now traveling to all the chapters worldwide preparing them for the future to place our own priests in all the key parishes."

The men looked around in confusion. Milites Domini had never had anything to do with day-to-day Church functions.

"I will soon travel to America to put a plan in motion, a plan started years ago. Its goal is nothing less than the salvation of the Western world. To achieve this great goal we will bring the world's most powerful nation and the world's most powerful church under one roof. Brothers, I tell you, in the near future not only will the world's greatest army be marching for our cause, but we will control the Vatican and the very papacy itself!"

At first the men sat in stunned silence, but after some minutes, when they realized what Alvaro was saying, one-by-one they stood and clapped, then the clapping turned to pounding on the table, and this warmed Alvaro's heart. The ancient symbol for Christianity was a fish, but that fish must be consumed by more aggressive fish. Alvaro needed sharks. Fight fire with a bigger fire, he always said. These men had the zeal and like sharks, they had the taste for blood.

CHAPTER XLIV

Love ... destroys the in-between which ... separates us from others.
—Hannah Arendt

The Vatican City

Annalisa received a message summoning her to Cardinal Roncalli's office. After the vandals had robbed her apartment, she had taken temporary residence in a Vatican City apartment. News of the incident had made the papers, including the racial slur scrawled on the wall. The police had investigated but produced no leads. Her few friends had been outraged; most others were quietly smug or silent on the subject.

Roncalli looked weary today, and she knew why. The news had not reached the press, but word of the Church's financial catastrophe was leaking out around the Vatican. Annalisa had seen the worry on Roncalli's face over the past months before hearing the rumors.

"I want you to take a trip with me to the Trastevere," Roncalli said with a tired smile.

"Oh?" Annalisa said.

Roncalli engaged her with small talk that lasted the entire car ride to Piazza San Cosimato. Walking through the square, Annalisa saw many residents she knew. They greeted her warmly. Roncalli remained talkative, and soon Annalisa was standing in front of her apartment. She turned and noticed a crowd of people had followed them from the Piazza. She looked at Roncalli.

"Just follow me," he said.

They walked up the stairs, and the people followed behind them. They arrived at the door to her apartment, and Roncalli opened it. Inside she saw more residents, all people she knew. One man who had been polishing a table jumped up when she entered and turned to face her with an embarrassed grin. Annalisa walked a few steps farther into the room. The apartment was completely restored and refurnished. Annalisa walked around touching the new items then stopped in front of a wall shelf. On it stood the carved mahogany bust of her mother, the one possession she was sad to have lost.

She turned and addressed the swelling group of neighbors now crowding the apartment. Her tender smile and the single tear that coursed down her left cheek spoke her gratitude better than any words could convey.

Signora Sicali, a neighborhood woman, stepped forward and spoke. "Eminenza, when we learned what happened, we were ashamed. What kind of people would do such a thing? Since you moved here, things have gotten better. You teach children, advise any who ask you, and even sick people, people you never met, have been healed."

"Like my Stephania," Signora DeRosa chimed in. "Miracles followed you to the Trastevere."

"We collected money," Signora Sicali said, gesturing around the room. "And we have some good workmen who live here," she said, pointing out some of the men.

"And this?" Annalisa asked, pointing to the bust.

"Ahem," Signor DePrisco cleared his throat, preparing to answer. "We have certain people who . . . uh . . . who have connections with the black market. The rest was only money."

After a small party and a many expressions of thanks from Annalisa, the neighbors left. Only Annalisa and Roncalli remained. "I know the Vatican has been difficult for you," Roncalli said. "I'm sorry I've not been more help. So many problems — the Ecumenical Council, the financial disaster — have occupied my every minute, but no matter. Today, the people who count most, those whom we serve, honored you. You changed their lives. None of those fossils in the Vatican could boast so much. If you ever despair, think back on this day, think of the love these people showed you. Will you do that?"

Annalisa hugged him and clung to him in silence. *Now why am I surprised,* he wondered. *After all, she is only human.*

Rome

That evening, after the party, Annalisa left her apartment. She was going back to the Vatican to gather her belongings. Two men tailed her as she crossed the dimly lit streets. They had been following her for three days, waiting for the right moment, and luck was with them. It looked like she was going to pass right in front of the alleyway in which one of them was hiding. Just before she was going to walk by, one of the men called out.

"Say, sister, got a light?"

Annalisa turned and saw a rough-shaven man. He had no cigarette. She held his gaze as he neared. "I am not a sister, I don't smoke, and neither should you.

You've had tuberculosis, and," she said, "you don't really want to do what you are about to do."

Before the shocked man could ask how she knew all that, the second thug came up from behind and clamped a hand over Annalisa's mouth. The men dragged her into the alley. It was very odd; she did not put up a struggle or attempt to cry out. They laid her on the dirty pavement. The second thug pulled out a knife and held it to her throat as he kept her mouth clamped with his other hand. "You make one sound and I slit you, understand?"

Annalisa made no response. She seemed limp. The second thug motioned with his head for his crony to come near. "She looks good for a priest, ah? Always wanted to fuck a black bitch; now I can fuck a goddamn priest at the same time. Too good to pass up. Waddya say?"

The other man looked nervous. "That wasn't what we was told," he said in the other's ear. "We're supposed to rough her up, break an arm maybe, but we wasn't told to do that."

The second thug shook his head. "Fuckin' idiot. You really think they care? I ain't lettin' this one go." He stared at Annalisa like a starving wolf looking at fresh kill.

The other man's breathing grew shallow; something felt wrong. She still did not look afraid even as his cohort began tearing at her simar. She clenched her torn robe and shook her head no, not in protest but . . . as if warning him! No fear in her face, just a warning look.

"You're somethin', lady," Annalisa's assailant said. "Keep it like this, nice and quiet."

The other man could not stop fidgeting, and he kept looking over his shoulder. "No, no," he said. "This is no good. We gotta split."

"You fuckin' nuts?" the second man said, trying to concentrate on Annalisa. "You're gonna end up worse than her if you don't do what I tell you."

The other man punched away at his palm with the fist of his other hand. "Don't you feel it? This ain't right. Somethin's gonna—"

"Pay attention to your friend," Annalisa said. "He is listening inside himself. This is not meant to happen. You are letting yourself be used to a bad end, and you are in great danger because of it. You have a chance to leave now. Take it."

"Used?" the assailant laughed. "Used? I'm enjoying this. And you," he said to his partner, "you shut the fuck up or I'll cut your throat."

As he stood above her unbuckling his belt, a shadow passed across their field of vision with a swooshing sound followed by a shattering noise. The assailant's head snapped back then drooped at an awkward angle. He emitted a crackling, gurgly sound and a spray of warm liquid spewed from his throat to coruscate in the moonlit alley. The remaining man glanced down and saw the shards of the fallen terra-cotta roof tile. He looked up but no one was visible on any of the upper stories. He looked back at Annalisa and started to shake.

"A waste," she said. "Go now, and tell those who sent you their time is not yet come."

He ran. Annalisa would not report the incident or speak of it to anyone. The man was dead, and those who sent him would soon learn how their plans got out of hand. But it was not lost on her that her enemies grew bolder, and that meant they grew desperate.

CHAPTER XLV

Worry is interest paid on trouble before it falls due.
— W. R. Inge

Rome

The New Year of 2028 was bringing bad news for American intelligence. Robert Avernis read his quarterly briefing:

Unprepared Western nations are verging on a catastrophe greater than the one Hitler posed in 1933. Where he threatened, intimidated, then hijacked a nation of 75 million, the Islamo-fascists have done the same to a religion of 1.2 billion. Hitler did not live to see nuclear weapons, terrorists have the potential to acquire them . . .

Israel was on increasingly hostile terms with its neighbors over water rights for dwindling sources in Gaza and the Jordan River area. Iran was using the situation to further its dominance in the Islamic world. Aggressive rhetoric was coming from Tehran and its allies in Baghdad.

Tehran had finally brokered the exclusive oil pact between the Islamic countries and Asian nations despite repeated warnings by the Americans through diplomatic channels that it could precipitate dangerous circumstances. The American economy was already suffering from reduced oil flow, and the militant candidates supporting President Davidson were gaining momentum going into next November's elections.

A troubling type of terrorism different from the Muslim fundamentalist variety was also maturing in the twenty-first century. The PNC (Poor Nations' Coalition) was a mysterious network of people, perhaps 50–100 in number, from predominantly Third-World Christian countries. They were demanding reforms in the international economy and a redistribution of wealth to redress the worsening gap between rich and poor countries. Their targets cut across all the developed nations, and the Catholic Church was a favored victim for kidnappings and ransoms.

Avernis received credit for the Celine episode in Rome. The information off Celine's STAT had provided some valuable information. It confirmed the

Iranians were behind the arms shipments to Nigeria. In fact, she had been in Rome handling one such shipment. The Italian authorities would now tighten up port inspections.

They also got some names. She had met with one Moustafa, apparently a top operative of the rebel Nigerian Front against Neo-Colonialism. rebels. Avernis remained suspicious of the whole episode with Celine, how smoothly it went and her cozy attitude toward him, but before the STAT transmissions stopped, they had picked up a name: Alhaji. Alhaji was apparently an N-FAC leader, and Moustafa, the man Celine met, was a high-ranking subordinate. True, there were thousands Alhajis in Nigeria — the name meant one who has made the hadjj or journey to Mecca — but it was a start. N-FAC was striking Western targets in Nigeria from oil rigs to corporate headquarters. The information provided by the STAT he planted on Celine had yielded their only break so far in the operation.

Avernis' personal life was in as much turmoil as the world's political situation. His budding relationship with Teresa had cooled off ever since he left her in the restaurant. She was friendly, but always had something going when he called her. Finally, he stopped. The mysterious symbols had ceased being found months ago, so he had little excuse to see her.

Things around the Vatican were tense. Roald Zugli confided to him that the Church had lost a fortune six months ago. They were trying to cover it up, but they were hurting . . . severely. Avernis was glad he wasn't on their payroll, but now he understood why the pope, Roncalli, and Mannheim looked tired and drawn so much of the time.

One day, Roncalli called him into his office. "I have a very confidential matter to discuss with you," the cardinal told him. "It's so delicate, I cannot even involve Commander Zugli. Robert, I'm turning to you as a friend."

Avernis respected Roncalli. "Whatever I can do to help, Your Eminence," he replied.

"Thank you. You know that the Church suffered an enormous financial loss last year. I've come to believe we were victims of foul play. I think at least one of our own cardinals may be involved."

Avernis took in a deep breath. "What makes you think that, Your Eminence?"

"That's just it," Roncalli said. "I have no concrete evidence, only suspicions . . . about Cardinal Van Kluysen." Avernis let out a low whistle. "Yes, I know," Roncalli said. "Hard to believe, but Van Kluysen was quietly reprimanded in the past for minor irregularities. He enjoys Mannheim's protection, and because he has a financial background from his family business in Belgium, Mannheim made him prefect of the bank."

"You don't think Cardinal Mannheim was involved, do you?"

"I'm not sure," Roncalli said. "I don't think so. He's hindering internal investigations, but he's probably trying to avoid personal embarrassment since he put Van Kluysen in office. He's an ambitious man, but I don't see him doing anything to harm the Church for personal gain. Van Kluysen is another story. He's greedy, very greedy."

"What can I do to help?" Avernis asked.

"Whatever you can do to prove or disprove my suspicions," Roncalli said. "I realize this is irregular, calling you in like this, but I cannot even talk to Zugli since he technically answers to Mannheim. I can't make such accusations to the internal investigators. It would cause a political uproar for one cardinal to accuse another without evidence. You are an outsider who's inside. If you can find a way to help, any way, you'd do us a great service."

Avernis sat in thought for some time. "Cardinal, you realize I can't involve the CIA in any way, but I'll try to help. I have to think this through. This has got to be very discreet so please, don't ask me any questions until I come to you with an answer."

Roncalli agreed. Avernis would now have to contact a cousin he had scrupulously avoided since coming to Italy. It would put his job at risk, but a crime that affected so many must not stand. He would do it for the Church.

CHAPTER XLVI

... dreames ben sometime—I say not all—Warning of thinges that shall after fall.—Geoffrey Chaucer

Rome

The sun-filled day brought forth abundant signs of life in the Trastevere as Cardinals Roncalli and Basanjo strolled through the colorful neighborhood. Old men with caps sat on benches smoking and pompously solving the world's problems in loud, argumentative voices. Children played soccer on stone-paved streets while mothers hung clothes out to dry in their courtyards.

The two prelates stopped at a fruit stand where Annalisa purchased some dried figs—excellent for the digestion, she claimed—and the vendor gave her a warm greeting. "Ah, Eminenza, good to see you. You still sure you're not Italian?"

"Hah! Not today, Flavio, maybe next week," and all the fruit mongers laughed. Annalisa explained the local joke to Roncalli. When they first heard her last name, Basanjo, they were certain that she *must* be Italian. She did not understand until someone scribbled down on a piece of paper: *Bisanggio*. "See," they said. "That is surely an Italian name."

"I can see why you moved here," Roncalli said. "You have more friends in Trastevere than in the Vatican. It was a good idea for you to get out of there. It can be a little stifling," Roncalli mused as they came to sit on a bench and eat the figs.

"Even more so for you, Pietro," she remarked.

"Oh? How do you mean?"

"Perhaps it is time for you too to get out of the confines of the Vatican."

"What, and move to Trastevere?" he asked, confused by her comment.

"Hah! Now that would be something," she said. "No, I mean finally expressing your true feelings about your calling, about the Church. I know how difficult it was for you to be quietly isolated all these years because of your views."

"How did you know that? Is this some clairvoyance on your part?"

"Hardly," she said with a smile. "It comes from conversations with Desmond."

"Desmond O'Keefe? So the old lad's been talkin' now, has he?" Roncalli said, mimicking the Irishman's brogue. "A dear, brilliant man he is, but he loves to gab, and he's not above bein' a wee bit melodramatic now and again."

She laughed at his impression of the monsignor. "He is a good friend and concerned for you, and in this case he is right. May I tell you a secret someone once told me?"

"Of course."

"In this world," she said, "we attract our opposites in measure. Light attracts darkness, and you are trying to bring to light ideas that are meant to liberate people, liberate their understanding of God and the Church. Those who don't want that will always oppose you."

She had his attention. Her unsolicited advice had been very helpful before.

"If you had been too outspoken before now," she said, "you would have been suppressed, but now it is time for you to give full expression to what is in your heart."

Not completely sure where the conversation was leading, Roncalli said, "If your comments are related to the synods and the Ecumenical Council, I am encouraged. We are getting more resistance than ever here in the Vatican, but we're making progress."

"Ah, your opponents suffer from the Vatican paradox," she said. "The harder they try to define people's beliefs, the less people believe in *them,* but I think many bishops will support a new way; the people are ready for change despite the Vatican's resistance."

"How did you come to have a pulse on Church politics?" he asked her. "I always thought insulating yourself from that business was the reason you spent so much time in the library."

She smiled and shook her head. "No," she said, "I needed an education." and she pointed around to the surrounding neighborhood. "But my real education has been here, talking to the people on the streets, or back in Africa, listening to the hopes of the people there."

"And what do they tell you?" he asked.

"Their lives and goals seem as different as the mountains from the sea, but inside," and she thumped on her chest, "inside, what they really want is a spiritual presence in their lives that is living, not dead; close, not remote. What they're getting are cynical dogmas from people whose belief is lukewarm in their minds and stone cold in their hearts."

"You are referring to the Vatican when you say that," he remarked.

"Have you ever noticed the unhappy people working in the Vatican, how closed and hostile they are to outsiders?" she asked with a sad look in her eyes.

"Well, there is certain business we conduct that must remain confidential."

"Of course, but there is secrecy about *everything*," she said, "a hesitation about even saying hello because that may lead to conversation. Have you ever wondered about that?"

"Mannheim and Tormada are dictators. People fear them," he said.

"It goes beyond any individual, Pietro. It is a culture of silence. Do you know why?"

He shook his head. "No, maybe I have lived around it too long. Do you know?"

Annalisa picked up a small wooden stick and scratched randomly at the dirt as they spoke. "I think, maybe, it is because they are so out of step with the world they are embarrassed." She continued to pick at the ground. "I visited the catacombs. There old Rome is buried by this new earth, but only in the Church is the new buried by the old. Old ways bury new thoughts. Does that not seem contrary to the natural process?"

As Roncalli considered her statement, a soccer ball rolled up to the bench by Annalisa's feet, followed by five or six neighborhood boys. They shouted for the Eminenza to throw out the ball, and she had them line up in the proper positions. She gave the ball a surprisingly strong overhead toss, and the boys kicked their way merrily down the street.

"It's a paradox, true," Roncalli said as the boys' shouts faded among the dingy, time-worn buildings. "There's little democracy in the Church — that is why democracy-prone Americans like myself are often regarded with contempt here — but the unity of faith under Church guidance has kept Christianity from fragmenting out of existence."

Annalisa nodded her head. "True, but today we have coldness and fear in the Vatican," she said. "It is a culture of closed doors. I believe it feels itself to be at odds with a more questioning, rational world, a world that seems to pick at its foundations."

"How far should we carry change?" Roncalli asked. "By tampering with our doctrines, aren't we forcing God into our own image, our concept of the moment?"

"Hah!" she chuckled. "I apologize, Pietro. I was not laughing at you, but do you really think our dogmas have any effect on God? All that changes is our view of Him. Only His view of *us* remains the same. God is what He is despite our theories."

Roncalli's brow furrowed at her last comment. This was the first time Annalisa was expressing her leanings on a broad Church matter.

"It is said God exists beyond time," she said. "No yesterday, today, or tomorrow, just now, everything is now. So why did He give us time? Why is life sequential to us?"

Roncalli chuckled. "Were physics and philosophy part of your studies too? You question in the manner of Socrates."

"Neither physics nor philosophy, Pietro, and I never read Socrates," she laughed. "But think of it. Through time, we are given the opportunity to act and then to meet with the results of our actions — our errors or successes — on another day, at another time."

"What is the purpose of such a process?" he asked.

"That's just it," she said. "It's a process, *a learning process.* We have an incredible power to create, even to create our own reality by our choices. Time gives us the ability to look backward at the results of past choices. We see how our successes or failures were created from good or bad choices, and we learn. We learn to choose responsibly for the future."

"What are you telling me, Annalisa?"

"Pietro, you have an important task, and the time to act boldly is now. See what the Church's past choices have created, and do not constantly second-guess yourself. Use your good instincts and intentions. Move forward. Now, I also have something specific I want to tell you."

Roncalli's expression was cast in uncertainty. "What's on your mind then?"

Annalisa placed her hand on his and looked him in the eyes so he would know she was lucid and certain about what she was going to say. "A dark man, a bishop, I believe, will approach the pope. I am not sure what he wants, but I caution you: beware of him. He will seek something from the Holy Father. I cannot tell you what will be offered or what will be said, but Pietro, whatever you do, do not let the pope bargain with this man. It would be the downfall of the Church."

Roncalli knew Annalisa well enough by now not to ask from where she had come by this information. The question was, could he believe it? Annalisa, if not prophetic, was exceptionally perceptive. Use your instincts; act boldly, she had told him. She saw to the core of his problem and he knew it. She had been correct about so many things, why should he not take her warning on faith?

It was an ominous end to a peaceful afternoon, but then again, peaceful moments had been few and far between for a long time now. Roncalli thought long on her words until finally, with growing resolve, he nodded his head and said, "I will stay alert. If any such moment presents itself, I will do everything I can to protect the Holy Father and the Church."

CHAPTER XLVII

. . . till one day the sun shall shine more brightly . . . shall perchance shine into our minds and hearts, and light up our whole lives with a great awakening light. — Henry David Thoreau

The Vatican City

After the meeting with Roncalli, Annalisa was walking across the Cortile di Belvedere, when a cardinal in a passing group of prelates groaned out in pain and collapsed to the ground. Annalisa rushed toward the stricken man. "Please, I may be able to help," she said. "Can someone call for medical assistance?"

Annalisa saw the fallen cardinal grimacing. His body writhed, tensed in pain and twisted like a piece of licorice. She closed her eyes then ran her hand up and down his back. After a minute, she whispered, "You have a benign growth inside near your spine, but the nerves are calming now. Try to relax," she said, and she placed her hands on him for several minutes.

The observers saw the tension drain slowly from his face, and his body ceased to quiver, finally straightening out to the point where he could stand. When the paramedics arrived, there was not much for them to do. They performed routine tests, and advised him to see his doctor.

The two cardinals accompanying him led the ailing man to a bench. His fine white hair was parted to the left under his zucchetto. He was of medium height, although he seemed shorter owing to a stoop in his posture. He wore glasses over brown eyes that gazed in wonder at the African cardinal.

"You're Cardinal Basanjo," he said in English. "We've not met. I am Cardinal Berletti."

"I am pleased to meet you, Your Eminence," Annalisa replied in Italian, pointing to the ground where he had lain, "but next time I hope for a less eventful encounter."

"Ah, you've learned Italian." The cardinal let out a hearty laugh for someone who was on his knees only a few minutes before. "Annalisa, if I may I call you by your Christian name," he said, "you mentioned a growth by my spine. How did you know that?"

Annalisa smiled, eyes skyward as if searching there for an explanation. "I saw it as a picture in my mind, and then my hands were attracted to the area with a pull . . . like a magnet."

The cardinal looked around at the other men. "I indeed have a benign growth near my spine located in such a way that they are afraid to operate. It sometimes causes paralyzing attacks, but only my doctors know about it. It cannot be felt by hand, it is too deep." He then looked at Annalisa. "I heard that you healed the pope. I did not believe it then, but I think I do now."

"No, Your Eminence," she replied. "I have never healed anyone. Only God does that."

"Yes, but He acts through human agents and even then too seldom these days," Berletti said in a sad voice. "You must have done something to be a worthy vessel of His blessings."

"Hah!" Annalisa laughed. "Few here think there is anything blessed about me."

"I am sorry for that," Berletti said. "I know you have spent much time alone in the library since you arrived. I think we have lost something from your absence."

"I study to better serve the Church, Your Eminence."

"Would you mind if I visit you some time?" Berletti asked. "I would like to talk more."

"I would welcome that, Your Eminence," she replied.

He said, "Please, call me Giacomo."

As they parted, one of the nearby cardinals said, "It seems you've made a powerful friend today. Berletti's name is often mentioned as one who could be the next pope."

"Hah! I am happy to work for one pope at a time," she said.

The cardinal gave her a skeptical look and walked away.

A few days later, Cardinal Berletti indeed made good on his desire to see Annalisa again.

"I apologize for my rudeness in not visiting you before," he said. Annalisa brushed it off with a nod of her head. His visits became a frequent occurrence. He usually came by himself, but sometimes he brought other cardinals for belated meetings with their African colleague.

Over the ensuing months, Annalisa and Berletti drew closer, talking about a great variety of subjects, particularly her view of God and her desire to be constantly in His presence.

"Why have you shut yourself away?" he asked. "Yes, we made life difficult for you, but perhaps you cloistered yourself to avoid the duties of a position you did not want?"

"I may not have wanted this, but God did, for whatever His reasons," she said. "No, my studies are my only way to understand and try to communicate in a world of older, European men who want nothing to do with me."

Berletti confessed to only now realizing how alien the Vatican must seem to her given her background, her sex, and even her age.

One day she came near him, placed a hand on his back, and asked him, "Do you want to eliminate the problem with your spine? You can, you know. You are a good man, a little set in your ways, cranky at times, no? But you do not have a bad bone in your body." She closed her eyes and was quiet for a few seconds, then she said in a soft voice as if to no one in particular, "Just a shift in your conception of God."

And Cardinal Berletti became Annalisa's first Vatican student to learn about healing. During those six months, they talked. Sometimes she would lay hands on him and tell him things. His intermittent attacks of paralysis ceased. "Your tumor no longer is present," Berletti's astounded doctors told him one day. Cardinal Berletti, perhaps the next pope, wept. He thanked God for showing Himself in so personal a way, and he embraced Annalisa.

After a moment, he pointed through the window to the dome of St. Peter's and said in a whisper, "I am a man who thought he was dwelling in God's house," then he held his hand over his heart, "but now I know God truly dwells in mine."

Annalisa smiled realizing the importance of this day; it was the turning point in her emotional isolation in the Vatican.

CHAPTER XLVIII

Forewarned is forearmed — Cervantes

The Vatican City

Seeing Bishop Alvaro waiting in the anteroom to the papal offices, Pietro Roncalli knew at once he was the man about whom Annalisa had warned him. Roncalli had never met Alvaro, but he was aware of the shadowy Milites Domini order.

Milites was more a myth than a reality to most people in the Church. Few knew anything substantial about them. They were known to be ultra-conservative. They had a number of Vatican cardinals who were admirers of their program and they had the support of the last two popes. Clement accorded them a great deal of respect, but Roncalli had the impression that Milites only revealed the tip of its iceberg to the Church.

An American bishop friend of his once told Roncalli that a high-ranking Milites official had visited his diocese in Miami. The visit was preceded by a call from a now retired Vatican cardinal. The cardinal told Roncalli's friend to provide the Milites visitor with anything he needed and *stay out of his way*. That kind of language had only confirmed to Roncalli that there was more to Milites than met the eye. And speaking of eyes, what was wrong with Alvaro's?

Alvaro had dark, curling salt-and-pepper ringlets cascading to the bottom of his neck. His skin was deep olive in color but the look around his eyes defined the dominant expression on his face. His thick, low-hung black eye-brows formed prominent ridges over deep-set orbs.

From certain angles it might appear he was eyeless, possessed of cadaverous sockets, but in direct light, Roncalli saw the man's green irises as he looked up at him. Alvaro looked altogether like one of those medieval priests who had accompanied the conquistadors to the New World. He would probably have enjoyed torturing Indians to convert them, from what Roncalli observed.

"Bishop Alvaro," Roncalli said without offering the man a hand, "I will tell the Holy Father you are here."

Alvaro nodded without so much as a word. Roncalli knew the meeting had been arranged for the pope to see Alvaro alone, so he needed to interject himself quickly. He stepped inside the papal study and closed the door. "Papa," he said, "I must talk to you on an urgent matter."

"Yes, Pietro, but I have an appointment now."

"I know, Papa, with Bishop Alvaro. He's waiting outside. It's about him I must speak to you."

Clement looked puzzled, but he motioned for Roncalli to sit in the chair next to him. "Very well, Pietro, what is troubling you?"

"Papa," Roncalli replied, "I will be direct. I believe Alvaro has come to seduce you with an offer, a very appealing offer. He will want something in return. Do not bargain with him. If you do, it will be a calamity for the Church."

Clement studied Roncalli's face. *Probably to see if I'm sane*, Roncalli thought.

"How do you know this, Pietro?"

Roncalli spat it out: "Annalisa. Annalisa had a premonition, and I trust her."

Clement leaned back on his chair with a deep sigh.

"All I ask, Papa, is that you make no commitment to Alvaro before discussing this with me," Roncalli said. "If he makes you an offer like I described, Annalisa would be correct."

Clement nodded his head. "After what happened in Lagos, I cannot discount anything Annalisa says. Very well, no matter what Alvaro tells me, you and I will discuss it."

Roncalli exhaled in relief. He went outside, ushered Alvaro back in, and closed the door so the pope and the bishop were alone. Two hours later, the door opened and Alvaro walked out by himself. For a split second, he sized up Roncalli with a neutral expression, then continued to the door and left without a word.

Roncalli knocked, then entered the papal study.

"It was just as you said," Clement said, his hands shaking. Roncalli sat next to him, and Clement told him of the meeting. "Being a non-secular order with many businessmen in their ranks, Milites is quite wealthy. Alvaro has offered to replace most of the money the Church lost in the debacle."

Roncalli raised an eyebrow. That was a tempting offer indeed. Missionary work had all but halted, and a number of dioceses around the world had declared bankruptcy. The individual dioceses were struggling on their own because the remaining money was being used to support the Vatican City environs. Some were even talking about auctioning off Vatican art treasures to raise funds.

"What did he want in return, Papa?"

Clement exhaled deeply. "The right to select thirty cardinal electors."

Roncalli gasped. "Papa, he wants to elect the next pope!"

Clement nodded. "Yes. Still, is it too high a price to pay to keep the Church operating?"

For three hours, Roncalli gave an impassioned plea. "Papa, don't usher corruption back into the Church. Let any one man become pope-maker and we return to the days when despotic emperors controlled us," Roncalli declared. "We cannot let the papacy be bought. If we drive out the Holy Spirit, there is no Church to save. In our final days, Papa, could we face our Maker if we allowed this to happen?"

Clement listened, face cupped in his hands. He swayed in his seat, waging his own inner spiritual battle, surveying the paths before him. Minutes later, he gave Roncalli his decision.

Two days after Alvaro departed Rome, a papal legate delivered a sealed message to him in Toledo. It read: **We decline your offer as not being in the best interests of the Holy See.**

Alvaro crumpled the note and called Van Kluysen. "Clement has refused us," he said. "Prepare yourself to approach Mannheim."

CHAPTER XLIX

Silent, nameless men with unadorned hearts. —Don Dellilo

The Vatican City

Alvaro said what?" Mannheim asked Van Kluysen. The pastel shades of Mannheim's gray-blond hair and pale skin faded against the icy blue eyes that now lit up with cold fire.

"Milites Domini are the only ones who can bail us out," Van Kluysen declared. "The only ones who have the means, the common goals, and the shared interests we have. They are offering to restore to us a good portion of what we lost."

"Restore?" Mannheim said. It sounded as much an accusation as a question.

"Yes. And they are not talking about a loan," Van Kluysen said.

"But they are talking about a *price*," Mannheim said. "What is it?"

Van Kluysen responded without hesitation. "They want, among other things, the right to select the next thirty cardinal-electors."

Mannheim stood, balled his fists on his desk, and leaned forward at a forty-five degree angle. "They dare make me this proposal? You dare *bring* this proposal to me?"

He walked around his desk to stand over Van Kluysen, and he stood in such a way that the seated Belgian had to rotate rather uncomfortably while looking up at him. "In the nineteen-eighties, during the first financial crisis," Mannheim said, "Milites Domini brought in money and bought themselves a personal prelature. Now the Milites bishop answers only to the pope. This time they want to buy the papacy and the entire Church!"

"Heinrich, they are just asking for the right to select some cardinals," said Van Kluysen.

"My God, man, I thought you were intelligent," Mannheim said. "They already have the affinities of fifteen to twenty cardinal-electors. Add thirty more directly loyal to them and they form a voting block that can control election of the next pope."

"But Heinrich, once a pope is elected he is beholden to no one. Any promises made during election become null and void," Van Kluysen said.

Mannheim grunted. "You fool," he snapped. "Don't be naïve. If one of their new cardinals is elected, you can be sure he will be totally indoctrinated by them."

"One of their newly-appointed cardinals being elected is unlikely," Van Kluysen replied.

"True," Mannheim said. "So that means they will want to have strings over the rest of us. What are the conditions of this 'donation?' Do we get the money in one lump sum?"

"Well, no, of course not. They will put it in incrementally."

"Yes, to keep their leverage on us." Mannheim snapped. "And tell me, what if we do not agree to let them select the cardinals?"

Van Kluysen's gaze immediately sunk to floor level. "They will not give us the money," he replied. "But, Heinrich, think for a minute. Milites shares our outlook. They are helping us bog down Clement's council. We all know you will be a contender at the next election, so what if their voting block were used to support you?"

Mannheim bristled, stood erect, and said, "If I will be pope it will be because of who I am. I will not sell my papacy to Milites Domini and become their dog on a leash. You tell that son of a Spanish whore Delgado that if he has the best interests of the Church in mind he will float us a long-term, low-interest loan with no conditions. Interest I will pay them, homage I will not." Mannheim stopped yelling for a minute and considered Van Kluysen with laser-blue eyes. "Tell me, where did Milites get that kind of money?"

The question took Van Kluysen by surprise. "Ah . . . well, you know, they don't have the restrictions of the religious orders. Over the years, their highly placed lay associates made them a fortune in investments and donations."

"Indeed," Mannheim said with a caustic bite. "Maybe *we* should have hired *their* advisors. But I'm doing arithmetic in my mind. Milites would not bankrupt themselves to control the papacy. If they gave us a billion, they would have to have a significant sum left in their till. I don't think even their shady deals netted them that kind of money."

Van Kluysen's eyes drifted southward to the floor again. His skin flushed and he broke out in a sudden sweat. "What are you getting at?" he asked.

That Flemish son-of-a-bitch, Mannheim thought. Somehow, Milites Domini had swindled the Church and was now trying to buy the weakened papacy! He could smell the whole sordid plot. With Van Kluysen's legendary greed, he knew the Belgian had to be in on it, but it might be better to keep that to himself for the time being. Then again, maybe not.

Mannheim thought carefully about his next move. For over two years, the

Vatican had been able to conceal the true extent of its losses because it was not required to make public disclosures of its finances. Also, the convoluted web of entities through which the lost investments had flowed obscured the Church's involvement.

If he ousted Van Kluysen, or went public with his suspicions about Milites, it would bounce back on him and taint his bid for the papacy because Van Kluysen was known to be his man. Mannheim himself might even come under suspicion if he did not handle this right. Besides, he had no solid evidence, not just yet.

"Come back tomorrow," Mannheim said to the Belgian. "I'll have an answer for Milites by then."

At 11:00 a.m. the next morning, an ashen-faced Van Kluysen read the paper Mannheim handed him. "Wh-what in God's name are you saying here?" he asked in a tremulous voice.

"I'm saying in *my* name that you colluded with Milites Domini to defraud the Church of a billion dollars," Mannheim snarled.

"This is preposterous," Van Kluysen protested. "I never—"

The palm of Mannheim's hand cut through the air and ended Van Kluysen's reply. "Save that bullshit for an idiot like Clement. If this letter goes public, you have two fates in store: jail for your crime or death because you're a key witness against Alvaro." Mannheim knew the Belgian was easily intimidated, and this was his ploy to get a confession.

One mental flash of Alvaro's sinister eyes was all it took for Van Kluysen. "Oh, dear God," he whined. "I feared this. You're right, you're right, Alvaro will kill me."

"No, he won't," Mannheim said, "not if you do what I tell you. This letter is an insurance policy for both of us. If either of us should have a heart attack or a car accident, I've made arrangements for this letter to be made public. Of course, you will add your confession to it. That way Alvaro will truly get the point of his dilemma."

For the next hour, Mannheim instructed Van Kluysen how they would proceed with Alvaro. Van Kluysen groaned. "I can't call him and say that, I just can't," he said.

"Stop whining," Mannheim snapped. "You had enough balls to steal the Church blind; show some guts now. I'll handle Alvaro, if he tries to create a problem, if he tries to undermine me, he will find himself with more than a disenfranchised order. Now do it!"

An unconvinced Van Kluysen placed the call under Mannheim's scrutiny. Alvaro was waiting for a report on the meeting. Van Kluysen fought to keep his panic under control. It took an eternity for his trembling finger to punch out each number on the keypad. Alvaro answered after two rings. Van Kluysen tried to keep a firm voice as he related Mannheim's response. The Spanish bishop's reaction was not at all what Van Kluysen expected. There was a long silence on the phone. When he finally spoke, the controlled anger and venom in his voice was more disturbing than if he had screamed at the top of his lungs.

Alvaro said, "Tell Mannheim this much and no more: if he exposes us, we'll say he was in on it. Things are in motion. Buy time and we'll see how this all plays out." *Click.*

Things were in motion? Van Kluysen had no idea what Alvaro meant, and he did not want to know. He related Alvaro's threat to a sullen Mannheim then left his office. He went home, took a sedative, and went to bed. He did not pray before he retired; he had not prayed for some time. After all, would God really want to hear from *him*?

CHAPTER L

"There is one who will cross this bridge I will make,
a leader, that much I saw, but like Moses was unable to enter
the Promised Land, I will not be there at the crossing."
—The vision of Pope Clement XV

The Vatican City

Clement's Ecumenical Council finally got underway in the spring of 2028. It had been over three years since he had announced his intention to bring all of the world's prelates together to decide the course of the Church for the twenty-first century. The conservative bloc of the curia bureaucracy, traditionalist bishops, and Milites Domini had been effective in obstructing the process. Only Roncalli bringing the bishops to Rome ended their efforts.

The bishops' synods had been a preliminary skirmish, but the Ecumenical Council was the real battleground for reform in the face of fierce opposition. Although progressives outnumbered the conservatives in the synods, there was a problem for the reformers at the full Ecumenical Council. The conservative bishops had united with their counterparts among the College of Cardinals and traditionalist elements from the religious orders.

The reformers had their platform on the table, but the conservatives were on the home turf of the curia. They were effectively blocking adoption of new policies on birth control, female ordination, and other issues. Bitterness among the factions threatened to boil over.

Clement, inexplicably, continued to remain neutral. When Roncalli urged the pope to break the logjam and move the reform agenda forward, Clement said it was not the head but the body of Christ that should make the decisions this time. Roncalli knew as long as the pope clung to this attitude, anti-ecumenical forces would greatly dilute, or possibly even discard, any reforms.

Annalisa was more of a listener than an active participant in the various debates, but she was noticed by the numerous prelates trying to size her up. After all, they were naturally curious to understand the views of the only female in their ranks. The fact that she could speak in five of the language groups, including Latin, elevated her stature. If she did speak on a subject, it was always in the form of questions that elucidated facts and promoted clarity in the discussions.

"Do you believe that birth control is related to the overpopulation problem?" "Did the early Christian Church employ women as deaconesses?" "Are you sure canon law really says that?"

Such were the humble questions she asked, but over time and by osmosis, many began to realize that her command of Church history and theology was substantial. In addition, stories of her healings, never made public before, had been filtering through the Church grapevine. All this made for a mystique developing around her; she did not have to say much to make an impression on people, the impression was made just by her presence.

The months passed on. It was Wednesday afternoon on a late summer day, and the sky was graying. A hint of coolness was in the air, a harbinger that perhaps the fall would come sooner this year. Cardinal Roncalli knocked on the door of the pope's room. The pontiff had retired for a brief nap at two-thirty, but Clement was now forty minutes late for the mass the two men were to celebrate in the private chapel of the papal apartments.

Sister Florenza, the pope's housekeeper, had not known about the mass and she told Roncalli the pope must still have been sleeping as he had not yet come out of his room. Roncalli knocked on the thick door to the bedroom. No answer. After several more knocks, he tried the door, which opened without difficulty.

"Your Holiness?" he called out softly.

No answer. He walked farther into the room so he could see the pope's bed. The pope was still sleeping. Roncalli almost hesitated to wake Clement, but the pope had a meeting with some Anglican bishops in less than thirty minutes. He went to the pope's bedside and called out his name. The pope did not move, so Roncalli gently shook the covers to wake him. Still, the pope showed no sign of stirring.

The gentle nudges became firmer with anxiety. Roncalli then took the pope's wrist between his fingers and inclined his head to the pontiff's chest. In a loud but even voice he called out, "Sister Florenza, get Dr. Solari and Cardinal Torante immediately."

Less than one hour later, Dr. Solari backed away from the bed and removed the stethoscope from his ears. He turned to Cardinal Roncalli and shook his head with lips solemnly pursed. Calls were then made to Cardinal Mannheim; Cardinal Forletti, the dean of the College of Cardinals; and Roald Zugli. Archbishops Longo and Stasena, the vicars general of the diocese of Rome and the Vatican City, were pulled from meetings. Also summoned were Archbishop Giotto Riccio, the powerful *sostituto*, or head of the first section of the Secretariat of State; the prefect of the papal household, Bishop Turlogh Murray; and Filotemo Saure, the major penitentiary.

When all the men had assembled at the quiet bedside, Cardinal Torante, the camerlengo, or chamberlain of the Church, pulled the sheet down from over the pope's face.

"Achille Della Campania?" Three times he called out the pope's baptismal name, then he tapped the pontiff's forehead with a silver mallet. Upon receiving no response, he turned to the other men in the room and said, "The pope is truly dead."

The men nodded their heads. Torante then took the Piscatore, the Ring of the Fisherman, off the pope's finger, and using a key, he exerted force against it until the gold rim bearing the pope's name broke off. He held it up to the others to examine, and with the destruction of the ring, the procedure was complete. Thus, the Church officially acknowledged the death of Clement, fifteenth in the two-thousand-year-old line of popes to bear that name. Dr. Solari claimed the apparent cause of death was a massive heart attack.

"God rest his soul," and that solitary expression of impassioned loss was from the mouth of Cardinal Roncalli, who stood alone, facing the others gathered on the opposite side of the room.

BOOK THREE

The Blood of Fallen Angels

CHAPTER LI

Reason is our soul's left hand, faith her right.
—John Donne

The Vatican City

Bleak and somber days preceded Pope Clement's funeral in the Vatican. The cause of death was listed as myocardial infarction—a heart attack—and some noted that the burial had been a peculiarly hasty affair. Annalisa said a prayer for Clement as she sat, head in hands, in a room of the library. She then picked up a book to read, and the tarot card she used as a bookmark fluttered to the floor just as Monsignor O'Keefe walked in.

The Irishman bent down to retrieve the card for her. "What have we got here?" he asked. Seeing the image on the card, he froze. "*La Papesse*, the female pope," he said, translating the title after a moment of speechlessness.

The card depicted a blue-robed woman wearing a jeweled crown. The crown, vestments, and title of the card indicated a female pope, but underneath her crown, the woman's hair was hidden beneath a nun's wimple. "I recognize this," he said to her. "This is a card from the old Marseille Tarot. How did you come by it?"

"When I first moved to Rome," Annalisa told him, "the first day I arrived actually, I met a poor woman in the Trastevere. She gave it to me."

"Why?" he asked her.

"I am not really sure," Annalisa replied. "I gave her money. She seemed destitute. She had me pick a card from the deck. She wanted me to keep it. She said things to me in Italian, but I did not speak the language then. Is there something about the card?"

"I know something of the tarot," O'Keefe said. "This card is a symbol for female spirituality, the lost Goddess. It's one of the more peculiar cards of the old-style decks. The newer versions call this card the High Priestess and her manner of dress is very different."

"Peculiar, you say? Why is this card peculiar?" Annalisa asked him.

O'Keefe studied the card. "Most tarot cards correspond to actual historical figures such as emperors, empresses, knights, or popes, and there never was a female pope, you see?"

"Perhaps medievals had no other way to represent female spiritually,"

Annalisa said.

O'Keefe's mouth puckered into a small circle. "Oh, but they did. Many ways, in fact. A Madonna-like figure was the classical symbol during that period. There was the legend of a female pope, Pope Joan, but that was likely a fabrication by a medieval monk. I also recall that a Sister Manfreda was elected pope by a sect of Lombards called the Gugliemites back in the 1200s, but that was an obscure event and had no status in the Church. No, these cards predate those events. This card always raised questions—why was a female depicted as pope and why does she wear a nun's whimple under her miter?"

"What do you think?" Annalisa asked with a curious half-smile.

"I always felt the tarot's symbology was concealing something," O'Keefe said. "So, one day I used my resources here at the library, my access to restricted materials."

"What did you find?"

O'Keefe's eyes glanced sideward. "Things that the Church would not like," he replied.

"Are you able to tell me?" Annalisa asked.

"You know," O'Keefe said, "there was a time when we would have been burnt as heretics for discussing these subjects."

"Heretics," she repeated. "You mean the Inquisition. Oh, we are probably safe now."

He rubbed his chin and said, "Don't be so sure about that. Tormada probably keeps some stakes and a can of lighter fluid in his closet just for special occasions. Yes, I believe the cards represent a secret, heretical Gnostic Church that once existed in southern France," O'Keefe said. "Different sects, collectively called Albigensians, took root in the area of Provence. These people practiced a simpler, some might say purer, form of Christianity. Their Church was called the Church of *Amor,* which is to say 'Love,' and that is *Roma* spelled backward, you see? They stood in opposition to the practices of the Church of Rome, which they thought to be in error and corrupt."

"What were their beliefs and practices?" Annalisa asked.

"They taught that each person had Christ potential to become godlike by the action of the Holy Spirit working through their minds and hearts," O'Keefe said. "They thought Jesus was fully human and divine, the highest expression of God's light on earth. They believed he taught inner mysteries meant to unlock the divinity within each human being so that they too could become vessels for the outpouring of divine light. This was not unique: it was a mystical wisdom taught in all lands, in all ages, by different revealers of the Word."

O'Keefe noticed the goose bumps rising on Annalisa's arm. "It is rumored that women headed this Church from time to time as well as men," he said.

"Female popes," she interjected.

"Exactly," O'Keefe said. "They also roamed the countryside and practiced healing"—he was not unaware of the irony of telling this to her, of all people—"but the most astonishing thing is how they came by these ideas."

Annalisa leaned forward, hanging on his every word.

"It is said that none other than Mary Magdalene came to southern Gaul, modern France today, along with a young woman believed to be her daughter, the child of Jesus."

Annalisa seemed to go rigid. *"No child,"* she said under her breath.

"What?" O'Keefe asked her.

"I . . . well, that Jesus had a child sounds strange," Annalisa explained.

"Anyway," O'Keefe said, "some believe the heretical Church exists even today, hidden and waiting for—"

Just then, Roncalli burst into the room with a violent thrust on the door. He had dark circles under his eyes, and his face looked drawn and pasty, as if he had been losing weight. O'Keefe knew he was exhausted from battling the conservatives in the Ecumenical Council. Now, with Clement's passing, it seemed the rug had been cruelly pulled out from under him. Clement had not exerted his authority in the reform battle he had initiated, but his presence had been a constant check in the minds of Church conservatives. With Clement gone, they could now question the papal intention behind every issue.

"The American bishops have a secret plan to break from Rome," he declared.

Now O'Keefe's face paled. "My God! A schism? Is that possible? Don't they realize what that would do to the Church in these precarious times?"

"I know Desmond, I know, but the Neanderthals in the curia have totally frustrated the progressive bishops. The Americans know the College of Cardinals will certainly elect a conservative pope." Roncalli ran his fingers through his wavy hair, which had gone considerably grayer in the past three years. "How much longer can they have intolerable doctrines and practices shoved down their throats? We've lost our last chance at reforming the Church."

"Surely there must be room for compromise somewhere?" O'Keefe asked.

Roncalli shook his head. "With Milites Domini pushing the traditionalists, they seem as if they would be content with a smaller, pared-down Church that maintains their vision of doctrinal purity."

"Yes," O'Keefe said. "Preparing for Armageddon, they are."

"I cannot understand Clement," Roncalli suddenly blurted out as if talking to himself. The sudden shift in topics left Annalisa and O'Keefe momentarily confused. "He gave birth to a magnificent idea and then abandoned it right from the beginning, when it needed to be nurtured. He left it for the vultures to pick. Why? I don't understand. Why?"

"Pietro, please sit so we can talk," Annalisa said, gesturing to a chair.

When Roncalli sat, she reached across the table and put her hand over his. O'Keefe looked at her face as she attempted to comfort her friend. She was now in her midforties but still looked as young and lovely as the day she had arrived on the plane from Africa. She was demure, even deferential, yet, almost imperceptibly, even hardened veterans of Vatican politics were quietly coming to respect her.

"Pietro," she said, "you know Clement was inspired. God inspired him with a particular vision, a particular role to play, and that changed everything. Clement sensed the boundaries God set for him in that role, and I believe Clement acted within those boundaries. "

"I don't follow you, Annalisa," he said in a fatigued voice.

Her hands, warm to the touch, remained on his. "I mean that Clement saw himself as the builder of the arena," she said, "but not the emperor who would control the outcome of the games. He wanted to leave the outcome to the combatants, and perhaps that was wise. Anything worth struggling for has more meaning to us. If he had intervened and made decrees, how lasting would the reforms be in the hearts of the participants? People resist things that are forced on them."

"But that is what popes do. They make decisions and enforce their views," Roncalli said.

"Yet those things Clement set in motion, Pietro, they may not all have been his views."

"He told you that?" Roncalli asked, snapping into alertness. "He told you he did not believe in those things he set in motion?"

Annalisa shook her head and said, "Clement was never explicit, but I believe he saw his role restricted to setting the wheels of the Church in motion to make up its own mind."

"Perhaps you are correct," Roncalli said, rapping his knuckles against the table. "It is always a battle. I shouldn't complain, and I am prepared to carry on, but the next pope most certainly will be a conservative. Be sure *he* will not be hesitant to enforce *his* will, and then"— a bitter look appeared on Roncalli's face—"then I fear our efforts will turn into one great public announcement that we do not care enough to change."

"When things look their worst, good people must exert their faith, Pietro. God always shows us a way, we just have to find the open door."

Roncalli said, "Then I pray that when we enter the conclave, the doors of the Sistine Chapel are open wide."

CHAPTER LII

What happened in the past is lived again in memory.
—John Dewey

Rome

It was a lucid dream where one is aware of the dreaming, as if one's consciousness were both the actor and the camera recording the events. . . .

They were in a room with a dirt floor. Teresa heard a beautiful woman with reddish-gold hair speak. "You have missed the real meaning of the Master's teachings, Peter."

Teresa knew herself to be sitting in a group of nineteen people, twelve men and seven women. The surrounding walls were made of crude clay and straw. They wore robes of rough wool. Teresa viewed the scene through the eyes of a dark-skinned young woman in the group. She even had a name—Tezrah.

"We know the Master has confided in you, Mary," one of the men said to the red-headed woman. "Tell us how our brother Peter is in error."

Mary had a gentle smile and seemed to speak with calculated deference so as not to offend the men. "The Master has stressed two things above all to apprehend God and the Kingdom of Heaven: to love and to seek answers within ourselves. Brother Peter, you would organize communities ruled by councils and bishops. You would teach them the parables and rituals mimicking the Master's life, but these are external things.

"Soon, you will need—you will become—a priesthood interpreting these things. You will replace the Sanhedrin and the Romans with a new authority, a new hierarchy. We will fall into the trap of the oppressors."

"How dare you compare the Jewish priesthood with the Romans!" Peter shouted.

"How so?" Mary replied. "In both of them there is neither love nor insight as the Master teaches. Love opposes their need to control. Intuition runs counter to the logic by which they justify their rule over people's minds and bodies. Gnosis, insight into the nature of God, shows the unity of all things. Slavery, war, the oppression of women and the weak—these things could not stand in the face of that reality."

"What would you have us do then?" Peter asked with undisguised contempt.

"Stop despising women for one thing," Mary said. "The Master wants us to integrate our male and female natures. Only then can we become whole spiritual beings. We must help people see this in their own souls, but as guides or helpers, not as priests or lawgivers."

"This is too difficult for the masses to comprehend," Peter said. "Without a visible church, without leadership and a unified creed, these ideas shall wither under opposition."

"The Way is not meant to create a new religion, but to awaken spiritual beings lost in forgetfulness," Mary said. "We all reach the same door by different paths, and the world is transformed one soul at a time. Your way will demand one path, if not now then soon to come. This will lead us back in a circle of ignorance to where we sit today."

"All these qualities you speak of are womanly in nature," Peter said. "How do you expect these ideas to stand in the face of Rome and the Sanhedrin?"

Mary replied, "The Master trusts in the power of the feminine, why can you not? Once Sophia and Logos, Wisdom and Reason, reigned together, but masculine ways have usurped rule of this world. Masculine logic explains only the visible phenomena of the world; feminine wisdom is an intuitive vision of the real nature of things. Only through wisdom do we experience gnosis, experience the True God. You must intuit awareness of the True Father-Mother God so you must bring the feminine back into your soul."

Peter grew stubborn. "Do you seek to confound us with these strange ideas? This god you speak of is not Yahweh, the God of our fathers. Your blasphemy will lead us to ruin . . . "

At that point Teresa awoke, or left the scene might be more accurate, it was so vivid. She found her Vox-Corder and dictated the experience while it was still fresh. This was no idle dream. It was saying something, and maybe Monsignor O'Keefe could help decipher it.

The Vatican City

"I found more symbols, Desmond, only this time in my own room!" Cardinal Roncalli exclaimed to Desmond O'Keefe. "I'm coming to see you. Call Avernis and ask him to be there, but only him. I want no one to know of this before the conclave, not even Zugli."

"Peter," O'Keefe replied, "the young woman who has been deciphering the symbols just walked into my office right now. I believe you've met. Her name is Teresa Ferentinos."

"Ferentinos, the reporter I met in Nigeria? Desmond, what on earth are you thinking?"

"Teresa is a personal friend, Pietro, and a highly accredited religious scholar. You know I'm short on staff. She has maintained every confidence to date and done a fine job."

Roncalli was momentarily silent. "Very well, I'll be right down."

When Roncalli arrived, Avernis was already present.

"Your Eminence," Teresa and Avernis said, simultaneously standing up to greet him.

"Please, be seated," he said. "I want everything said in this room to stay here until I authorize the release of this information, is that understood?" Everyone nodded. "Good. Now if we can't find who is doing this, at least we have to try and understand their message. Perhaps that will lead us to the perpetrator. Please look at these." Roncalli pulled the objects out of a box.

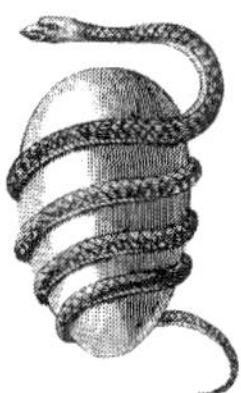

"Unbelievable!" Teresa said. "I recognize both these symbols, and I'm inclined to interpret them here and now because of a dream I had last night. I just told the monsignor about it."

Roncalli and Avernis looked puzzled.

"You should hear this," O'Keefe said. "Play it for them, Teresa."

Teresa turned on her Vox-Corder, and for thirty minutes they listened to her vivid recount of her dream. Roncalli looked alternately shocked and absorbed in what he was hearing. "These symbols have meaning to me in light of my dream," Teresa said as she turned off the recorder. "It's almost as if I had the dream just to interpret them. Sounds crazy, no?"

O'Keefe said, "Karl Jung coined a word to describe how external events and internal thoughts coincide in order to address issues or problems held in our minds."

"Yes, it's called synchronicity," Teresa said. "Anyway, I believe I was present at a discussion between Jesus' disciples in my dream. In fact, *I felt I was one of them* along with six other females. The dialogue was mainly between Saint Peter and a woman. I believe the woman was Mary Magdalene. The argument was spiritual in nature.

"Mary said Jesus taught people to develop insight into their souls to gain wisdom about the cosmos and experience of God. Peter felt this was too difficult for the masses. Mary argued that Peter would merely replace Jewish rituals and priestly hierarchies with Christian ones. His way would perpetuate ignorance by having people look outside themselves for answers."

Roncalli's face was flushed. "Are you all right?" O'Keefe asked.

"Yes, thank you. Must be an allergic reaction to something." Roncalli took a tissue from a dispenser on O'Keefe's desk and wiped the perspiration off his brow. "Please, Teresa, tell us how this relates to the symbols."

"Again, these are gnostically themed symbols," Teresa said, "and again, they may be considered pagan or evil, but we always need to be mindful of their original meanings."

"Give us dual interpretations then," Avernis suggested. Roncalli and O'Keefe agreed.

"All right then," Teresa said. "The figure on the left is the dragon, or worm, Ouroboros. Dragons and serpents, called worms by the ancients, were often related in symbology. You see how it's devouring its own tail. It could mean that listening to the voice of evil leads to our own downfall or destruction, like Eve in the Garden."

"Looking at the symbol, that makes sense," Avernis said.

"Not to a Gnostic," Teresa replied. "To them the serpent was a symbol of wisdom, not evil. They taught that the jealous, vengeful Creator God of the Old Testament was a false god. He was not the True God of love Jesus revealed. A good and true God could not create this imperfect world."

"What?" Avernis exclaimed. "Early Christians believed that stuff?"

"Gnostic Christians *and* Gnostic Jews," Teresa replied. "We would never have known if not for the lost texts accidentally recovered in 1945 at Nag Hammadi in Egypt. The material was so complex that even today only a few scholars know the whole story of it. To Gnostics, the serpent in the Garden was the True God's liberating force of awakened enlightenment. It opened our eyes to the hidden knowledge that a false god keeps us imprisoned in a world of evil. To Gnostics, Ouroboros would mean that *failure* to listen to inner wisdom would perpetuate a vicious circle of spiritual darkness, just as Mary described in my dream. The false god is an analog to our egos that keep us lost in illusion. The True God is our higher self, the connection with the divine that transcends ego."

"Hmm, deep thinkers, weren't they?" Roncalli remarked. "What about the other symbol?"

"It's called the Orphic Egg," Teresa said. "Gnostics believed that heavenly beings emanated or projected successive copies of themselves. A lower emanation of the Holy Spirit called Sophia, or Wisdom, made an error which birthed the false Creator God of the material world. Her burden thereafter was to make things right. The egg is a universal symbol of the creation. Where the Church's interpretation of the Orphic Egg would be the evil serpent engulfing or strangling the world, the Gnostic view would see the serpent as Wisdom rising to enfold, enlighten, and correct the imperfect creation."

"In your dream Mary says that feminine intuition and masculine reason once ruled together," O'Keefe observed. "Many believe the root psychological sickness of this world lies in our fragmented nature. The enlightenment of Wisdom you mention is evident in Mary saying that we have to reintegrate the qualities of male and female to become whole, enlightened beings and experience God. Very interesting dream."

"So, are we dealing with heretics, feminists, psychologists, or prophets?" Avernis asked.

"Maybe all of the above," O'Keefe said.

"I read Teresa's reports on the previous symbols," Roncalli said. "Adding it all up, here's what seems to be the dire message: a primordial power of evil is incarnating and on the move. It may take any form, male or female. Its intent is to engulf the world in evil. The more benign interpretation is that a forgotten power, feminine in nature, is issuing from God to lead the world to some new understanding, some unknown direction. The first version is blasphemous, the second heretical in the eyes of the Church."

"The third possibility is that some lunatic is trying to rattle your cage," Avernis said.

Roncalli sighed. "Teresa, Robert, thank you for your help, and especially you, Teresa, for using discretion. I'm sure this would have made a good story for your TV network. If you don't mind, I need to speak with the monsignor alone now."

When Teresa and Avernis left the office, Roncalli said to O'Keefe, "No symbols for months, now this on the eve of the conclave. Why now? Mannheim and the others are whispering about Annalisa. Since she's been here the Church divisions have deepened, we're tottering on financial ruin, and these symbols started appearing the same time she arrived."

"The issue is the prophecies, true?" O'Keefe said.

"Desmond, did I bring the Great Deceiver into the Church? I know she has helped me; she seems kind and good and she heals people. Can that be evil? But the reforms I'm pushing—will they unravel the Church? Am I a pawn as they are saying? The Church might rip apart now in the wake of Clement's death."

"That could happen without Annalisa," O'Keefe said. "Forget the prophecies for a minute. Her enemies want her out. One day you'll have to back her to a greater degree than anything you've done. You see it coming. You need to believe in her or not. You'll have to choose. Perhaps there is a message in Teresa's dream. Don't rely on people or prophecies or anything external to yourself. You're a good man. Use your own instincts."

Roncalli nodded. "Teresa's story affected me deeply. I felt almost ashamed, like I was Peter in her dream and my obstinacy was suppressing something beautiful."

"They didn't call Peter the Rock for nothing," O'Keefe said, "but I believe that given the right circumstances, even that stubborn old man would see the light and do the right thing."

"Whoever is behind these symbols," Roncalli said, "I'd like to know what they know that we don't."

"We'll find out one day," O'Keefe said, "and I'm sure it will surprise the hell out of us."

"Is it my imagination or are you avoiding me?" Robert Avernis asked Teresa after they exited Monsignor O'Keefe's office.

Teresa looked down at her feet thinking what to say. "What do you do here?" she asked.

Avernis wrinkled his forehead. "You know I work for Vatican Security."

"But Americans never work on Vatican Security. You're the first," she said.

"So what?" he shot back.

"Does your job entail leaving me in the middle of dinner to meet an attractive woman in the Via Del Boschetto? And who were the men in the car you met before seeing her?"

Avernis' mouth hung open before his words came out. "*You followed me?* Why?"

"Reporter's intuition," she said. "Since Nigeria I had the feeling you've been concealing things. We were starting something that night, and the way you left so abruptly . . . I wanted to understand, and I didn't feel you were being upfront with me. You're either some kind of spy or a womanizer who goes to extreme lengths. Want to tell me about it?"

Avernis was shocked, but then he had just seen her almost psychic intuition at play in O'Keefe's office. "I can't answer those questions," he replied, trying to sound indignant.

"Really?" she said in a tone calculated to underscore the awkwardness of his response. "Well, you know where I live. Call me when you feel like talking." She turned and walked away, leaving him feeling small enough to crawl through a keyhole . . . and she knew it.

CHAPTER LIII

Nearly all evils in the Church have arisen from Bishops desiring power *more than* light. *They want authority, not outlook.* —*John Ruskin*

The Vatican City

Cardinal Mannheim had turned his office into the equivalent of a campaign headquarters. Cardinals were not supposed to solicit votes for themselves or anyone else; such activity was forbidden during a *sede vacante,* the time between the death of a pope and a new electoral conclave. "But," Mannheim said, "I *must* win this election. We've set too many things in motion, and we must rid the Church of the nun. That's the first action I will take as pope."

"Yet Berletti is your immediate problem," Cardinal DeGolia said. He was a gifted speaker but also a slow-moving, phlegmatic man. People were usually disarmed when talking to the prelate whose comically blasé attitude was legendary in the Vatican. This quality made him the ideal person to gather information on potential candidates for the papal election conclave to be held in a few days.

"Do you have anything to tell us, Aldo, or would you prefer we get you a file to do your nails?" said Henri Villendot.

The other men snickered at the jibe highlighting DeGolia's lackadaisical attention. As usual, DeGolia took the comment stoically, showing no sign of offense. "Ah, thank you, Henri, but I have already bitten them to the quick," he said. "Now, to matters. Heinrich, do you remember how a reporter once asked Pope John how many people work in the Vatican and he replied, 'about half'?"

Mannheim nodded. "A clever joke, but not a bad assessment, yes."

"Well, therein lies part of your problem," DeGolia said.

"How is that?" Mannheim asked.

DeGolia smiled as he delivered his next statement. "My dear Heinrich, it's either your blessing or misfortune, as it were, to be born a German with all the methodical efficiencies that come along with that birthright."

"Damn it, get to the point, Aldo," Tormada interrupted. "What the hell are you saying?"

DeGolia paused for a few seconds before resuming, if for no other reason than to annoy Tormada even further. "Most of the cardinals admire the job you have done as secretary of state, and they respect your credentials — "

Mannheim himself now interrupted DeGolia. "But what?" he said.

"But many fear your style may be too driving and dictatorial as pope," DeGolia finally responded. "They all remember Pius and how insufferable life was during his reign."

DeGolia's reference to Pius XIII, the pope before Clement, could be taken as either flattering or unflattering depending on one's point of view. The staunchest of traditionalists, there had been no ambiguity surrounding his reign like that of Clement's, but he was so demanding and inflexible that he was nicknamed "Il Duce," a reference to Mussolini, by the Italian cardinals.

"Things are close, Heinrich, but Berletti has the edge," DeGolia said. "I did hear Sosa's name mentioned as a possible compromise if you and Berletti are deadlocked."

"What of the Milites Domini cardinals?" Tormada asked.

"You mean Toladana, Alfieri, and that crowd?" DeGolia said. "I cannot say at this point."

"Alvaro's been avoiding me," Mannheim said, looking crossways at Van Kluysen. "We cannot count on Milites Domini." Clement's death had allowed no time to play out the duel with Alvaro. It was a standoff until after the conclave. Mannheim's threat would prevent Milites from using the stolen money for the election, but if Mannheim were elected, he would gain greater leverage on them.

Mannheim sat behind his big ornate desk in the high-backed chair and began directing the other cardinals to action. "Henri, call Berlinguerre, he owes me, and tell him to put pressure on Despine and Gonçalves. Giacomo, get a hold of your friend Parellos. As metropolitan of Antioch he has the respect of the eastern cardinals. Aldo, we know Park from Korea wants to be prefect for the Far Eastern Churches. Tell him he has the job if he can deliver any votes."

And so it went as Mannheim broke every pre-election protocol, but they all knew what was at stake — not just their jobs but the Church and the civilization it supported, for they had no doubt their vision was the true road to salvation.

LoPresti then brought up the subject of the Cardinal Apprentice again. "We can't be rid of her soon enough. She's seduced Berletti just as she did Clement and Roncalli. And what if Berletti becomes pope? Can't we use the information we have to be rid of her now? Nothing else has worked, even those thugs that Silvestro's contacts provided."

Tripalini had contacted some shady characters he had known from his hometown in Milan, but something had gone terribly wrong. The two thugs they sent were supposed to rough up the witch, but they tried to rape her and one of them ended up dead. More proof of her evil powers, but the cardinals decided more physical violence might backfire. As they had pondered what to do next, investigations they had launched about her in Africa had finally paid off, yielding some shocking information.

Mannheim turned to Trevi and said, "Those sworn affadavits from Nigeria, you have them in safekeeping and readily available, yes?"

"I do," Trevi replied.

"Hold off for now. If I'm chosen," Mannheim said, "it will carry more weight to eliminate her as pope, but if things go against us, we can still make the case at any time with our information in hand. Whether God sees fit to see me on the papal throne or not, the nun will be excised from the Church like the cancer that she is."

"Amen," was the collective response, and then the men went about their business of making Heinrich Mannheim the new pope.

CHAPTER LIV

The Barbarians, then, as they did not apprehend God, went astray . . .
—Anastius, the Librarian

The Vatican City

Threats, bribery, poisoning, fist-fights, and mob action; all had played a role in papal elections of centuries past. Modern elections had been less eventful, but it was a troubled new world, and this was destined to be the most widely watched papal conclave in history.

The great nations wondered whether the Church could regain its equilibrium and become a positive force in precarious world events as it had done a generation earlier during the decline of Communism. Islam waited to see what sort of man would lead the religious arm of the Western world, a world they were challenging on every front. The poor of the world desired a Church that would hear their pleas for help, and the intelligentsia wanted to know how the Church would address the scientific scholarship that was eroding the underpinnings of the Bible and Christian faith. Even Wall Street was curious to see if the Church could weather its financial crisis, a problem that had slowly leaked out to international business circles. Everyone had a stake in the upcoming election. It was a sign of the times that so many projected their fears and hostilities, their hopes and their dreams, on an ancient, tired institution that purported to express the will of God.

The day commencing the age old ceremony of electing a new pope had finally arrived. As required, it began fifteen days after the mass of the Holy Spirit was performed. One-hundred-forty cardinals in scarlet cassocks with white lace trim had started their procession from the Hall of Benedictions to the Sala Regia. From there, they filed into the Sistine Chapel under the sonorous hymn of "Veni Creator Spiritus."

Only one-hundred-twenty cardinals actually proceeded to the conclave to vote. The rest were over the age of eighty and not eligible as cardinal electors. The Latin term *conclave* meant "locked key" because the cardinals were literally locked in an annex room until a pope was elected. Once the cardinals assembled in the Sistine Chapel annex, each of them swore an oath of complete secrecy about the conclave proceedings. All the world would ever know about the results of this historic gathering was the name of the new pontiff, nothing more.

"Extra Omnes!" the conclave marshal shouted, and all unauthorized people had to exit the room. Besides the cardinals, canon law allowed the presence of four masters of ceremony attached to the papal household and sacristy, an ecclesiastic chosen to assist the cardinal dean, and confessors for any cardinals who wanted to partake of that sacrament. Two medical doctors, several cooks, and some housekeepers were also allowed to stay.

Three people then locked the door from the outside: the prefect of the pontifical household, the commandant of the Swiss Guards — in this case Roald Zugli — and the delegate from the Vatican City state. Security kept the media, spectators, and the visiting public confined to the area of St. Peter's Square. The people in the chapel annex were now cut off from all communication with the outside world. All they had was one telephone in case of emergencies. They were in virtual solitary confinement until they elected a new pope.

Annalisa was both fascinated and respectful of the ceremony surrounding the election. She missed Clement, but she was not sad at his death. It was part of the natural cycle, and God had granted Clement the rare gift of realizing his earthly purpose before his passing.

The high walls and ceilings of the room echoed with the droning of numerous small conversations. Cardinal Forletti, the dean of the College of Cardinals, now called the conclave to order, and the deep, rumbling voices faded to silence.

Forletti reiterated the words of the ecclesiastic who had left the room prior to the locking of the door: "It is incumbent upon you to act with right intention for the good of the universal Church, *solum Deum prae oculis habentes* (having only one God before your eyes)." The first ballot voting then began.

Each cardinal filled out a small rectangular ballot, folded it down the middle, then held it high for all to see. One by one, they knelt in brief prayer at the altar of the chapel and recited this oath: "I call as my witness Christ the Lord who will be my judge that my vote is given to the one who before God I think should be elected." Each man then dropped his ballot onto a plate known as the paten. Forletti would then slide the ballot from the paten into a chalice.

The ballots were counted by three Scrutineers and verified by three Revisers. Forletti announced the results. There were twelve candidates, none receiving the required two thirds of the vote to achieve election. The voting would go to a second ballot. This came as no surprise to Annalisa. Roncalli had explained the election procedures to her. He said that often, despite the oath, cardinals would vote on the first ballot for their patrons, to repay favors, or to express support for a fellow countryman.

The serious voting began on the second ballot. The field narrowed to four candidates: Cardinals Mannheim and Berletti, the two candidates who received the most votes on the first ballot, and two new nominees. The other nominees were Cardinal Toladana, who had close ties to Milites Domini, and Cardinal Dinesewec, a Czech with a Jesuit background.

Once again, the results were tabulated, and once again, no candidate received the requisite votes, although Berletti and Mannheim far outstripped the other candidates, with Berletti the leading ballot-getter up to that point.

The voting adjourned for the day, and the cardinals called for the doors to be unlocked so that they could retire to the Domus Sanctae Marthae, their temporary residence during the conclave. Annalisa met with Cardinals Roncalli and De Faissy in De Faissy's room.

"Eventually it's going to come down to Berletti and Mannheim as everyone expected," De Faissy said.

"Conservative or fascist," Roncalli quipped. "What a choice."

"Pietro, just be thankful Toladana got nowhere," said De Faissy.

"Toladana? That was just Milites Domini making itself visible, sending a message that its votes could help *someone* get elected," Roncalli said.

"Pietro," Annalisa said, "about Cardinal Berletti. If it comes to him, I know he does not share your views, but I assure you he acts according to his conscience, and he is a fair man."

Roncalli smiled. "I know you are close to Berletti, and I do respect him, Annalisa, though I could never envision change as part of his papacy. It is the willingness to change that we need most."

"I think we need divine intervention here," De Faissy said. "That's about the only thing that can change the direction in which the Church is heading, and I once thought we were so close."

"So close," repeated Roncalli, and lacking anything more to say, the rest faded to silence.

✠

Two days and numerous ballots later, the world still had no pope. The lines had been drawn many votes back when Berletti and Mannheim emerged as the only serious candidates. No other contenders had appeared on the last fourteen ballots, but neither of the vying cardinals could gather the eighty votes necessary for election.

Berletti was able to rely on sixty-eight votes; the Milites Domini cardinals had declared for him. Mannheim would not forget that fact in his struggle with Alvaro after the conclave, but due to strong-arm tactics by Mannheim, his fifty-two votes were holding firm.

Inside the conclave, electioneering was prohibited, but outside, during the breaks for prayer and contemplation, the Mannheim faction was lobbying relentlessly and illegally. They were in a desperate situation. After the next ballot, one of two things would likely occur. Seeing an endless deadlock, the cardinals could decide to change the election requirement to an absolute majority rather than a two-thirds vote to elect. In that case, Berletti would certainly win. Mannheim's supporters could block the move to switch to a majority election, but the probable outcome of that would be the election of a compromise candidate, perhaps the Portuguese cardinal, Sosa. Either way Mannheim lost. Roncalli and De Faissy took some measure of comfort knowing that if they had to have a conservative pope, at least it would not be Mannheim.

The current conclave proceeded as before in a deadlock. Cardinal Forletti exhorted the members of the assembly to examine their consciences as he prepared them to vote on the question of reducing the electoral requirement from two thirds to an absolute majority.

De Faissy, who had once been a student at the École Des Beaux Arts in Paris, had been doodling intently all day on a pad of paper, perhaps in resigned disinterest at the proceedings. Roncalli was finally curious enough to lean forward and look over his shoulder. On the paper were seven figures drawn caricature style with small bodies and large heads. There were frantic beads of sweat flying off their brows, and each of the figures had a caption below it. De Faissy had not lost his touch. All of the figures were quite recognizable.

The scowling face of Cardinal Tormada with his thick, dark eyebrows was labeled "Anger." The sunken cheeks and eyeglasses of Van Kluysen, who was suspected by many of having profited from his position as guardian of Church finances, bore the title "Avarice." The face of Villendot, whose esteem for himself was strictly unilateral, seemed to be longing for a papal miter just beyond his grasp. He was labeled "Envy." The jowly face of the rotund LoPresti was tagged with "Gluttony," while the rather handsome Trevi, who was said to have a fondness for the ladies, was called "Lust." The yawning and bored looking Cardinal DeGolia earned the epithet "Sloth" and was the most humorous of the animated lot.

The last face had a distant expression and his head bore a crown. The fasces emblem of the Roman emperors rose over the shoulder of the diminutive body. It was Cardinal Mannheim. He was "Pride," and there was nothing humorous about his face.

Still, Roncalli had to put a hand over his mouth to stifle a laugh. It was so perfect, the way De Faissy had captured them as the Seven Deadly Sins, and seven deathly worried Sins at that. But Roncalli did not have the chance to savor his friend's artistry because at that moment something peculiar happened. A man wearing a suit and tie marched down the middle of the Sistine Chapel right up to Forletti, the cardinal dean. The man approached the startled Forletti then barked out, "Gentlemen, or should I say Eminences, your attention please."

Cardinal Forletti stood and started to say, "What is the mean —"

"SHUT UP AND GIVE ME YOUR ATTENTION!" the man said as he pushed Forletti back into his seat.

A cardinal started to move toward the single telephone in the room, the only means of communication with the outside world. It lay on a table behind the stranger and Forletti. As if expecting such a move, the man drew a gun from under his jacket, placed it on Forletti's temple, and gripped the cardinal's shoulder with his free hand. With Forletti in tow, he whirled around to face the man going for the phone.

"Now I must tell you that if you reach for that phone, if anyone starts to pound on doors, if you shout or even talk without my permission, I will shoot Cardinal Forletti. I will then proceed to kill anyone else in range." The man rotated the weapon in a semi-circle. "And that means quite a few of you," he concluded as his gun crossed the paths of numerous bodies.

CHAPTER LV

His small boat was little more than a carved out log and they poled him through the swamp to the misty shore where lay the camp of the Huns. Alone he went to talk with the Great Hun and lo, the next day the savage, bloody army turned its face from an Eternal City whose people and timeless treasures lay prostrate and open to the depredations of the barbarians. None can say what powers of heaven or earth the pontiff used to ward off the scourge of the East, but all are praising God and the pope for their salvation.
— Popular account of the mysterious meeting between pope Leo and Attila that saved Rome from disaster in the sixth century AD

The Vatican City

The room full of cardinals sat very still. The intruder looked around and seemed pleased. "Good," he said. "Now we will use that phone you were so anxious to grab. Cardinal Forletti, I want you to make a call, and I will tell you what to say."

Cardinal Roncalli stood up. "Sir, you are profaning a house of God by this action."

"So you would care to be nearer to God, would you, Cardinal?" the man replied, training the gun on Roncalli. "Because I assure you, if you say one more word, you will be. Good, yes, sit down. Stay there and keep your mouth shut! Now Cardinal Forletti, about that telephone call . . . "

After receiving instructions from the gunman, Cardinal Forletti picked up the black telephone handset. The line beeped until the voice of Turlogh Murray, the papal prefect, answered.

"Turlogh, I need you to do something," Forletti said, his voice remarkably steady. "We may be able to complete the election today, but we have some unusual questions pertaining to canon law. We need outside experts. There is a Dr. Zabaglia in Rome; I will give you his number. He may need to bring some associates. Please have him come here immediately and call me back."

The cardinals sat in quiet shock. Ten minutes later, the telephone rang. "Yes?" Forletti answered. "Good, thank you." The man prodded Forletti's arm. "Turlogh, please tell Colonel Zugli to expedite their entry. We want to conclude today if possible." Forletti hung up. "He said Zabaglia will be here as soon as possible," the cardinal reported to the gun-wielding man.

"Very good," said the man. "You held up well, Cardinal. Now everybody sit back, and if you cooperate, you may still get to elect yourself a pope."

An hour later, four men with briefcases were ushered to the entrance of the Sistine Chapel, where they were greeted by Bishop Murray; Tiro Fanile, the Vatican delegate; Roald Zugli; and four Swiss Guards.

"I am Dr. Zabaglia," said the spokesman, a dark man with bushy eyebrows. "I believe our assistance was requested by the cardinals."

"Si, Dottore," replied Zugli. "We will get you in immediately, but first I must check your brief cases. A necessary formality, you see."

"Of course," Zabaglia said. "Gentlemen," he said, addressing his companions, "if you would." The men set their brief cases on a table to the right of the main door of the chapel annex.

In a synchronized action, the snap of brief case latches echoed through the hallway. Each man lifted the lid of his brief case with one hand while inserting his other hand inside. The next thing Roald Zugli and his men saw were four semi-automatic pistols pointed directly at their heads.

"Colonel Zugli, we have no wish to shoot you, so each of you turn and place your hands above your shoulders on the wall."

Zugli and the other men stood for several seconds in stunned silence.

"NOW, COLONEL!" The loud command got their attention, and the Guards complied. Zugli was obviously seething, the lines of his lean face drawn tight with rage and impotence.

One of the four strangers proceeded to frisk and disarm the guards while his comrades stood back and covered him, weapons trained on the helpless captives. They even checked the religious men just to be sure. Zabaglia then pulled the four Swiss Guards to one side, separating them from Zugli, Murray, and Fanile.

"Now, I believe you gentlemen have the keys to unlock the door. Please do so," he ordered.

Zugli hesitated.

Zabaglia sighed. "Colonel, if you are worried about the safety of your cardinals, we already have a man inside. Oh, you haven't figured that out yet? Let me also inform you that if you do not cooperate, we will shoot all of you and get in anyway."

Zugli nodded to Murray and Fanile. The men produced their keys and unlocked the doors. The marauders then herded them inside, driving them like cattle. Like the Goths who once sacked Rome, the armed men marched triumphantly across the hallowed floor of the Sistine Chapel, trampling the pride and sanctity of the Roman Church beneath their feet. Straight to the front and center they strode, with arrogant purpose and without hesitation.

Zabaglia turned to face the captive cardinals. "Sit!" he commanded in English, "and place your hands on the railings in front of you. Everyone!"

They did as they were told. Zabaglia gave a curt nod to the men on either side of him. Off to the wings of the chapel they went and proceeded to slap dull globs of grayish clay on the columns along the entire length of the room. When they were finished, they returned to Zabaglia's side, and one of the men whispered in his ear.

"Very good," Zabaglia said. "We are now ready to introduce ourselves," he exclaimed to the cardinals in a loud, strident voice that resounded through the sacred space. "We are the Poor Nations Coalition, usually called the PNC for brevity's sake. You have, perhaps, heard of us."

Roald Zugli was most definitely aware of them. They had already kidnapped and ransomed Catholic bishops on two continents. Leo Dusayne and others had shared intelligence on the PNC with him on several occasions. They were the most shadowy and unusual of all the globe's assorted terrorist organizations. The limited information available painted them as a small, multinational group of highly committed intellectuals numbering between fifty and one hundred members. Often from upper-class families, most with Catholic backgrounds, they had a capacity for armed action not usually found in people with their upbringing and intelligence.

All their prior actions had demonstrated incredible planning and forethought. They had not struck with anywhere near the frequency or randomness of most terrorist organizations, but when they had acted, the results had been spectacular. They once held the entire National Assembly of Argentina hostage and then, a year later in Malaysia, a conference of central bankers from the G-8 nations was briefly added to their list of unwilling detainees.

People had died because of them, both their own members and some of their captives, but the PNC had succeeded in gaining publicity and large sums of money for their cause. What intrigued Zugli was that the intelligence sources believed a good deal of the purloined funds had actually gone to support popular movements, both militant and nonviolent, in numerous Third World countries.

"Many of you are saying to yourselves, how dare we violate your conclave, what do the likes of us have to do with the Church?" Zabaglia said. "Well, I'll explain it to you. You are a very important part of a global system enforced by the industrialized nations. Each year that system condemns millions around the world to poverty and death."

Zabaglia looked around at the blank-faced figures in scarlet cassocks. "Oh, come now, as if you were not aware! You support reactionary governments despite the fact that many of your local priests are good people. You force policies on the gullible like no birth control or abortion, policies that keep them ignorant and impoverished. You collect their hard-earned money, yet you give nothing back."

He looked at Forletti, the cardinal dean, with undisguised disdain. "A bunch of fossils sitting here in splendor while the world goes to hell around you," he declaimed, pointing out the priceless wonders of the Sistine Chapel. "The planet is running out of fuel, water, and food while the West controls seventy-five percent of the world's resources. Do you know what that is? That is rape, that is murder, that is greed gone wild."

Zabaglia now stepped down from the raised steps in front of the altar and slowly walked along the wide aisle between the areas where the cardinals were seated.

"Do you know what I hate most about you?" He stopped and looked directly into the frightened eyes of one cardinal. "You are hypocrites," he said, answering his own question into the face of another prelate while continuing down the aisle.

And so it went with Zabaglia strolling up and down, back and forth, delivering his tirade personally to each cardinal he would approach. "The banks, the governments, the corporations — they, at least, do not disguise their greed and rapacity, but you, you men of the Church, you are supposed to nurture the spirit, uplift the people. Bah! All you do is pacify them to their state of misery. You are the heroin of the Western world posing as heroes. No gender pun intended, madam," he said, spying Annalisa in one of the rows.

She had her eyes closed. Zabaglia gave a rueful snicker and continued on with his peripatetic lecture. "You have all sinned, and you must atone," he said, voice rising in pitch. "You are big on that, yes, the concept of sin and atonement? Well today you will say many Hail Marys and you will perform an act of contrition. Now let me tell you how that will be done."

Zabaglia walked back to the front by the altar. His dark gaze was dull but missed nothing. His eyes were shark-like, reflecting the inexorable need to fulfill its nature: feed then move on to the next prey.

"In this room are those who control the Vatican purse strings," he said. "I want one hundred million dollars transferred from the Vatican Bank to foreign accounts in the name of several entities. This money will be converted into gold. When I receive confirmation that the gold deliveries have been physically received, we will leave and you may elect your pope."

Zabaglia smiled, appearing quite pleased with the flow of events. "Actually, we were hoping you would have a pope by now, but you took so long we could no longer wait. If everything goes well, the whole process should be complete in a working day, and since you are a sovereign nation with your own central bank, there is no need to involve the Italians or any other governments."

"That is impossible," a voice called out.

"Identify yourself," said Zabaglia, "and you'd better have a good reason for your statement."

"I am Cardinal Mannheim, the secretary of state." He stood up and spoke firmly. "The Vatican lost huge sums of money a few years back, and we never recovered them. What you demand would bankrupt the Church. We do not have that kind of money."

"Well, complain to your broker then, but get me that money!" Zabaglia screamed. "If you do not comply, I have this chapel rigged to blow by remote detonation. Although the world may miss Michelangelo, I seriously doubt they will mourn your loss when you go up in smoke with him."

There was a disturbed buzz of voices at that threat.

"I still do not believe we have sufficient cash on hand in the amount you demand," Mannheim said, looking at Van Kluysen, who shook his head in affirmation of Mannheim's statement. "The Church you believe to be so rich is tottering financially."

One of Zabaglia's cohorts motioned to him, and they conferred in whispered tones. When the conversation ended, Zabaglia faced the cardinals again, appearing angry but determined.

"Do not negotiate with us, you glorified priest. You still have the ability to borrow from the Italian banking network with one or two phone calls. It is one more step in the process, but you *will* get that money."

"We cannot do this!" Mannheim said. "It would ruin the Church."

"What?" Zabaglia said. "What did you say?" He rushed over to Mannheim, grabbing the shoulder cape about his simar and dragging him to the center of the chapel. He held his gun to Mannheim's head.

Zabaglia looked like a coiled snake ready to strike, but Roncalli stood up and said, "You will need Cardinal Mannheim! If you shoot him, you will not have one of the men whose authority is needed to achieve your goal."

The tension in Zabaglia's body seemed to slacken ever so slightly, and it was at that moment a voice said, "Is it money you want, or is it justice?"

The entire room looked at the only female present. "Do you want mercy for poor people or simply the power to kill?" she added.

Zabaglia looked at Annalisa incredulously, then he burst out laughing. "And here I thought you were sleeping! So, you are the celebrity cardinal, the woman from Africa. We have all read about you. Now what the hell do you want?"

"I want to talk to you in private," she replied. "I listened very closely to what you had to say. Yes, I was born in Africa, in a mud hut under a grass roof. I spent my whole life with the poor people you talk of. Does that earn me the right to have fifteen minutes of conversation with you?"

"Conversation? About what?" said Zabaglia.

"About your concerns," said Annalisa.

"My concerns. My concerns. What do you know of my concerns?" he said. "Do not waste my time or you will have this gun at your head instead."

"Hah!" she laughed. "Did you know some of the cardinals here might like that, particularly the one whose head you have your gun on now? It is the only way they could be rid of me."

Whether it was her ability to be humorous under such circumstances or the desire to hear what she could possibly tell him; whether it was her courage or simply her attractiveness amongst these dour relics, Zabaglia decided to listen to her.

"All right, Madam Cardinal, step down here and we will find a place to talk."

As she walked toward Zabaglia, Roncalli caught her by the arm and said in a low voice, "Annalisa, what are you doing? These men are killers. If you say something that displeases them they might shoot you!"

She smiled, patted his hand, then continued moving toward Zabaglia. He let go of Mannheim and motioned her toward a side chapel where they would be neither seen nor heard by the others.

"Cover them, do not let them speak to one another, and do not tolerate any problems," he ordered his cohorts. "This will only take a few minutes."

Over an hour passed, and Roncalli was inwardly frantic. What was he doing with her back there? Then Zabaglia appeared around a corner. He motioned one of the other men to join him. Roncalli was sick to his stomach. Zabaglia looked . . . contented, satisfied, nothing like the man who almost pulled a trigger on Mannheim. Oh, God no. The bastard! Could he have . . . ?

Two more grueling hours passed until, finally, Annalisa and the two men emerged from their seclusion. The two men went to talk to their three companions. The men spoke together for almost thirty minutes, and at times the three who had not been with Annalisa appeared to argue with the two who had. Finally, their conversation ended, and Zabaglia gave a nod to the African cardinal.

She drew herself up to speak and be heard by her fellow prelates. "These men have agreed to leave on condition we provide them safe passage. We are a sovereign nation and have the right to make such an arrangement. No one was killed, no damage has been done, and they are dropping the demand for money. They are willing to end the matter now. Will you all agree and abide by that?"

A stunned silence overtook the chapel. "That's it?" Mannheim asked, the confusion and incredulity apparent in his voice. "No other conditions?"

"Only that Colonel Zugli must call the Vatican heliport and have them land the helicopter in the courtyard near the chapel," Annalisa said. "He will go with the men to insure they are not intercepted. If we uphold our end, he will be released once they are free. Colonel?"

"If that will guarantee the safety of the cardinals and avoid destruction of the buildings, I will comply," Zugli said without hesitation.

"If I believed they would harm you, I would never ask you to do this, Colonel," she said with a smile that imparted as much comfort to him as the occasion would allow.

"One thing I must know," Zugli asked. "How did they get their man in here?"

"Apparently, they were following the doctor who would normally attend the conclave," Annalisa said. "Last week he was unknowingly administered some bacteria in his food to make him ill. Another doctor from his office, one with whom no one here was familiar by sight, was to substitute for him. They intercepted and held that man, replacing him with their own colleague. As a sign of good faith, they have given me an address where he will be found, bound and gagged but alive."

Zugli bit his lip and nodded. No one would have missed the kidnapped man, because he was supposed to be part of the sequestered conclave. Zugli had also seen the unusual gun the first intruder had used when Zabaglia forced him into the conclave room. He guessed they had all fashioned crude weapons entirely out of plastic and wood parts to escape the metal detectors. Conclave attendees were not physically searched, a practice he would change if he made it back alive.

"Now," Annalisa said, raising her voice to be heard, "as the acting head of the See of St. Peter, does the College of Cardinals agree to what I have told you?"

One by one each head adorned by a red biretta nodded and expressed his assent.

Zugli made the required call for the helicopter. Within twenty minutes the whirring noise of the choppers was heard. Zugli turned to Mannheim and said, "I hope to make it back to see you again, but caution the others — I do not to think it advisable to make the outside world aware of what transpired today. It will do the Church no good to make public this violation, and right now, the knowledge of the event is limited to this room."

"Agreed," Mannheim said. "God be with you, Colonel."

"And also with you, with all of you," Zugli replied, and then he was blindfolded by the terrorists.

The intruders disarmed the explosives, relinquished their captives, and started an orderly exodus from the Sistine Chapel, but then one more extraordinary thing happened. As three of the terrorists guided Zugli out to the helicopter, the two who had spoken to Annalisa lingered momentarily, *knelt, and kissed her hand!* Then, as swiftly as they had entered the chapel, they were gone.

The room now seemed to flow inward on Annalisa as cardinals, Swiss Guards, and even common cooks crowded around her like specks of matter gathering to herald the birth of a new sun. Wonder and bewilderment commingled in their eyes.

"What happened back there?" they asked." What did you say to those men? Why would they just leave? Tell us, please," they clamored. She was inundated with questions until she raised a hand and silenced them."

"I am sorry, I cannot tell you," she said.

"Cannot tell us?" Voices collectively raised in indignation and surprise.

When the noise subsided, Annalisa spoke in a slow, calm voice. "I pledged that I would not discuss the details of my conversation with them."

"Pledged?" Tormada cried. "You bind yourself by a pledge to such men?"

"A pledge is a pledge," she replied, "and I am bound not only to them in this matter." She let that statement linger for a minute and seep into their consciousness before she added, "What was said in there will be made known in time, but not now. Please, ask me no more."

"Ask her no more," said one cardinal, "but do recognize the hand of God in this matter."

It was Cardinal Sterri, a man well-steeped in Church history. He turned in a circle as he addressed the crowd surrounding Annalisa. They all stepped back a few paces to give him room. "When Rome lay prostrate before the ravages of the Huns, Pope Leo went alone to talk to Attila. All the riches of Rome lay at the barbarian's feet, and yet he turned from the Eternal City, turned and never came back. I believe this day we have seen the sword of the Hun turned once again by the Lord's intercession through his chosen messenger."

The men stared at Annalisa. Some perceived a brightening of the light in the room, though daytime had long been driven out by the dark blanket of night.

"What are we to do now?" a voice among the cardinals called out.

Pietro Roncalli took a decisive step to the center of the room, in front of Annalisa. In a commanding voice he said, "We do what God and the Church have mandated for us. We elect a pope. After these four days in the wilderness of doubt and indecision, a path has been shown to us. My brethren, if we look into our hearts, I believe we will see, by the grace of God, we have among us one who was meant to be pope." A chill passed along the collective spines of the assemblage when he turned to look directly into the eyes of Annalisa, Cardinal Basanjo of Africa.

CHAPTER LVI

Christianity is really a man's religion; there's not much in it for a woman except docility, obedience . . . downcast eyes and death in childbirth. For the men it's better: all power and money and fine robes, the burning of heretics—fun—fun—fun!—and the Inquisition fulminating from the pulpit.
— Fay Weldon

The Vatican City

One day you'll have to back her to a greater degree than anything you've done. . . . You need to believe in her or not. Roncalli remembered O'Keefe's advice about supporting Annalisa against her enemies. Under the crucible of the day's events, Roncalli distilled his inner feelings about the African cardinal and made his choice. The moment he turned to her and declared it was her destiny to be pope, his eyes locked on Annalisa's. In that moment they were both transformed forever, bound and intertwined like threads in a tapestry of God's creation.

Could anyone describe the energy emanating from the two of them, let alone see it? Perhaps not, but people felt it. Maybe it was from witnessing a scene of deep emotion; maybe it was something else. Yet all present had experienced salvation that day and the answering of a prayer in the form of a small African woman.

Who can say what thoughts were in the minds of Roncalli and Annalisa, but at that very moment, their lives were repatterned to create a living work more magnificent than the inspired ceiling of the Sistine Chapel. Annalisa looked upward, and her gaze fixed on the hand of Michelangelo's God reaching out to humanity in his depiction of *The Creation of Adam.* Next, Roncalli lifted his face, and soon the entire gathering of cardinals inclined their heads to see what had captured her attention.

Whether or not the cardinals saw the promise of rebirth and renewal in those images, a feeling started to seep into the chapel. *"Meant to be pope,"* some began to repeat Roncalli's words, and a number of heads began to nod in acceptance.

Trevi looked at Mannheim and saw the fury on his face. Mannheim's eyes spoke his thoughts— *they're trying to elect her by acclamation!* Trevi knew Mannheim had given him a silent command.

"Listen to me!" Trevi called out in a jarring voice that broke the invisible wave gathering in the hall. "How can you talk of electing a woman—*this* woman—pope?"

"Canon law prohibits the discussion of electing candidates in conclave," said Villendot, following on Trevi's heels. "Why are we even talking about this?"

"We are talking about this because of what we just witnessed." To the surprise of all, it was the leading contender, Cardinal Berletti, who spoke.

"Even if she were to be nominated or elected," cried out LoPresti, "would she accept?"

In a quick voice, firm and unwavering, and to the great amazement of everyone, Annalisa said, "Yes."

Roncalli, acting with determination, pushed to resolve the matter immediately. "We have been at an impasse for days," he said. "Before the interruption, Cardinal Forletti called for contemplation of our direction, as is our custom at such junctures. Therefore, I propose we convene outside the chapel to discuss what has occurred here."

The rumble of many small debates filled the room until the elderly Cardinal Sato from Japan was able to get the attention of the group. "I, for one, am tired from the long day and our ordeal, but I feel the need to discuss these extraordinary events with my brethren while the experience is still vivid in my mind."

There was strong agreement to that sentiment despite the opposition of Tormada and LoPresti. Forletti, the cardinal dean, said, "I agree that our best course of action is to persevere. We will reconvene in the Aula, where we can continue to discuss how we may proceed. However, while we are still in conclave, I suggest we decide whether to allow election of the pope by absolute rather than two thirds majority."

They did vote, and over two-thirds of the cardinals agreed to put the absolute majority rule into effect. Whereas the Mannheim faction had hoped to prevent this before the terrorist intrusion, the tired and traumatized cardinals now wanted to end the election as quickly as possible. The motion passed. It would now take sixty-two cardinals to elect a new pontiff, and Berletti had had more than that number on the last ballot. Annalisa was now a wild card thrown into the equation.

The one-hundred-twenty cardinals in the conclave, though hungry and weary to the core of their being, then proceeded to the Aula, the papal audience hall. Their deliverance had inspired them, and a sense of destiny now drove them. They might well be the midwives called to birth the most significant event in the Church's history since the Nativity of their Lord.

Walking to the Aula, Mannheim and his six collaborators held a hasty conference. "I am in a very difficult position as a contender," said the German. "I cannot appear to attack her directly, but we must pull out all the stops. If she rides this emotional tide, it spells real trouble for us."

"Then no waiting until after the conclave. We use the information from Africa now," Tormada said.

"Agreed," Mannheim said. "If things start to swing her way, we use it. Aldo, you are the most effective speaker, you do the talking."

"Oh, I will speak for you," DeGolia said, "but no matter what I say, remember what just happened. She saved our lives too. I am in awe, even if you are not. Did you ever stop to think she might truly be someone special?"

"Don't be a fool, man! She is devilishly clever, and we badly underestimated her," Mannheim said. "She's no saint. God talks to no one anymore, not since the days of the prophets. At best she is just a crafty and disarming actress. At worst she is the Great Deceiver, but mark my words. She has a hidden agenda and it spells ill for the Church."

"The others are lost in euphoria," said Villendot. "We need to burst that bubble quickly and stop this slide from becoming an avalanche."

"We are up against something more serious than we imagine," LoPresti said. "Remember the demonic symbols that warned us of her advent. Stop the Great Heretic by any means necessary, I tell you." But the others did not have time to respond because the cardinals were now filing into the Aula.

Cardinal Forletti had given instructions for sandwiches to be prepared so that the cardinals could eat without interrupting the discussions. After a brief prayer for the safe return of Colonel Zugli, when everyone was seated, he said, "The question we must address is the candidacy of Cardinal Basanjo, whom Cardinal Roncalli, I presume, intends to nominate on the next ballot."

Roncalli rose from his seat. "Your Eminence, if I may?" He received a nod of approval from Forletti. "I must ask the question of why this body would debate the candidacy of Cardinal Basanjo. The custom is to present a name and that name shall be considered. I see no reason why this candidate should be treated differently."

"There is every reason she should be treated differently," Trevi said, standing to speak. "She is a woman, in case you had not noticed, and there has never been a female pope. I am not even sure if electing her is canonically feasible."

"She is a cardinal and a bishop, and therefore eligible," said Cardinal De Faissy, quickly interjecting his opinion. "As far as any other canonical requirements related to her gender, they would have been superseded when Clement decided to invest her in those offices."

Forletti held up a hand to halt further discussion. "Cardinal Taquin, you are a canon lawyer, what do you say on this point?"

The Swiss cardinal rose and said, "Cardinal De Faissy is correct. We must look back at the late pontiff's actions. Clement waived those canon laws that on their face proscribed Cardinal Basanjo from holding ecclesiastical office. That is to say, gender requirements for this individual were waived the moment the pontiff created her as cardinal. The effect is that she stands as both cardinal and bishop, and she is as eligible to be pope as anyone here, canonically speaking."

"We can speak about legalities all day," Tormada said, "but who is she really? What do we really know of her beliefs? After all, we are talking about electing the spiritual and temporal head of all Christendom. I may disagree on issues with other candidates here, but at least I know of them, of their ideas, of their experience. What do we know about Cardinal Basanjo except that she enjoys reading in the library?"

A clamor of arguments broke out among numerous small groups. Some questioned the propriety of the proceeding; some wanted to reenter the conclave and vote. During the bickering a soft voice kept speaking out, "Please, please, if you will," until eventually, the group calmed down and focused their attention on Annalisa.

"My name has been put forth and many questions have followed. Some of you know me, many more do not, but that I am here at all is unusual, you agree? If I am to be considered, I want to feel I was accepted or rejected based on your understanding of whether or not I can lead the Church. So, despite being treated as an exception, I will answer any questions you care to ask."

Cardinal Forletti was the first to respond to Annalisa's statement. "Cardinal Basanjo, I for one believe there is something unfair about raising you to a level of scrutiny to which no one else must submit. However, I also see the inherent wisdom in your offer because you acknowledge the reality of concerns among your fellow cardinals that might hinder your candidacy." Forletti gazed at the group of prelates and seemed to look particularly long at Mannheim. "The time for this questioning should be of limited duration, not more than thirty minutes, is that agreeable?"

The nodding of heads indicated general assent to Forletti's suggestion. Roncalli knew what Annalisa's opponents hoped to do. The venal group surrounding Mannheim was trying to take that shining moment of their liberation at Annalisa's hands, drag it down, soil it, and demean it in the electors' eyes. They wanted to take the focus off her miraculous life and drown her in a wave of dogmatic smoke and political trickery. It was too late to stop it. He could not change things now. She had offered to put her head into the jaws of the lion.

There was one thing he could do though. "Your Eminence," he called out, addressing Forletti. "If I may?" Forletti gave him an approving nod. "Your Eminence has pointed out the aspect of unfairness surrounding this procedure. In order to balance the scales, I suggest that those who know Cardinal Basanjo be allowed to speak in her favor where appropriate during this allotted time."

Forletti smiled and nodded. "I think that would be very appropriate Cardinal Roncalli. How does that sit with you?" he asked, addressing the assembly.

No one could really disagree with the suggestion and still appear impartial, so there was no dissent. The questioning then began. Cardinal Mendoza, one of the Milites Domini cardinals, posed the first question. "Cardinal Basanjo, as pope would you uphold the traditional Church position on abortion and birth control?"

"As some here have pointed out," Annalisa said, speaking slowly and in an even tone, "I am a cardinal who has spent a great deal of time in study and reflection. The first thing I tried to do was learn many languages. I did this so I could understand and look into the hearts of my colleagues when they spoke to me." She stood and walked slowly to the center of the room so she could look at, and be seen by, all of them. "I never had to consider abortion or birth control in a policy sense, and it seems our Ecumenical Council has not been able to address these questions either."

She placed her palms over her chest with fingers spread. "In Africa, I always dealt with immediate issues of life and death, of sickness and healing. But if you ask me about abortion, about female clergy or celibacy, I have the same response: like everything else, I will go to God for my answers and we will watch for validation in the lives of the people. Decisions we make that do not improve and uplift people would not be the will of God, you see?"

A wonderful response, Roncalli thought. Annalisa fended off repeated attempts to restate the same questions with a shrug of her shoulders and a kindly tilt of her head. She merely extended her arms with palms outward in a gesture that said, *Sorry, I have already given my answer.*

Eventually, her opponents relented because they would simply expose themselves as biased and hostile if they persisted in the same line of questioning.

Cardinal DeGolia then asked, "Cardinal Basanjo, do you really perform miracles?"

"No," Annalisa said. She paused and let the single word linger in the echo of the room. "Only God performs miracles. That God allows me to assist Him in helping this world, that is what I consider the real miracle."

"Well," said DeGolia, "I for one do believe you perform miracles, indeed I do. The real question is from where do those miracles come?"

Roncalli knew where DeGolia was going the moment he heard that last phrase — the report.

"Cardinal Basanjo, is it not true that your predecessor, the late Cardinal Onomoh, conducted an investigation of your activities?"

Annalisa answered directly. "It is true."

"And why do you suppose he would do that?" DeGolia asked rhetorically. "Was it because of rumors that you practiced shamanism and people feared the evil nature of your works, fears grounded in the fact that from a young age, you were raised by a shaman in your village?"

Annalisa showed no outward loss of composure from DeGolia's strident questioning. "If you were to condemn every African who was born with a shaman in his or her village, or who was influenced by native religion, there would be no room in the Church for a single man, woman, or child from that continent."

She looked around the room so that every cardinal felt he was being addressed personally. "The old *ogun* in my village worshipped nature, as most native religionists do. God's hand created everything, including nature, so the *ogun* really worshipped the same God we do according to his background and understanding. He was not evil; he only helped people. Now, that is more than I can say for those who call themselves Christians but whose actions are not in harmony with their words, you see?"

The cardinals stirred, and Roncalli was amazed. The quiet nun was out-dueling the noted orator DeGolia. He had attempted to indict her by association, and she had thrown the onus right back on him by a finely worded allusion to the base motivations of her interrogators. DeGolia felt the sympathy of the room going against him, and he looked like a feeding nocturnal predator suddenly exposed to the light. He glanced at his cohorts. They, too, knew they had to change directions.

LoPresti stood up next. The gluttonous cardinal's rotund face had a drooping cant about his nose and mouth that made him look like he was sneering at lowly peasants. "How well spoken, Cardinal Basanjo," LoPresti chided. "Yet I must bring the attention of the Church to a source of wisdom far greater and older than yours. A number of you have heard of the Breverarium."

A bolt shot through Roncalli. *The prophecies?* Of course. LoPresti was the only other active churchman besides Desmond O'Keefe who had been on the secret commission that made the compilation years ago. The obese cardinal intended to bring matters to a head.

"The Breverarium is a compendium of all Christian prophecies since the dawn of the Church," LoPresti explained. "Those of you familiar with it know many of its predictions have been astonishingly accurate. Of late I have been drawn to the prophecies, perhaps because of the great turmoil we have been experiencing in recent times."

A wave of uneasiness swept through the room as soon as LoPresti mentioned predictions. Roncalli's lips twisted with disdain. Even an indirect allusion to the future, and look at the reaction. It was a sad measure of the lack of confidence and the absence of optimism that had characterized the foundering ship of the Church for so many years.

"Allow me to recall some passages that may well refer to the times in which we live," the obese cardinal said. *"The church will suffer great ills; a torrent of evil will open a breach on her, but the first attack will be against her fortune and her riches.'"*

LoPresti let that sink in. Roncalli's fingers ground against one another. LoPresti's quote seemed to make a clear reference to the severe financial dilemma in which the Church had been mired for several years.

"The prophecies predict the downfall of the Church and the papacy in this very decade," LoPresti said. "They speak of the last two popes. Listen: *'And De Gloria Olivae shall hasten the downfall.'* De Gloria Olivae, the Glory of Olives. Have we seen him yet? Did you know the late Clement's family were olive growers?

"And Petrus Romanus, the last pope," LoPresti intoned. "Now, the Breverarium links Petrus Romanus with a she goat, a female goat. Cryptic? Yes, but where in any rank of the Church is a female?" Instead of answering his own question, LoPresti looked around the room then finally let his eyes rest on Annalisa. "One last thing. Many of you know that demonic, heretical symbols have mysteriously appeared around the Vatican coinciding with Cardinal Basanjo's arrival. You also know the Breverariun predicts the advent of the Great Heretic in our time."

Roncalli sprang from his seat and addressed Forletti. "Your Eminence, I must protest. Though the information in the Breverarium is eligible for viewing by the members of this college, it has always been the practice that the information it contains be viewed and discussed with utmost discretion. It was never meant for use in a mass forum where it might be quoted out of context, as Cardinal LoPresti uses it, to cast doubts on another cardinal."

"Out of context?" LoPresti shot back. "That is your opinion, Cardinal

Roncalli, but the Church's problems began with her activities in Africa. At best, we are talking about making an inexperienced young woman pope, an unknown element in these precarious times. You make assumptions of her sanctity, but I tell you the wicked hide behind the holy!"

Before Roncalli could respond, DeGolia interjected. The time had come to deliver the deathblow. "The illusion of sanctity, an unknown element," he repeated his colleague's words. "Cardinal LoPresti speaks the truth. Who is this woman who would be elected pope? It's been reported that her mother was a Muslim, not a crime, certainly, but how would that upbringing affect her views as the defender of the Christian faith against Islam?"

Roncalli shouted at him. "The report to which you refer also mentions miraculous acts of healing attributed to Cardinal Basanjo. Your characterizations are statements of slander!"

"No, Cardinal Roncalli, they are statements of fact, and there is more," said DeGolia. "A pope is responsible not only for upholding the faith but also the morals of the Church. Does anyone dispute that? Well, it seems that Cardinal Basanjo bore a child out of wedlock as a young woman. We have sworn statements on this. Is that a moral example for a pope to set for young Catholics? Is that a legacy we want our next pope, this 'Lady of Miracles' to carry?"

Enraged at the smug face of Mannheim, who appeared pleased at the work of his minions, Roncalli stood up and strode to the center of the room. Facing the assembly he said, "This is an outrage. No conclave has ever put a papal candidate under such scrutiny. Besides, I have read the report on Cardinal Basanjo and there is no mention of a pregnancy."

"Nonetheless, it is true, Cardinal Roncalli," but this time the voice came neither from LoPresti nor from DeGolia. Roncalli looked around in shocked silence as Annalisa completed her sentence. "May I speak now?"

The attack on her had been vehement, but her voice sounded neither weak nor pathetic. Something about the calm, quiet way she responded commanded authority. The fluid emotions contained in one-hundred-nineteen gathered hearts shifted again at the sound of her voice.

"As for the Muslim part, yes," Annalisa said. "My mother was a Muslim, so I see Muslims as people, not as enemies. That perhaps puts me in a position to deal with them out of love and respect, which, if I recall correctly, is what the Lord asked of us, yes?"

Annalisa came to stand beside Roncalli. She smiled and patted his hand. He nodded and took his seat. "I did become pregnant at sixteen, but not by choice or accident. I was raped."

Her eyes were not downcast, nor did her voice indicate shame. When she spoke, all sound faded to stillness and all thoughts lay frozen in shock. She looked at Roncalli. He tried not to let her see how grief-stricken he was. God, they were exposing her to so much pain. He tried to put on a face that would encourage her; it was clear she intended to play this out.

"I was raped, and as Cardinal DeGolia said, there is more. It was not a bandit or an overzealous boy who raped me."

Roncalli touched her arm. "Annalisa, you do not have to—"

She raised a hand and looked at him, and her eyes spoke her determination. "If you . . . if *they* want to know who I am then I must tell you this," and then in a voice for all to hear she said, "It was my own uncle, you see. *My mother's brother raped me.*"

CHAPTER LVII

You would have thought the world was coming to an end.
— Woman interviewed by a World Magazine *reporter during the pandemonium in St. Peter's Square at the announcement of the new pope*

The Vatican City

"*It was my own uncle, you see. My mother's brother raped me.*"Her words gripped the room with complete silence as each man tried to process the images through his mind. Many averted their eyes from her. Mouths opened forming crinkled O shapes that expressed emotions they were too stunned to utter. Mannheim, Tormada, and LoPresti too, were shocked at images of a violated young girl, though they were oblivious to the irony that a hundred and nineteen inquisitors were violating her again.

"I was sent to a convent in another village by the nun who was my spiritual guardian. My child died at birth. It did not live . . . it suffered from defects and that is why it died, you see."

Many of the cardinals now shook their heads in abhorrence; others buried their faces in their hands as she spoke.

"Did this taint my 'purity'? Does it affect my ability to be a cardinal or pope? Well, I think it was the most humanizing experience of my life. You are surprised?" she asked as many of them looked up again upon hearing her words.

"You must understand my world as a child. I lived in a place of outward silence and inner peace you might call the prayer state. Imagine a monk in a solitary cell devoted to constant prayer, oblivious to the outer world. That was my world, even though there were people around me. You mentioned people fearing me? I rarely spoke, and one person's silence is always a vacuum to be filled by another person's fears, you see?"

Annalisa's eyes closed, perhaps in remembrance of the life she was now recounting, and her body appeared to sway gently. "I was the opposite of most people. 'Normal' people have only flashes of ecstatic experience while I, by contrast, had only glimpses of their 'real' world. The trauma of my rape ripped me from my inner dwelling; it placed me squarely in the world of sight and sound and violence. For that I hated my uncle more than for the violation of my body. Can any of you understand that?"

As her eyes opened, everyone's gaze was fixed on her.

"I was torn from a paradise of innocence, but I worked my way through rage to forgiveness of my uncle, and it was from that time forward that God made me a healing instrument for His will. It was only from that time of realization and forgiveness that I embarked on a mission of healing in God's name. Do you find that strange, fantastic?"

The cardinals remained frozen, unable to speak, but she spoke and answered for them. "It *was* fantastic, fantastic and wonderful, and when God expressed His healing, it was not just *through* me, but also *for* me. It was my lesson in this life, my personal challenge revealed. I learned we are born to act in this world and be of this earth. I waded through fear, through bitterness, through anger and disillusionment to understand that I was being called upon to change. Hah"—she emitted a laugh that startled them—"you all think God does not want us to be evil, but the funny thing is, He does not want us to be too holy either."

Even the seven cardinals, her enemies, did not think to interrupt her, so enthralled were the prelates at her story and her words.

"Oh, I was holy, so holy," she continued, "but God does not want mere holiness from us," she said. "He does not want us to sit in a monastery or a cave and pray all day. I was strongly awakened to that knowledge by my uncle's deed. God wants us to *act,* to manifest His power of heaven on earth through our bodies and souls. From that time on, that is what I have sought to do. Jesus said of his miracles, 'Greater things than this shall *ye* do, for I have gone to my Father in heaven.' He is telling us he opened a gate, a channel to the Divine, for all of us to participate and become mediums of healing. As a result of all this, I came out from the monastery of my mind and into the world."

Like the learned rabbis of the Bible listening in amazement to the young Jesus, the stultified minds of the cardinals appeared both piqued and intrigued by her words.

"Imagine," she said. "What a wonder that even the worst evil, rape by a trusted uncle, ultimately works to the purpose of God as it did in the case of this young girl, now a woman, who stands before you. Let those of you who worry about the *apparent* power of evil in this world take comfort in that fact. Evil itself dances to God's purpose, and the Comforter He has sent dwells in the testimony of our own experience."

The small woman then folded her hands and walked back to her seat. They all looked at her now as she passed them, and many were not afraid to let their tears fall. Even Mannheim and his circle sat in awe for many minutes as each man took time to look inward.

Cardinal Berletti was the first to stand and break the ethereal silence that had descended over the room like a misty veil. "I have heard enough. I have experienced healing at the hands of this woman. I saw her save the Church this very day, as did all of you, and you have now heard her words. I know in my heart such a person was meant to lead God's Church. I ask in all gratitude that those who supported me now support Cardinal Basanjo. I withdraw as a candidate. My brethren, the time is come: the Holy Spirit must sit once again on the throne of St. Peter!"

The cardinals were stunned. Berletti's action had a great impact on every man in that room. He was sure to have been elected on the next ballot, and now he was stepping down in favor of Annalisa. The Holy Spirit to which he referred now moved men in ways not seen for millennia.

Cardinal Forletti, the presiding dean, now instructed the College of Cardinals: "This extraordinary session is at an end. We will now return to the conclave. If no other candidates are put forward, only Cardinals Basanjo and Mannheim will stand. The pope will now be elected by an absolute majority plus one, which is to say sixty-two votes or more."

DeGolia looked at Mannheim for any signal to speak again, but the solemn look on the German's face told him the time for maneuvering was over. The die had been cast; now fortune and the conscience of cardinals would elect the next pope.

The assembly filed out of the Aula. It was remarkable, Roncalli noticed, but no one spoke as they proceeded back to the conclave. Perhaps each man wanted to seek inner counsel for the decision he would shortly make. That was certainly his own preference as he reentered the Sistine Chapel, where, by the will of God, history might be made this day.

✠

Everything that could be said had been said; every emotion from the base to the sublime had been experienced during the course of this portentous day. The hearts and minds of men were now sorted out by a seminal event of extraordinary proportions.

Humanity was periodically given collective opportunities to move forward and evolve, or to stagnate and regress. Roncalli perceived this as one of those moments. He would have thought that the signs were clear—their salvation from the terrorists at Annalisa's hands, the testimony of Cardinal Berletti, Annalisa's own words—but then he recalled the rejection of Jesus and so reminded himself of the way of this world.

Many answered the same call as Roncalli. Others heard with deaf ears and retreated into fear or the safety of tradition. Still others were guided by the unrelenting ambition for power. Whatever the reasons were, realignments occurred in the conclave along diverse paths.

Many honored Berletti's request. Most of them were men familiar with Annalisa's healing acts through Berletti himself. Others recalled her contributions at the Ecumenical Council sessions and admired the diligent way she had pursued her studies in theology and canon law. Some Third World cardinals defected from Mannheim. In Annalisa, they saw an exceptional person from their own ranks who might balance the scales of the Church and accomplish a dream of equality they longed to fulfill. Annalisa's supporters admired her courage and believed she was attuned to the will of God. They differed only in their hopes of how that attunement would express itself in their particular lives.

The Milites Domini cardinals went over to Mannheim, as did those who saw a loss of influence with Annalisa's election. All who feared change and what it might bring in its wake if a woman were to wear the ring of the fisherman also allied with the German.

One by one, the cardinals filed by to place their ballots on the silver plate. The counting began, and then they made a recount, indicating it must have been a close vote. A third count was made for additional certainty, then the camerlengo, Torante, gathered all the ballots. He placed them in a furnace with a chemical additive that would cause white smoke to appear to the outside world, announcing that the Church had a new pope.

Forletti stood up and walked toward the seated cardinals. He gave a nod of acknowledgement to Cardinal Mannheim, but then walked past him to the delicate black woman sitting with hands folded on her lap and eyes closed.

At the sound of his approach, she opened her eyes. The cardinal dean's voice, made deep and sonorous by the cavernous hall, intoned the words: "Annalisa, Cardinal Basanjo, by the grace of God you are chosen bishop of Rome and pontiff of the Holy Roman Church. Do you accept your canonical election as Supreme Pontiff?"

In answer to Forletti's question, she closed her eyes once again, and with the slightest of smiles, her body began a gentle rocking. "I accept," she said.

"By what name do you wish to be called?" he asked.

"By my given birth name, Annalisa," she replied.

"Then you shall be known as Pope Annalisa the First," he said, announcing her papal name to the cardinals.

Each cardinal then lowered a purple canopy over his seat so that only Annalisa's remained folded, and it was done. The world had its first female pope. *And may God watch over her,* Roncalli prayed in silence.

The camerlengo then led Annalisa before the kneeling cardinals to a room adjacent to the chapel called the Room of Tears. There she was asked to choose from three sets of vestments, each of them white, the color reserved for popes alone. No one really knew how that room got its name, but as soon as the camerlengo left, Annalisa cried. She cried, and then she laughed. She wept again, softly, and then her emotions merged into a sobbing laugh of relief.

She donned the smallest alb and chasuble, but they still hung from her body like adult's clothing on a child, dangling and drooping, snowy white against her dark skin. It was never contemplated that those vestments should contain a female form. Her hands clenched at the loose fabric. "Now," her voice rasped at the empty room. "Now, let it begin." A burning look of passion came over her face . . . and anyone seeing her that way might have thought her possessed.

She finally emerged from the room, clutching the pectoral cross about her neck. The white smoke had alerted the world that there was a new pope, so the crowd and the media had already started to assemble and was overflowing St. Peter's Square. The camerlengo led Annalisa upstairs to the balcony of the papal apartments in the Apostolic Palace. Roncalli and Berletti accompanied them at Annalisa's request, as did Antonio Scolari, the senior cardinal deacon who would announce the name of the new pope to the world.

Annalisa smiled at Berletti and Roncalli, squeezing each of their hands as she waited in the room while the camerlengo stepped out onto the balcony. He leaned into the microphone and shouted *"HABEMUS PAPEM!"* which is to say, "WE HAVE A POPE!" The roar coming through the walls of the Apostolic Palace almost caused Annalisa to step backward, but there was no going back now. She walked onto the balcony, flanked by her entourage.

It was 7:30 p.m. and the sun was still out, but the light was mixed with shadows of approaching night. For a moment, there was a pronounced silence as the crowd strained to see the face of the pope. Who was the small, thin figure swimming in the loose white chasuble? The face looked very dark. Was it some trick of the shadows?

The pope reached up behind his head and seemed to be adjusting his skullcap, but then a mass of shoulder length black hair cascaded down from underneath the headpiece. A distinctly feminine shaking of the head sent the locks whipping from side to side, floating in the breeze for all to see. The crowd gasped in a shock that faded to momentary silence.

The sparks that ignited the bonfire of emotion in St. Peter's Square started at the front of the crowd nearest the balcony then spread toward the rear like a great, backwashing wave.

"A woman! The pope is a woman!"

"It's her, it's the female cardinal!"

"The African cardinal! The one they say does miracles."

"Glory be to God, the new pope is a woman!"

"My God, my God, they have elected a woman pope!"

Roncalli had no idea how the people would receive a female pope. They had elected her by the narrowest of margins, and so she ruled over a Church divided. Like the Caesars and Pompeys of ancient Rome, Roncalli listened closely to the Roman masses. Would it be the protest of silence, the growl of disapproval or . . . ?

Scolari, the cardinal deacon, now went to the microphone and announced the name of Annalisa I, the new pontiff, but the startled silence had given way to an eruption of cheers, and the crescendo obliterated his voice. The noise became voluminous and defined, and it was clear.

Hysterical, heartfelt joy exploded in the square, and with it, Roncalli's spirit carried upward. It was liberating. A miracle! The rumor of miracles had swirled in the air about Annalisa and now . . . now she was pope. As twilight grudgingly gave way to evening and the flood lamps were lit to shine on the balcony, Roncalli flung thinking and analysis to the wind. His feelings merged with those of the multitude in the square below. He stood tall behind Annalisa, a guardian at her back. A halo of light gleamed from her white chasuble and made her look like an earthbound angel. Beams from that light shone through loose white sleeves that hung like wings beneath her outstretched arms, and some of that light . . . some of that light penetrated through to cast its glow on Pietro Roncalli.

The rumor of miracles—a young British reporter named Teresa Ferentinos had first brought that rumor to the world's attention, and now she was in St. Peter's Square experiencing the greatest miracle of all. Once again, she stood in proximity to the woman whose life she seemed destined to chart.

When the pope first stepped onto the balcony and unpinned her hair to let the world know a woman would sit on the throne of St. Peter, Teresa was broadcasting. She signaled her cameras to keep rolling while she stepped out of the picture. She sat on a nearby stairway and cried, not even sure why. Relief, elation, triumph, wonder—it was all of these things.

Life took on new color, a sense of excitement and suspense at the possibility that God was extending His hand from the unseen to the visible world in the form of an exceptional woman. And He had given Teresa her small part to play. After two millennia, the feminine qualities of love, mercy, and nurturing would finally lead the institution that was supposed to embody those virtues. Was the Gnostic prediction of transformation coming true?

Flashing cameras strobed through the square like a display of electric fireworks never seeming to end, and the crowd roared on. It was a jubilee. Teresa was struck with an insight about this celebration. People were pinning their hopes and dreams of deliverance from this troubled world on that small figure engulfed in white light. Tonight's joy could become a great weight; did Annalisa realize that?

Teresa said a silent prayer for the pope. As she composed herself to cover the event, she said out loud, "Be careful, Annalisa," and she wondered if someone would whisper in Annalisa's ear the same admonition given to Roman generals during their triumphal marches two thousand years ago: "*sic gloria transit mundis*, remember thou art mortal, and all the glory of this world is fleeting."

CHAPTER LVIII

A letter is an unannounced visit, and the postman is the intermediary of impolite surprises. —Friedrich Nietzsche

Qom, Iran

Ayatollah Havenei opened the suitcase and found two million two hundred and forty thousand dollars and a note. An Irishman from the PNC had delivered the suitcase.

"Why should I not kill you?" Havenei asked the man. "Your people betrayed us."

The Irishman shook his head. He did not seem affected by the threat. "No betrayal, changed circumstances," he said in a thick brogue. "We're givin' yer money back. I suggest you read the note. Now, if you wants to kill me, you'll have that war on your hands you threatened us with, but I heard you was a smart man. You has to ask yerself, what have you lost? Is it worth it? And remember, we know where you live. You can't say the same fer us. We're willin' to call it quits."

Havenei stared at him. The man was brave. He did not blink. When he first heard the news of the failed operation, Havenei was furious. When he heard they elected the nun as the pope, he was beside himself. She was the very reason he wanted to punish the Church. He knew they made the popular nun a cardinal to strike at Islam in Nigeria. Now they were trying to push the knife in deeper by making her pope. It was exactly what they did when they elected a Pole to bring down communism in Poland.

Havenei had vented his anger prior to the PNC man's arrival. He knew these men were dangerous. He could not afford to start a war with them to distract from his grand plan. They had returned his money, so he had no real cause, but he was perplexed and infuriated. They had penetrated the Vatican and given up! Why?

"Leave," he told the Irishman. "I should have known better than to trust infidels, but there will be no war since you have returned our funds." When the man was gone, Havenei opened the suitcase and read the note.

We are returning your money with eight percent interest. Do not say we are not honorable. As for the operation, the African cardinal who has now become pope is a holy woman and a prophet. Make no mistake about it. We were told things only a prophet could know. We will be ceasing any further attacks on the Church.

How had she made hardened men cower and run like beaten dogs? The Christians were nearly as opposed to women in their ranks as Muslims. He had heard the stories of the shaman who raised her in the dark arts. Perhaps she was no prophet, but a devil.

He had sought to cripple the Church by stealing its money and its ability to fund its proselytizing in Nigeria and around the world, but perhaps she would accomplish his agenda for him. The Church was deeply divided over her papacy. Still, she was the wild card in world politics no one had predicted, and no one knew what to expect. There must be something extraordinary about her yet to be revealed. The way she turned the PNC terrorists was almost supernatural. Havenei did not understand her, and that worried him. He decided the best course was to wait and watch . . . and he would watch closely.

CHAPTER LIX

. . . do not give what is holy to dogs . . . do not give pearls to swine.
—The Gospel of Thomas

The Vatican City

Meteoric and *astonishing* were the words everyone used when referring to Annalisa's rise from obscurity to the papacy, and now she had to select the people who would help her govern. A change in the Holy See automatically vacated all positions in the curia. The new pontiff then staffed the vacancies with appointees of his—now her—own choosing.

Monsignor O'Keefe agreed to assume Roncalli's former role as the pope's personal secretary. Only Annalisa could have lured O'Keefe away from his beloved library. Cardinal Berletti took Tormada's position as prefect of the Doctrine of the Faith, Archbishop Maccario would now oversee the Vatican Bank. Roncalli became substitute for General Affairs, or sostituto. Many considered the sostituto the real fulcrum of power in the Vatican. He was the equivalent of the chief of staff to the U.S. president, the indispensable focal point who controlled both the people and the documents that would come before the pope's eyes.

The sostituto's position nominally came under the secretary of state, that office went to Cardinal De Faissy, but not before Annalisa offered to let Mannheim keep his former position, to the surprise of all. When she asked O'Keefe his opinion he said, "Secretary of State, eh? A powerful position. Be careful not to put all your eggs in one bastard," but it did not matter. Mannheim refused.

"Her election must not stand," Mannheim declared to his six cohorts. They then made a decision that was the equivalent of Caesar crossing the Rubicon. They began contacting the nearly half of the college of cardinals who had voted against Annalisa, Mannheim planned for his showdown with Alvaro, and they placed calls to every bishop around the world who stood for traditional Catholic values.

"When do we make our move?" Trevi asked.

"She will reveal her true colors at the Ecumenical Council, I know it," Mannheim replied. "At that time, when they see her real agenda, then we move."

Annalisa called Desmond O'Keefe into her office. She told him of her intentions for the Ecumenical Council. Annalisa was about to cross the threshold that neither Roncalli nor Clement had dared to tread and do it in a way they never dreamed. O'Keefe recalled Roncalli telling him the words of the former pope, Clement: "There is one who will cross this bridge I will make, a leader, that much I saw, but like Moses was unable to enter the Promised Land, I will not be there at the crossing."

Annalisa would now complete the process Clement had started but would not finish. Clement's words now seemed prophetic, and O'Keefe focused on the part about the Promised Land. He knew the Hebrews did not enter Israel without the shedding of blood. He was certain that blood in one sense or another would be spilled over what he had just read.

He looked at Annalisa. Without any doubt in his mind that some force had guided her to this moment, he asked her, "Why are you here; what is it you intend for the world?"

Annalisa looked at him. Perhaps it was a trick of the light, but her face seemed different to him, more than human. "Why, Desmond, you know quite well. You've seen the symbols appearing in the Vatican, for *I am come to open the gates of hell.*"

O'Keefe sat numb and trembling, hearing her words as her vice-like eyes locked into his soul. He would not divulge her secret until she told him the time was right.

CHAPTER LX

From fanaticism to barbarism is only one step. —Denis Diderot

Toledo, Spain

MID-TERM VICTORY
FOR DAVIDSON!

(UP WASHINGTON 11.15.28) The campaign strategy that pundits labeled risky eighteen months ago paid off for president John Davidson today. He tirelessly campaigned to elect congressional allies and he succeeded, cutting across party lines to do so.

Davidson forcibly addressed the fear and anxiety of the nation in an era when long term recession borders on depression. His one word campaign slogan, "ENOUGH," summed up the mood of a nation tired of terrorism, suicide bombings, and being the world's whipping boy for Third World and Islamic countries.

Davidson characterized past foreign policy as criminally weak in light of Iranian efforts to divert oil from America's pipelines. The conclusion three months ago of the Iranian/Islamic oil agreement with the Asian bloc countries under China gave Davidson's warnings an urgency that translated into votes. The deciding factor was the huge campaign war chest Davidson amassed that allowed him to stage a phenomenal advertising blitz sixty days prior to the elections . . .

That last sentence in today's newspaper gave Bishop Alvaro great satisfaction as he sat and read in his Toledo office. The huge sums of money Milites Domini funneled to Davidson had paid off. It had been a risky move, but great deeds were not done by the faint-hearted.

Rebuffed so far in his efforts to control the Vatican, Alvaro took comfort that the most important part of his plan was in place. Islam was a blight that had to be eradicated. It had ceased to be a religion; it had become an ideology, and its central tenet was destroying the West. Its adherents were brainwashed into a deep, abiding hatred of anything non-Islamic, anything modern, and anything democratic. They could not keep to themselves, wallowing in their own backwardness. Their hatred and hostility had forced them to attack every other religion in the world: Christianity, Hinduism, and Buddhism. They struck, then hid like cockroaches among the so-called legitimate Islamic nations who gave them aid and sustenance.

All the while, the weak, socialist Western countries played the corrupt United Nations game, pretending the enemy states that harbored the terrorists were not enemies. Iran, Saudi Arabia, Pakistan—they were all the same. They claimed to be friendly while their religious schools churned out Christian haters, while they funneled money and intelligence to the terrorists and sheltered them.

Cockroaches. Those lowly insects gave him the idea that had turned into his grand plan. He remembered that day in New York walking to Milites' North American office when he passed a brick townhouse. He saw the building enveloped in plastic. A machine was pumping smoke into it while the supervisor of the crew stood out front.

"What is that?" Alvaro inquired, pointing at the building.

"Fumigation, Father, fumigation," the man replied. "Cockroaches."

"It kills cockroaches? How does it work?" Alvaro asked.

The foreman spit a wad of phlegm on the ground. "It's the only way to go, Father, when you get run over by the little bastards — s'cuse my English. You can step on 'em, use traps, whatever. It ain't enough. Sooner or later, they overrun you. Only way to put an end to it is get 'em all at one time. That's what this baby does. Nuke's 'em all at once."

Nuke them all at once—Alvaro took the image as a divine metaphor. The West had the capacity, but not the will. How could he give them the will to end the threat for good? He had found the answer, and the proof was in now front of him. For the sheer pleasure of it, he picked up the newspaper and read it again.

CHAPTER LXI

Change means movement, movement means friction.
— Saul Alinsky

The Vatican City

Pietro Roncalli looked around the crowded basilica in excited anticipation. Annalisa had done it. She had broken the deadlock and made the Ecumenical Council happen. Under Clement, the conservatives had managed to block the Council's moderate reformist agenda formulated at the earlier bishop's synods. Annalisa had made sure the agenda was heard and a balanced analysis was presented. She personally participated in all work sessions, and she spent many solitary hours in prayer and contemplation.

"The time for study and discussion is over," she had announced to her advisors with a casual smile. "This is a great work we must do." She was ready to lend the weight of the papacy to the issues before the Council. She showed the draft of her speech to Cardinal Berletti, the new prefect of the Holy Office who had replaced the still irate and obstreperous Tormada.

Popes customarily ran speeches and apostolic letters by the prefect, who was supposed to assure consistency with Catholic doctrine. When Berletti saw the draft of Annalisa's speech, he spent many hours behind closed doors with her. He tried his best to change her mind or at least soften her position on many of the issues. "You are a new pope, a young pope, and you will put great pressure on yourself and the Church the moment these words become public. These matters stretch the tranquility of current doctrine."

"The world is ready, Giacomo." That was the extent of her reply.

"I have grave reservations about your decisions and the effects on the Church," he said, "but when I stepped down in hope of seeing you elected, it was for a reason. Now I must learn to exercise that trust we talked about so many times before; from this there will be no turning back."

So it was after all his years of struggling, Pietro Roncalli found himself listening to Pope Annalisa deliver her first address to the Ecumenical Council on November third of 2028 in St. Peter's Basilica. The Church teemed with prelates from around the world: metropolitans from the Eastern churches in their black phelonia and high headpieces, patriarchs in golden vestments, cardinals in red simars with white, watered lace, and bishops in different colored pallia. The church was a living kaleidoscope of ecclesiastic colors.

On a dais before the altar of St. Peter sat the African pope, white vestments now altered to fit her diminutive form. Roncalli, fingers grinding within the clenched ball of his hand, sat thinking of the miracle of Annalisa's election . . . but this was a different day. Over time, even miracles succumbed to the weight of rationalized doubt. The euphoria had passed, and the mundane pressure cooker of problems, politics, and squabbling was boiling over once more. The eyes of the world now watched every move and utterance of the new pope, ready to see how she would meet the daunting challenges before her. This was her first real-world test.

"The papers are already saying hers is the papacy that will decide the fate of the Church," Cardinal De Faissy commented to Roncalli. He read from a newspaper clipping in his palm. "Church on the precipice . . . She could propel or retard the role of women in the new millennium . . . could advance or destroy the hopes of all Third World peoples to secure a place of respect in the eyes of the world and in the depths of their own hearts. They put much on her, Pietro."

Roncalli nodded. More than anyone, he was aware of the mounting expectations being heaped upon the shoulders of the small, delicate woman who stepped up to the dais and stood before them so early in her reign as pope. "Even so," he remarked, "she's allowing news coverage of the Ecumenical Council."

"Yes, that's a first," De Faissy replied, "and much to the chagrin of the traditionalists."

Annalisa was opening the Vatican to the world at large, and the media, insatiable for information about the new pope, responded in a massive way. Teresa Ferentinos sat in a booth with a contingent of UNN personnel watching Annalisa on the monitors. The network was using Father John Royer to assist Teresa with a theologian's analysis of the proceedings. The packed basilica grew deathly silent as Annalisa started to deliver the speech that would set the tone of her papacy:

"Peace be with you, my brethren. In the two thousand years since Jesus taught, have average people moved closer to God? Have wars stopped? Are people healing one another? Where are the prophets? A bishop once told me that God speaks to no one any more. Does this seem like spiritual progress to you? Early Christians

called their spiritual movement 'The Way'. What 'way' did Jesus teach, what path to divine knowledge was lost that unleashed a torrent of miracles in those days? Perhaps in these questions lie the answers to why so many people are falling away from the Church."

Roncalli could feel the audience bursting with an overwhelming sense of anticipation. How would this forty-three year old woman bear up under such tremendous demands? Could she make the hard decisions and still keep the Church united? She had started aggressively, almost challenging the gathered establishment.

"Let us speak of truth, for ultimately, that is the goal that we pursue. The Church makes two assumptions about the world: first that God has created a fixed, knowable truth, revealed it in the scriptures, and left humanity to discover precisely what that truth is. Second, the Church believes that truth and God are both external to us."

Teresa Ferentinos sat in the UNN news booth. Even from up there she sensed restlessness among the Church elders, a powder keg of tension waiting to ignite.

"These notions have caused people to believe that absolute truth is something 'out there' to be found in the scriptures as occasionally captured by prophets or witnesses. But let us look at truth in another light. What if there is only one absolute truth and that truth is God? *What if His truth is not* outside *of us but* implanted in all of us, waiting to be remembered?

A large portion of the audience stirred. Father Royer said to Teresa, "These things she speaks of have no theological precedent. It's very unusual."

" What if the prophets were just those of us who accessed the truths available to all humanity if we but had the courage to look within and the means to understand. For truth, like God, is a mystery. It does not come into the mind literally and obviously; it comes in dreams, images, and symbols. It is a constant process of revelation, an ever present, parallel reality seeping through to help us to evolve and guide our lives."

One could hear a faint rumbling begin. Roncalli cupped his mouth and whispered to Segri, "This is profound. It runs counter to everything they believe."

"Herein lies the clue of what direction the Church can take to truly help its people. Instead of dwelling on rituals they do not understand, instead of forcing dogmas and practices on them that are abstract to their lives, we can help them seek answers within. We can help them interpret their images and metaphors in a way that directs their lives, for though our paths are many, the place to which we journey is the same."

The low, impatient grumbling of the prelates was now being magnified by the basilica's stone walls. Roncalli looked at Segri in apprehension.

"If you doubt my words, ask yourselves why so many seek to become whole in a psychiatrist's office instead of the Church. The Church offers no answers; psychiatrists help but they have no spiritual orientation. Human beings are fragmented, and we have misdirected them. Truth is an unfolding story we uncover through our intuition and perceptions, an unveiling process leading to ever-higher plateaus of understanding.

"Let us then never believe a *truth is* the *truth, but rather what we call truth is our best understanding at the time. Truths, therefore, are superseded by newer and more accurate truths, until we realize the One Truth—God—by total absorption into His heart. As for that state, we will know it only it when we attain it."*

At those words, there was an audible disturbance in the audience. Umberto Segri, the Venetian Patriarch, came to sit behind Roncalli and De Faissy. "Trouble," he whispered. "The conservatives are expecting the worst. They're planning to do something."

"Do what?" Roncalli asked.

"I couldn't learn any details," Segri said. "We'll have to wait and see what happens, but they've gotten wind of her decisions."

"In God's own image were we made, and that image is contained in each of us: we are as cells in the universal Body of Christ's Church. Just as the cells of our individual bodies must constantly change and renew themselves for the organism to live and grow, so too must the Body of Christ change and renew itself or die."

Roncalli saw that some were already shaking their heads as if to say, *Here it is. We told you so.* Listening to the conservative prelates bristling around him, Cardinal De Faissy said to Roncalli, "I hope this was not a mistake—a young, inexperienced woman making such sweeping theological statements. Who would have dreamed she had such boldness in her? Did becoming pope transform her?"

"No, but I think she's transforming the papacy," Roncalli whispered back. "I think we're seeing a different face of the same woman. The time for caution and pretense is over. She knew that, and now I know it. Remember the tale of the emperor's new clothes, how the deluded people applauded out of compulsion and habit until someone said, 'Look, the Emperor is naked?' Today, she's telling the world the Church is naked."

Up on the dais, Annalisa was concluding her speech. "*I ask each of you to recognize that we were made by God for the purpose of moving toward His perfection. When we see suffering and disease, guilt and poverty, loneliness and discrimination, we must not stand still but move in different directions. These afflictions are born of our faulty understandings and perpetuated by our fear of change.*

"People have asked throughout the ages: What God is it that abides by the suffering, violence, and cruelty of this world? We see these things operating in nature as well as in the human condition, so we cannot say human failing or sin has caused this imperfection. It seems rather that imperfection is inherent in the very fabric of the world. If God is truly perfection, but the world that we live in is imperfect, then some force stands between us and the truth and this world is an illusion, an aberration from God's reality. What is it that bars us from the truth? What forces stand between us and God? These are the questions we must answer.

"Today we will speak of new directions to seek the truth. We will speak of lifting barriers to liberate human energy and allow it to move in a new direction. We now give answers to the questions before this Council," the pope said, "with the highest and best understanding available to us."

In the UNN booth, Father Royer spoke to Teresa with anticipation in his voice, "This is very controversial theology. Some will say it borders on heresy. She's been building the theological platform for whatever she's about to do, and by the tone of it, she's readying them for something they may not like."

"Here it goes," Teresa said. "What is she going to do?"

"Something very different, I think," was all Father Royer could say in reply, and they both inhaled deeply, waiting for what would come.

CHAPTER LXII

God is a comedian playing to an audience too afraid to laugh.
— Voltaire

The Vatican City

It was one of the most anticipated moments of the twenty-first century. One by one, the pope addressed the list of controversial issues that had plagued the Church for so many years:

Female clergy: "Women will be allowed to hold all ranks within the Church hierarchy. Seminaries will begin accepting worthy candidates without unfair hindrance." (A collective groan.) "If Mary the mother of Jesus were to appear before us today, would you deny her Holy Orders based on her sex?" the pope asked.

Clerical celibacy: "Clergy of all ranks will be allowed to marry if they choose, providing that the Church is not financially responsible for the maintenance of the family beyond the salary of the clergyman or clergywoman. ("No, no!" came the shouts.) "Marriage was allowed in the early Church," the pope said, "and nothing is more distracting from devotion to God than the deviant paths created by repressed human needs."

Homosexuality: "The Church need not condone homosexual lifestyles, but we can no longer condemn homosexuals. We must go on record strongly opposing abuse and violence against them. As for ordaining homosexuals, that will be a matter of review on a case-by-case basis between an archdiocese and an individual parish with right of appeal to the Vatican. The wishes of the parishioners would be paramount in determining the need for or acceptance of a homosexual clergy person. ("Outrageous!" the clergy howled.)

"The character of a relationship is more important than the outward sexuality of it," the pope continued undaunted. "If the individual seeking ordination believes in relationships characterized by love, fidelity, and devotion, that person should be given the opportunity for a life in the service of Christ regardless of sexual orientation. The Church forgives heterosexuals who lapse from such relationships and praises those who do not. The same must be true of homosexuals. To condemn them is to condemn ourselves, to praise them is to praise ourselves."

Birth control: The Church will henceforth cease its opposition to birth control.

(Betrayal! came the most vehement cries yet.) "Uncontrolled reproduction is not multiplying the fruit of the earth, my brethren, but rather diminishing it. The population explosion causes poverty, famine, and war, and this is not a path, intended or unintended, direct or indirect, that the Church should ever promote. Even the issue of abortion can be partially addressed by responsible birth control."

As the pope spoke, some bishops and cardinals stood up and started to walk out of the room, and this caught Teresa's eye.

Abortion: "Abortion," the pope said, "touches at people's very core because each side perceives it in terms of life and death, or control thereof. The Church will continue to discourage abortion but only in the form of private counseling between a priest and parishioner. The Church will drop its intransigent public stance on the subject and the clergy will be instructed to support the final decision of any woman or couple after clerical counseling on alternatives to the abortion procedure." (Now the protesters almost drowned Annalisa's voice.)

An increasing number of prelates were rising from their seats and making their way out. *There were too many to be just taking a break for the restroom,* Teresa thought.

Poverty: "Charity is fine and has its place," the pope said, "but providing opportunity for economic growth is a more fundamental response to the problem. The roots of poverty are many, but the remedy is singular. If I give a man some money in alms, the money is soon gone. But if I give that man a job, the money replenishes itself along with the man's self-respect.

"The Church cannot assume the responsibility of governments in this area, but a community that shares its wealth and labor to support its members did characterize the ancient Church. Drawing from that example, we might strive for a system, a kind of volunteer corps staffed by skilled and spiritually motivated people, where the Churches would invest in selected Third World areas to start communal industries. The people of those communities can be trained as employees, but they would also own *the businesses. As these industries became profitable, they would repay the loans to the Church to create a revolving investment fund.*

"This is not possible today given the current state of Church finances, but articulating the intent and principle of the idea is important. It will remind people that material and spiritual growth are connected. Economic prosperity promotes higher levels of education. In turn, education and economic well-being afford people the time and motivation to engage in spiritual growth."

From her position in the booth above the assembly, Teresa observed Cardinal Mannheim stand and walk out of the basilica with six other cardinals. As the pope continued her talk, more prelates methodically stood and followed Mannheim in a steady stream until close to half the congregation had left. A loud buzz grew among those remaining, but the pope did not falter in speech or appear distracted, a feat that must have required monumental concentration. "Are we actually witnessing a walkout?" Teresa inquired of Father Royer as part of her on-air commentary.

"It . . . it must be," he replied. "This is completely unprecedented," he stammered, and she saw he looked shaken.

"Father," she said, turning her mike off, "I know something big is happening here. We have to keep calm and describe what is occurring to the best of our ability, okay? That's what we're here to do. Are you with me now?"

He nodded and took a deep breath to compose himself. "It's a protest by the traditionalists. I can see that much now."

Teresa held his hand. "When we're back on air, give us your best analysis of what occurred. Take your cues from me, all right?"

He bit his lower lip and nodded his assent.

The pope was finishing her speech, and the camera switched from the floor to the team in the booth. The audio and visual were now fully on Teresa and the priest. "It seems that some sort of walkout or protest has occurred by a large number of prelates," Teresa told the global audience. "Father Royer, can you tell us about the pope's speech and what happened here?"

The television viewers could not see it, but Royer's hands were scrunched-up spheres. Teresa gave him a supportive look as he began to reply. "Well, now we understand the reason for her comments on the nature of truth—she just changed precepts held sacred by the Church for millennia. What surprised me, however, was the scope and depth of the changes she proposed. This pope was an experiment by the Church in many ways, the first woman, the first African, and as such one might have supposed she would walk lightly."

"And apparently we have just seen a negative reaction to her decisions, or, perhaps to *her*," said Teresa. "Can you analyze her speech and isolate the elements that may have caused so many prelates to leave in what appears to have been a shocking protest?"

"The pope has gone beyond the recommendations embodied in the majority opinion of the reformers," Royer said, and to Teresa's relief, he seemed to have recovered from his initial distress. "The emphasis on subjective intuition instead of Church teaching to approach the mystery of God, the relativity of truth, but mostly the reference to 'forces' that created an imperfect world—these are all statements that fly in the face of settled theology."

"Where does the Catholic Church go from here?" Teresa asked.

"I wish I could answer that," Royer said. "Certainly, the authority of this pope has been called into question by the bishops who walked out, and that is a very grave concern."

The pope had concluded her speech and was stepping off the dais to greet the remaining Church officials. The prelates, almost to a man, were kneeling and crossing themselves as she passed. Many reached out to kiss her hand.

"Again unprecedented," Royer said. "It's a gauge of the emotion that must be sweeping the basilica at this moment, or else a calculated show of support for the remarkable actions of this pope. But it also demonstrates how deeply the Church is divided."

Teresa thanked Royer for his analysis as the camera lingered on the scene for some time. Finally, the camera switched back to fix solely on Teresa as she concluded the broadcast. "We have just witnessed a watershed in the history of Christianity. The hopes of millions were uplifted today, but at the expense of the harmony, and possibly the unity, of the Church. What effect this pope will have on the Church will no doubt be the subject of future reports."

A close-up still picture of Annalisa flashed on-screen to be viewed by millions around the earth. Her face was impossibly young looking, too beautiful to be a pope, yet on this day she had indelibly printed her signature on the Church in a way no other pontiff had done before. Teresa now did a voice-over while the pope's image dominated the TV screen.

"The world seldom hangs on the cliff of a drama as great as this one. How this chapter will unfold in the book of human history is a story for another day. For UNN, this is Teresa Ferentinos. Good night."

CHAPTER LXIII

Gone is the belief that adulthood is, or ought to be, a time of internal peace and comfort, that growing pains belong only to the young.
—Lillian Breslow Rubin

The Vatican City

Cardinal Roncalli read the *World Magazine* article to the group assembled in the papal study on the third floor of the Apostolic Palace. The pope herself was there, and so were Cardinals Berletti and De Faissy, Monsignor O'Keefe, and the patriarch Umberto Segri.

WAR IN HEAVEN

by *World Magazine* staff correspondent Dru Sarech

Less than three months after the pope's phenomenal address to a full Ecumenical Council gathered in Rome, the Catholic Church under Annalisa I is facing an ecclesiastical civil war the likes of which has not been seen since the Protestant Reformation.

Angered by the unprecedented sweep of reforms announced at Vatican III, a number of bishops led by former Vatican Secretary of State, Heinrich Cardinal Mannheim, and totaling as much as forty percent of the prelates in the Church, have announced their intention to disregard the reforms instituted at the Council. The bishops, whose dioceses are concentrated primarily in Europe and North America, have formed an opposition called the Holy Orthodox Catholic Church, the first step, perhaps, in a complete split with Rome. They are ordering priests to conduct local church affairs as if the Ecumenical Council never took place.

This sets the stage for a potential schism, the most dreaded word in Christianity. If the rebellious bishops do not relent, the pope may be forced to excommunicate them and all members of the Church who follow them.

In what must be a bitter pill for the pope, her own Archdiocese of Lagos under Bishop Ogunsanya has joined the ranks of the protesters. The majority of the people in Nigeria, however, remain supportive of Annalisa, according to UNN polls.

The complaints against the new pope by her detractors are widespread and bitter. "It is not just the changes in practice," said Bishop Tomas Dueren of Vienna, "her theological statements are of grave concern. She seems to be exalting man without the mediation of the Church and God's grace. That is arrogant presumption at best, heresy at worst."

"Rubbish," replies Archbishop Silvio Marcen of Manila. "They cannot make such accusations about her theology based on her pronouncements at Vatican III. Her perspectives were brilliant and uplifting, and I heard nothing to support these spurious claims."

The majority of parishioners around the world seem to share in Archbishop Marcen's feelings about the pope. "I think she is wonderful," says fifty-two-year-old Anita Trosten, a devout Catholic from Philadelphia. "I really believe attendance has increased in our church solely because of Pope Annie. She is trying to show us a more enlightened way, but I guess some people prefer to look backwards."

Some of the people to whom Mrs. Trosten may be referring have been picketing in front of Catholic churches with placards saying, THE POPE IS A BABY KILLER! and POPE ANNIE—SOFT ON ABORTION.

Yet in Latin America, where overpopulation is choking the lifeblood of many poor nations, it is "Viva Annie!" "Finally a pope who seems to understand us," said Elario Torrez, an itinerant worker who recently lost the second of six children due to inability to obtain proper medical care. "Maybe the Church will now be a help and not a hindrance."

Annalisa seems to be a figure either loved or loathed in the popular mind. She elicits emotions like no other public figure on the world stage today, even in the infancy of her papacy. It has been widely rumored that the pope is a miracle worker and that, in part, was the reason for her unprecedented election by the normally conservative College of Cardinals. Many of them, however, are said to view her as an impetuous upstart.

"The Church is financially unsound, fragmented, and wavering. If she does perform miracles," said an anonymous Vatican insider, "she better pull one out of her miter, or she may be the last pope to preside over a unified Church."

"If they persist in this course, Mother, you *will* have to excommunicate them," Segri said. Those close to her called Annalisa "Mother" at her request. The word pope in Italian is *papa*, which derived from the word for "father" in Greek. She explained to them that she was obviously no papa, but mother would do nicely to describe her status.

"Mannheim runs his opposition Church from here in the Vatican!" Segri said. "The audacity! We cannot function like this. You must expel them and appoint new prelates."

"No, Umberto, no one gets excommunicated while I am pope," Annalisa replied. "If none are lost in *God's* eyes, how can *we* presume to lose them? For too long now the Church has compelled people with the yoke of its authority rather than convinced them with the validity of its ideas. We will not excommunicate, but we will respond."

"How?" De Faissy asked.

"By persuasion," Annalisa said, and then she pointed to two suitcases in the corner of the study. "We will go out to the churches," she said. "I knew there would be a strong reaction to the decisions made at the Council, there had to be. That is the way of the world."

"A schism in the Church is the most serious thing that can happen, and that is just where we're heading," Roncalli said.

"That is why I am proposing to leave the Vatican for the next six months to travel to parishes around the world," Annalisa said.

"Six months!" O'Keefe exclaimed. "No pope leaves the Vatican for that length of time."

"How many popes were faced with a schism?" Annalisa replied. "The opponents of change will seek to confuse the people. If we provide them a chance to make up their own minds, if we are to renew the Church, we have to be among the people as much as possible."

"You packed your bags for a tour without telling any of us?" Monsignor O'Keefe asked.

"Well, not exactly." The pope smiled. "The suitcases are empty, but I will fill them as soon as we discuss our plans."

Over the next several hours, she outlined her ideas. At the conclusion of the discussion, she said to them, "This whole episode is difficult but necessary. Yet it is also an opportunity." She looked at Roncalli. "Yes, it will be a struggle, but out of this will come a new consciousness of what it means to be a Christian. A Church that does not periodically reexamine itself, its practices, and even its beliefs, is a dead relic, not a living body."

The pope now started gesturing with her hands. It was rare that she spoke so emphatically. "It is especially important that this process of reform occurs with the participation of the people. The controversy our detractors have created will ensure that participation. The Church must now grow from this experience, or most assuredly, the Church will die from it."

CHAPTER LXIV

But this people hath a revolting and rebellious heart. — Isaiah 5:23

The Vatican City

Cardinal LoPresti addressed his colleagues in the apartment of Cardinal Villendot. "We have an *antipope* on the throne. I have been seeking guidance. It is customary for a pope to write a last epistle, a letter to his future successor giving such advice as he deems necessary. I found a letter from Pius to Clement." LoPresti then started skim reading to other cardinals.

Evil forces will engulf you in a great storm. Only your faith in God will sustain you and the Church during these dark days. Beware: assassins will attempt to end your life . . . some will try to damage the Church from within, to destroy it like a cancer. Many will seek to force you away from our traditions and articles of faith . . . they will implore you to modernize the Church, to end celibacy, to allow women to enter the Priesthood, even to support the use of artificial birth control. Know that they are in the service of the devil and heed them not.

A close adviser shall be your Judas . . . a viper, seeming to act for good purpose, yet even he is not the Deceiver of whom the prophecies warned but a mere forerunner. The world shall descend into conflict. Economies will grind to a halt in America and the West from lack of oil. Nations shall be bankrupt. The sleeping Czars of Russia will return to communism . . . there shall be war and rumblings of war. The crescent and the cross shall collide. Amid this ruin shall the Great Deceiver come as a peacemaker.

You shall lead the Holy Church in the end of days. The great evil of Revelations shall come to pass . . . the Great Deceiver will enthrall the world . . . hell will reign on earth. Large parts of the world will be destroyed and slide into oblivion . . . great portions of all things living will perish.

"This is quite foreboding, Gianmarco," Mannheim said to LoPresti, "but I remember this letter. It was supposed to have been from Pius to Clement when Clement assumed the papacy, but Pius' people disavowed its legitimacy when it somehow became public. It was said to be a forgery."

"I was close to Pius," LoPresti said. "I asked him one day about its authenticity. He would not answer me, though he did not deny it. I never understood why, but he would say nothing about it. Whether Pius wrote it or not, he did not reject its content. And what if someone else wrote the prophecy; does that make it untrue?"

LoPresti picked up his copy and began reading aloud, skimming the lines. "Corruption of the Church, straying from the faith, ending celibacy, ordaining women, permitting birth control—it's all happened!"

DeGolia said, "But this business of an assassination attempt, that never happened."

"No?" LoPresti asked. "Do we know that? Clement almost died in Africa. Perhaps that illness was somehow induced. It did pave the way for the nun's entry into the Church. And how do we even know his eventual death was natural?"

That took the others by surprise. They paused to consider the implications.

"Now listen," LoPresti said. "'A close adviser shall be your Judas yet even he is not the great Deceiver but a forerunner.' We have a perfect living analog for this figure."

Mannheim stared wide-eyed at LoPresti. "The Judas—*Roncalli!*" he exclaimed, spitting the name out with a throaty exhalation of breath. "The architect of this whole disaster. The advisor who swayed Clement, the one who paved the way for Annalisa."

LoPresti nodded in agreement and said, "Those symbols cropping up, things she hinted at in the Council, I fear she intends to reopen the Pandora's Box of Gnosticism, the most dangerous heresy the Church ever faced," and the already ashen-faced cardinals blanched to new shades of pale.

"We must stop her," Mannheim declared. "And I have a plan. Leave it to me."

The outskirts of Rome

Mannheim watched the car drive up to the small chapel on a hill outside of Rome. He cupped one of the flowers growing from the vines on the side of the chapel's stone walls then broke it off and kept it in his hand. He walked inside and sat down.

A few minutes later, a dark man with baleful eyes and a venomous cast to his mouth entered the room. For a second, the two men glared at each other until Mannheim said, "Don't play your intimidation games with me, Alvaro. I'm not Van Kluysen. Sit."

Alvaro waited a minute to distance his compliance from Mannheim's command, but he did sit as he was told. "You have a hell of a nerve stealing the Church's money," Mannheim said. "Under other circumstances, I'd have you defrocked and thrown in jail."

"But you won't, will you?" Alvaro said.

"No, I won't, because we have a greater threat facing us," Mannheim said. "I can use your stolen funds to correct it. I will see this heresy dead and buried," and he threw the flower from his hand onto the table between the two men. "We are going to use the money to buy me the papacy."

Alvaro looked at him with a down-turned mouth. "I already tried that."

"Yes," Mannheim said, "but that was with Clement. Things are different now. The Church is breaking apart under the African woman. Also, I'll not be heavy-handed like you were. I won't demand to be pope in exchange for the money. I won't have to. At the end of her papal trip, the woman will have ground the Church to dust. I will then broker the deal that solves the financial problem. The entire Vatican will be grateful and see me as the savior who can return the Church to normalcy. She'll be pressured right off the papal throne."

Alvaro considered Mannheim's statements. "What is in this for Milites Domini?"

Mannheim made an ironic little smile as if he had known the question was coming. "Plenty. You get to keep your position, your order, and any money you had before your theft. You also stay out of jail. But those are all negative incentives. I'll make sure some of your men get key positions in the curia when I'm pope."

Alvaro sat, thinking.

"Look, Alvaro, we need to be realistic," Mannheim declared. "All our previous plans were nullified by her election. We face a common threat greater than any the Church has ever known. The Muslims and other terrorists are attacking on all fronts, the Church weakens by the day, and now the papacy itself is leading the charge into the abyss. Supernatural forces are at work, and the prophecies support that view. Since the day she arrived, demonic symbols keep appearing around the Vatican, reaffirming her evil."

Alvaro nodded, indicating for Mannheim to proceed with his train of thought.

"Despite our differences," Mannheim said, "we are cut from the same cloth. If

I were pope, I would rid the Church of its liberal elements and negate Vatican III. I would create modern crusaders out of local Christian youths in battleground countries to combat the Muslims. These are all things you want too."

Alvaro, ever the chess player, was thinking several moves ahead. He had already accomplished one goal by getting Davidson elected. He had hoped to have someone under his control assume the papacy, but the African woman had changed everything. If he could not use the stolen funds to put a minion on the papal throne, a strong ally as pope was an acceptable alternative at this point. His goal was spiritual renewal of the Western world before it lay down and committed suicide before its enemies. He had to keep his purpose in sight and not deviate down blind alleys of pride. Pride was Mannheim's province; purpose belonged to Alvaro.

"We have an agreement," he said, and Mannheim took the flower back into his hand.

There was no handshake to seal the bargain; Alvaro was not his equal and Mannheim would not condescend. No matter. Uneasy pacts are best cemented by mutual need; both men knew that without saying.

CHAPTER LXV

When you do not know what you are doing and what you are doing is the best—that is inspiration. — Robert Bresson

The Vatican City

We put up a slew of new security cameras, but whoever is doing this is smart," Avernis said. "These were posted outside the headquarters of the Congregation of the Doctrine of the Faith," and he pointed to the two images on the desk of Roncalli's office. O'Keefe, Roncalli, and Teresa viewed the images, one a picture, one a symbol.

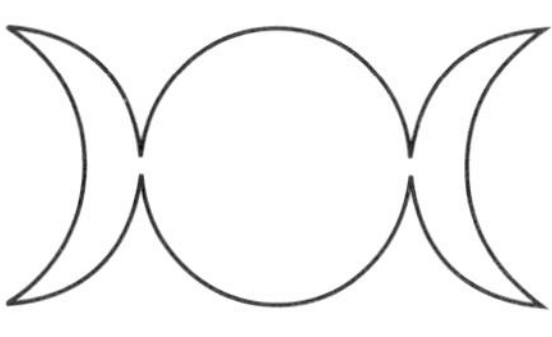

"Teresa already has some information for us," O'Keefe said.

Teresa nodded. "These images seemed fairly straightforward compared to the others in this series of bizarre appearances. The one on the left is called Papal Triumph. It's part of a painting from the 1500s seeming to show Gnostic influences. The Gnostics were expelled as heretics, but they were never completely silenced. Of course, the unusual aspect here is readily noticeable. The pope is a woman. It is the Church personified in a *female pope.*"

"This is the first object that makes sense to anything in our experience," Roncalli observed. "We have a female pope now. All the other symbols have been abstract."

"Perhaps," O'Keefe said, "or perhaps they seem abstract because we don't completely understand what is being said."

"True," Teresa said. "Now, the second symbol is known as the Triple Goddess. The moon was always a symbol of the divine female. In this case it shows a waxing, full, and waning moon. That relates to the female divinity's evolution from growing to full to mature."

"But how can God evolve?" Avernis asked. "I thought God was perfect."

"It's a paradox," O'Keefe said. "God chose imperfection to complete His perfection. Gnostics believed the divine plan called for Sophia, the female aspect of the Deity, to lead the fall into material creation. Her intention was to experience material existence."

Teresa cut in. "The myth can also be interpreted to say that she was seeking the divine in the material."

"True," O'Keefe agreed, "But instead, something unexpected occured. The mixture of her spiritual force with matter generated darker counterparts on this plane, the Archons, pseudo-spirits you might say. These forces and the lower vibrations of the material plane limited the spirits, causing them to forget their divine origins. Humans became the vessels containing their divine spiritual essence. Our destiny became a struggle to regain full spiritual awareness by overcoming the darker forces that limited higher consciousness."

Avernis pinched the bridge of his nose between his fingers and closed his eyes.

"Robert, Are you all right?" Roncalli asked.

Avernis sat in a chair. "Give me a minute," he said. He looked as if he were in deep thought. "Something came to me just now." He looked up at the puzzled group. "We've concentrated on the meaning of the symbols and catching whoever is placing them, right? But what about considering *where* the objects were placed?"

"I don't follow," O'Keefe said.

"Okay," Avernis said, picking up a pencil and making energetic, staccato taps with it on a nearby table. "The Church has always been characterized by a male power symbolized by the pope, but Abraxas symbolizes God as male *and* female, power and wisdom. Perhaps placing Abraxas in the pope's apartments is reminding the male-dominated Church of God's female aspect. Now the Monad, the second symbol, suggests that heaven reflects a perfect male/female balance. That balance is reflected on earth by the perfection of Adam and Eve in Garden of Eden."

"I get it!" Teresa said. "That's why it was placed in the *Vatican Gardens.*"

"Right," Avernis said. "The third symbol, the Sacred Marriage, describes God actually incarnating, not only as a male figure, but also as a female. Why does God incarnate both as male and female according to the Gnostics? To correct the imbalance between everything the two sexes represent—logic, order, and power versus intuition, creativity, and feeling. The merging of these two divine incarnations, these divine qualities, is a most holy event. St. Peter's altar is the holiest place in the basilica, does that make sense?"

The others encouraged him to keep going. "The Orphic Egg and Ouroboros both display the serpent," he said as the tempo and excitement in his voice rose. "Teresa told us the serpent is a Gnostic symbol for wisdom, a feminine quality, which they associated with the Holy Spirit. Ouroboros, the serpent devouring its own tail, says if we don't learn to use wisdom, we will devour or destroy ourselves. The egg encircled by the serpent means wisdom can protect the earth, the material creation. Conversely, the whole earth may be in danger if we ignore our intuition."

"Okay, I see a relation there," Teresa said. "In my dream, Magdalene claimed that feminine intuition was the path to the wisdom of God, but why were the symbols placed in Cardinal Roncalli's apartment?"

Avernis took a deep breath and exhaled. "This may sound far out, but I feel this one was almost a personal message to the cardinal. Remember we discussed how each of these symbols could have dual meanings, one good and one evil? I think it's telling you, Cardinal, that you face a crossroads where you must make a choice. You have to distinguish between good and evil, and in this choice it admonishes you to seek the path of wisdom rather than reason for your answers."

Avernis was on a roll, speaking like a man possessed of a vision. Roncalli, who was silent for a time, said, "Go on," signaling that he was taking him seriously.

"In the final symbols, the female pope is the only one to correspond to an identifiable event," Avernis said. "Annalisa is now pope and she is setting out to transform the Church. The Triple Goddess image is about evolution. It represents the feminine principle rising, coming into its own, you see? Why was it placed at the doctrinal headquarters? Because it's telling us new beliefs are being born to replace the old dogmas."

Avernis then ended his monologue and looked uncertainly at the others. "Am I insane? I can't believe I just spewed all that out. No idea where it came from." The others stood by in silence. Avernis' fingers fidgeted, and he hung his head down, avoiding eye contact with the others.

"I think," O'Keefe said, "you have provided us with a great gift of insight, Robert."

"Unusual," Teresa said, "but it sounds right."

Avernis looked up. Teresa had an admiring look in her eyes he had not seen in months. Roncalli appeared contemplative, and O'Keefe was smiling, but each of them was clearly giving credence to his interpretation.

"I thank all of you for your efforts," Roncalli said. "Please, if I may be alone with Monsignor O'Keefe for a while." After Teresa and Avernis left, Roncalli turned to O'Keefe, "Desmond, how do you feel about what Robert said?"

O'Keefe put a hand on his friend's shoulder. "Peter, there is much I don't understand about all these events, but one thing I know. God can speak in any way through any mouth. Teresa's dream and what we just heard from Robert were inspired. Everything points to Annalisa. Use your feeling as he told you, not your logic about what he said. You, above all, have been torn by doubt about Annalisa. The days ahead will further test you. Is she the savior or destroyer of all we know? Whatever her intention, whether she succeeds or fails will have much to do with your support . . . or your opposition."

Roncalli thought on O'Keefe's words for a long while. After a time he said, "This much I know—someone or something is knocking at my door, and I have got to listen. I'll *learn* to listen."

CHAPTER LXVI

Christianity has not been tried and found wanting;
it has been found difficult and not tried. — *G. K. Chesterton*

Harlem, New York

Desmond O'Keefe closed his eyes as the limousine glided through the streets of New York. He had never been more tired in his life. For more than five months he had been on the road with the papal "renewal tour" as it had come to be called. Every inhabited continent on earth had been visited during that time, country-by-country, city-by-city, parish-by-parish.

It was not just the travel that was so tiring, it was the nature of the work. Nothing short of a revolution was occurring. A new Church with new practices and a new outlook was taking shape with each talk the pope gave. The pressures of answering the hard questions and dealing with the deeply rooted fears and emotions of a billion Catholics were overwhelming, and this new evangelicism was not limited just to Catholics.

People of all faiths were turning out to listen, each of them curious for their own reasons, each going away touched by some aspect of her message. And it was working. The people were responding to the pope's vision of Christianity. The rift in the Church was being played out for the world to see as dissident bishops argued with the pope in the Churches themselves, in front of the eyes of the ever-present television cameras.

Desmond O'Keefe watched, studied, and listened to the new pope carefully. He knew her teachings were heresy. She had said or done nothing explicit, nothing concise and dramatic that sent up red flags. The story was in the total sweep of what she was doing, and it was too large for most people to intellectually encompass.

She refused to issue any theological decrees, always letting people make their own decisions. It was subtle, but she stood almost as an opposite pole to the Church, saying, "Here is another vision of reality, of spirit, and a way to experience it." She was offering them *experience*, not faith, knowledge by direct experience as opposed to mere belief. He was observing history in the making, but he suspected something far more profound was happening.

"Why did you choose me to sit by your side during these times?" he asked her.

She looked at him as if she were surprised by the question. “It’s not all given to me yet, but you know me. Of all of them you remember, don’t you?”

He did not respond. He kept his mind on immediate matters. The papal tour had been successful, but the physical and emotional toll was enormous, at least it was for O’Keefe. He peeked through a half-closed eyelid to glimpse the pope staring out the window of the limousine. How did she stay so energetic? The entire burden of these many grueling months had rested almost solely upon her. She seemed to thrive during this time, tireless, undaunted, and never faltering in her course.

“Oooh,” she crowed, looking out the car window like a little girl at Disney World for the first time, “look at that skyscraper, those crowds.”

Childlike yet changing the world, such radical contrasts—what she really was and how she appeared, what she really intended and how she acted. Did her knowledge give her vision, or did her visions give her knowledge? He pondered that rhetorical question for a millisecond before falling asleep.

✠

The pope’s car stopped at a small convenience store for O’Keefe to buy some aspirin. He stepped out and noticed three young men hanging around the sidewalk.

“Is you somebody?” one of the boys asked him, pointing to the limousine.

“Whad’ all these people up here today?” said another. “And Spics man. Look at ‘em, up an’ down the street. Wassup wit dat?”

“Shit man, where you ignorant niggers been?” said the third. “Don’t you know the pope is here? That’s the black pope in that car!” Why you think all these Spics and white-breads here today?”

“That indeed is the pope,” O’Keefe said. “She’s speaking up the street at the Church.”

“The black pope! C’mon man, that her?” the first one said, and just then, Annalisa rolled down the car window and waved at them. “Damn, lookit that,” he said.

“Don’t approach the car boys,” O’Keefe said, “security won’t like that, but why don’t you come to the Church to meet her?”

“No shit?” the interested boy said. “I gotta see this. Black pope in Harlem. Goddamn!”

The Church to which O’Keefe referred was the African Methodist Church of Zion, and in addition to the people of Harlem, whites and Hispanics from Lower

Manhattan and the Upper East Side were flocking to the Church to see the new pope. So many people came that the television news networks set up a special outdoor monitor as a courtesy to the public, which had spilled over the Church steps and onto the street.

Inside the church the pastor, Reverend James Harley, was finishing a brief speech just as the papal entourage arrived. He explained how the pope of the Catholic Church had personally called him one day and asked if she could meet with any and all people who would be interested in an "old time" Christian service. He then introduced the pope, who walked in from a door at the side of the church connected to the rectory. An unsure, embarrassed clapping started to rise from the congregation, but some hand motions and a light shaking of the head from the pope told them no applause was necessary.

The pope wore simple white vestments and a white zucchetto, or skullcap. She had effectively forsaken the crown-like papal miter since taking office, saying its regal appearance created an emotional barrier between her and the people. Annalisa sat in a seat that was placed in front of the congregation to the right of the altar. Monsignor O'Keefe and a local Catholic priest sat on either side and slightly behind her.

"Hello," she said as her voice carried through the clip-on microphone and echoed into the loudspeakers. "I am the bishop of Rome, and the bishop of Rome is usually called the pope. In southern Europe, people call the pope *Papa,* from the Greek word for "father," but as you see, I am not a father. In Italy, they sometimes refer to me as *la papessa,* "the popess." In my country, Nigeria, they do the simplest thing—they call me Mother, and if you like, you may call me that too. Is that all right with you?"

Heads in the crowd smiled back and nodded.

"Good," said the pope, and she clapped her hands together softly. "Today I would like to take you back two thousand years to recreate the experience of the early Christians. When they gathered in those days, their meetings were a little different from our services today."

The pope stood and walked down the aisle to be closer to the audience. She continued speaking as she strolled among them. "They would speak of their lives, you see, and they would try to apply spiritual solutions to their problems. It took faith, trust, and courage for these early Christians to speak in public of their problems, their failures, their shortcomings."

The pope looked directly into the eyes of the seated listeners. She gave them a warm smile and asked, "Could any of you do that in Church today?" Eyes flitted around the room at one another in questioning glances, but no one responded. "The reason they were able to do that back then was because Jesus' message of love was still as warm and real in their hearts as the freshly baked loaves of bread they all shared during the gathering."

The pope stood up, put her hand on the shoulder of a middle-aged black lady, smiled at her, then said to the congregation, "You see, it takes trust to tell your problems to others, trust they have enough love to care."

The pope walked back toward the front of the Church and turned to face the seated people. "Now today they no longer throw Christians to the lions, but life still has sharp teeth. Difficulties will always be around us: it was so then, it is so now. Will anyone here today trust enough to talk of something that bothers them? If you do, I will try to demonstrate how the ancient Christians might have helped."

Only one individual raised a hand. It was a thirteen-year-old boy. He seemed excited and he said, "My mamma doesn't want me hangin' with the gang but you're nothin' around here if you don't run with them."

The pope nodded her head, waiting to see if the boy had more to say. The boy's mother spoke up instead. "He gets good grades. The gang makes fun of him because I make him talk good English. He's a smart boy, but I know he'll wind up dead or in jail if he hangs around with those thugs. In fact, some of them are in here now," she said, and she jerked her head in the direction of three boys who had just walked into the Church.

The pope nodded and asked the boy to come forward. He did, and she put out her hand, which he took without any trace of self-consciousness. "What is your name?" she inquired.

"Darnell," the boy replied.

The pope closed her eyes. "Darnell, you feel confused?" she asked him. "Scared, but you don't know what to do?"

The boy stood frozen. He was looking at the three older boys in the audience and he trembled. Annalisa heard him whisper "*DeMont*," and he managed only a nod in response.

"Do you know you already have an answer to your problem?" she said.

The boy turned toward her, unsure exactly what she meant.

The pope patted the boy's chest right above his heart. "Right in there are all the answers to your questions. God puts them there; the answers are in all of us, and if we learn how to ask, if we learn how to listen, we will hear those answers. Do you dream, Darnell?"

"Yes, ma'am."

The pope looked at the congregation. "One of the practices of early

Christianity we have lost was interpreting our dreams. Dreams are a language by which our innermost feelings are run through the divine . . . let's call it the divine *processor*, to use a modern computer analogy."

The pope then turned her attention back to the boy. "Darnell, would you mind sharing one of your dreams with us?"

After a moment of quiet thought, he said, "Okay . . . I s'pose."

The pope patted his shoulder, encouraging him to start whenever he wanted. "I'm in a garage with some of the gang," the boy said. "All of a sudden, I know somethin's gonna happen. I yell for everyone to get out and the ceilin' comes down. No one wants to go back in with me when it's all over, but I gotta go in. When I get inside, everythin's different. It looks like one of them buildings I seen at the airports for planes—what you call 'em?"

"Hangars," Monsignor O'Keefe said to help the boy with his story.

"Yeah! Hangars," Darnell said, excited that they knew what he was talking about. "The garage and the low ceilin', they're gone, see? I see high ceilings and lots air above."

The pope smiled. "What was your feeling as you stood in the hangar?" she asked him.

"It was real good," he said. "Yeah, like I was excited and everythin'."

"Is that all?" the pope asked.

Darnell gave a nervous glance at the three boys then said, "Yeah, I s'pose so."

The pope looked at the congregation. "The priest or an elder of the old Church would lead discussion about the dreams. If you please, I will try to do that today."

O'Keefe looked at the people. At the beginning of the tour, this whole subject had been foreign to him, so he'd no idea how the audiences would react. He had found that in each case, they were captivated, and today was no exception.

"Darnell is in the garage with the gang, that is the world he is in," the pope said "But he realizes there is danger in the gang's world and, sure enough, the ceiling comes down. But there is good news in this dream, Darnell. You had the *desire* to get out of that world in time to escape uninjured." The pope smiled and tussled the boy's hair. "When the dust clears, you go back in and realize the gang world was a limitation. The low ceiling and small garage boxed you in, kept you limited, but now you see the world you really want, the spacious building, the clear sky, the room to grow on a solid foundation that will not collapse. Things will get better because you have the desire to change pulsing deep within you."

The pope kept silent for a few seconds to let the people absorb her comments.

"What do you want to be, Darnell? What do you want for your life?" she asked.

With no hesitation, Darnell spoke up. "I want to draw things for people to build, you know, big buildings and things. I want a nice house that I would draw myself."

"An architect, you mean? A person who designs and draws plans to make buildings, that is what you want to do?" the pope asked.

"Yeah, that's it!" the boy replied. "I saw a show on TV how they make those tall buildings like in downtown, the sky-skyscarr—"

"Skyscrapers," O'Keefe chimed in.

"You got it," Darnell said with a grin, but he peeked sideways at the three older boys.

Annalisa turned Darnell's head away from the boys and held his eyes with hers. "If that is what you want, Darnell, you must hold that vision. See yourself drawing those homes all the time. In your mind, see yourself in your own new home like you already live there. See yourself working in your home, drawing plans for other people's houses."

"How do I do that?" Darnell asked.

The pope tapped her index finger against the side of her temple. "Imagination," she said.

"But that's so hard to do," he said. "I mean, it ain't nothin' like that here in Harlem."

"Not so hard as you think," the pope said. "You can see yourself selling drugs, getting into trouble with the police, can you not?"

"That ain't hard," the boy said.

"So, ask yourself, which thoughts make you feel better—thinking about being an architect in your own beautiful home in a nice neighborhood, or thinking about gangs and drugs?"

"The new home," he replied.

"Good," said the pope. "Then work hard at that idea, and be conscious of your thoughts. Go to the library. Find pictures of buildings and homes. Every time bad thoughts come into your head, chase them away by seeing yourself directing people to build those places. Maybe one day someone will take you to a real architect's office and make your dream more real."

A well-dressed man in the audience then raised his hand. "My name is James Buford. I belong to an organization of African-American professionals. We work with young children from hardship areas. We have an architect in our group, and I'll bet he would love to take Darnell to his office sometime."

The pope clapped her hands and said, "Wonderful! Would you like that, Darnell?"

"Cool!" said Darnell, eyes wide with delight, this time ignoring the three boys.

The seated congregation clapped with enthusiasm at the turn of events.

"You see, my friends," the pope said, "that is how the early Christians met and helped one another. In the Catholic Church, we are now working to reclaim this spirit, this type of experience at our Sunday gatherings. I hope all churches would consider this practice."

And when the pope finished her talk and retired to the rectory, O'Keefe brought in three boys, the boys she had waved to from the limousine on 136th Street, the boys who had given Darnell such apprehension. A boy named DeMont spoke. "You, ah, you said things. We was thinkin,' we, uh—can we talk which' you?"

Annalisa spent several hours with them, even ordering hamburgers from McDonald's for them to eat. As O'Keefe listened, he knew she was reaching one of them. He could see it on the boy's face. *That is how it must be for her to instill the new way*, he thought. *She must reach the young.* The media followed up on the story eight months after the meeting. DeMont, the young man with all the questions, had landed a good job with the help of the Church, and he was free of the migraine headaches that had plagued him for years. He prayed regularly in the manner the pope taught him, and she called him from time to time to encourage him. The press dubbed the story the "Big Mac Miracle."

The other two boys had not really listened when the pope spoke; they had just gone along for the free food, they said. DeMont did not see them much anymore. When the pope was asked about the Big Mac Miracle and the two boys who remained unaffected, she replied with a wry smile that when certain people hold a deep desire and are willing to accept God's help, even a cheeseburger can be the bread of life, but, for other people, a Big Mac is just a Big Mac.

CHAPTER LXVII

I know that every good and excellent thing in the world stands moment by moment on the razor-edge of danger and must be fought for . . .
— Thornton Wilder

Newark, New Jersey

A few days later, the pope made her last U.S. appearance, the final stop on her tour before returning to Rome, and there occurred the incident that received the greatest amount of press coverage. The pope was in Newark, New Jersey, in one of the Orthodox Catholic churches that was refusing to conform to Vatican III, and in this church the rebellious clergy had the support of the mostly conservative, working-class parishioners.

Annalisa stopped for a second before crossing the threshold of the church and closed her eyes as the information came to her. *This is where they will make their final assault; this is where the world is watching.*

"Are you all right, Mother?" O'Keefe inquired.

The pope nodded her head and proceeded inside.

Of all the television coverage of the papal tour, UNN, as usual, had garnered the largest audience of viewers around the globe. Important Church prelates in the Vatican, including seven very tense cardinals, watched Teresa Ferentinos's televised commentary of the event. The cameras showed Annalisa trying to conduct a service in much the same manner as she had done in New York, but several people kept interrupting her. The seven cardinals in the Vatican leaned forward in their chairs as an agitated parishioner stood up to speak.

"This is the best chance we have to expose her," said Tormada.

"Sshh," Mannheim hissed with his finger to his lip. "Listen. It's starting."

The room was quiet as the men watched the television screen.

Parishioner: I'm sorry, Your Holiness, but many of us did not come here to celebrate mass. We are upset about where you are leading the Church. For instance, you have publicly criticized the doctrine of papal infallibility. Your own College of Cardinals is firmly opposed to your view. How do you explain your statements when we have been told for years that the pope is infallible in matters of faith and morals?

Teresa Ferentinos, UNN anchorperson (*voiceover*): *An irate parishioner has interrupted the pope. This is the first time we are aware that an ordinary lay member has conducted his or herself in such a manner toward the leader of the Church in public.*

Annalisa: You see, when the Church makes an infallible pronouncement through the pope, it takes away choice of conscience on the part of the faithful. Now, Jesus taught by example, not by coercion. He did not point spears at the backs of his disciples and force them to follow him to martyrdom. Why, then, should the Church point the spear of infallibility at the minds of its people and force them to believe us? Belief is *earned* by credible ideas, not *forced* by commands.

Ferentinos: *A clergyman is now jumping into the argument.*

Priest: You dismiss our dogma and doctrines, yet they have defined who and what we are for thousands of years. Why would you destroy our faith?

Annalisa: True faith is flexible, not dogmatic. It is open to reason, even to doubt. True faith is a premise, an initial assumption about the reality of spirit. No, I do not encourage blind obedience and acceptance of Church dogma, but I do encourage people to use faith in the scriptures as a starting point for their spiritual journey.

A Bishop: You call for a reexamination of basic Christian belief and deny the Church's authority. How can you say that is not destroying faith?

Ferentinos: *Remarkable. The pope has knelt down in front of a row of parishioners, looking them in the eye, speaking directly to them above the rumbling of the congregation.*

Annalisa: I encourage people to accept Church teachings provisionally, but take personal responsibility for their own spirituality. That means question and test the teachings yourselves. Practice your spiritual beliefs so you can say with certainty they work or they do not. This hypothesis of faith is validated by personal experience. Faith and belief only graduate to knowledge through practice, and knowledge is certainty. Start with your faith in this manner, seek with heartfelt sincerity and I promise, each of you will be transformed.

Another Priest: We face a threat from Islam. Your self-examination will cause confusion during these dangerous times.

Annalisa *(standing up again):* There is no threat from Islam, Father. There is a threat from certain people who justify their goals in Islam's name. Religion is an excuse for, not a cause of, worldwide conflict. I call for a spiritual renewal, and spirituality transcends religion. Religion too often tells us what to do, tells us what is good and what is bad. Spirit is no respecter of religious judgments.

If we all build on the spiritual core buried in each of our religions, the world will come together, not fly apart.

"She certainly knows how to speak to a crowd," DeGolia said, watching closely as the televised pope moved around her audience. "All that studying she did as a cardinal — it seems her erudition paid off. Her grasp of history and theology is nothing short of remarkable. Still think she is a—what was it—a jungle monkey, Francisco?"

"SHUT — " Tormada's angry response was cut off by an upheld hand and withering look from Mannheim, who did not want to miss any of the drama on the television.

Ferentinos: *A man is now standing to question the pope. He appears to be another prelate of the Church.*

Bishop: I am Archbishop Castellani from the Diocese of Newark. It disturbs me that you exalt man's position in God's hierarchy. You leave belief as a matter of individual decision. What use is the Church in a world where each individual is a church unto himself?

DeGolia, watching the events in far off Rome, started to ask his colleagues, "This bishop, is he one of the ones who is supposed to—" His question was cut short by Mannheim's palm waving in the air and an affirmative nod of the German's head. Mannheim never took his eyes off the pope's televised image as he gestured to DeGolia.

Annalisa: Your Excellence, it has ever been this way: the final decision about what to accept as the truth of God rests with the individual. That is called free will, and if God has granted it, the Church should not presume to take it away.

Archbishop: There you have it! By granting humanity such power, you de-emphasize the person and authority of Christ. That is the very definition of anti-Christian.

Annalisa: You misunderstand. What I de-emphasize is the Church's idolatrous notion of Jesus standing separate from us and above us. *(An angry roar erupts; it takes several minutes for the pope to be heard again.).*

Ferentinos: *Some here may be adverse to her teachings, but I notice many others silencing those trying to cut in and interrupt the pope's reply.*

Annalisa *(voice loud and firm):* When we idolize someone, we relinquish our own power. Jesus was divine, and he came to reveal the divinity within each of us, not to set himself up as an object of blind worship. He wanted us to emulate him, not idolize him.

Archbishop ***(amid angry shouts from the audience):*** Blasphemy! That I should have lived to hear a pope say this!

Ferentinos: *This is really quite remarkable. A pope of the Catholic Church having to defend herself from charges from her own clergy that, in essence, seem to be saying she is a heretic!*

Annalisa ***(ignoring attempted interruptions):*** Blasphemy, Your Excellence, is using Jesus' divinity to make us less than we were meant to be. He wanted us to be like him. He taught prayers, meditations, and imparted spiritual guidance for each individual to find his or her path to God. That is what we have forgotten, and that is what I urge you to remember.

Archbishop: I never believed I would hear a pope of the Catholic Church say the things you have said. What is it then that you *do* teach?

Annalisa: That the Church will impart wisdom, knowledge, and guidance to its members as a conduit for help, not as a dictator of beliefs.

Bishop: These are not the traditional ways and views of the Church. You are covering your apostasy with smooth-sounding ideas.

Annalisa: I take exception, Your Excellence. It is *you* who are concealing the truth of what the Church is. Church intellectual history is vast, and its thinking broad. The truth is that each of us is free to determine our vision of God.

Ferentinos: *In what is the most dramatic moment of this confrontation between the pope and her rebellious clergy, the pontiff, for the first time, has accused her accusers. She seems to have paused to let the force of her words sink in.*

"You see what she is doing?" Tormada asked his fellow cardinals gathered around the television. "She seeks to undermine overall confidence in the Church."

"Satan is ever insidious," LoPresti added with pious certainty.

Annalisa: Hear these words once spoken by the great explorer Magellan: *'The Church says that the earth is flat, but I know that it is round. For I have seen its shadow on the moon and I have more faith in the shadow than in the Church.'* Is that what we want, Your Excellence, that we drive the people to have more faith in shadows than in the Church?

Archbishop: That is not—

Annalisa ***(talking right over the Archbishop to conclude her point):*** The earth is neither flat nor the center of the universe! The Church is neither infallible nor superior to the individual!

Hearing the pope's words in Rome, DeGolia said, "The British newscaster was correct. The accused has indeed become the accuser." And, as usual, his colleagues were none too happy about his observations.

Ferentinos *(voiceover, camera panning to show facial close-ups of the audience):* *The pope seems to have stopped replying to the bishop and is now speaking directly to the people in her audience.*

Annalisa: Today, people's faith has been depleted by empty ritual on one hand and misdirected science on the other. Listen to what Jesus would have told you: grow still, and empty a place within your being. Envision whatever symbolizes God for you; with that vision, and with fervent desire in your heart, create that space and He will come, He will fill it. That is a living religion!

Ferentinos: *The emotional charge in the room has shifted, and the angry voices have died down.*

Annalisa: The Church is like a signpost on a wilderness road. It helps to indicate direction, but never confuse the signpost for the destination. Jesus did not come for you to bow before him. he came to remind you, he came to illuminate your rightful path home. Those of you who would reclaim your spirituality by his words, stay with me and upon that rock we will rebuild our Church!

Ferentinos *(in a hushed voice)*: *The bitterness seems to have subsided. People are listening intently to the pope. They are transfixed by the power of her words. There is nothing more to say.*

After a time, Monsignor O'Keefe stood and addressed the gathering. "Ladies and gentlemen, at this time the pope will begin celebration of the mass. For those of you who wish to stay, we invite you to join us."

And at that American church in Newark, New Jersey, in a parish that had severely questioned the pope and put the unity of the Church at stake, only a fraction of the people departed, and many of those were recalcitrant clergy. But the vast majority stayed and celebrated mass. Many lingered even later to personally speak with the pontiff. It was almost midnight before the last people left, and the pope had spoken to each one of them.

Teresa Ferentinos summarized events to a global audience that had persisted through outlandish hours to watch history being made. "Even as a reporter, I could not remain unmoved by today's extraordinary happenings. One might feel we are reliving the age of miracles: the Catholic Church elects a female pontiff, the new pope reverses many Church practices against the huge weight of tradition, and the Church heads for schism. Yet now, it seems to be reuniting under a new vision." As she spoke, a man placed some papers in front of Teresa.

"Who could have foreseen that this pope, this small woman from the back-country of Africa, would stand up to the theologians, the Church hierarchy, and the sheer weight of history to transform the Church and bring it into the modern age?" Teresa picked up the papers just placed on her desk. "We have new information from polls taken by several sources around the world. Churches in dioceses protesting against the pope and Vatican III are emptying at prodigious rates in favor of the churches remaining loyal. I think perhaps future generations will mark this as the day the tide of Christianity turned, here, at this small church in New Jersey."

CLICK.

"Enough!" Mannheim barked at his colleagues, his fingers still smashing at the remote control to erase the pope's image from the screen. He too sensed the turning of the tide. Again, that woman had thwarted his plans. He had counted on a fragmented Church to plant the seeds of his future papacy—his papacy and her demise. He knew his opposition Church was dead. Now there was but one way open. *I have the will and way, but not yet the means,* he prayed in silence. *Give me a sign, O Lord, and let me move swiftly to action in defense of the faith.*

CHAPTER LXVIII

Two vipers tangled into one. —Percy Bysshe Shelley

Qom, Iran

Cardinal Mannheim was not the only one who sensed a turning tide in the Christian world. Ayatollah Havenei had watched the events with awe and dismay, and he had made his decision. He summoned Alhaji Kadir al Kadu, the head of his client N-FAC terrorist network, to Qom.

"Alhaji, what we feared years ago has come to pass," Havenei said. "As a nun, this woman caused problems among your people in Nigeria. Now they have made her pope knowing her mother was a Muslim. Can there now be any doubt about their motives? Not only do they want to tip the scales in the battleground of Nigeria, but they are aiming to blunt our plans around the globe. She will use her charisma to take aim at the entire Muslim world."

"We have warned all along about this Yoruba woman and her potential for trouble," Alhaji said.

Havenei agreed. "My mistake was taking her too lightly. The action I am now proposing is a monumental but delicate matter. The time had to be ripe and now it is. Your fighters in Nigeria have grown stronger but do not yet have the popular support you need. If Nigerian Muslims were attacked by the Christians they would unify under your leadership because only you have the organization."

"What are you proposing?" Alhaji asked.

"That we kill two birds with one stone by eliminating the Nigerian pope," Havenei replied.

Alhaji raised both eyebrows. "How?" he asked.

"It must be done publicly, in open sight, and by Nigerian Muslims who must give their lives," Havenei replied. "This will precipitate Christian attacks in Nigeria, and Muslims will flock to your banner for protection and retaliation. Moving from guerilla war to open war will at the very least disrupt America's remaining oil supplies and at best lead to our mutual control of the entire country."

"And we eliminate the figurehead of the 'Muslim' pope too," Alhaji said.

Havenei nodded. "Are you prepared for such a plan?"

Alhaji answered promptly. “Not only prepared, but I can fill in important details for such an operation. For one, I even have the personnel in mind. One of my best fighters is a man named Hakim. He is the perfect profile for a suicide mission. Years ago he was nearly killed, hacked up by villagers after his unit attacked a Christian village. The machete marks he bears scarred his soul as well as his body. He does not care about his own life, and he is tough. He will understand the glory of this action; he will die as a martyr of martyrs.”

“Excellent,” Havenei, said. “Prepare him and two others. Do not divulge their target until the last minute; this operation must be secure and never traced back to this conversation. Now, how to stage this? They must get to her in the Vatican, and security is tight.”

Alhaji thought for a minute. “Many in her own Church still hate her. One such man is a bishop in Lagos. I have a contact who could approach him.”

“That is too risky,” Havenei said. “This bishop may decide to alert them.”

“What if he does?” Alhaji said. “They simply tighten their security and we wait for another day. But I don’t think he will. My contacts know the bishop. He thinks her the devil’s spawn, and she took a cardinal’s position away from him. He and others would like to see her dead as long as they don’t have to pull the trigger. As for my men, they are hardened. If they are captured, they’ll swallow poison pills before they talk.”

Havenei debated the idea. “If a bishop could somehow get your men near the pope—let me think on this and we will talk more.” And Havenei did think on it, long and hard.

CHAPTER LXIX

Power corrupts the few, while weakness corrupts the many.
— Eric Hoffer

Tehran

Today was the day for which Reza Gorbani had been waiting. Havenei and the council were inducting him into their ranks as the new Ayatollah Gorbani. Havenei was now imparting the religio-political vision and secrets of the Ruling Council to him.

The old ayatollah rose slowly from his seat and moved around the long oval table to stand by a wall underneath a huge geo-political map of the Middle East. "America made both military and political mistakes. I am a man of God, not a soldier," Havenei proclaimed with pious modesty, "but when they invaded Afghanistan and Iraq, they should have sealed the borders. They did not, and many fish escaped the net. One big one came to us."

Havenei smiled like a man reliving a pleasant memory. He traced the Iraqi-Iranian border on the map as he looked straight at Gorbani, the new member. "I now entrust you, Reza, with information that must never be revealed outside this room. Before Allah, should you ever betray this information, first your body then your soul will burn in torment."

Gorbani nodded, his face looking sufficiently solemn. Satisfied, Havenei continued his history lesson. "When the Americans invaded Iraq for the second time, Saddam Hussein knew he was finished. He did not want to be caught with the weapons of destruction they accused him of having, so he divested himself. Hussein was a devil, but a clever one. He circumvented his top leadership because he knew the Americans would catch them and make them talk. He took junior grade officers in the Republican Guard, put them in civilian clothes, and made them truck drivers.

"These men delivered the Iraqi weapons program to Iran in trucks, buses, and other civilian transport. We received biological agents and weapons-grade nuclear material; the drivers' reward was death. By agreement with Saddam, we killed the couriers. No one lived to talk, and we hid the weapons away until this day."

"Saddam was our enemy," Gorbani observed. "Why would he give us such weapons? Why not give them to an Arab country like Syria, or to an Arabic liberation group?"

Havenei smiled and looked around the table at the bearded, turbaned men. "Saddam knew he would never rule Iraq again. He wanted revenge on America. Al Qaeda was scattered and on the run, the other Arabic countries were weak and too vulnerable to Israeli intelligence. He knew we were the strongest power left in the region. He knew the weapons would be safest here, and he knew our hostility to the West was constant. Besides, we were the only state that had a fledgling nuclear program that could make use of his gifts. We let them lie dormant in the desert until eight years ago."

Havenei lifted his palms upward in praise. "Allah works in mysterious ways. Our enemy delivered us the means to defeat our enemy!" he proclaimed. "We are on the verge of doing what no Islamic nation has ever done — bringing the West to its knees."

"Allahu Akhbar," several of the men intoned.

Havenei's fingers swept over the map from Iran to Iraq. "When America and the West abandoned Iraq, we increased the infiltration of our clerics into the country. The Iraqis have a nominally nationalist government but we assumed de facto control through the activity of the madrassahs and the ulema. If the civilian authorities ever crossed our allied Iraqi ayatollahs, the government would collapse in a matter of weeks."

Gorbani nodded. Everyone knew the religious schools and courts were the real power in Iraq, but he had learned an astounding new fact today—his country had biological and nuclear weapons.

The West had known about the Iranian nuclear program some decades ago; they did not know about the dormant cache from Saddam. By opening up their original program to inspection, the Iranians had fooled a UN that seemed willing to be fooled. After the dust settled, the Iranians started utilizing the hidden Iraqi technology. *The question*, Gorbani asked himself, *is how will we use them?*

"When the Americans pulled out of the region," Havenei explained, "the liberation groups we support reorganized and carried the war to Western soil. The bombing and terror campaign has disrupted the Western economies, but we must cut off their remaining oil supplies to truly change the global power balance."

Gorbani considered the statement. The West was staggering along on a trickle of oil supplies from the nearly exhausted reserves of non-Islamic nations from the old OPEC. The West was in a catch-22: terror attacks and a dry oil spigot had caused deep recession, and the bad economy slowed their efforts to perfect replacement energies. Only Nigerian oil was providing them any bridge out of their dilemma.

"We have concluded our pact with China despite America's threats," Havenei said. "China and the Asian nations have enough demand to make up what we lose selling to our godless enemies in the West. Iran and the Islamic bloc will grow stronger while the West collapses. Iran will become the regional power in the Mid- East, and through the Islamic bloc we can assert global influence."

Gorbani's forehead furrowed as he mulled over everything he had heard.

"Is something wrong?" Havenei asked.

"The West is weakened, but they are not toothless tigers," Gorbani said. "We can always disavow support of the paramilitary liberation groups, but after publicly spearheading this agreement with the Asian countries . . . "

"You fear they will attack us," Havenei said. "That is unlikely, but that is where Saddam's gifts come in. They lost their chance to disarm us. If they ever assault Iran, we will unveil our secret weapons. They will never risk attacking once they find out what we possess."

Gorbani raised a questioning eyebrow. Havenei spoke of defensive uses, but with these weapons in hand and the growing boldness of the council, they were just one situation away from using the weapons offensively, perhaps through the terrorist paramilitary surrogates.

"Do not worry," Havenei said. "None of this will come to pass. The Europeans never had the stomach for confrontation, and the Americans have become just as weak."

"Pardon my ignorance," Gorbani said, "but can we count on that?"

Havenei smiled as if indulging him. "An exclusive oil pact is simply free trade. We have attacked no one—what justifies an attack on us? The Americans will paralyze themselves over banal legalities even while we are strangling them. I can hear them now—no justification for attacking a sovereign nation; the immorality of large nations attacking smaller ones—no, Reza, Americans seek quick victories for immediate causes. Protracted struggles are too abstract for them. They have no patience or will for it."

"Yet there is a hawkish president in America," Gorbani said. "The frustration in the United States is high. He has gained support."

Havenei nodded his head. "Davidson, yes, we know. He makes noise, but our assessment is that he still lacks popular support. Even if he tried, the world would not condone an attack—we have done nothing—and if America were to attack, we have deterrents."

Gorbani tried not to show his doubt on his face. This was a risky global strategy based on dangerous assumptions. They were underestimating what people could do when you leave them no alternative. In his view, America, at least, was ripe for a reaction.

"Our chief concern now is Nigeria and its new oil finds," Havenei said. "We cannot let their oil continue to reach Western hands. Shut down Nigeria and we effectively close off the West's last pipeline. Our Nigerian clients will soon be moving toward a general armed conflict, and civil war should disrupt much of the oil flow even before they seize power."

Nigeria was just a pawn in the greater game, Gorbani knew. His colleagues were intoxicated with the centuries-old dream of *Dar al-Islam*, or bringing the *kufr*, the unbelieving nations, under the rule of Islam. That was the ultimate goal.

Most Islamic extremists thought this goal was achievable. The Muslim population in key Western countries was already substantial. In Britain and France, it had reached twenty percent by 2020 thanks to unchecked immigration policies. This fact had kept French foreign policy toward radical Islam in an appeasement mode for decades. In America, prisons and inner cities were churning out Islamic converts by the thousands, recruited mostly from poor, disaffected minorities.

These trends would be telling over time, but Havenei was of no mind to wait. To Gorbani's way of thinking, he was becoming dangerously aggressive. Havenei was old, and he wanted to be remembered as the new Saladin before he died. He was like a man in a fast car speeding up a mountain to catch the sun, but the sun was in his eyes. Gorbani hoped that in his blindness he would not drive them all off the cliff.

CHAPTER LXX

. . . we put faith not in a heretic, but in Christ's gospel.
— Saint Augustine

The Vatican City

An eager Pietro Roncalli sat over lunch on a Vatican garden patio listening to Desmond O'Keefe recounting stories about his trip around the world with the pope. "One time, in Germany," he said, "neo-Nazis were holding up placards calling her a nigger, actually shouting that at her. She walks right up to them — almost gives Zugli a heart attack — and asks one of them, 'Do you know me?' He's too cowardly to answer her, but he tries to stare her down. She stares right back at him. After a minute or two, he breaks it off, and she says, 'Hah, I thought so. You must have been thinking of a different nigger.'"

Roncalli's eyes widened as O'Keefe spoke. "I can tell you, Peter, it took superhuman forbearance, or perhaps it was pure love, but you can't know the half of what she endured. People didn't just attack her teachings. It got very personal at times. So she says to the whole pack of thugs, 'You know what I admire about you? You put *so much* energy into your hatred. If you ever care to go in the other direction, you would all move mountains and become holy men. Come see me if you care to move mountains.'"

"And how did they react?" Roncalli asked, fascinated by the account.

"Well, you know, these are big, violent, skin-headed thugs too macho to show any feelings," O'Keefe said, "but I heard one of them say '*mutig*' in German."

"What does that mean?"

"Literally? It means courage," O'Keefe said. "They were saying she had guts."

Roncalli shook his head in wonder. "That's probably the highest compliment any of those people could have given her. Some wine?" he asked, holding the bottle up to O'Keefe.

"No, thanks, Peter," O'Keefe replied. "Me old father once said he hadn't touched a drop of alcohol since the invention of the funnel. I too drink big but only at big occasions."

Roncalli laughed and poured him some San Pellegrino instead. He was happy to see O'Keefe looking considerably better than when he had returned from the papal tour. The pressure on that trip must have been enormous. Roncalli had risen each morning wondering if there would still be a Church. He had wanted to be with Annalisa, but the pope wanted him to guard the lions back in the Vatican. The lions, however, had been tame. Mannheim and his circle had been quiet.

"The rebellious dioceses are dying out," Roncalli told O'Keefe. "Church attendance is way up on all continents, and many dioceses are taking in money again. We're still in a financial bind, but those monies are helping."

"The amazing thing, Peter, is that she did it all without excommunicating anyone, without splitting the Church apart," O'Keefe said.

"She told us she would never excommunicate anyone while she was pope, remember?" Roncalli reminded him. "Winning by force of faith and ideas, not by coercion," Roncalli said, repeating the pope's oft-quoted words. "In hindsight, it was the *only* way, Desmond. Any other pope would have resorted to excommunication and broken the Church apart."

"Well, she showed a genius at politics too," O'Keefe remarked. "After the tour she let the people of the troubled dioceses vote on who they wanted to lead them, the rebellious bishops or ones conforming to Vatican III. It was a master stroke, I tell you."

Roncalli laughed in agreement. "Mannheim and his group are ready to capitulate. Most of the rebel bishops are out of jobs and pleading to the Congregation of Bishops for relief."

"How strange," O'Keefe said. "A short time ago it would have been her who was excommunicated for heresy."

"What?" Roncalli said.

O'Keefe looked at his friend. "I said she would be excommunicated. You see, Peter, Mannheim and LoPresti are correct. Our pope, Annalisa, is a heretic."

CHAPTER LXXI

We too have accepted the faith . . . in one God, in Jesus Christ, in the virgin birth and the resurrection . . . but . . . following Jesus' injunction to seek . . . we have been striving to go beyond the church's elementary precepts to attain spiritual maturity.

—Response of the heretics to Irenaeus

The Vatican City

The pope is a heretic. The words lingered in the air. O'Keefe was surprised at Roncalli's calm reaction. "Go on," was all the American cardinal said.

"You see," O'Keefe explained, "she doesn't come right out with grand theological pronouncements, except to the extent she had to at the Ecumenical Council. She doesn't frontally assault people's beliefs, and her approach is not abstract or intellectual."

"What does she do then?" Roncalli asked.

"She teaches spiritual truths the way people can best grasp them," O'Keefe said. "She teaches pragmatically and by example."

Roncalli clasped both hands to his chin. "Explain that."

O'Keefe thought for a minute. "Take prayer, for example. She has little regard for petitioning the Lord with prayer. She sees the human soul as individualized parts of God, not creations separate from Him. Since we're of God's substance, His perfection and knowledge lie dormant within us. Real prayer is connecting with this inner knowledge, remembering our sleeping power. It's not praying for something outside of us; it's realizing everything is already within us. It's knowing our desire is already accomplished and manifesting it."

"She believes that we're of the same substance as God, that we're consubstantial with Him? That's blasphemy," Roncalli said. "It places man and God on the same level."

"Oh, no," O'Keefe said, shaking his head. "We may be the parts but God is the whole and the whole is always greater than the sum of the parts. We are part of His plan but not the planners. Aspects of God will always remain unfathomable to us."

"This way of prayer you speak of, how are the results of these prayers manifested? Is this the way she achieves her miracles?" Roncalli asked.

"Annalisa says miracles are not always great, instantaneous events heralded by thunder and trumpets," O'Keefe said, raising his arms in the air in a grandiose gesture. "Watch for subtle changes in attitude, emotions, and direction, she said. Over time, small shifts translate into great changes. If we pray for an alcoholic, that person might experience a breakdown that translates into a willingness to finally listen, which translates into reasoning and then recognition of the problem. That process results in action, a change of direction, the first step in reversing the person's dissolution."

"So learning how to recognize answers is just as important as knowing how to ask the questions, is it?" Roncalli asked.

"Exactly," O'Keefe replied. "We meditate and learn to have faith in our connection to God. We learn to see the signs of our prayers being answered. Our faith then graduates to experience of a prayer answered. That experience leads to the knowledge that God works through us as mediums or co-participants in shaping reality. Slowly and subtly through teachings like these she's altering people's perceptions, turning their faces toward a different direction to find God. That direction is not toward the Church, Peter. It's inside each of us. Personal experience of God is the goal . . . *gnosis.*"

Roncalli raised an eyebrow at that statement "But I remember something of the Gnostics from our study of heresies in the seminary," Roncalli said. "They didn't believe the god of the Bible was the True God. They believed the world was created in error by an inferior god."

"Actually, they believed the Creator God of the Old Testament *was* the inferior god," O'Keefe said. "Jesus' God of love in the New Testament was the True God. But the error that led to the material creation was committed by powerful spiritual beings projected from the True God's substance. These beings became the First Souls, became the first incarnated beings."

The words struck some chord in Roncalli. *"The First Souls,"* he whispered.

"You haven't heard the term before yet you recognize it, don't you?" O'Keefe said. "And there's a reason for that, but we won't go into it now. The Gnostics believed that God's creative pattern was balanced between forces that could loosely be described as masculine and feminine."

"Like the yin-yang principle of Eastern beliefs?"

"Yes," O'Keefe replied. "You know that the central Gnostic story concerns Sophia, a feminine aspect of God. She created outside the balance of the natural order, that is, she created without her masculine counterpart, the Christ. Her actions led to the rise of the false god that created our imperfect world, the Archon Jehovah of the Old Testament, a blood-thirsty, jealous, ego-oriented god. Sophia and her spirit grouping then became trapped in the illusion of the material world they had inadvertently created."

"Yes, but why would the True and Perfect God allow this to happen?" Roncalli asked.

"I questioned Annalisa directly on this matter," O'Keefe said. "How can human beings, as imperfect as we are, be any part of a perfect God? I asked. She laughed. 'God was bored,' she said, 'and imperfection makes for excitement.' I know, it sounds like a flippant answer to a deep question, but hear the rest. How best to explain it? Do you remember your classic American television shows from thirty or forty years ago, Peter? There is one they still air occasionally on the science fiction channels. It was a series about space travelers, and they had a hologram machine on their ship."

"A holodeck," Roncalli said. "We're on the verge of realizing such technology this decade, so I understand. I remember that TV series. They holographically created any desired scenario and actually lived inside it, relating with the characters and objects they created. Totally real and interactive, for all intents and purposes."

"Yes." O'Keefe smiled. "Now, why do you suppose someone would create a holodeck?"

Roncalli shrugged. "For the most vivid experience of a lifetime, a fantasy come true."

O'Keefe nodded. "As it is above, so it is below," he said, paraphrasing an ancient wisdom saying. "God is all-knowing and all-powerful, yet knowing something intellectually and knowing it through direct experience are two different things. God, the Great Mind, projected Himself into the individual angelic spirits as a way to experience His all-encompassing Oneness. He can only know Himself by seeing Himself through the vantage point of individualized spirits. These spirits know themselves to be God, yet know themselves to be themselves. Without that sense of self, these spirit projections would be automatons, artifices, not true companions able to contemplate God."

"But where does human existence fit in to this plan?" Roncalli asked.

"The *I Am* expressed into the *We Are,* remember?" O'Keefe said. "The whole universe is God's holodeck. To further extend His experience, He allowed the individual spirit parts of Himself, through the medium of the soul and the agent of free will, to project as physical beings into the material universe. This 'holographic' world was so real, and we became so immersed in the program, we forgot it was just that—a cosmic program. And it was perfection! A game becomes real when you forget it's a game — the All-Knowing Programmer becomes His own characters."

Roncalli touched a hand to his forehead. "And *our* purpose in this?" he asked.

"Ah, there's the question," O'Keefe said. "Creation is complex, and I can only guess."

"Then by all means, take a guess," Roncalli said.

O'Keefe closed his eyes, pausing before responding. "Humans may be the only beings with free will," he said. "I don't think that even the powerful spirit intelligences truly possess it."

The fingers of Roncalli's hands formed a steeple shape, touching against his lips as he thought on that statement. "Why the special treatment for us?" he asked.

"If God's intent is to experience His creation," O'Keefe said, "I suppose that we were the next logical step in that process. Beings with free will are free to forget God. Isn't that what we did? We became immersed in materiality and forgot who or what God really was; we forgot our own origins. Only in that way could God, through us, experience what He created as independent beings; or, more accurately, as beings with the *perception* of independence."

O'Keefe noticed Roncalli's forehead furrow in contemplation of the paradox.

"Look," he said to Roncalli, "experience is *discovery.* But how can you discover something you've already created? An artist creates a painting, but to discover and experience his creation, he'd have to immerse himself so deeply as to *forget* he's the artist and *become* the painting. He'd have to *project himself into* the painting just as God projected His spirit into us."

Roncalli shook his head. "More than a little insanity involved in that," he remarked.

O'Keefe chuckled. "Crazy, wild, adventurous — those are some of the terms by which the ancients referred to the *Great Involution,* or God projecting his Mind and Spirit Essence into material creation. The tarot contains a card called the Fool. It's number is zero, the card of infinite possibilities. It shows a seemingly absentminded traveler about to step off a cliff. The Fool is God. The precipice is God falling into the unknown experience of the created world. So the ancients knew that forgetting was a conscious choice, you see? It was a necessary choice, made by free will, to allow Spirit to have experience. They also knew it was an 'insane' paradox as you put it. It's the paradox so many religions speak of, that the world is *Maya,* an illusion. It's God's illusion that he is no longer God, but rather billions of sparks of light encased in fleshly forms."

"What is the role of salvation in all this?" Roncalli asked. "What was the meaning of Christ's sacrifice?"

"Salvation," O'Keefe said, "is not necessarily bodily resurrection, but enlightened remembrance of our real nature, our true origin in God. Christ's sacrifice was to come from the higher realms and suffer this dense plane to awaken us to our true origin. The Greeks called it *anamnesis,* remembrance, the opposite of amnesia, or forgetting. It's a concept that runs back through the Gnostics to Socrates and beyond. So there is *involution* from spirit to flesh then *evolution* from flesh back to spirit when we reawaken."

Roncalli sighed. "So, we involuted from perfection and awareness to imperfection and ignorance, is that what you're saying? That means evil and suffering were the price we paid for experience, discovery, and adventure? That means shadow and ignorance are inevitable consequences of living, no?"

"Yes, that's true," O'Keefe replied, "and the goal of the Gnostic was to attain that moment of true enlightenment that would bring divine recollection. Remembrance brings comfort, certainty, and an end to suffering, an end of the need to keep reincarnating in the material plane. It's God's safety valve back to Himself."

"Hmmph," Roncalli exclaimed. "It seems a very high price to pay."

"From our limited point of view, perhaps," O'Keefe said. "But if we're really made in God's image, then maybe God is growing and evolving just as we are. He could be actualizing the potential of His subconscious, the base material of creation. Perhaps God enters the created universe through us to bring unconscious matter to full consciousness."

"To create heaven on earth? Is that what you're saying?" Roncalli asked.

"More than that," O'Keefe replied. "The veil separating heaven and earth would be lifted. A fully awakened humanity would not only bring the consciousness of heaven to earth, but of earth to heaven. God would have His full experience of materiality and all matter would be spiritualized."

"And humanity is the tipping point between heaven and earth," Roncalli said.

O'Keefe pondered the statement. "I think it's more accurate to say that humanity is the battleground between heaven and the forces seeking to keep us from remembering our divine origins."

"What forces?" Roncalli asked.

"The forces," O'Keefe said locking his hands together like a clamp, "that seek the status quo of a world that controls us by misleading thoughts, habits, and perceptions of reality."

Roncalli slumped down in his chair. "You're correct about one thing at least—this is heresy, Desmond. What will you do about it?"

O'Keefe swallowed hard then said, "Nothing. I'll let it unfold, Peter. I believe in her. If she is a heretic in your eyes, then I am too. The question is what will *you* do?"

Again, Roncalli surprised O'Keefe. There was neither anger nor shock on his face. He simply nodded at O'Keefe's confession. "If we were to go public with this conversation, with the pope's admissions to you, it would likely fulfill the prophecies, destroying both the Church and the papacy. Clement, Gloria Olivae, whose successor will destroy the Church, the Great Heretic—I shudder at those ancient prophecies now."

"Yes, but there are other prophecies to the contrary — Gnostic prophecies," O'Keefe said.

"Really?" Roncalli closed his eyes. "And which are correct? Is she a savior or the Great Deceiver? She may not even know herself — you once said that. If I erred by bringing her into the Church, I've unleashed a power that could destroy us all."

"When Jesus walked the earth, many thought *him* a sorcerer too," O'Keefe said.

Roncalli sighed and looked out the window. O'Keefe could see that his friend faced a monumental decision, both personally and for the Church he so dearly loved. He had invested his faith in Annalisa and her papacy, but now he clearly discerned that her papacy and the Church were on opposing paths. If he, of all people, were to publicly declare against her, it could reignite the opposition that might bring her down, and the Church with her.

When he finally spoke, his voice was drained, as if he had emotionally retreated to a place where he hoped to find an answer. "I need time and prayer to seek guidance on this, Desmond. When I decide, you'll be the first to know, but it will be another day. It will have to be another day," and he left the room looking very small and worn as he passed though the tall doorway.

CHAPTER LXXII

there was . . . oblivion which deceives
and draws down to itself the hearts of men.
— The Vision of Paul the Apostle

The Vatican City

A few days after their conversation, Cardinal Roncalli entered Desmond O'Keefe's office, his voice full of excitement. "Desmond, I've been struggling about our recent conversation. Just as I was reaching my point of greatest despair, I received this anonymous letter in the mail. You're the only person I'm showing it to. Tell me what you think."

O'Keefe pulled out his glasses and adjusted them, took the note, and began to read:

> *Cardinal Roncalli,*
> *Do you see a pattern in the events surrounding you? A fragment of an ancient document lost somewhere in Jerusalem holds the answers that you seek. It was in the possession of a Father McPherson, who died retrieving it. McPherson hid the fragment somewhere before his death. Find this document and all your questions will be answered, not only for you but for the entire world. You will recognize the document by its opening words. It claims to be by the hand of Mary Magdalene. Use extreme caution. At least one man has died trying to bring these words to light.*
>
> *A Friend*

"Remarkable," O'Keefe said, putting the note down. "Any idea who sent this?"

"None." Roncalli shook his head. "It was postmarked in Rome, but that's all. I have enemies. This letter may be leading me on with general suggestions like the games that phony fortune-tellers play. They could be setting me up for something. What do you make of it?"

O'Keefe sighed, looking at the mixture of anticipation and anxiety on his friend's face. "Hard to say. So many mysterious symbols, messages, and happenings—it's almost as if we're being led somewhere. It could be a wild goose chase, but if there's any chance something exists that can shed light on all the questions we face, it should be worth pursuing."

"I don't understand how ancient writings of Mary Magdalene could have any bearing on current events," Roncalli said, "but I agree with you. Things are happening for a reason. All my life I searched for truth. I haven't found it yet—not in the Church, anyway," he said in a sad, resigned voice. "Doubt has plagued me all my life, Desmond, but if this lost document can shed light on the truth . . . well, I'm going to send Robert to Jerusalem to investigate."

O'Keefe smiled. "A wise choice," he said.

Roncalli cupped his hands to his face. "What does she want, Desmond? If she's not deceiving us, what does Annalisa want?"

"She . . ." O'Keefe took a deep breath as if he had an answer but was reluctant to speak it. "I think she has a message to deliver. We have to learn its meaning on our own, but I do know she would prefer not to be here."

Roncalli raised an eyebrow. "Not to be pope, you mean?"

"Yes, but not just that," O'Keefe said. "I mean she wants to go forever within that 'still place' she talks about. I tell you, Peter, the woman longs for the sweetness of holy oblivion."

"Oblivion," Roncalli repeated. "We face a fork, Desmond. One way may be doing God's will; the other may lead to our own oblivion if she is other than what we believe. Tell me, why did you become a priest, Desmond? Was it a calling? Was it destiny?"

O'Keefe did not answer his question directly, but instead offered Roncalli a glass of wine, which the cardinal accepted. After they each had a few sips, O'Keefe spoke wistfully, gazing out his office window.

O'Keefe cracked a wry smile and said, "Why did I become a priest, you asked? Well, Peter, me boy, I'm Irish you see, so the matter was easy: I couldn't figure out a way to drink for a living, so I became a priest."

Roncalli laughed. "We're either going to rise with this pope or go down as the biggest fools in history, but I've come to believe that I *know* this woman; somehow I know her and she is good." He grasped the stem of his wineglass and raised it high. "Here's your chance to both sin and be a priest today, Desmond. Raise your glass and drink with me."

And the men raised their glasses and toasted: "To truth . . . or oblivion."

CHAPTER LXXIII

The voice of thy brother's blood crieth unto me from the ground.
— Genesis 4:10

Jerusalem

I'm curious why the Vatican is reopening this inquiry," Inspector Lev Bronstein said to Robert Avernis as the secretary's typing clicked away in the background of his office.

"Reopening?" Avernis said. "Who was inquiring before?"

"I remember them, not their names," Bronstein said. "Hang on." He flipped through the dossier on his cluttered desk. "Oh yeah, Miguel Rosario and a Monsignor Jan Voorstrand."

Avernis shrugged as he jotted the names in his notepad. Neither man was familiar.

"They looked more like Vatican types than you," Bronstein said.

Avernis smiled. "How's that?"

Bronstein leaned back in his chair and folded his hands in his lap. "You know, somber, serious, never smiling."

Avernis chuckled. "Yeah, the Vatican can do that to you." He couldn't tell the inspector that he was CIA on loan to the Vatican. People automatically assumed the CIA was present to spy on them. But he was indeed here on behalf of the Vatican; Roncalli asked him to do this as a personal favor. For some reason Roncalli felt he was better suited to find information on the mysterious missing document than Vatican Security. "So what did those guys ask about?"

"Obvious stuff," Bronstein said. "Actually, I had more questions for them than they had for me—why was McPherson here, why might someone be chasing him, did he have known enemies? You know, things like that, but they knew nothing."

Avernis questioned the inspector for nearly an hour in the drab, windowless police headquarters, but got only hypothetical scenarios—happened at twilight, no one directly witnessed the death, people heard a scream for help in Arabic, saw McPherson's body below the ramparts with two men who may have been Westerners, may have been robbers, may or may not have had something to do with his fall—lots of maybes. The cause of death was clearly a fall from higher up, but whether he was pushed from above or fell climbing, no one was quite sure.

"Have you seen the site yet?" Bronstein asked.

"Only in pictures, but I'll be there later today. Why?"

Bronstein shrugged. "Whether you're above or below the point where the body was found, there's not much around there to attract anyone. Below are some old ruins, above is the back of the Al Aqsa Mosque. Always made me feel like there was some connection between the priest and the two men near the body."

"Wouldn't a field inspection and forensics indicate whether he fell climbing up or fell from above?" Avernis asked.

"It was dark when we arrived. Had to examine the place under poor lighting conditions. After that it was turned over to the Palestinians."

"What?" Avernis said.

"You didn't know?" Bronstein said. "It happened in a Palestinian-administered area. Since it didn't involve an Israeli citizen we decided not to press the matter given relations between us and the Palestinian Security Forces."

"And what about the body and the physical effects?"

"All in the hands of the Palestinians," Bronstein said. "I assume they shipped the body back to the family, but as for autopsies and physical evidence, they had it all."

Avernis tugged at his chin. If he had known this, he would have started with the Palestinians. Bronstein read his thoughts. "If you want to see the Palestinians, I suggest you contact your patriarch, Hieronymus. He's one of them."

"Yeah," Avernis replied, "he's on my list. Anyway, Inspector, one last question—what's your gut tell you on this one? Accident or homicide?"

Bronstein did not respond immediately. When he did he was slow and cautious in his speech. "The logical part of me doesn't like that question. I never had a chance to gather evidence and do proper police work, but you asked for my gut. There was more to this than just a mere accident. Why did the two guys run? Maybe they didn't want to get involved, but what were they doing in a deserted area at twilight? And, according to witnesses, they appeared to be searching the body. To rob him? If they were Westerners that's unlikely. A lot of ifs. That's all I have, sorry."

Avernis thanked the inspector and went to see Hieronymus, who saw him immediately. The patriarch did not have anything of real value to add to the story. He had questioned the Palestinian Authority investigators but that yielded scant information. "They just don't have the resources," the patriarch said. "They were more preoccupied with the Israelis and their own radicals than with the death of a foreign priest. They treated it as accidental."

"But what was he doing here?" Avernis asked.

"I checked with his bishop in Ireland," Hieronymus said. "Apparently Father McPherson had a fervent calling to come to Jerusalem, call it a personal spiritual crisis if you will."

"Sounds as if he may have been unstable. The Israelis told me he was dressed as an Arab. Isn't that odd? Could he have committed suicide then?"

Hieronymus paused, then shook his head. "His bishop said McPherson was always steady as a rock. As for the dress, Westerners often feel insecure in East Jerusalem with all the rising tensions in the Muslim world today. Maybe he was afraid of being attacked."

"So you think Muslims may have killed him?"

"Unlikely, particularly as he was dressed as an Arab," Hieronymus said. He then placed a call to one of the Palestinian Authority investigators with whom he had spoken a few years ago and arranged for Avernis to meet him.

An hour later, Avernis met Mr. Ghassan from Palestinian Security. His hovel of an office made Bronstein's seem palatial. After conversing with him for thirty minutes, Avernis realized that the patriarch was right. It had been a shoddy investigation by the Palestinians about a death that held no priority in their minds, but he did get some useful information. McPherson's death was caused by trauma consistent with a fall from a height. The area where McPherson died was below a promontory jutting off the Temple Mount in back of the Al Aqsa Mosque. The craggy-faced Ghassan told him it was unlikely that McPherson had accessed the plaza atop the promontory from above.

Ghassan displayed some pictures. "See here. The only real way to access the upper landing is from inside the mosque, but that area is restricted. He would never be able to pass there even if he were Palestinian. The people who heard him shout were workmen fixing the door into the mosque, and they didn't see him pass through. He must have climbed up the south wall on the scaffolding that was there at the time. See it there running up to the landing? If he fell, he likely slipped climbing that scaffolding. It is unlikely anyone pushed him from above. The workmen would have seen that happening."

Looking at the pictures, Avernis had to agree. The last thing Ghassan mentioned was a little slip of a note found in McPherson's pocket. He still had it in the dossier. "It said: *Ali Wafa, the Last Supper.* Avernis asked Ghassan if he knew what that meant.

"The only Ali Wafa we know of is a merchant in the lower city near to where the western wall turns to the south," Ghassan said, stroking the stubble on his cheek. "I did speak to him. He said he had never met the dead man and had no idea what the note was about."

"Did you believe him?" Avernis asked.

"Yes," Ghassan replied without hesitation. "Ali is a cautious man. He's one of the few Christian merchants in the area so he's extra careful about how he conducts himself in these times. Besides, in this business you learn to read people. He seemed genuinely ignorant of the dead man when I showed him a picture."

Avernis thanked Ghassan and went straight to Ali Wafa's shop with the directions Ghassan had given him. Ali's goods were mostly displayed outdoors in front of his shop. His business was at one end of a row of eight merchants, all selling substantially the same lines of tourist merchandise—vases, plates, mass-produced artwork, prayer beads, and numerous other items.

Ali was a short, pleasant septuagenarian with thick-rimmed glasses and a faded old vest that made him look every inch the small shopkeeper. Avernis made it a point to buy several items for which he had no use. No better way to ingratiate yourself to a small merchant than to buy his goods. He struck up a conversation, then mentioned the McPherson incident, claiming he was a friend of the family. He told Ali that the family had always harbored questions and was having difficulty coming to closure over the death.

Ali was sympathetic but seemed at a genuine loss to help. "I never met the poor man, a priest I understand, and I'm a Christian, you know, but I don't know why he had my shop's name on his person."

"The note mentioned the Last Supper," Avernis said. "Does that mean anything to you?"

"Of course I know what it is," Ali said, "but what he meant by this I have no idea."

The thought had crossed Avernis' mind that Ali might be some sort of antiquities dealer on the sly, perhaps even the source of the document, but there was big money in that illicit business and neither Ali nor his shop looked very prosperous. "Have you heard of Mary Magdalene?" Avernis asked, seeking a reaction. The little man's expression was neutral when he answered uncertainly that she was a biblical figure, wasn't she? Avernis didn't detect any physical tip-offs from the response.

Avernis thanked him and started to walk back to his hotel as the late afternoon sun sank behind Mount Zion. He hated to disappoint Cardinal Roncalli, but a five-year-old case was a cold trail to follow. McPherson's bishop claimed that an epiphany caused the priest to travel to Jerusalem; someone else claimed he was transporting ancient documents, then he was dead.

Something was going on beneath the surface in this one. Avernis could almost feel the threads of this incident undulating in the wind around him, beckoning him to tie them together, but at this point that would take a miracle.

CHAPTER LXXIV

[Synchronicity is] a meaningful occurrence.—Karl Jung

Jerusalem

Robert Avernis sat on the collapsed wall of an ancient stone building in the archaeological park beneath the south wall of the Temple Mount, where Father James McPherson had met his end. He stood up, balancing himself on the old stones, cupping his eyes against the midmorning sun. He made a panoramic scan of the surroundings. It was the first time he had ever been in Jerusalem, but he had a nagging feeling of familiarity.

Starting last night in the twilight zone between sleep and wakefulness, his mind started identifying places around the city. The thing was that these sites no longer existed—they were part of *ancient* Jerusalem. Early in the morning, he visited the patriarch's library. He was able to confirm a number of ancient structures said to have once existed on the Mount of Olives and the Temple Mount in the exact areas where he had envisioned them.

Something extraordinary was stirring within him, something containing information from somewhere, even his logical mind had to admit that now. He sat upon the stone wall and shut his eyes. Threads of the mystery still fluttered at the edges of his consciousness, only this time they began to weave together—priest in possession of a document . . . priest found dead probably climbing wall to escape pursuers . . . no document on the body . . . *Ali Wafa, the Last Supper . . .*

The facts then faded and a vision formed of a beautiful young woman. It was Teresa, but different from the Teresa he knew. Behind her stood two men and, behind them, a lone woman. The men were Roncalli and O'Keefe but he only sensed that because they did not look like the two men he knew. They were dressed in ancient robes. Of the lone woman in the distance behind them, all he could make out was her long, reddish-gold hair.

"The vessel of gnosis, Caius, seek the receptacle of knowledge," the Teresa figure whispered to him. Avernis' eyes opened, surprised at the vividness of his vision, and the first thing he fixed on was the cracked remains of a huge urn resting against the opposing wall. His mind made the connection. He couldn't believe his eyes were confirming what his mind had told him, but he ran all the way to

Ali Wafa's shop. Once there he asked the shopkeeper, "Do you carry any goods depicting the Last Supper, particularly urns or vases?"

"Why, no," Ali said. "Christians don't visit here much any more because of problems between the Arabs and Israelis. I'm the only Christian here and I have to be careful myself. Ali isn't even my real name; Philip is my name. I just use a nickname to fit in better. I stopped displaying vases two years ago. They never sold well anyway."

"Where is your old merchandise?" Avernis asked with urgency in his voice.

"Some of it's stored at the back of my shop. Some of it I sold in Tel Aviv."

Avernis slipped Ali a hundred Euros to let him rummage through the small warehouse at the rear of the shop. Ali was happy to accommodate. The place was a jungle of sundry merchandise with items piled on top of one another. Much of it was ceramic or pottery, and he moved carefully so as not to break anything. He searched for nearly two hours. He had seen plates with Last Supper images painted on them, even a few tapestries, but he was beginning to despair at the notion that what he sought might no longer be around after all this time.

Then he lifted a tarp at the back of the room, and his eyes opened wide. Underneath stood three vases, each with a depiction of the Last Supper painted across it! He lifted the first vase, turned it over, and felt inside. Nothing. The same with the second. He had a dizzy sensation, and he closed his eyes in prayer as he lifted the third vase. He shook it and he heard something inside. He reached in and pulled out a plastic tube. He breathed hard as he opened it. His hands shook as he read the contents.

The scroll contained in the vase, the knowledge contained in the receptacle. The symbology of the vision that led him here was not lost on him—Jesus' gnosis deposited in the vessel of Mary Magdalene, the beloved disciple shown by his side at the Last Supper! He now had one more stop to make before going home.

CHAPTER LXXV

I shall manifest the forms of the gods and teach them the secrets of the holy way which I call Gnosis. . . . .
—The Naasene Gospel

Tel Aviv

I was wondering if I might see you," Dr. Gallie Herron said as he greeted Avernis into his Tel Aviv apartment. "Monsignor O'Keefe told me you were someone special."

"Really?" a surprised Avernis said. "Can't imagine why he'd say that. Maybe he meant I'd be carrying something special. He told me to show you a fragment of ancient writing. I have the original and a quick translation that was recently wired to me from the Vatican."

"Okay, let's get to it, I have a doctoral thesis to review shortly," Herron said, sounding a bit curmudgeonly. The graying Herron looked like a professorial version of Ernest Borgnine, the old pre-holofilm movie actor, with his gap-toothed grin and fleshy nose. Avernis took out the sealed tube and opened it. He handed the contents to Herron, who took it to a desk and placed it under a magnifier. Herron adjusted the desk lamp and then leaned forward, resting both cheeks on raised arms, and began to read.

Mary Magdalene, companion of Jesus of Nazareth, by my hand is this written. Let none bear false witness in my name, for you shall know me by the truth of my words.

What are your dreams O sons of Adam and daughters of Eve? For your dreams are closer to reality than this world of flesh and blood. We have wandered into a cave and dwell among the creatures of the dark thinking this to be life. But the Christ, through the person of Jesus of Nazareth, did introduce a light unto the world that you might glimpse the truth of existence outside the cave. Still, the creatures of darkness will not relinquish. They will seek to pull us back from the light, to dim its glow, and to extinguish its flame.

They attack through our minds like parasites, and darkness follows in their wake. It is a darkness of false perceptions that transforms their hosts into oppressors who give themselves openly to the powers and authorities. Even close followers of Jesus begin to succumb, for darkness enters by ignorance and illusion and leads to error.

There are seven dark Archons in the lower heavens that hold you in bondage; there are seven dark emotions in the souls of man, and there are seven dark images to be overcome. Of the Archons and the emotions elsewhere has been written. Of the images I say to you beware—The Trickster, Death the Destroyer, The Punisher, The Prostitute, The Damaged Child, The Betrayer, and over all of them stands the Antichrist.

The Christ Jesus did awaken me to my true self. He rid me of these seven shadows to reunite his spirit and mine. The two became one again. So it must be with all humanity. The Sophia and the Christ, the man and the woman, the mind and the heart—the two shall become one. But who shall live to tell of these things? For I see the course that matters shall take. The Way of the Lord shall fall under the shadow of the Archons from whom it was meant to liberate. The Church shall become the abode of the beast and the light shall be grievously oppressed.

My life and my name shall be forfeit, but I shall return, black of skin, the three alphas of God in my name, and I shall assume the place of my detractor, Peter. Then the message shall be given, the secret Church shall become visible, the hidden shall be revealed, the First Souls shall rise, and the god of this world shall be overthrown. Blessed is the True God who dwells beyond the world and its snares.

Herron made several passes of the single Greek scroll. He bit his lower lip, stood up, and walked over to a phone. "Ava, this is Dr. Herron. Do me a favor, please. Tell the committee I had an emergency. I'd like to push the dissertation back two hours, okay? Thanks, Ava. Herron then turned to Avernis. "Sit down, young man. We've got some talking to do."

Avernis took a seat, wondering at Herron's sudden change in demeanor.

"Where did this come from?" Herron asked.

Avernis, unsure of what to say, gave minimum information. He related that the Vatican had received a tip about a document in Jerusalem related to Mary Magdalene without mentioning the McPherson history. "Monsignor O'Keefe wanted your opinion or interpretation of the contents and said you were the best man to contact in Israel."

"Well, he was right," Herron said without missing a step. "I assume the Vatican will have it dated, but my bet from the script, the tone, the Greek idiom and the content is that this is a real first-century work. There's a constant black market in antiquities in these parts, but this . . . it's exceptional. Do you know what you're holding? Did you read it?"

"I read the translation," Avernis said. "Not wanting to sound stupid, Professor, but it didn't make much sense to me. Let me take that back—on some level it seemed eerily familiar, but not in a way that I can logically relate. I'm no scholar or expert."

Herron cleared his throat then ran fingers through his thatch of grizzly hair. "I don't know what you recognized in it, but let me give you the historical and religious context. This is the first document ever purported to be written directly by Mary Magdalene, a woman almost completely blotted out of history. The recovery of Gnostic gospels at Nag Hammadi, Egypt, in 1945 started to bring her back to life. In fact, those gospels shocked scholars because they portrayed her as Christ's leading disciple. Some of them even hinted that she was the embodiment of the Holy Spirit, Sophia, just as Jesus embodied Christ."

Avernis put a hand to the side of his temple to aid his remembrance. "Sophia, yes, someone I'm working with mentioned a relation between her and Mary Magdalene. Anyway, this scroll contains some strange ideas. Maybe Monsignor O'Keefe anticipated that. He was hoping you could provide some commentary or interpretation of the text."

"Ha, he did, did he?" Herron snickered. "Son, the contents of this are pure dynamite. It would take teams of scholars a long time to analyze it and determine the chances that Magdalene really wrote it. If we could only recover the entire text. Regardless, this single page alone is loaded with novel psychological insights and material that sheds light on religious mysteries and philosophical dilemmas that have plagued the world to this day."

Avernis scratched his cheek. "That was a mouthful, Doctor. Can you do a little deciphering for me before leaving for your appointment?"

Herron laughed. "I'm a little excited. Don't see stuff like this every day. Okay, I'll make a laser copy and write out a brief outline. When you get back to the Vatican, have O'Keefe call me in a few days and I'll have a lot more to talk about."

"Deal," Avernis said, happy to know he could come away with something on such short notice. "By the way, Doctor, what is your field of expertise?"

Herron smiled. "You might call me a brain picker. I'm an evolutionary psychologist among other things. I study the development of human consciousness. Since that is strongly tied to spiritual mysteries, I'm also a religious scholar, so I'm versed in Aramaic, Greek, Hebrew, and Latin. Now let me get to it so you don't leave empty-handed."

"Just pretend I'm not here," Avernis said.

"No problem with that. I'll just treat you like my wife treats me," Herron said. He pulled his glasses down to the tip of his bulbous nose, cocked his eyebrows, and looked Avernis straight in the eye. "But Mr. Avernis, I should tell you right now that if this document is truly written by Mary Magdalene, the Vatican has a real problem on its hands."

"Oh? How so?" Avernis asked.

"Well," Herron said leaning back in his chair, "for one thing this reinforces the view from the Nag Hammadi discoveries that Mary Magdalene was the second most authoritative figure in Christianity. The popes, as heirs to Saint Peter, won't like that much."

"I see," Avernis said. "So that's the big problem in this?"

"No. There's something much worse in here from the Church's viewpoint," Herron said. "This document, as it stands, is pure heresy coming right from the mouth of Jesus' closest companion, you see? I think that's a bit of a problem for the Church, don't you?"

CHAPTER LXXVI

Then Jesus said "Behold, Father, she wanders the earth pursued by evil.
Far from thy Breath she is going astray. She is trying to flee bitter Chaos,
And does not know how she is to escape. —The Gospel of the Naasenes

Tel Aviv

Okay, I've broken down the document for you," Gallie Herron exclaimed after forty minutes on the Vox-to-Text computer. "I'll give you a rundown before I leave."

Avernis took a seat next to the Israeli scholar, who displayed his notes on a large computer monitor. "There are half a dozen key parts to this," Herron explained. "The cave allegory in the first paragraph—the idea that the phenomenal world our souls fell into is not the true reality but a poor reflection of a more perfect reality—that idea is both Platonic and Gnostic. But what follows is purely Gnostic."

"Gnostic? You're kidding?" Avernis said.

"Why, you know about the Gnostics?" Herron asked.

"I'm learning about them," Avernis said. "The Vatican has a renewed interest in them."

"Is that so?" Herron said, his eyebrows rising. "Perhaps O'Keefe can enlighten me when I speak with him. Anyway, the part about 'creatures of darkness' is an allusion to the Archons that she mentions later. The Archons are forces that created the material world and seek to keep spirit imprisoned in the confines of the material or astral planes. They are opposed to Christ, who tried to free humanity by reminding it of its true spiritual origin. The next part is most astonishing, though. She claims the way the Archons manipulate us is through the creation of false perceptions of reality in our minds."

"What does that mean?"

"To a Gnostic," Herron said, "reality meant that everything is encompassed by God. It's a continuous wave of omnipresent light, no past or future, but everything happening now. Some modern physicists—my wife is one—have postulated the same thing. Gnostics believed that all of our minds are a reflection of God's Mind yet we don't perceive or act like God. The reason is intervening forces, what the document refers to here as parasites, that come between us and the Divine Mind. These forces are expressed in the natural world—*gravity*, for example, that traps universal light locally; *time* that makes the omnipresent now seem to have a past, present, and future; *matter* that gives the illusion of solidity to an energy that is not solid; a *collective unconscious* harboring ancestral animal memories that warp our perceptions; and, above all, an *ego* that makes us psychically believe we are separate and flawed in the face of a true, perfect unity."

"The Gnostics thought real beings were behind these natural laws?"

"Some surely did," Herron said. "And it's not an impossible notion. My wife could tell you about dark matter and dark energy, invisible phenomena that comprise ninety percent of our universe, invisible forces that have a huge effect on shaping our physical world. A lot of people believe God created the cosmos; even many scientists perceive an '*intelligence*' behind the creation, but maybe there were plural *intelligences* involved. Who's to say God didn't create a spiritual life as varied as physical life? We have legends of fallen angels, fallen meaning imperfect. Perhaps they were symbolic of powerful, intelligent forces exercising free will but creating imperfectly—as in our world."

"Excuse me for saying so, but you don't sound like a scientist," Avernis remarked.

Herron laughed. "I take that as a compliment. I'm also a Kabbalist so I have sympathy for Gnostic views. The Kabbalists and the Gnostics were essentially Jewish and Christian sides of the same coin, but we digress, and I have to go soon. Now, Magdalene says here that even some of Jesus' closest followers succumbed to the errors and illusions of the world. I take this to mean that certain disciples, particularly Peter, Andrew, and James, never understood the inner truth of Jesus' message. Some of the Nag Hammadi gospels were pretty pointed about that. By not doing so they perpetuated the repressive, old patriarchal and hierarchical patterns of the Jewish priesthood and the Roman authorities.

"The icing on the cake was Constantine making Christianity the Roman state religion. The literal, authoritarian interpretation of Christianity triumphed by marrying the Roman power structure. The author of this scroll stunningly prophesizes this in the fifth paragraph where she says '*the Church shall become the abode of the beast and the light shall be grievously oppressed.*' This orthodox state Church systematically eradicated the secret mystical traditions along with Magdalene's name and Jesus' Gnostic legacy."

"My God," Avernis said. "That would make the Church heretics and the Gnostics the true Church! Monsignor O'Keefe once told me how the Church feared that."

"Ironic, no? Originally Gnostic and orthodox Christians were two strains of the same religion: one esoteric, relying on inner mystical experience; the other external, relying on ritual and dogma," Herron said. "The Gnostics considered the outer Church to be a primitive stepping stone toward personal revelations about God, but as the external Church became more dogmatic and tied to the Roman Empire, it could no longer tolerate those who didn't conform to its beliefs."

"So they exterminated them," Avernis said.

"Yes," Herron replied, "over a long time, ending with the Cathars in medieval France, the last Gnostic Church."

"What about these 'dark images' mentioned in the fourth paragraph?" Avernis asked.

"Those are negative archetypes," Herron said. "Think of them as obstacles from our collective unconscious animal mind hardwired into our psyches. They represent traps we face in the course of our lives. *The Trickster* is the dead ends, the illusions, and betrayals we face; *The Punisher* is guilt that holds us back and causes many complexes; *The Damaged Child* is arrested emotional and psychological development; *The Prostitute* is the way we sell our souls or higher purpose to get by in the world, and so on. The Gnostics considered them psychological manifestations of the Archons."

Avernis could only shake his head in wonder that a woman dead for two thousand years could identify things it had taken psychologists all the ensuing centuries to rediscover.

"Sounds bleak, though she gives us the way out here in the next to last paragraph," Herron said. "*'The two shall become one . . .'* she means that we must integrate our hearts and minds, our spirits and our psyches to become actualized human beings and perceive reality as God perceives it. She says Jesus awakened her by ridding her of these complexes, these Archontic images in her mind. Just as Gnostic legend claims, she says here that Jesus and she were *'reunited.'* That means they were together before. It can only refer to the legend that the indwelling spirits of Christ and Sophia were embodied in Jesus and Magdalene."

"Is that significant?" Avernis asked.

Herron folded his hands, and his face took on a soft, reverent expression, losing some of the hardness Avernis had sensed earlier. "That's perhaps the most important statement in the entire scroll. Gnostic Christians, certain Jewish sages, and the spiritual mystery schools of the ancient world held a common, sacred tradition. It concerns the feminine aspect of God, variously called Sophia, Wisdom, Earth Mother, the Great Goddess, or the Holy Spirit.

"The tradition says that certain actions by Sophia inadvertently led to the creation of the Archontic forces. These forces created this flawed material world and its animal life-forms, including hominids that they evolved from lower primates. The first 'humans' were little more than animals. The Archons derived their power from the psychic energy they parasitically drew from base human emotions—fear, anger, anxiety, images of pain and pleasure. They came to be worshipped as fearful gods like Jehovah of the Old Testament."

"That's quite a statement from a Jew," Avernis said.

"A Jew who has studied the veiled wisdom of the Kabbalah," Herron said. "Anyway, Sophia became trapped in the material plane as the world soul. The Christ came down and awakened her. Seeing the brutal, mechanistic world she had unintentionally created, she planted the divine spark of her essence in the human animal. This energy lay within like the coiled serpent of the Yogic kundalini, slowly rising and evolving the human nervous system to prepare it for the inflowing of divine consciousness.

"After a time that divine energy awoke in Adam and Eve, the first conscious and self-aware humans, and we come to the events captured in the Book of Genesis. The divine energy climbed up the spine to the crown of the head, symbolized by the serpent rising in the Tree of Knowledge. Sophia's force, which lay slumbering under the layers of ego and the collective unconscious, raised the human *animal* to consciousness as human *beings.*

"The Archons are shaken by the sudden awakening of their servants. Jehovah, the Chief Archon, as Genesis relates, decides to cast them out lest they eat from the tree of life and 'become as one of us,' note the plural tense used for the seven Archons. The Archons work to prevent them from realizing their true immortal origins. By thrusting humans into a world of toil and tribulation, they keep them focused on their material needs instead of their spiritual nature."

Herron looked at his watch. "I really need to go, but we're at the end. *'I shall return, black of skin, the three alphas of God in my name*—she seems here to predict her death and reincarnation, but in the last paragraph, *'and I shall assume the place of my detractor, Peter'*—I have no idea what that means. The secret Church becoming visible and the hidden being revealed may mean a resurgence of gnosis, but I never heard of the First Souls. And that, I'm afraid, is all I can offer before I leave."

The two men stood and shook hands. "Dr. Herron, I admire all the knowledge you brought to bear to interpret this text," Avernis said. "No wonder the monsignor had me come here. I'll relate everything you said to him, but I have one personal question before you go. What good did it all do? Jesus and Sophia, I mean? Whether you take this myth literally or symbolically, look at the state of humanity today."

Herron smiled and placed a hand on Avernis' shoulder. "Evolution, my friend, is not a straight line; it has steps forward and steps back with dead ends along the way. Our evolution is retarded by the Archontic forces. But myths, despite the fact that characters may be exaggerated or fictitious, are the highest form of truth since they describe the forces that shape our lives. Understanding the essence of a myth brings knowledge and wisdom, and knowledge is transformative. There's a branch of science called memetics that demonstrates how knowledge can become wired into our minds and transferred almost like DNA."

"Yes," Avernis said. "I remember the *hundred-monkeys* incident. When one monkey on an island learned to wash sweet potatoes, a few learned directly, but at a point they called the 'ninety-ninth monkey', the behavior became universal. It exploded throughout the entire island and then to neighboring islands like the ability was telepathically transmitted."

"Exactly," Herron said. "When a critical mass of knowledge is reached, it becomes encoded in the collective consciousness. It can take time, but don't underestimate the transformative power of knowledge and ideas. After a relatively brief exposure to Christianity, the Vikings, once the most savage of warrior races, became the modern Scandinavians who are among the most peaceful and cultured people in Europe. Think what the recovery of Jesus' true teachings could do with the knowledge they'd bring.

"It could mean a new world view, a new paradigm of thinking, a new way of perceiving reality. It might even allow us to *create* a new reality. New, positive archetypes would come to dominate the human mind. There are seven counter archetypes to the dark images mentioned in the scroll. O'Keefe can tell you about that, I don't have time now, but such knowledge found and taken to heart could usher in the next stage of human evolution."

Avernis felt something coalescing in his mind as he put together pieces from what he'd learned about the Gnostics from Teresa and now Dr. Herron. "The myths, the forces, the direction of humanity—somehow, it's all starting to sound right, to sound familiar," he told Herron.

"This document has significance beyond what you could imagine at first glance," Herron said. "If we could only find the rest of it," he mused, "but the announcement of this single page alone will cause unpredictable reactions, so take caution. I sense something is brewing in the Vatican that has to do with this document, and I hope it will be for the good."

Something was indeed brewing, and all Avernis could say in response was, "Amen."

CHAPTER LXXVII

Fanatics have their dreams, wherewith they weave a paradise . . .
—John Keats

Tehran, Iran

Madness, Ayatollah Reza Gorbani thought as he listened to the senior members of the Iranian religious council sitting around the oval table. There was madness in men when they twisted history into signs from God assuring them of their dominance in the world. How many other would-be conquerors went to their graves ignoring the reality that God rarely weights the scales of fate all on one side?

Havenei was so anxious to play the modern Caliph Baybars, so anxious to be the one to defeat the Western crusaders. They were dangerously overreaching. Gorbani raised his hand; Havenei recognized him.

"My esteemed teachers," he said. "I am the youngest man present and perhaps that makes me naïve. It is true American power has diminished in the past two decades. Their economy has been in a long-term malaise, their political will has been weak, and, as you said, their investment in military technology has declined significantly since the second Gulf War. Perhaps they cannot even field the kind of army they had two decades ago, but they are still dangerous."

He looked around the room. All of the gray-bearded men sat with folded arms and proud, self-assured faces that looked as if they were indulging him. "I mean no presumption," Gorbani said, "when I remind you of the old wounded tiger story. The Americans still possess the greatest destructive power on the planet. They know we have funded attacks against them and their Israeli allies for years. They know we subverted them in Iraq. They certainly know our oil pact with Asia was aimed at them. Now you are planning to provide chemical weapons to the Palestinians and other jihad fighters to finish Israel. Do you really think the trail will not lead back to us?"

Ayatollah Havenei patted the Quran on his desk. "What is your concern Reza?"

"My concern is that we go too far," Gorbani replied. "We are slowly achieving our ends. Why risk American retaliation?"

Havenei shook his head. "They have neither the means nor the will to retaliate."

"You followed their elections as well as I did," Gorbani said. "They elected a man who promised to reverse their slide and pursue an aggressive foreign policy against us."

"Yes," Havenei said. "A maverick who would have to control both American political parties to get anything done."

Gorbani knew he was witnessing the classic Islamic mistake about America, the same one that got Saddam ousted. They believed a bureaucratic machine of weak-willed politicians ran America, but now the American people were angry. The people could well force their politicians into acting, something his colleagues could not understand because the people in Islamic countries never made a difference.

"You overestimate America's position," Havenei said. "It takes oil to wage war. Only Nigeria and the near-exhausted Latin American supplies are providing limited amounts to the Americans. If they still threaten us, we will defend ourselves with nuclear and chemical weapons. Besides, by attacking us, they risk confrontation with China. China will not want the oil pact broken by force. This is our best opportunity. We can overthrow the Israelis and cripple the West for good. We will solidify a preeminent position in Islam for generations."

"Exactly," Ayatollah Charubey chimed in. "Water has become as important as oil in the Mid-East, and, once again, we are sitting in the right place. Almost half of the dwindling Israeli water supply comes from aquifers lying under Palestinian Authority territory in the West Bank. Arabs are more unified than ever against Israel because of Israeli demands for the resource. The power balance has shifted. This is our best window to achieve our ends."

"We are spreading propaganda against the Israelis," Havenei said. "We will demand they relinquish all water rights to the rightful ownership of the Palestinians. Remember too, Russian communists are once again a concern to the West, and with them and the Chinese looming in the background, the Americans will be paralyzed and unable to move against us."

It was no use arguing further. They saw the hand of God in these events and there was no telling them otherwise. Gorbani held his tongue through the rest of the meeting.

"Dangerous, dangerous games," Ayatollah Reza Gorbani muttered as he entered his apartment, slammed the door behind him, and slumped on a sofa. Fatilah entered the room.

"What is wrong?" she asked as she rubbed his shoulders, encouraging him to talk.

Gorbani did just that, ranting away at the stupidity of the senior clerics. "There are great gaps of logic in their game of brinkmanship," Gorbani said. "The West may not react the way they think. America is desperate now. We could be pushing two super-powers into each other's faces, and Havenei's willingness to use our chemical and nuclear weapons . . ."

There it is, Fatilah thought. *What I've waited for all these years.* Gorbani spoke on, and Fatilah forced herself to hear it all, but he had already spoken the magic words. The world became different for her in that moment, bright and sweet with the fragrance of a desire near fulfillment. She made a show of sympathy for the man whose bed she had shared for years. She feigned enthusiasm in their lovemaking, and when he fell into a deep sleep, she was careful not to make any noise as she slipped out the door. She paused and spat over the threshold. Appropriate, since she would never be returning.

✠

An hour later, on the outskirts of the city, she knocked on a door. A man asked a question in Farsi and she answered correctly. The door opened and she entered the sparsely decorated room of the safe house. "So," the man said, this time in perfect American English, "You're the one we've waited for all this time."

Fatilah nodded, then instructed the agent to transmit her information. He removed a stucco panel and pulled a concealed omnisat radio from inside the wall. "Omar has returned," he said when the transmitter was ready. "Repeat, Omar has returned. Darius is hot and spicy, Darius is hot and spicy. He's delivering spice to David via Ishmael, he—"

A series of noises suddenly interrupted his transmission. Fatilah recognized the sound of rifle butts banging on the single reinforced door. "Quick," she said. "Buy me time."

The agent ran into the next room and started pushing furniture against the door. Fatilah took her earrings off. She opened one of the disk-shaped earrings, pulled out a small, clear silicon chip, then put the earrings back on. Her eyes made a frantic search around the room. She spotted a white-painted metal grating covering an air return. The agent was shouting in the next room, and she heard the door splintering. Fatilah pulled some nail glue out of her bag and applied it to the back of the studlike chip. She pressed it against the bottom of the flat-rimmed grating.

Buy me time, she prayed as she waited for the glue to set . . . shots in the next room . . . and when the stud seemed firmly attached, she dabbed over it with white nail polish. It was passable. It looked like a protruding fastener, similar to the one at the top of the grating. The agent cried out. They were inside! Fatilah pulled out a vid-phone and punched in some numbers. Holding the vid-phone in such a way as to be heard and seen, she kept speaking even as she walked into the room with hands in the air.

The agent was a bloody mess lying on the floor. When the secret police approached her, she stared them hard in the eye, unblinking. They were not going to intimidate her. Apparently, they realized that too. A rifle butt caught her on the jaw and she slumped to the floor, praying the nail glue held as she lost consciousness.

CHAPTER LXXVIII

War never takes a wicked man by chance.
— Sophocles

The outskirts of Tehran, Iran

Robert Avernis gazed at the majestic Alborz Mountains as the helicopter began its approach into Tehran. His eyes blanked out on the white slopes at the upper levels. He had no sooner returned to deliver the Magdalene document to a grateful Cardinal Roncalli when Leo Dusayne called him over to the Rome station to attend an astonishing briefing.

"Celine was a mole, Bob, a high-level mole," Dusayne had explained. "Only the director and the president himself knew about her. Her old man was apparently a real bastard. He frequently beat Celine's mother, and the doctors think that triggered the woman's Parkinson's disease. The Iranians offered him a low-level government job fifteen years ago. He took off for Iran with Celine's younger sister while Celine took care of the mother in France. She was boiling with hate for the father when she approached us.

"She wanted her sister back. She also wanted revenge on her father and all the 'woman-hating Iranians,' it says here in the dossier Langley released to us. We planted her as a top secret sleeper with one primary mission—get conclusive proof the Iranians have weapons of mass destruction. She did good. She got their trust, worked her way in, and cultivated an affair with an up-and-coming ayatollah who now sits on the clerical governing council."

Dusayne closed the dossier. "We received a transmission from Iran night before last. Before it broke off, it indicated the Iranians have nukes and chemical weapons. They may soon be providing some of that material to Palestinian terrorist groups for use against Israel. Fatilah and the safe house were under attack when the transmission ended. You need to find out if she is alive. If you can extract her, do so. If not, get whatever evidence is available about the Iranian WMD program. That info goes straight to president Davidson. He's assumed a vital interest in this operation."

Avernis was entering Tehran as a member of a Vatican and French diplomatic delegation. The French were finally cooperating with the United States after seeing the tide of terrorism rolling over the West in the aftermath of the Iraqi pullout two decades ago. Fatilah's last action was to call the French embassy in Tehran on her vid-phone, state her name, and declare that she was a French citizen. She claimed she was either going to be killed or arrested by the Ministry of Justice, a euphemism for the Iranian Secret Police.

Avernis was trained to read body language, and Mr. Sadegh's language spoke a bucket full of bullshit. Sadegh was an official from the Ministry assigned to meet with the French, and his office was the spartan model of a true bureaucrat. They conducted the meeting in English with Sadegh stubbornly denying any knowledge of Fatilah Celine Marchand Jahani.

"But she called us on a vid-phone," Monsieur Lussier from the French embassy exclaimed. "We have the video on record to show you. She was alive and being handled by armed men before the phone was turned off."

"Who were these men?" Sadegh shot back. "If there is any truth to this incident, the woman could have been abducted by thieves. Why she says police I don't know, but we are holding no one by that name or description."

She's still alive. Avernis made the instant assessment based on what he was seeing and hearing from Sadegh. Besides, logic dictated they would not have killed her yet. They would want to know what she knew, what she communicated to whom, and over what period of time had she been passing information. They were likely torturing her at this very moment.

After twenty more minutes of Sadegh's stonewalling, the meeting ended. The French promised to keep pressing the matter, but Avernis knew that would come to nothing.

Avernis gave a barely audible sigh. It was time to hunker down for Plan B. He was going to be in Iran longer than he wanted.

Washington, D.C.

"History indeed repeats itself," National Security Advisor Rachel Worth heard president John Davidson say to the assembled group. Ms. Worth's fingernails dug into the palms of her hands, and the confining, windowless walls of the subterranean situation room were not helping her anxiety. This was going to be the most important meeting of the National Security Council she had attended since Davidson had assumed the presidency.

"Two thousand five hundred years ago," Davidson said, "Alexander the Great and the Greek army broke the back of the Persian Empire, ending centuries of despotic incursions that threatened to obliterate European civilization even as it was being born. We find ourselves in a curiously similar position today."

As promised in his election, Davidson had fully committed himself to reversing America's downward spiral. His answer was the Davidson Doctrine, which he was repeating right now to the NSC members. "The Persian threat is once again on the rise," he said. "We backed down from moral, political, and military commitments that allowed our enemies to run amok, and we have paid a dear price. Terrorists and their sponsor states have tried to isolate America by singling out our cities and our economy with a particular vengeance. This we will stop. Offensive action is the only response to terrorism. We must take the fight to their soil. Any government or country aiding and abetting terrorism has forfeited its right as a sovereign state under international law. Now, we have just such a situation with Iran."

He nodded at Rachel. "We have received reliable intelligence confirming that Iran is in possession of nuclear and chemical weapons," she said. A chain of murmurs swept across the room. "We believe they have a medium-range missile delivery system for the nukes that is at least regional in capability though in what numbers we can't be sure. What is more troubling are the less conventional means of delivery, particularly in the wrong hands."

Everyone in the room knew what that meant. Depending on the type of thermonuclear device in question, an object the size of a baseball could wipe out the heart of any major city.

"Our sources tell us the Iranians plan to put chemicals in the hands of Palestinian terror groups for use against Israel." Again, Rachel paused for the buzzing to subside. "The CIA's assessment is that Iran itself is unlikely to use the nukes conventionally for other than defensive purposes, probably as a form of blackmail to protect against retaliation for their aggressions, but they could disburse material and technology to terrorists." Rachel gestured to CIA Director Paul Hobson.

"The Iranian's agenda is to dominate the Islamic world," Hobson said. "They want to be the country that brings America to its knees. Iran has been the prime funding source for the terrorism hitting our cities for the past decade. They destabilized Iraq. Most recently, they instigated the oil pact with China and other Asian nations. They're feeling strong, and they're apparently raising the ante in a game they believe they can win."

Now the president took the lead again. "Ladies and gentlemen, an ant cannot kill a man, but, given enough time and enough ants, they can nibble the feet right out from under him until he falls. Of course, that assumes the man stands still and doesn't stomp on the ants, and America will no longer stand still. The way to stop ants is to kill the queen, and it's now or never. Our objective is regime change in Iran."

Rachel felt elevated tension in the room, but the president had picked most of the NSC members because they shared his views. They would back him one hundred percent.

Davidson pointed to an electronic map of the Middle East occupying the giant wall screen to his left. "Fortunately, we foresaw the possibility of confronting Iran when I took office. I had Secretary Forrester negotiate a deal with the Armenians to allow bases, if necessary, to stage an invasion of northern Iran. Christian Armenia is gravely concerned, being surrounded as it is by hostile Muslim states."

Rachel saw the looks of surprise on some of the faces in the room. The secret Armenian deal was a brilliant coup for the new administration.

"The Armenian agreement will give us leverage with the Turks to open up another front," Davidson said. "It's time to stand up and be counted. The Turks won't want to be on our bad side this time, particularly if the Armenians stand to reap the benefits as our allies. We can expect to have two land fronts close to Tehran in the north and west and numerous amphibious assault points along the Persian Gulf to the south. Sound like a plan, General?"

Joint Chief General Richard Sturmer nodded. "It opens up real possibilities, sir."

"Mr. President, may I ask a question?"

Rachel looked at Vice President Earnhardt. Davidson had had to choose him as a running mate to blunt criticism from liberals that his administration would have no moderate views. He was perhaps the only man in the room not solidly behind the president.

"Mr. President," Philip Earnhardt said in flat, midwestern tones, "You spoke of regime change, and now we're discussing invasion plans. Why not try and accomplish our objectives by a show of force rather than the force itself?"

"Good God, Phil," Secretary of State Kanellos said. "We've engaged in empty bluster for two decades. No one takes us seriously anymore. As long as the ayatollahs run the country, we have a problem. They have WMDs and a plan to use them. Now is the time to strike a mortal blow at terrorism. We've got the goods on them."

"*Do* we have the goods on them?" Earnhardt said. "What intelligence do we have?"

"A direct report from an agent close to the Iranian Ruling Council," Director

Hobson answered. "Soon, we hope to have an actual recorded admission by one of the ayatollahs."

"Based on the information we have now," Davidson said, "I'm ordering Operation Alexander the Great to go into effect—the quarantine and neutralization of Iran."

"Mr. President," Earnhardt said, "I get the feeling I'm the only one here who wasn't informed of these contingency plans, so pardon my questions. First, if the Iranians have WMDs and we invade, will they use them against us or Israel? Second, how will the Chinese react? Will they see it as a threat to their new energy source? And finally, can you get this through Congress?"

He just doesn't get it, Rachel thought. When the president responded, she could tell he was trying not to condescend.

"Phil," he said, "In case the Iranians try to use their weapons, I'm ordering a Hammerhead-class sub to the Gulf along with the third Mediterranean carrier group to dissuade them. The Iranians have gone too far this time. They lied about their weapons programs, and soon we'll have proof of their criminal intent. We're protecting both ourselves and the world against their threat. The Chinese won't go to war under such circumstances. As for Congress, we must act now to contain the emergency, but when the facts are out, I'll get enough votes to protect the American people. We did well in the midterm elections."

"Mr. President," Earnhardt said with a tone of increased urgency, "You are going to aim over a hundred nuclear missiles at Iran. That is dangerous in the extreme. Can't we at least keep the Hammerhead away and opt for conventional means of containment?"

Davidson slapped a hand down on the table. "The Iranians are playing nuclear blackmail. We have to show them they cannot succeed at that game by calling their bluff with a serious deterrent. I'm going to send them the following message through back channels—if they should use chemical or nuclear weapons at any time, they will pay an unthinkable price."

There were more discussions. Earnhardt pointed out that a war could drain America's critically low oil supplies. Davidson declared it was a necessary risk and the army would make use of caputured oil refineries. Another of Iran's provocations was the Asian oil pact, which Davidson intended to break. Earnhardt was plainly outnumbered, and Operation Alexander the Great was set in motion. Rachel was nervous but proud to serve under a president who stayed true to his word in a crisis. He asked her and Director Hobson to stay on after the others left.

"Paul," he said to Hobson with urgency in his voice, "I need that evidence from Iran to clinch our plans, and I need it now. Do we have our best operatives on this?"

Hobson did not want to divulge Avernis' abbreviated CIA resumé. "Sir, we have a very sharp young man leading the effort," was all he said, and he prayed his words would be proved out.

"Good," Davidson replied, "Because the future of our world rests on his shoulders tonight."

CHAPTER LXXIX

Can your conscience allow you to demand such a price?
—Dictionary of Fact & Fable

The White House, Washington, D.C.

Virginia Davidson had been one of the brightest lawyers in her law firm before she became the First Lady. During her husband's election campaign, she was one of his best advisors. Tonight her concentration was on her third drink, and she was not a drinker.

"Talk to me, Ginny," Davidson said to his blond, attractive wife.

Virginia put the glass down on the coffee table. "I have reservations about all this," she said in a cultured southern accent. "I don't want my children to grow up knowing their daddy was the one who unleashed the bomb. Is there no other way?"

Davidson sighed. "It's my children for whom I'm doing this. I've thought on these things a very long time. You know that, Ginny. We've always discussed our politics openly since we met. You fully acknowledged this necessity might come."

"I did," Virginia said, "yet somehow it seems different now that *our* finger is on the trigger."

"Is it more moral to shirk the responsibility and leave it to someone else?" Davidson asked.

Virginia did not answer.

"For two decades now, I've watched these terrorists whittle a great nation down to the bone. From the time we abandoned Iraq and emboldened these murderous bastards, look at what has happened. We have bombings every week, our economy is in shambles, and now they are trying to cut our remaining oil supplies."

"We left ourselves open to that," Virginia said.

"Yes, we did. A free market economy is not a bullet train on a straight track; it's a locomotive going around bends. That doesn't change the fact that we've been targeted by an ultranational movement bent on our destruction. We've pretended for years a minority of the Islamic world is the problem. Here are the facts—twenty percent are actively killing us and fifty percent tacitly support the twenty percent. Islam has become less a religion and more a fascist ideology, a cult of war and martyrdom. And where are the moderates? Are they closing down the madrassahs that breed hate?"

"I understand that," Virginia replied. "Maybe that is where we should direct our efforts."

"Too late," Davidson said. "Besides, those hate schools reside within their boundaries. We can't invade every country and change the curriculums."

Virginia shook her head. "How did we come to this?"

"How? The same way Europe came to the brink of destruction with Hitler," Davidson said. "Since World War Two, Europe has been socialist to the core, and socialism is inherently weak in the face of foreign threats. Our own liberals in this country are close to socialists, cut ideologically from the same cloth. That sums up the state of the Western world. Great nations with heads buried in the sand. Iran has the bomb because we closed our eyes and played the UN appeasement game."

Virginia shivered. "I do shudder to think a government like Iran's can now spread nuclear technology to the terrorists."

"If you have moral hesitation against using such weapons, they don't," Davidson said. "And I would not be the first to use such weapons. Truman did it."

"I know it was a morbid impulse," Virginia said, "but I pulled classified archives of the Hiroshima blast." She did not describe the images that haunted her mind. It wasn't so much the charred, surreal magnitude of destruction from the aerials. It was the people.

Charred bodies, bodies looking like their insides were turned out, and some of them were still alive, shambling along in parodies of human form like a horror movie that Hollywood special effects could never hope to recreate.

She did not tell these things to her husband. All she said was: "You should view the archives. I ask myself what sort of race are human beings that we can drive ourselves to perpetrate such an act?"

Davidson closed his eyes. "I don't want to see it, and I certainly don't want it to happen here, on our soil, to our children, but that's what they want to do to us. They're insane, and it often takes insanity to combat insanity."

"But we were in a global war then and . . ." her voice trailed off weakly, ending her tenuous plea to deter the inevitable.

"Come on, Ginny, you know better. What do you think we're engaged in now? It's even worse now, more insidious. Americans think conventional armies slugging it out in the field is the only type of activity defined as war. What we have is a long-term guerilla war of attrition coupled with the threat of nuclear attacks by the guerillas. This is a whole new paradigm for war."

Virginia picked up her glass and took another drink. "I know my history, John. Guerilla wars were always lost by the stronger countries because they would not escalate to the level necessary to win," she said. "They bound themselves by convention so as not to be criticized by the world community, or their own people, for that matter."

"Exactly. But the war has come to our soil, and people are no longer seeing it as an abstraction. That is what got me elected, narrowly perhaps, but we're here."

"Yes," Virginia said. "We are here. The question is what do we do?"

"I know what to do," Davidson said. "These terrorists have attacked, murdered, and destroyed with impunity for too long now. They hide and get support among the so-called moderate Muslims and they turn world opinion against us, the ones being attacked, saying everything is our fault.

"They even have misguided people in the Western countries reciting that mantra. We sit here quaking over the day they use a nuclear bomb while some Americans spout these insanities. The terrorists have to know that the game is over. We will destroy their cities, their cultural centers, and their way of life if they don't desist. I will not sit by and have the rats slowly gnaw our bones because we were too afraid to lift our hand."

Virginia took a picture of their children off the table, held it to her breast, and let her head fall toward her lap. Davidson came over and put his hand under her chin. When he lifted her head up, her bleary eyes glistened with tears. "Ginny, what's wrong?"

She embraced him, placing her head on his chest. "My head tells me you're right, but my heart prays to God for forgiveness."

"Forgiveness for what?" he asked.

He felt her fingers dig into the sides of his ribs. She tilted her head up to face him and said in a soft, hoarse voice, "Forgiveness for not seeing another way."

CHAPTER LXXX

For false Christs and false prophets shall rise, and shall show signs and wonders, to seduce, if it were possible, even the elect.
— Mark 13:22.2

The Vatican City

Annalisa was conducting a meeting in the papal study with Cardinals Roncalli and Berletti and Patriarch Umberto Segri when her eyes went blank and she sat bolt upright in her seat.

"Mother, what is it?" Roncalli asked.

Annalisa's eyes closed and she was silent for minutes while the men looked on, puzzled and alarmed. When she spoke, her voice was a low and breathy. "Trouble. A great storm is coming. I must leave the Vatican soon for the East. I know that much. That is when it will begin. You all will be called upon."

A great storm? Roncalli wondered. *This is a premonition.* He left the room that afternoon greatly concerned, for history had taught him to trust the pope's predictions.

Two days following Annalisa's vision, news broke that America was blockading Iran, and a great earthquake shook Rome. All around the city, buildings crumbled while flames and smoke rose like sacrificial bonfires for the gods. The dome of Saint Peter's cracked; many clergy were killed as Vatican buildings fared little better than the rest of Rome.

After burying their own dead, the pope instructed all Vatican clergy to go out into Rome to aid the sick and dying. The pope herself walked the streets in the hardest-hit areas, and wherever she went, the people took great heart. There were claims that upon touching her, many were healed of fractured bones, and they walked despite injuries that had kept them prostrate.

Then came rumors of war. The Iranians accused America of warmongering and Israel of genocide, of stealing precious water from Arab mouths. The Americans dispatched a fleet to the Persian Gulf, and public sentiment in North America ran high against the Muslims and China. The Americans accused them of economic genocide, of stealing precious oil from the American economy. China responded with harsh words and warnings to the Americans.

During a pause from their own efforts in a devastated part of the city, Roncalli and Zugli met with Leo Dusayne. They sat under a large, old tree in a park filled with people too afraid of aftershocks to reenter their homes—what was left of their homes, that is.

"The pope wants to know the truth of what is happening, Leo. What can you tell us about the Middle East crisis?" Zugli asked.

Dusayne said, "The situation is grim, Roald. Iran has nuclear and biological capabilities. They seem emboldened because the Chinese are warning us off any actions against them. The Chinese are feverishly building up their economy, and they think we want to put them down by breaking their oil pacts with the Arabs."

"What of the other Arab states?" Roncalli asked.

"This crisis over water resources really played into the Iranian's hands," Dusayne said. "They're inciting old fears in Israel's neighbors. We're even worried they're going to pass biological agents to the Palestinian terrorists."

"What about Havenei?" Roncalli asked. "What kind of man is he? Will he negotiate?"

Dusayne thought for a second. "Remember ancient Rome, when the emperors poisoned or killed their relatives out of fear that their relatives were trying to kill *them*? Caligula, for instance?" Roncalli nodded, and Dusayne continued. "Well, the Iranian regime also feeds on itself," Dusayne said. "Havenei killed rivals and associates alike to get where he is. He thinks he's God's right hand. He is fanatic and given to extremes. That profile makes for irrationality, and, as any of our analysts will tell you, cultivating irrationality is the most dangerous kind of political strategy."

While Dusayne spoke, the drone of machinery permeated the air as heavy equipment moved dusty clouds of collapsed rubble at the opposite end of the park. "This time around, we have a president who won't back off," Dusayne said. "If Havenei deploys weapons of mass destruction, the Americans, or even the Israelis, will go nuclear on him. Then America, China, and the world will be in a very dire situation. It's a scary scenario."

Just as he finished his statement, a nearby underground gas main exploded in a plume of fire. People screamed and huddled together in the face of one more onslaught on their senses, one more disruption of their crumbled worlds. As the fire leaped into the air, Roncalli recalled the saying that Christian Rome would be as a light unto the world—surely this could not be what they had meant.

✠

After Zugli and Roncalli briefed Annalisa on their conversation with Dusayne, she announced her intention to leave for Iran immediately. "Open up channels to Tehran," she ordered over the protests of most of her advisors.

Many in the Vatican started to wonder if the prophecies were coming true. Umberto Segri approached Roncalli one day. "I found a chilling passage in the Breverarium. Let me read it:

BEFORE THE RESURRECTION, THE ENDING OF THE LINE SHALL LEAVE THE SHAKING DOME ON THE HILL.

PETRUS ROMANUS, THE BEGINNING OF THE END, SHALL LIE WITH THE BEAST WHO COMING FROM THE EAST WILL OPEN THE BOX OF PANDORA.

THE DARK ONE WILL TRIUMPH AND LEGION WILL LIE UNDERFOOT; THE CHILDREN OF ABRAHAM REUNITE.

THE SHE GOAT OF SATURN SHALL BE LED FOR SLAUGHTER BY THE SEVEN SINS.

"It's very foreboding," Segri said in a heavy voice. "Annalisa was born in January under the sign of the Goat, under Saturn. I don't quite understand the seven sins, but St. Peter's Dome on the Vatican Hill has already shaken and cracked. Annalisa is leaving for the East. The children of Abraham reuniting must refer to rallying the Arab League against Israel."

"What are you trying to say, Umberto?"

Segri sighed, and when he spoke, he did not look Roncalli in the eye. "The world was troubled before Annalisa became pope, Pietro, but look at things now. The Church and the world are in chaos. And the prophecies . . . Clement being the second-to-last pope paving the way for Petrus Romanus, Annalisa about to treat with the beast who, armed with Armageddon weapons, will unleash a nuclear or biological Pandora's box . . ."

"And the Dark One will triumph," Roncalli said, completing Segri's thought. "Umberto, since she was a nun, everyone has been divided on whether this woman is a saint or the devil in disguise. I had many moments of doubt, and I know what the prophecies seem to be saying. But I believe in her, believe in her goodness."

Segri closed his eyes in a look of tired skepticism

Undaunted, Roncalli said, "Yes, there is turmoil, but the great come in the wake of turmoil. Our world evolves during times of challenge. Great people meet those challenges, exceptional people define them, and in doing so they transform us. Remember, Jesus said, 'Think not that I am come to send peace on earth; I came not to send peace, but a sword.'"

Segri looked at him in surprise.

"Umberto, you were correct," Roncalli said. "These troubles all happened during Annalisa's papacy, but it is because *she was meant to be here,* now, during these times. I believe she will prevail in what she sets out to do, and I believe we will be transformed because of it."

Segri marveled, looking at the resoluteness in his friend's eyes. This man who had been so careworn years past, so torn with indecision, now radiated a strength that calmed Segri's own restless mind. Indeed, perhaps Pietro was right, perhaps people *could* be transformed—anyway, he prayed it was so.

CHAPTER LXXXI

. . . a double face, a charming Janus, and underneath, the house motto: "Be wary". —Albert Camus

Tehran

The Delta Force commander signaled Avernis to stay low. He crouched behind the shrubs opposite the home where the Iranians were holding Fatilah captive. After holing up in Tehran for days, Avernis' American ops unit got their first break from the Israeli Mossad. The Mossad had a better intelligence network inside Iran than the United States and they came through with information on Fatilah's location.

Time was of the essence, so they had made only minimal reconnaissance of the walled compound building in which the Iranians were holding her. They had no idea where she was located in the building, and that was problematic. Avernis glanced at Avram Loschman, the Israeli Sayeret Matkal man assigned by his government to assist the Americans.

Avram told him Fatilah's sister had put the secret police on to her, the same sister she had returned to save. *The father must have done a number on the sister from the time she was young*, Avernis thought. He almost choked on the bitter irony of it. He could only imagine the betrayal Fatilah must have felt; he prayed she was still alive.

"Time," Avram said. "Wish me luck."

Avernis clasped his forearm and nodded. Avram walked down the street of sparse, widely spaced buildings in a rather common residential neighborhood. He hailed the two guards at the front gate in Farsi and presented his papers from the Ministry of Information. At that moment, the Delta Special Forces took out the perimeter guards with silenced weapons. Avernis moved forward with them to the wall. He was armed with Avram's silenced Galil MAR assault rifle. Avram asked him to carry it for good luck since he had to use an Iranian-issued weapon.

The Special Forces men unfolded adjustable platform ladders and placed them against the eight-foot-high compound walls. Avernis mounted one and crouched just below the top of the wall, waiting for Avram's signal. They heard Avram's voice engaging the men at the other side of the courtyard. Avernis waited for what seemed like eons until he heard Avram's signal words in a raised voice. He pushed up the ladder, and using the platform step, he launched over the wall and into the courtyard with six Delta Force soldiers.

Avram had drawn the four Iranians in the courtyard to the opened front gate, so there were six to eliminate including the two gate guards. The sound of the men landing on the ground attracted the Iranians. They turned and received a volley of silent bullets. Taken by surprise and caught in a cross fire between Avram and the Delta Forces, all the Iranians died except one. Avram had bashed one of the gate guards with his gun butt, immobilizing and disarming him.

The Deltas trained their weapons on the house while Avram questioned the guard by holding a knife to his throat. It did not take long to make him talk. "She's on the first floor in a reinforced room with a steel door, down the hall, third door on the left," Avram said.

They were readying to use the guard to gain entry to the building when the front door opened. Two men stepped out. Seeing the intruders, the first man started to raise his weapon, and the Deltas cut him down. The second man stumbled back, wounded but alive, and crying out an alarm.

"Go!" Avernis shouted, and the men rushed forward through the door.

Shots rang out as the Deltas swept through the house. Avernis plowed forward to the steel door with the Deltas' demolition man. The Israelis had prepared them for just such a barrier. They had suffered a failed mission years before in the Nachshon Waxman rescue attempt because of inadequate munitions to blow the door. Not this time. It blew swiftly.

Avernis rushed in, gun raised, just in time to see two men, one of them pointing a gun at Fatilah. The Delta took out one man and Avernis fired at the other, but the Iranian shot at Fatilah before collapsing. Avernis saw a red light flashing. Someone in the building had pressed a button and alerted the inner guards. They had lost the element of surprise.

He rushed over to Fatilah, who was shackled to a bed and groaning. He froze. A pool of blood was soaking the filthy bedsheets. The single bullet fired by the guard had struck her.

"Find the keys!" he called out to the Delta as he bent over to examine Fatilah. Her face was battered and puffy from beatings. They had cut off most of her hair and it felt like she had broken ribs. The bullet had caught her in the chest, close to her heart, and he knew she was dying. He did his best to staunch the blood with the medpac they carried. "Fatilah, Celine, it's me, Robert, from Nigeria, from Rome, remember?"

Her glassy eyes were trying to focus on him. "Robert?" she repeated in a soft voice. "I . . . I see you now. I remember." She coughed, and blood oozed from her mouth. "They sent you. I'm glad. I want to see a familiar face at the end."

"No endings, Fatilah. We're going to get you out," he said.

She shook her head. "No, Robert, I will die here. I feel it all slipping away," and in that moment she told him about the location of the chip. When he had it all down, she said, "I told you we would meet again. I liked you, Robert. I'm glad they sent you. I knew what you were when they had you meet me in Rome."

That explained why it had been so easy to plant the STAT, but he had figured that out when they told him she was a mole.

He held her as her body arced in pain. "Would we have been friends or lovers, Robert?"

He touched her cheek and felt her tears flow between his fingers. Her life force hovered between two worlds, and she started to ramble. "This world . . . ah . . . no more . . . sisssterr . . ." and the sadness of her death and betrayal overwhelmed him as her breathing stopped.

Avram came into the room and put a hand on his shoulder. "We must leave now," he said.

Avernis nodded. "Yes." He leaned forward and kissed Fatilah's forehead. "Time to go."

Washington, D.C.

Avernis returned to Washington on a new Air Force Rapier rapid flight jet. National Security Advisor Rachel Worth greeted him in the waiting room outside the Oval Office. "Mr. Avernis, it's a pleasure, sir."

"Thank you," Avernis replied.

"The president wants to thank you personally," Worth said. "They've already extracted the contents of the chip you retrieved. It's crucial to justify the actions we're taking against Iran."

Avernis nodded.

They spoke for a few minutes, then a man who looked like Secret Service opened the door to the Oval Office. "The president will see you now," he said to Avernis.

President Davidson sprang up from his chair with the same energy Avernis saw him during his election campaign. "Mr. Avernis, am I pronouncing that correctly? Your nation owes you a debt of gratitude, sir."

"I hope this information helps, Mr. President. A brave woman died for this. She's the real hero, not me."

"Yes, I'm sorry about that," Davidson said. "We've been fighting an undeclared war for two decades whether the public admits it or not. We have to win this war. The information you brought back will silence the naysayers and the weak-kneed among us who always find excuses to undermine our security. But surely, I'm preaching to the choir."

Avernis studied the president. This was a strong-willed man used to having his way; Avernis could see that in his bearing and hear it in his voice. Authority and command would be default settings for him. Yet there was something else evident in his blue eyes. He had will and purpose, not in a general sense, but more like an agenda. Then again, what politician did not? Avernis stopped playing psychic and answered Davidson.

"Mr. President, national security is the whole point of my job description. Those of us in the field appreciate your support."

His brief audience with the president then ended, and Rachel Worth escorted Avernis out of the Oval Office.

"Ms. Worth."

"Call me Rachel."

"Thank you. Rachel. It's not often a field agent gets to meet the commander-in-chief. What kind of man is the president?"

Rachel smiled. He was unsure whether she thought the question naïve or forward, but she responded nonetheless. "He's unlike any president or politician in recent times. His goal in life is to halt the country's tailspin and restore America's greatness. You can count on him to prosecute this war without hesitation, even if it costs him reelection."

Perhaps she might want to take her answer back if given the chance. It probably disclosed more than she wanted. How could Davidson change twenty years of problems as a one-term president? How could he end what he had called a two-decades-old war? Unless . . . unless he really meant to invade Iran, not just blockade it. But did he believe a regime change would end global Islamic terrorism?

Maybe that was what he had seen in Davidson's eyes—he wanted to go down in history as the man who stemmed the terrorist tide, and he was planning something decisive. Whatever Davidson's plans were, he would have to execute them swiftly and decisively. His moment for greatness or defeat was coming. Either way, it pointed to one fact—America, and the world, would soon be in for one hell of a ride.

CHAPTER LXXXII

Thou hast filled my nostrils with the breath of remembrance,
that I recall a bond made in heaven before time began,
and the first spark of light was yet to ignite the flame of the universe.
—Anonymous

The Vatican City

The night was blacker than anyone recalled, and a previously unknown comet streaked across the sky, mystifying scientists around the globe. On this night, at Roncalli's request, Annalisa gathered Roncalli, O'Keefe, Teresa, and Robert Avernis in the papal study. "I know you have something you want to show me," she said to Roncalli.

"Yes," Roncalli said, and he produced the Magdalene document along with the notes Dr. Herron had given to Avernis. "This is the first chance I had to show you this."

Annalisa looked at the scroll in his hand and nodded her head. "Read me the first seven words of what you hold," she told Roncalli.

The cardinal carefully unrolled the scroll and read, *"Mary Magdalene, companion of Jesus of Nazareth—"*

". . . by my hand is this written. Let none bear false witness in my name, for you shall know me by the truth of my words." It was Annalisa who completed the paragraph word-for-word, not Roncalli.

"You cannot have seen this yet," Roncalli said. "I've shown this only to the people in this room who have worked on deciphering the Gnostic symbols found in the Vatican."

Annalisa stood, walked around to the front of her desk, then sat on it to face the people seated around her. "All my life," she said, "I have known I was building toward some purpose, some task. In the still place, a hidden voice spoke to me from the far bank of a river, a voice whose master I had longed for my entire life. Tonight he came to me like the low rumbling of an earthquake. 'YOU HAVE FOUND WISDOM; YOU HAVE FOUND YOURSELF. KNOW THEN YOUR ORIGIN, YOUR SIN, YOUR DESTINY.' That is what he told me.

"His figure emerged emitting rays of pure whiteness. He is the one missing among us, the one no longer in body, and he said, *'Remember me; accept the burden as I have done. Lead them home.'* And he no longer eluded me, for now I fully remembered. The threads of a thousand past lives connected within me at that moment in space and time. Barriers between past, present, and future crumbled to reveal the forces that shaped me, my purpose and my burden, my errors and my atonement.

"The destiny etched into my being, the surface of which I had scratched all my life, now lay exposed. My conscious mind, my soul mind, and the One True Mind merged into full unity. In that instant, I knew myself fully for the first time. I know the debt I must repay to heaven and earth. The document you hold is but a copy. You will find the full, original version in southern France in the Black Mountains. Its discovery will change many things."

"How can you know that the lost gospel lies in France?" an incredulous Avernis asked.

Annalisa looked at him quizzically. "Because I know myself; I have remembered. Do you remember who you are, any of you? You will soon, if not now. Your minds may question this, but your hearts know it to be true. The world faces great danger. The opposing forces rise in strength."

"The Magdalene letter speaks of seven dark images, the psychic manifestations of the Archontic powers," Robert said. "Dr. Herron told me that when Sophia rises to restore the lost knowledge, seven new images of light will replace them. What are they?"

"Your Dr. Herron sounds like a smart man," Annalisa said with a wan smile. "Make sure he is on the recovery team that goes to Carcassonne, France, to unearth the gospels, Desmond. You too, Teresa. Without you they won't find the lost texts you so carefully concealed two millennia ago."

All Teresa could do was gape at her, dumbfounded along with the others.

"The seven images of light you wanted to know of— The Wise Man, The Wise Woman, The Hero, The Healer, The Mystic, and the Couple."

"That's only six," Robert said.

"Well the seventh, of course, is the hidden God, the True God who shall be revealed with the restoration of the secret Church," Annalisa replied. "The time is upon us where humanity leaps forward or falls into darkness. Each of you must play a role in this quest, though this may seem preposterous to you. You feel insignificant in the vastness of creation, but each life is crucial, none more than yours, for the qualities that define the First Souls are templates for humankind.

"Please," she said, "hold hands with me." O'Keefe dimmed the lights without being asked to do so, but no one spoke out, no one questioned anything. Annalisa uttered some strange words to ease them, to guide them, and after a while their eyes blanked in the dim light, then closed. Soon all sense of surroundings vanished. After an indeterminate time, as if connected by an etheric thread, a common vision began to form in their minds:

They perceived themselves as bodiless points of light circling one another like elegant glowing butterflies. Each of them experienced a sense of belonging, an inner peace like none they had ever known. Any feeling of separation was absent. Then they gathered and merged into one greater light, and the light faced a dark void. First one ray, then another, then all of their light ventured into the black hole. Their light was drawn downward, so subtly seduced that they were barely conscious of the pull. They had been weightless, but soon they could feel the tug of gravity. The force drew them down in a tube-like vortex, and they felt ever heavier, taking on mass and substance and finally, form.

They knew themselves to be different now, as if looking at creation from an opposing vantage point . . . a view from the far side of heaven. They were aware that theirs had been a grave choice, only now fully understanding what they had done when they followed her, called Sophia. They knew they had forsaken the realm of the spirit and entered a trap, emerging into the dark world from a one-way membrane, a cosmic valve that let them in but now barred their return to the light.

And instantly they became aware, in a brief moment of insight, of the "god" of this world and his angels, forces that were birthed from Sophia's spirit energy mixing with the chaotic substance, and that chaos itself was formed of the shadow created the moment Sophia dreamed of separation, of creating apart from the divine unity.

For a time they remembered their spiritual home, they remembered the loving Father of All, but like the electric lights O'Keefe had dimmed, their divine recollection and the quality of its realness slowly faded like the memory of a childhood visit to a far-off place in the distant past. Was the memory real or a figment of their imaginations? Had they really been there at all?

And now they occupied separate forms as they took on the consciousness of material bodies and so, over time, began their descent. Speech replaced thought for communication. Divine origins were forgotten and replaced by fables, dreams, and myths. Divine knowledge was obscured and replaced by faith, philosophy, and religion. The souls' power over matter was lost and replaced by the inferior labor of material devices. Spirit, once master over flesh, became subjugated by it.

And the god of this world replaced the memory of the True God, and he demanded worship and obedience claiming, "I am God and there are no other gods before me."

Now a montage of images flashed rapidly across their minds— the march of human history, for they were now in time, not beyond it. They relived origins lost in the shrouds of time, glimpsing the mysteries of human life. Their countless incarnations, countless lives flickered in then out of focus, highlighting the paradox of human existence, the immortality embodied in the fragility. Then the procession of images halted.

They stood in a familiar place looking at a scene that clutched at their heartstrings like a dying love. They were all there, in Palestine, all the disciples walking with Jesus. They saw Peter weeping in helpless rage, and they gasped inwardly, for they knew him to be Pietro Roncalli! They saw the downcast young Teresa and Robert Avernis . . . only here they were a Hebrew girl, Tezrah, and a Roman soldier named Averna. And old Desmonus, the Greek philosopher, turned to them with a pained face and said, "the authorities come," and they all knew it was Desmond O'Keefe speaking.

And there was one other. Jesus held her in his arms and said, "Regard well, and be not afraid, Mary." Jesus smiled with a tenderness that belied the gravity of what was happening, for the soldiers were already coming for him. And Jesus spoke for everyone to hear, "I tell you that I am but the half. The gates of hell shall not release its captives until Holy Wisdom does come to the world, for they may not understand me except thorough the Holy Spirit." He held Mary's hand up for all to see. "Behold the Wisdom, Sophia. What I endure tomorrow so too shall she endure one day, but her suffering shall be greater. She shall be rejected, scorned, and forgotten. But as I shall rise and return, so too will she. One day she shall return and right the errors committed by her and against her . . . and his words faded as their attention focused on the woman.

Mary Magdalene, companion of the Savior—Annalisa! They looked at her hands, now pale white instead of black, but tinged with the color of the warm Palestinian sun. Her sorrow did not dim her beauty, neither did the light cease to sparkle on her red-gold hair as she gazed at Jesus through teary eyes.

No one knew how long they were in the throes of the vision, but after a time they returned to the world of the senses. Teresa wept steadily; Avernis could not console her. Avernis and Roncalli looked dazed. Only Annalisa and O'Keefe seemed to retain their equilibrium. No one asked any questions; they sat in the silence of their own thoughts.

O'Keefe spoke and he gestured his hand toward the pope." I shall return, black of skin, the three alphas of God in my name . . . **A**nn**A**lis**A**," he said, emphasizing the three vowels, and they all looked at the pope.

With a soft, deferential voice O'Keefe said, "The mind is a poor medium to absorb such monumental things as we have seen tonight. I counsel that you all go home now. Reflect on what you've seen; seek one another out in the coming days as you feel moved to do so."

Annalisa then spoke. "The world seems random and confusing, and we seem like flowers uprooted in a storm," she told them, "but truthfully, we have written our own story unnumbered ages ago. Soon we will all pass through the shadow. At times during our trials ahead, it may seem the sun will not rise on us another day. In those hours look within and build your understanding upon what you have seen this night. There you will find the answers to your questions, for the threads of heaven are woven within you."

Annalisa made four rotations of her hands, two of the left hand and two of the right, and four small crucifixes materialized out of thin air! "Take these and remember me. We will not all be together again in this lifetime as we are tonight, but be sure, we are never apart."

And as they stood in awe with the electricity of their experience still vibrating within them, she saw their expressions and smiled. "Life is a strange and marvelous thing, is it not? Good night then, and God bless you."

After her four companions departed her, Annalisa relived the part of her vision she did not divulge to them. Everything around her had melted away then reformed. Annalisa turned, and in that rotation, the world remade itself. She saw herself in the Vatican. She saw the gun pointed at her. In slow, exquisite detail, the bullets issued from the barrel. She watched as the first one glided purposefully into her body, followed by others. The pain was excruciating as vessels burst, bone shattered, and the connection of body and soul failed. It was given to her to know all this, and in accepting, she could conclude her journey. She could fulfill the great purpose toward which she had moved all her life . . . *all of her lives.*

Yet off to one side another path beckoned her. She saw herself there growing old as the pope, beloved and adored by a doting humanity for the good works she would do. She would have years of friendship with Peter, with *Pietro*, mending the wounds of their old enmity, consummating a two-thousand-year-old healing, then dying gently one night many happy years from now.

She stood on the cusp, shaking. Tonight the last veil was torn from her vision; she could ascend and shred the last bonds of her earthly dream. She could realize the ultimate promise of the still place, but she must endure one last trial to complete the purpose for which she had entered the world eons ago.

All night she kept her mind on he who had prepared the way before her. He had been the first of them to awaken. She saw the path he walked cutting through every plane of existence, traversing life and death, and now she owed it to the souls of this earth to tread there too. Soon she would pass through the depths of the shadow, but the reward was to bring the certainty of God's love to this earth, and so she made her choice.

CHAPTER LXXXIII

. . . on either side of the river was there the tree of life . . . and the leaves of the tree were for the healing of the nations.— Revelation 22:2

Tehran

An infernal heat blew in from the east the day the pope arrived in Tehran, in old Persia. The only person to accompany her was Monsignor O'Keefe. He thought the pope would have wanted someone with more experience in matters of state, perhaps someone from the Vatican diplomatic corps, but the pope had refused all advice. It did not matter what the experts told her; O'Keefe perceived that she had a clear purpose in mind.

The pope reached out to grasp O'Keefe's hands as the plane's engines died and the door started to jar open. "Do not worry, Desmond," she said. "Things can only get better from here on."

Her hands were so warm to the touch he almost didn't notice the searing heat blasting through the airplane door like the open gates of hell. At the top of the deplaning stairs O'Keefe saw the huge contingent of news media assembled on the tarmac waiting to cover the meeting between the "Angel and the Devil," as they had billed it.

In the foreground, a few civilians and many mustachioed military types in olive- green berets ringed a waiting Mercedes limousine. The pope walked slowly down the stairs. When a grinning Iranian minister embraced the pope, camera lights flashed up and down the line of photographers like a strobing snake. After shaking hands with all the dignitaries, the pope and O'Keefe were whisked away to Tehran to meet Ayatollah Ali Havenei, leader of the Revolutionary Islamic Republic of Iran.

The old Parliament building had impressive but oddly Greek looking columns bolstering the porte cochere. The media scene there was similar to the airport. A jovial looking Havenei beamed for the cameras and gave the pope a bear hug so strong that O'Keefe was concerned she might lose her balance. The translators were busy jabbering out Havenei's welcome for the benefit of the pope and the media. Members of the Sazeman-e Tablighat-e Islami, the Iranian propaganda organization, issued statements to the press after the two leaders withdrew into the building and retired to a private room.

O'Keefe waited in a small conference area down the hall. Fortunately, there was air conditioning in the building, which helped ease the fatigue from the trip. An hour passed, and then two. O'Keefe accepted some food — a seasoned rice dish and some pieces of freshly slaughtered lamb. The pope had been meeting with Havenei for over two hours after O'Keefe had finished his meal — it stretched to almost four hours. Finally, the large double doors of inlaid metal opened and the two leaders walked out.

The pope's expression was neutral. Havenei was not smiling, at least not until they stepped into the large gathering room with the domed ceiling where the press awaited them. Havenei spouted off propaganda about peace and justice and redressing imbalances created by Western imperialism. He said the pact with the Chinese was essential for all Third World economies, and he was supporting his oppressed Arab neighbors bordering Israel. He said the American-led blockade of Iran was inhumane, illegal — the act of international criminals.

The pope was very quiet. Her only statement was that the world needed to work harder to achieve peace and something must be done to break the deadlocked patterns of reaction between the nations. When asked if her meeting achieved anything, she made a terse response: "We shall see."

In the limousine on the way back to the airport, the pope said to O'Keefe in a low voice, "He will do nothing but what he wants to do. He met with me so he would have political cover, just as everyone has been saying."

"Did that surprise you, Mother?" O'Keefe asked. "This is a cynical man by the feel of him."

"Hah!" The pope laughed. "No surprise when people stay the same, only when they change. Desmond?"

"Yes, Mother?"

"How are you feeling?"

"Better. I was a bit nervous, but it will be good to go home."

"It is not over yet, Desmond. The forces of opposition are at their zenith now. The world is in great peril, and this man is at the center of it."

"But, Mother, you did all you could."

"No, I have not. There is always something more to be done, and now I want you to do something for me."

"Of course, Mother. I have complete faith in you."

Annalisa smiled. "Faith defines your soul, Desmond. Now, when we get to the airport, no matter what happens, stay calm. You will have to contact Berletti, De Faissy, and Roncalli as soon as you can reach a telephone. Tell them not to interfere. I expect their support, do you understand?"

"What are you going to do, Mother?"

Annalisa smiled and held his hand. "Hopefully, I am going to do some good." And that was all she would tell him.

The press was still at the airport en masse, and the same officials who greeted her were there to see her off—or so they thought. The farewell procession started on the path to the pope's waiting airplane, but, after a few steps, the pope said, "Ooh, what is that?" She was pointing to a military aircraft thirty yards off to the left. She diverted her course and walked straight toward it.

Everybody from the press to the Iranians to O'Keefe was confused as the pope made a beeline for the plane. They followed, clueless as to what she was doing. She arrived at the airplane and touched a hand to its hot metal skin. "Is this a jet?" she asked.

The bewildered interpreter repeated the question to her hosts. Heads nodded up and down answering, "Yes, yes." The pope reached up. She could barely touch the underside of the cockpit. She traced a curving line on down to the front wheel, then she stooped, almost as if she were praying. *That must be it,* they all thought, *she is praying this machine will never strike in anger.*

Her back was facing them, and her chasuble obscured their view. After kneeling in supplication to the metal god of war, she swiveled to her side and sat down facing the Iranians and the cameras. Her extended hand still touched the airplane's wheel. An American reporter was the first to notice what had happened. "Oh, God!" he shouted then pointed. "She's handcuffed to the plane. She's chained herself to the plane!"

Pandemonium broke out on the tarmac as the interpreter told the Iranians what had happened. They could not believe their eyes. Cameras clicked nonstop, and people shouted in dozens of different languages. The media formed a tightening circle around the scene, and the Iraqis were too startled for the moment to push them back.

The foreign minister, through his interpreter, demanded an explanation of what was going on. The pope waved her one free arm and called for quiet. Finally, the commotion died down, and she addressed the crowd to give the minister his answer.

"This world is headed for war because, once again, rulers ignore and deceive their people. I am speaking of all countries, East and West alike, that are involved in these shadow war activities. I will remain chained here taking no food and half a glass of water per day until either my life or the war games have ended."

The media scurried around like frenzied ants just sprayed with insecticide. Was this for real?

Annalisa's voice gathered more power and strength as she spoke. "The leaders of the nations are not doing enough. They must set aside egos and ideologies, racial and religious hatreds, economic interests and all the other excuses they use to put us, the people of this world, in jeopardy."

The press buzzed furiously as the pope spoke."Goddamn, this *is* for real," a voice was heard to say above the drone.

"This is not an action against the people of Iran. I do this for all peoples of the world whose leaders have used them as helpless pawns while playing politics with their lives. Let me be clear: when I speak of those leaders, I include all the ministers and presidents of the Western nations involved in this matter."

The Iranians were so stunned, they did not notice how close the cameras and microphones had come to the pope. People around the world were hearing every word she spoke.

"I am from a Third World nation that is equally divided among Muslims and Christians. My mother was a Muslim, and I tell you the preciousness of life knows no religious bounds."

O'Keefe knelt by the pope, trying to compose himself. He must have faith in her. She knew what she was doing—he hoped.

"If you are told this is a war over religion, that is a lie. If you are told this is a war of economic survival, that too is a lie. This is a war of beliefs. If you believe in scarcity, if you believe you can only live at the expense of others, if you believe humanity does not have the capacity to solve problems before exterminating one another, then *that* side will win."

O'Keefe could see anger mounting in the faces of the Iranians as their translator frantically tried to keep up with the pope's rapid commentary. Annalisa must have realized her time was limited before they stifled her; she picked up the pace of her speech as the Iranians grew more agitated.

"But if you believe that many people gathered together with the desire for love and justice can move the world in a better direction, than the *right* side will win. All you have to do is want it, and demand it, and it shall be done."

The weight and force of her words made the crowd lapse into silence.

"You, the people, must demand that peace be achieved or find new leaders. If I can burn here in this heat with no food until they come to their senses, you can do much more. Make your desire to live and coexist known. Show the rulers of the earth you can move the world for a just cause!"

Someone in the Iranian contingent finally woke up, saw the mesmerized media crowd inching forward, and ordered the military to start pushing the press backward and away from the airplane. The foreign minister was speaking furiously through the interpreter.

O'Keefe repeated his words to be sure she had heard. "They are very angry, Mother. They say this is improper and unseemly. If you do not produce a key, they will cut the handcuffs off."

Annalisa reached into her robe and pulled out a small capsule. She placed the capsule near her mouth, holding it between her thumb and her index finger.

"Desmond, have the interpreter tell them this: I hold a fast-acting poison in my hand. If they try to take me, I will swallow it. You tell them that."

"Mother! What are you saying?" O'Keefe asked her in near panic. "You cannot do this, if not for your own sake then you know the position of the Church on . . . on suicide."

Annalisa gripped his wrist and spoke softly to him. "Desmond, I am well aware of what the Church says, but what I do is no different from a person who dies trying to save someone from an onrushing train. It is sacrifice, not suicide. I would not take my own life in despair, but I would sacrifice it out of love, you see?"

O'Keefe hesitated then nodded his head. Had he just not proclaimed his faith in her?

"Desmond, when you get to a telephone, tell this to Cardinal Roncalli: I want no actions from the Church to dissuade me or publicly undercut what I am doing. Furthermore, I want each priest and bishop in every diocese across the globe to ask their parishioners to search their consciences. If they believe they have the right to not let the world be destroyed around them, then encourage them to act as they are guided."

O'Keefe, kneeling on one leg in front of the pope, seemed to be in a slight daze. The next thing he felt was Annalisa shaking him with her free arm.

"Desmond, steady yourself and listen to me."

His head snapped up and his eyes focused on Annalisa.

"Tell Cardinal Roncalli I have prepared a letter instructing him what to do. He will find it in the left-hand drawer of my desk in the papal study. Do you understand?"

O'Keefe nodded.

O'Keefe had the interpreter tell the Iranians the action she was prepared to take if they tried to forcibly remove her, and the Iranians immediately began yelling and arguing with one another. Their noise melded with the confusion in O'Keefe's mind. *What will come of this?* That was the last question he posed to himself before hands seized his arms and dragged him away.

CHAPTER LXXXIV

Until the day of his death, no man can be sure of his courage.
—Jean Anouilh

Tehran

It was going on the eighth day of her hunger strike, and the pope's intervention had changed the entire complexion of the prelude to the Third Gulf War. The average person did not know it, and no government would admit it, but the stream of events altered their course as they flowed around the island of defiance she had staked out on the tarmac of that airport in Tehran.

Washington was making plans to invade Iran but was rethinking its tactics around Tehran because of the pope's presence there. Both the Israelis and the Americans ruled out bombing Tehran while she was chained at the airport. This may have seemed favorable for Havenei, but Annalisa posed more problems than benefits for the Iranians.

Annalisa's demonstration not only blunted Havenei's propaganda thrust, she completely reversed it. Her captivity, though voluntary, reminded the world of the repressive nature of Havenei's regime and his own people's lack of freedom. Caricatures appeared in newspapers around the world showing a tiny, chained Annalisa, arms outstretched, holding a looming, sword-wielding Havenei at bay.

One leg of Havenei's strategy—uniting Islam through anti-Western, anti-Israeli propaganda—was starting to totter. Although Islam closed ranks in the face of what they perceived as Western domination, in their hearts they knew Havenei was another dictator bent on controlling every land in the region. The Islamic world started to show a shift of sympathy toward the pope upon learning for the first time that her mother was a Muslim. They also admired Annalisa's courage. Now when she spoke, the Islamic people listened.

Annalisa's message of peace for Muslim and Christian alike rang true to them. As the leading figure of a Western institution, she was the first to recognize the yearnings of the region's peoples for peace and dignity, and certainly the first to back up that recognition with personal sacrifice.

The Iranians had arrested O'Keefe, the pope's secretary. They interrogated him about a plot by the Western powers to plant the pope in Iran. By the fourth day of his arrest, the international outcry against keeping him from assisting the pope was so great they had to allow him to return to the airport.

The Iranians then decided to erect a tent around the pope over the concrete tarmac. They could not be seen as denying her basic human dignity, and, in order to relieve herself, the tent afforded privacy while bedpans and other toiletries afforded hygiene. In their own self-interest, they wanted to shelter her from the prying cameras of the media. She absolutely refused attempts to install air conditioning, however.

Within an hour after she declared herself a prisoner for peace, the Iranians barred the press from the area. They began to fear that media speculation about what was happening to the pope would give the West an excuse to invade Iran with popular support. They eventually allowed the press to return. They could stand vigil several hundred yards from the tent at specified hours. Each day O'Keefe was allowed to tell them the pope was safe on his way back from the tent; that way they could testify that the pope was not being ill-treated without getting too close to her.

The tent also sheltered her from the glare, if not the heat, of the brutal desert sun. She had not eaten for days and taken only sips of water. She refused to let doctors examine her. The Iranians grew extremely nervous. It was brutally hot on that tarmac.

"What if she dies on our soil?" Havenei roared at his military officers in their command-and-control office. "What are you doing about this? The woman is a thorn, and this situation must end! We have a war to conduct. We cannot have her around like a dagger in our midst."

"Allah forbid you should violate their religion, and she is the symbol of Western religion," General Sharazi said. "We must be very cautious."

"She has put a gun to our heads," General Khashenouri said. "If she does not eat, she will not last long. It has already been six days. If she dies here, the West has a martyr around whom they will rally like nothing we have seen. If we try to force her out, feed her, or even provide air conditioning she will swallow her pill and die anyway."

"Is there no way to simply rush her when she is sleeping?" Havenei asked. "She must be weak and tired. It should be easy."

"My men have looked for every chance to do just that, In fact they tried twice," one colonel said. "She never really sleeps; she just shuts her eyes like one of those desert animals, always alert. She keeps the pill right on the edge of her lips too."

Havenei said, "Have equipment on hand to pump her stomach out then." Allah's ways were strange indeed. He had plotted to have her killed and now he was trying to save her.

"The problem is, many poisons kill almost instantly, particularly in her weakened condition," Sharazi said. "We just cannot risk that."

"Well you had better find a solution, and soon," Havenei hissed in a susurrant voice that everyone in the room recognized and feared like the coiling of a mad snake. People had permanently disappeared after Havenei had spoken to them in that voice.

The majority in the room hoped the pope would just faint one day from hunger, but she had told them the pill would be down her throat if she felt herself coming to that point. None of them wanted to mention the irony that a capsule of powder was stalemating the most powerful nation in the Middle East.

Excited voices ended the debate. News had come in from the borders. An allied force of Americans, Australians, and British had just crossed the Iranian borders in three locations. Havenei slammed his fist on the table. He barked out commands to his military.

"We cannot match their forces conventionally, but we must expel them from holy Iranian soil. Have your armies delay them as much as possible. We will deploy the Black Hand brigades at once to go to the borders and the Great Satan plan will go into effect. I will visit the command-and-control site myself."

After Havenei dismissed the military, Genereal Sharazi pulled General Khashenouri aside, making sure no one else was in earshot. "Using chemicals and nuclear weapons on the Americans, launching chemical missiles at Israel? His entire plan is insane. Gorbani knew it and Havenei executed him for treason after that affair with the woman leaked out. Havenei underestimated the Americans, and now he's desperate to save his skin. He will pave the way for our annihilation."

"Not just us," Khashenouri said. "The Chinese are involved. We will be pushing two super-powers into each other's faces."

"The biological weapons are more virulent than ever," Sharazi said. "I have no faith they can control the release. They could unleash a plague. The world will not forget a people that do the things he plans to do."

"That assumes we survive what may ensue," Khashenouri commented.

Sharazi said, "The people would support us, but the clerics have always controlled the military. I believe our units would follow us, but no one else. How can we stop him?"

"Yes, how do we stop him, and can you trust anyone else enough to even pose the question?" was Khashenouri's reply. No answer was forthcoming.

CHAPTER LXXXV

Nearly all men can stand adversity, but if you want to test a man's character, give him power. —Abraham Lincoln

Toledo, Spain

Congress declared a state of war between America and Iran as the United States presented incontrovertible proof to the United Nations that the Iranian government possessed weapons of mass destruction and were planning to use them. They further indicted twenty years of Iranian complicity in the world's reign of terror.

Stock markets around the globe plummeted and recessions deepened in the industrialized nations. Trade agreements among the major powers seemed in jeopardy, and China was threatening "severe measures" if the allies extended their invasion into Iran. The CIA assessment indicated a high probability that Havenei would use chemical warfare to slow the allied advance.

These events should have scared the wits out of a sane person, but Bishop Alvaro was so euphoric that his patience and discipline broke down for one of the few times in his life. He picked up the phone and dialed the president of the United States. Davidson had given him a private, secure number to call at his home in Kansas in case of emergencies.

When Davidson received the call, he sounded a bit hesitant. The line was secure, and who would ever listen in on the shadowy ultra-secret leader of Milites Domini? Still, he would have preferred if Alvaro had just left him alone to do his work.

"Bishop, good day."

Alvaro wasted no words. "Tell me, John, is it time for that which we have awaited?"

Davidson would really have preferred not to have this conversation, but he remembered the man with whom he was speaking. "Havenei is playing into our hands. He will strike soon and then we will have the justification."

"Tehran and Qom," Alvaro said. "You must hit Qom, destroy everything."

Davidson's eyes tightened when he heard that. Alvaro had never tried to give him orders before or tell him how to accomplish what they had discussed. "Bishop, understand, we will use a neutron bomb. It will destroy people, not structures. Qom is like Mecca to the Shi'ites. Our purpose is to eliminate their desire and ability to wage terrorist war. We can't annihilate all of Islam. Why destroy their holy places and give the remnants a new cause?"

And Alvaro and the president argued briefly with the president finally saying, "Don't worry, my way will achieve our goals. Our only problem is the pope being in Tehran. That will delay us, and we don't have enough oil reserves for a sustained war. Hopefully, she can't stay at that airport forever. If she does, I know the Iranians will cross the line with illegal weapons regardless. Only that can justify hitting them with the pope there. When they do that, then we must strike a devastating blow, pope or no pope in Tehran. Exercise the virtue of your great patience for now."

The two men who listened in and recorded the conversation between Alvaro and the president should have been in shock, but their English was not very good. From what little they knew, it had something to do with bombs. They understood that word quite well. When their boss, Ubaldo Deci, had the tape translated maybe he would explain it to them.

CHAPTER LXXXVI

A power is passing from the earth.
— William Wordsworth

Tehran

The Iranians had forbidden O'Keefe from communicating with the press. They wanted no news of Annalisa's hunger strike to reach out and stir up more trouble. O'Keefe saw the pope daily, but they always escorted him back to his quarters under guard. They would march him right through the news crowd, and he was instructed to wave and tell the press the pope was fine. That was a problem, because today he had a communiqué from the pope. Wracking his brains how to deliver the letter, he nearly stopped in his tracks.

Teresa Ferentinos stood out front among the gauntlet of reporters lining his path. She was not supposed to be here. Her network had wanted their Mid-East desk to cover the trip, and Teresa was supposed to handle the Vatican. Their eyes locked, and O'Keefe smiled. He slowed his pace, and as he approached her, he pretended to stumble. He fell at her feet, and slipped a folded note on the ground in front of her, obscuring it with his hand.

Before the soldiers reached him to haul him up, the quick-thinking Teresa placed her foot on top of the note to hide the paper. The soldiers leaned in from behind and took O'Keefe by the arms. As they hauled him up, Teresa whispered *"Better late than never."*

The soldiers walked O'Keefe away without further incident. He could not help smiling to himself. The pope had validated his belief that he, Teresa, and the others were bound together in a great plan to seek the truth. Now, from out of nowhere, Teresa came when he was in need. Desmond O'Keefe smiled. They were like actors who had been awarded roles in an epic drama—and that meant Someone knew they belonged in this play.

The Vatican City

Sunday afternoon, Cardinals Roncalli and Berletti delivered a televised address in St. Peter's Square. Roncalli surveyed the multitude from the balcony of the Apostolic Palace. Every Christian Church around the world had held services this day, not to pray for the pope, she did not want that, but to pray instead for ways to achieve peace.

Roncalli began his address. "As you know, we have received news of the pope in Tehran." His voice carried over the massive PA system to reach the vast audience, and the crowd grew silent. "She is showing the effects of hunger, but is surprisingly well considering the circumstances. It is her wish that her actions make people of different countries aware of one another's problems. She reminds us that we are not powerless — we have the ability to help one another and heal the rift between nations."

Despite his comments, Roncalli worried for Annalisa. That summer heat in Iran was debilitating. Even a young, healthy person would be in danger with no food and minimal water.

Roncalli continued speaking to the audience according to the original instructions left to him by the pope. "The Iranian people have suffered under a repressive regime," he told them. "The wealthy nations consumed an inordinate amount of the world's dwindling resources, while corporations seeking to squeeze the last drop from remaining energy sources retard new technologies that could have eased the world's problems."

Roncalli paused briefly to let the challenge of the pope's statements sink into the global audience listening to her words. "If we want peace," he said, "we must demand that our leaders address the man-made causes of scarcity and not resort to war, the easy but destructive way to solve the very problems we have created."

Reporters related how many people in the audience had their hands folded and eyes closed, praying in the manner Annalisa had introduced into the churches: they translated their desires into the expectation that their prayers were already answered.

"Do you wonder," Roncalli asked, "how you, a mere individual, can have any effect on the governments that make decisions for you? The pope reminds us of our true power from the book of Mark: 'Verily I say unto you, whatsoever ye shall bind on earth shall be bound in heaven: and whatsoever ye shall loose on earth shall be loosed in heaven. Again I say unto you, that if two of you shall agree on earth as touching any thing that they shall ask, it shall be done for them of my Father, which is in heaven. For where two or three are gathered together in my name, there am I in the midst of them.'

"The pope says to you, '*There are no nations under God, only people.*'" Roncalli paused to let them reflect on the passion behind Annalisa's message. "'*There are no nations under God, only people.*' Those are the pope's own words," Roncalli told the gathering in conclusion, "but these are mine: *The time to act is now.* The pope is ready to sacrifice her life for all of us — what are we willing to do for ourselves? Peace be with you, one and all."

Stepping away from the balcony, Roncalli pointed back to the crowd and said to Berletti, "What shall become of the world is in their hands now."

✠

The people of the world took matters into their hands by answering Cardinal Roncalli's challenge in a swift and resounding way. In cities and nations around the globe, people marched and demonstrated. In most cases, there was little organization. Calls went forth to turn out and show support for peace. In Washington, D.C., on the third Sunday of Annalisa's captivity, two million people marched on the capital.

There were none of the usual steering committees and celebrity speeches. People stood up and spontaneously spoke their feelings over a PA system set up on the Washington Mall. Different religious denominations provided what little organization was present. The religious leaders gave enough structure to the enormous gathering so that no one had a sense of aimlessness.

Many of the placards people carried read: THERE ARE NO NATIONS UNDER GOD, ONLY PEOPLE, and the pope's words seemed to define the spirit behind the human outpouring around the world.

"Will any of this have an effect?" Cardinal De Faissy asked Roncalli as they watched televised pictures of the demonstrations. "You're American, Pietro. What will they do?"

"Most Americans are frustrated and believe someone has to stop Havenei," he said, "but despite that, they have turned out for peace in huge numbers like in other countries. Something unusual is happening," he said, pointing to the television set. "Such massive demonstrations just don't happen this way. There's no ideology of peace among those demonstrators, no organizers, no ten-point program for ending the conflict. The war came on too fast."

"What is it then?" De Faissy asked.

"Annalisa." Roncalli replied without hesitation. "No one else could have done this. It's almost as if they are motivated by blind trust in *her.* They have no idea how this war can end justly. They are making a leap of faith that somehow it will all come together if they follow her lead."

De Faissy watched the endless sea of people on the television screen ambling by the monuments in Washington, D.C. It was the largest turnout of humanity that the capital city had ever seen. "Yes, it makes sense," he said, "but will the governments listen?"

Roncalli sighed. "The huge numbers and passion of the demonstrators will set limits for the politicians. The people have taken away governments' blank checks to pursue this war, and so we might have hope. If there is any chance for peace, it lies with the people, the Islamic and Western peoples, for this is a two-sided conflict. Will the governments listen? Perhaps. Given time . . . and Annalisa is sacrificing herself to buy that time."

CHAPTER LXXXVII

Taste this, and be henceforth among the Gods thyself a Goddess.
—John Milton

Tehran

When Havenei saw newscasters reading the pope's smuggled letter on global television, he became angry. Before he went to his underground base, he decided to see the pope for the first time since she had chained herself to the jet.

The Iranians had repeatedly offered to set up an air conditioning unit, powered by an external generator, in her tent. It would prolong her life and it was good humanitarian fodder for the press. Annalisa refused and used the threat of her pill. She told them she came to accomplish a goal, not to acquire luxuries the average Iranian lacked.

"You will die," Havenei said to Annalisa. "You look dead now, and your death won't change my position. I tried to feed you, to release you; they all know that. They will blame your death on the misfortunes of war, not me. The West is responsible for this, for what they have done to us. Why not leave now, while you have life left in you?"

The pope took a small sip of water. Her eyelids were heavy; her skin and lips were cracked and bleeding. She said something, but the words were raspy, and he took a step closer.

"Not too close, Havenei," she told him with her pill poised near her mouth. "You have one last chance to stop and reconsider."

"Reconsider what?" he asked.

"You know what you are about to do," she replied.

"I have no time to trade riddles with a dead woman," he said.

"No, Havenei, it is you who will die," she said. "If you do not change your mind, if you do not alter your course, you will be dead within twelve hours by your own plan of destruction."

"You dare threaten me?" he said, raising his voice.

"Listen to the will of Allah, not to me," she said.

"What would a nonbeliever know of Allah's will?" Havenei asked.

"He is my God as well as yours," she said. "Remember. Twelve hours."

The three bodyguards with Havenei saw his face turn red as his fist raised and balled up to strike her. The shaking fist hung in the air until some rational part of his mind told him a blow would precipitate her death, and he had sworn not to make a martyr of her.

"No one gives me orders in my own country!" he shouted at the crumpled little figure in the dirty white alb. "If your military cannot shake me, then no foreign priest will interfere with my plans. This is *our* time now. The one with the will to move decisively shall prevail. In all Islam, you do me the honor of having the Great Priest of the West die on my soil."

When Havenei left and his anger subsided, he began to wonder about her warning. She could not possibly have known that he was about to unleash his chemical warfare, could she? The allies were pushing his border units back and precision bombing targets all over the country. The Anglo-Saxon invasion justified what he was going to do. The world would understand.

They could bomb all they wanted, but it took ground troops to secure territory. They would think twice about committing troops vulnerable to chemical attack. With the threat of China in the equation, he was betting that the West would not dare retaliate with tactical nuclear strikes. This was his best and, perhaps, only chance to make use of the tremendous investment in research, personnel, and ordnance his nation had created with great sacrifice during the past two decades.

The woman knew nothing, he decided; she spoke out of delirium. He would be the first Islamic leader to back the West down, and when he did, all the groveling Arab states would have to acknowledge him as the region's real leader. But the window of opportunity was narrow, and he had to move swiftly. China might not stay committed with potential nuclear conflict at risk. They might conclude he was standing to gain everything and they were not.

No, he would not die in twelve hours. But in two days, he would be master of the Middle East.

✠

Havenei was gone, and she let the weakness flow. Her heartbeat slowed and her blood meandered languidly her veins. Her respiration grew so faint she hardly noticed it. The physical world took on a feeling of unreality, and the light of the other world waxed brighter. She let herself drift . . . drift . . . drift . . .

I am floating, I am free.

Ah, gentle fool, you are dying. You have no idea. You are not prepared. You think you know God. Do you know what God is? Nothingness. Inertia. God is the void, loss of control, eternal sleep.

You know my body is weak; it is dying. Lies make sense to the weary and tired; it is then *you* come through the mind, through the door of fear. It is you who is of the void. You are the bastard child born from my error.

Why do you contend with me? What have your illusions brought you? Rape, shooting, isolation, others fearing you. It can be different. The cardinal is a handsome man, no? He would have you and you him. You can have a full relationship and wash away the stench of evil from lying with your own uncle.

There was no evil where there was no intention.

What brought that upon you, then, if not the aberration of your own thoughts?

Purpose. Awakening. It was you who did these things to aid my remembrance.

But it can end if you take all that you desire from the earth, for that is real, and when we exert our power here, we truly live.

You lie; your memory has died. You know nothing of the true power that lies above you.

There is nothing to remember. It is all here to be had, to be lived now. Here I rule.

A speck of a second that is matter is what you call life? That is your kingdom? It is you who lives on by a thread of illusion. Deception and fear give you life.

You think my existence is a lie? You deny that I exist?

We all exist in the force of God's Mind. Some things are eternal, some perishable. You are a construct, an artificial device like the staged rockets that propel men into space. Once you serve your purpose you will be jettisoned, discarded, and forgotten. We continue beyond you.

Why waste time striving with me? You are dying. Eat and live. Stop this insanity. You may have whatever you want. Food, companionship, adulation, life—all yours to have. Why waste yourself on others who do not even know you?

I am in them and they in me. Leave me now. My course is firm and has nothing to do with you.

But your blood grows cold and your heartbeat slows, your organs fail and you choke for a last breath. I will be back. I am ever the friend of humanity; you might yet live.

The light is the true life; you are but the shadow through which I had to pass to recognize it. Others will follow until the stream becomes a torrent and our exile is ended. This world of illusions and your reign of fear are ending. I shall think on you no more. Get thee behind me.

CHAPTER LXXXVIII

There is no armour against fate; Death lays his icy hands on kings.
—James Shirley

Ardashir, Iran

The Americans had escalated and brought nuclear submarines into the Persian Gulf as their push on land spilled over the Iranian border. The underground laboratories at Ardashir had the great honor of receiving a last-minute inspection by the leader, the Grand Ayatollah Havenei himself. Havenei strutted around the corridors from room to room making sure that all aspects of warhead placement and delivery systems were in readiness.

Havenei then settled in a conference room with the highest-ranking officers of his army. They were coordinating final plans for deployment of the forbidden weapons. At the moment, they were enjoying a hearty laugh over the prophecy of Havenei's demise. Bodyguards had let the story slip through the ranks, and, at first, Havenei had been annoyed. He later decided to let them jest. When the predicted time came and went, belying the pope's prophecy, it would add that much more to his aura of righteousness.

One level below the senior commanders, a group of soldiers was working in a corridor outside one of the storage containment labs. They were removing tanks of chemicals for use against the Americans, leaving the door of the lab open.

One of the guards was backing off from having placed a tank outside the open lab entrance. It was wartime, and he had forgotten to remove the grenades strapped to his combat belt. As he moved backward, the narrow, protruding end of the door handle's grip lever snagged the safety ring on one of his grenades.

When the pin and safety lever of the AN-M18 incendiary grenade made a tinny clank on the floor, the guard received a remote glimmer of what had happened in the synapses of his brain. He reached to his right side to feel the area where the door had caught on something, and then he felt the lever-less grenade strapped to his belt.

He screamed out to his comrades as he dropped to his knees, frantically groping and pulling at the grenade to find a way to block the rotator from igniting. It was a panicked and useless gesture.

When the grenade detonated, it ignited the other two explosive grenades he carried, setting off the chemical tank. The confined area of the corridor increased the force of the explosion so that the opened laboratory door fragmented and flew inward. Inside the lab, men were working with lethal biological agents in the robotic chambers. The material enclosing the chambers was bulletproof, but not designed to withstand large hunks of metal propelled at high velocity. The enclosure was pierced and so were the tanks containing the lethal agents.

It took only seconds for the ventilation system to suck up the deadly chemicals. By the time Havenei and his generals were questioning the explosions that rocked the bunker, the chemical, bacterial, and viral agents were airborne. It had been an act of careless stupidity and shoddy procedure, but Havenei would not have the pleasure of executing the guilty party. For one thing, the guilty party was dead, and for another thing, so was Havenei. As he was screaming commands, he started coughing, and a welter of blood rushed out his mouth.

There were still two hours to go on this, the day of which Annalisa had warned him. His last fearful thought was that if Allah were indeed on *her* side, where was *he* destined to go?

Tehran

It was close to midnight before the first radio reports reached Tehran from Ardashir.

The soldiers guarding the surface of the bunker at Ardashir reported losing contact with the underground complex. They also reported that all troops guarding the northern perimeter were dead. The prevailing winds that evening were blowing toward the north. The alarmed soldiers withdrew from the area before the winds changed. They knew what was stored underground.

The Tehran communications center was in the control of troops under the command of General Khashenouri. When his aide woke him, he went to the command center for a full briefing. They raised the troops retreating from Ardashir on the radio. Khashenouri instructed them to return to Tehran immediately and not to mention the incident at Ardashir to anybody under pain of death.

Khashenouri immediately contacted Sharazi by radio. Sharazi's troops were stationed between Ardashir and Qom, about one hundred and twenty kilometers south of the bunker. Khashenouri told Sharazi what he suspected. Sharazi set off for Ardashir with anticontamination suits. Khashenouri then proceeded to contact sympathetic ranking army officers. If Havenei were dead, they might finally act. He had them ready their troops pending confirmation from Ardashir.

Six hours later, in the early morning, that confirmation arrived. Everyone in the bunker was dead. Despite fire and explosions inside the bunker, they had identified the body of Ali Havenei. Khashenouri wasted no time. He arrested all of the officer corps in Tehran loyal to the clerics, then he arrested the remainder of the leadership council. The allies were mauling other loyal military units stationed near the borders. This made the job of the Tehran insurrectionists easier.

As the day dawned and it became evident Khashenouri and Sharazi had the situation in hand, they announced Havenei's death and the change in government to the entire country. They promised to end the reign of suppression. They asked the people to remain calm, but they could not stop the celebrations on the street.

The junta leaders immediately sent word to the allies requesting a ceasefire and a meeting to discuss a negotiated peace. The loyal army troops near the border were now caught between the insurrectionists in Tehran and the advancing allies. The new leadership offered them amnesty if they laid down their arms and went home. Most accepted the terms.

The suddenness of the events was at first too difficult for the world to believe, but over the next twenty-four hours, the reality sank in: the fanatical ambitions of Havenei were over. The world had escaped a nuclear and chemical nightmare by a matter of hours.

When General Thomas Daltry and the allies under United States Operational Command entered Tehran after the ceasefire, he was shocked to learn the pope remained captive at her own request. He was more shocked to see the sunken cheeks and emaciated body of one who was more than halfway into the other world. Daltry, a Catholic, leaned close to the pope to speak with her. "Mother, why are you still here? The fighting is over. Forgive us for this war; we had no choice."

With a shaking hand, the pope motioned to O'Keefe for some water. He cradled her head and helped her slowly sip the liquid. After several attempts, she was finally able to produce words. "General, there is no virtue in standing idle when a man like Havenei held a sword of destruction over the world. You and your troops must not be condemned, but the sin of war can only be lifted if the victors dispense justice and mercy."

Daltry held her bony hand, and her drawn face summarized his own sadness about the war and the loss of life. He nodded in agreement. "Do not trample on the pride of these people," she told the general. "They want peace. End the blockade. Commit to find peace with the Chinese, have the Israelis make a lasting peace with the Arabs. When I see that commitment, I will leave, and only then."

Daltry did convey what she said to his leaders, but the press conveyed her feelings to the world. The excuses for war were over. With unprecedented ferocity, the people and the media of the leading nations immediately bombarded their own politicians to find solutions to preclude further conflicts. Every government on earth felt their people's anger at having been on the precipice, even President Davidson's. He now had no pretext, no justification for his plans. He swallowed his frustration. The decisive blow would wait for another day.

The United States called for a summit of concerned nations to deal with the problem of declining resources. A precondition of the summit was acceptance of the principle that resources must be shared equitably. The Americans talked of providing large-scale desalinization technology to the Arabs and Israelis. In turn, the Chinese and the Islamic oil nations would revisit the question of international oil allocation. Each nation was backing off from a rendezvous with unthinkable conflict. The world acknowledged that a small woman lying close to death in Tehran had shamed the powers into a position of compromise. The race for peace was now a race to save her life.

On the eighth day since the cessation of hostilities, Cardinal Roncalli, who had come from Rome to be at the pope's side, whispered into her ear. "Mother, they are doing everything you have asked. I give you my word on this."

At that, the pope nodded her head. The medical team standing by with IVs and other equipment started to move in. The pope raised the powdered capsule she had clutched for so long and looked at it for a second. She put it in her mouth and swallowed.

O'Keefe lurched forward and cried out, "Mother, why? What have you done?"

The pope smiled wanly, motioned for him to draw closer, and said in a hoarse, barely audible voice, "Desmond, I have not eaten for almost a month—I need my vitamins, you see?"

CHAPTER LXXXIX

From envy, hatred, and malice . . . Good Lord, deliver us.
—Litany

Katsina, Nigeria

When Alhaji Kadir al Kadu learned of the downfall of Havenei and the religious regime in Iran, he knew they had all underestimated the Yoruba woman. She was the devil. Havenei was gone. That would be a crippling blow to his N-FAC organization as financial and military support vanished. Worse than that, the Nigerian Muslims were actually calling her one of their own.

She had changed the world's political landscape right under everyone's noses, but Alhaji knew that Christianizing Nigeria was always her prime target. The West accomplished their goals through religion where they could not succeed militarily or politically. If she survived her ordeal in Tehran, she would be more powerful than ever. Only killing her to incite a new war between Christians and Muslims would allow N-FAC to survive now.

Alhaji summoned his chief of staff, Moustafa. "The time has come," he told him. "Send Hakim and his unit to Rome. Once they are situated, keep them on standby. Inform them of the target only on my command, a few hours before the mission. And remember, none of them are to come back. They will die like martyrs and be forever glorified by all Islam."

Moustafa nodded. "It will be done."

Havenei had the woman in his grasp, yet now *he* was dead. She should die from exposure or hunger, but Alhaji knew she wouldn't. Havenei was gone, but the plan they made would survive him as long as Alhaji still drew a breath. Praise Allah that the Christian bishop had effectuated the conspiracy at the highest levels of his church. Fate was strange to bring him together with those he would normally hold as enemies, but Nigerian Muslims were in her crosshairs. Now she would be in his, but unlike Havenei, he would pull the trigger first.

CHAPTER XC

I love you when you bow in your mosque, kneel in your temple, pray in your church. For you and I are sons of one religion, and it is the spirit.
— Kahlil Gibran

The Vatican City

The world held its collective breath during the pope's first seven days in the hospital in Tehran. Her condition was critical, but by the end of the week, she turned the corner. She would live, and the world exploded in jubilation. Parties, speeches, events, and prayers of thanks erupted on a scale never before seen in corners of the earth as remote and as dissimilar from one another as night is from day.

When she returned to Rome, she wasted no time resting. "I want to invite representatives from the sciences and different religions to the Vatican. Now it is time to consolidate what has started." And so the Vatican soon found itself hosting one of the greatest religious and scientific events of the century.

His peers had considered Alberto Virgoli a little twerp throughout his early school years. Now, as a man of age forty-eight, he might be considered a big twerp, but that would be a shallow assessment based primarily on his appearance.

Alberto did have an odd ability to make the worst of his physical shortcomings. Born with unruly, straight black hair that parted with difficulty on the left, he somehow managed to latch on to a style where the lengthy top hair flew outward in weedlike protuberances that hung over the fuzzy, short hairs along his temples. The overall appearance was like a crop of mung bean sprouts glued to his skull then bowl-cut around the ears so that the top strands crawled outward in a series of wormy overlapping tendrils. Of course, his cowlick did not help either.

Add to his unusual coif a pair of thick-rimmed, thick-lensed glasses overwhelming a pointy, narrow little nose that screwed up in conformity with his off center, quirky smile and it seemed plain that Alberto was determined to showcase his physical deficiencies. It would be easy to tag him with the quality of twerpitude based on his looks, but Alberto was one of the most prominent biblical scholars in Italy, a formidable intellect who knew what he looked like and did not care.

His appearance was actually his own perverse litmus test of humanity. He found the people who enjoyed his company and admired his intellect despite his comical façade were the few true friends to be cherished. Unfortunately, he was in the Vatican listening to the pope speaking, and he had few friends here. Alberto, whose mother was Jewish and father Catholic, was a prominent biblical scholar often critical of the Church.

Alberto's sense of intrigue offset his unease. For the past week, he had attended the globally televised, Vatican sponsored Conference for Human Reconciliation. In attendance were people from every major religion and from numerous scientific disciplines. Alberto had been amazed at the discussions. Quantum physicists had shown ways to reconcile the six days of biblical creation with the estimated sixteen-billion-year age of the universe. Similarly, others offered plausible theories of how the fossil record could show human remains from before the Bible said Adam and Eve existed.

They introduced Pope Annalisa to give the final speech of the conference. The audience greeted her with a ten-minute standing ovation. She deserved every minute of it for what she had done during the war. The pope summarized the conference's efforts to distill a common essence out of each religions' spiritual core. The goal was to reacquaint people with the roots of spirituality before the onset of dogmas and the meddling of institutional religion.

It had been an inspiring exercise, but now they had come to a moment that riveted Alberto's attention. During a discussion about relations between the Western religions, arguments had broken out on the floor between Jewish and Muslim religious scholars. Some Christian groups also joined in the fray.

"MY BROTHERS AND SISTERS, PLEASE." The pope's voice quieted the crowd. The high-beamed rafters of the expansive papal auditorium swept upward, seeming to touch the foot of heaven. As she spoke, the small woman on the raised lectern appeared even smaller against the grand scale of the surroundings. "Is God Muslim, Christian, Hindu, or Jewish? If you know, please raise your hand."

Alberto looked around. Not a single hand rose.

Annalisa nodded. "We act like islands of ignorance in an ocean of God's light. We argue over whose teachers or prophets are greater and more pure channels of God's message, but the truth is that every religion in this world was built on the foundation of other religions and our prophets are but successive chapters of the same book." The pope left the lectern, microphone in hand,

and strode onto the stage where she could gesture without obstruction.

"There is a story you may have heard from the Hindu tradition. In this story, an elephant is brought to twelve blind men. Each man is led to a different location around the animal. They grope with their hands. When asked to describe the being they have just touched, each man describes that part they felt. And so, the trunk, the tail, the leg, and the ear became the individual realities of each man, yet the whole from which the parts derived was so vast, and they so limited in perception, that each presumed they had perceived the entire truth."

Many in the audience smiled at the truth and simplicity of the story.

"Spiritual truth is a mosaic that makes a mural, and God's prophets come in waves. Each revelation builds on prior revelations. If each wave raises our level of knowledge, one day the high tide of truth will engulf us—no more islands, just all God's ocean. Is it sensible to fight about the waves because we do not see the ocean of which they are part?"

A man stood and said, "Your analogies are fine, but these disagreements are ingrained and have produced real problems. For instance, how would you address the anti-Semitic elements of the New Testament?"

The question struck to the core of Alberto's life. He remembered the anti-Semitic taunts that left him stuttering as a child; he remembered the nightmares that kept him awake with the bedside light on. Alberto sat up and listened carefully.

Annalisa nodded. "Prophets speak the heart of God; their followers start religions. Religions edit or distort the original teachings, for they lack the inspirational experience of the prophet. That is why the scriptures of every religion contain elements of condemnation for other faiths. The Talmud, for instance, has harsh words about Jesus and his followers as bad as anything the Bible says about Jews."

She's right, Alberto thought. He knew the passages in his head.

"If God sees us equally," Annalisa said, "then all such passages must be disregarded as the transient errors of men. Dwell on the truth that unites, not the mistakes that divide."

Alberto's eyes followed the television cameras to a delegation of Jewish religious leaders led by the famous British rabbi Joseph Kleidermann. From his location on the balcony, Kleidermann stood and said, "Your Holiness, would you then, as pope, revise offending passages in the New Testament to reflect the truth as you have stated it?"

Like many present, Alberto drew his breath in from the unexpected challenge; he felt a personal stake in the answer.

The pope made her reply. "No Rabbi, I will not do that."

"Why not, may I ask? You have been quoted as saying, 'the Jewish *people* did not kill Jesus any more than the American *people* killed Martin Luther King,'" Kleidermann said. "If you believe this, why not change the passages in the New Testament that perpetuate these problems?"

Difficult question, Alberto thought. *How will she answer this?*

"I will not rewrite any gospels," Annalisa replied, "because it is not the place of any of us, Christian or Jew, to revise the history of our scriptures. The scriptures, you see, are a record of the truth as it was understood by the people who wrote them. Right or wrong, original or edited over generations, it was a record of their perceptions, and so tells something about their times and the states of their faith."

"Yet these errors perpetuate problems between religions," Kleidermann said.

"No, Rabbi, people perpetuate problems between one another. As for the scriptures, were we to rewrite any history of our striving, however imperfect that legacy may be, we obliterate the steps of our evolution. What great harm do we then do by erasing the footprint of our errors? It is by those very errors that future generations may avoid the trail of our mistakes and follow a more enlightened path toward God."

Alberto raised an appreciative eyebrow at her response.

The pope looked directly at Rabbi Kleidermann. "I would no more rewrite the New Testament than you would rewrite the Old Testament or the Talmud."

Alberto saw members of Kleidermann's rabbinical group nodding in agreement.

"I have an idea," Annalisa said with a wry smile. "What if leaders of each religion choose one topic a year, one unloving, negative thing about their religion they could correct. Absurd? I tell you, whittle man's rituals away and draw closer to God's word."

Alberto listened to the rumbling passing through the auditorium. *Was she making light of a serious situation?*

"Oh, I *am* serious," Annalisa said, looking toward the opposite balcony where Alberto sat.

A chill locked his spine, leaving him wide-eyed and frozen in his seat. *My god, is she speaking to me, reading my mind?*

Then Annalisa turned her head back to address the rabbis. "And coupled with each item we excoriate, let us choose one thing of beauty, one passage in our writings, one concept that promotes the universality of spirit and our underlying unity. If we were to do that, we would grind the shells of our religions down to their spiritual bedrock, and there we would find no Muslim, no Jew, no Buddhist or Christian. What we would find is *one people under God.*"

Annalisa raised her hand toward the balcony where the British and American rabbinical delegations were seated. Looking straight at them, she said, "I will start this practice here and now. I will write a papal encyclical to be read aloud in all churches and Sunday schools. It will proclaim that Jesus was a Jew, that Christians of that time were a part of Judaism, and that the brutality leading to his death was imposed by the dictates of the Roman Empire."

Rabbi Kleidermann slumped into his seat at the weight of her words.

"Christ forgave both Jews and Romans. If one part of the Bible forgives and the other condemns, be sure the forgiveness was from the mouth of Christ, but the condemnation from the mouth of man."

Not a rustle or a stir was heard until the pope spoke again. "It is the obligation of Christians to renounce hatred in words or actions against Jews or members of any other race or religion. Such attitudes may be born of the darkness within humanity, but they will not be justified by the light of God." Applause started to break out but was quashed by the force of the pope's voice. "They will not be justified by people who call themselves Christians while perverting the Christian ideal of love! And that is my beautiful thought from Christianity—love."

The entire room was silenced by the passion of the pope's words. Alberto sensed many of them were struggling with their own ingrained ideas as they listened to her.

"Practices, rituals, and nuances of belief divide us because they are based on abstract notions of God," Annalisa said. "But if humanity is God's highest expression on earth, then let us make religions of love, kindness, and service toward humanity. Therein lies the path to God, not the path of man's religion, but of God's spirit. Will you join me, Rabbi, in rising above the mistakes of our ancestors, not as Christian to Jew, but as soul to soul?"

Like a clinging mist, the question hung in the air, permeating the minds of the audience. The room remained utterly silent, waiting for the rabbi's response. History could be made with the next words spoken. Alberto's attention was transfixed on Rabbi Kleidermann. The rabbi's hands covered his eyes as if he were reflecting, but when he removed them—tears. The rabbi wept! In the manner of his British countrymen, with the knuckles of his fist, he started to rap in approval on the waist-high wooden railings that separated the seating rows.

The other members of his group joined him, and soon, a thousand others joined them as the room thundered with their blows of approval. The audience could no longer contain themselves. They rose and clapped without pause, and it seemed that if the world should end right there, no more perfect communion of souls could have occurred than at that moment when the love of a thousand hearts was released from an ancient bondage.

As Annalisa stood at the dais, soft sunlight refracted through the stained-glassed windows, filling the cavernous auditorium with a hazy aura. Alberto sensed a palpable feeling in the air. Perhaps long-buried hopes of goodwill were rising from their graves of despair.

"Now," Annalisa said, "remember that we are all Jews as children of the One God; we are all Christians when we seek God's expression in humanity; we are all Muslims as we make our love for God part of our daily lives. This day should be counted among the happiest days of our lives, and the power in your hearts has made it so. Peace be with you."

Then, Annalisa, the pope, stepped off the stage into the wings while people in the crowd repeated her benediction to one another. Many shook hands or embraced. Alberto bolted from his chair and ran to the door at the side of the stage. He opened the door, but two Swiss Guards halted him as the pope was starting to exit the building a few feet away.

"Th-th-thannnk . . . " Alberto said, tongue-tied and trying to blurt the words out.

The pope turned and walked toward him, reached over the restraining arms of the guards, and touched his hand. She looked him in the eye, and Alberto sighed in relief—*she knows what I am trying to say*, he thought. She turned, and the guards escorted her out. Alberto stood alone, lost in a sea of inspired emotions. Like so many present, he sensed that somehow, on some level, the world would never be quite the same after this day.

CHAPTER XCI

For in the days we know not of Did fate Begin Weaving the web of days that wove Your doom. —*Algernon Charles Swinburne*

Kaiserdorf, Germany

Heinrich Mannheim looked out the airplane window at a German landscape that seemed very different to him now. His mind kept drifting back to his conversation with five fellow cardinals immediately after the pope's reconciliation speech.

They had watched the Rai Uno Italian television reporter interviewing some of the scholars and scientists leaving the auditorium. "A great day for the human race . . .", "Never believed I would see this in my lifetime . . .", "Blessed with a great insight on the human condition by this remarkable pope . . .", "More in thirty minutes to dispel anti-Semitism and heal rifts than in the past thousand years—"

Mannheim winced. She blamed Rome for the crucifixion. She attacked papal infallibility, she altered the liturgy, she introduced occultism, and the world was bowing before her feet. One thing above all had stuck with him when LoPresti said, "She has pushed us back into darkness. She has marginalized you, Heinrich, the man who should have been pope." That comment got his attention.

How else would the Antichrist destroy the Church and the world except from within? And who else would she target in her rise but him, the one man capable of reversing this madness?

"It must stop now!" Tormada had shouted. "They have contacted us, we discussed the details. This is the time to act. This bishop in Lagos was God's answer to us. We cannot let this opportunity pass. We await you order, Heinrich."

Mannheim had sat quietly, but his blue eyes had glowed hotly against the paleness of his skin as his inner fire boiled emotion over to resolution. "I agree," he had said in a low, strangely melancholy voice. "We will do what we discussed, but wait one more day for my final word. I have an important trip to make in Germany. That also makes the day we strike the fifteenth of March."

Each of the men in scarlet cassocks had nodded his head, acknowledging the astounding appropriateness attached to that fateful date. "Amen," intoned the voices, and so the cardinals had left to go about their appointed tasks.

Cardinal Mannheim had searched his mind for the resolve he needed. How peculiar it is among men that so few are graced with the fear God puts into one's heart that propels a man along the narrow path to salvation. For what were all the horrors of this world except demons lurking purposefully at the path's edge to remind man that he lives in the constant shadow of God's judgment? Only the God-given grace of fear kept man from straying off the edge into eternal darkness.

The sound of the landing gear going down brought Mannheim's thoughts back to the present. When exiting the terminal, he inhaled, taking in the air he had breathed as a youth for the first time in many years. Someone called behind him telling him he was blocking the door. Mannheim nodded. It was time to move, and he started to walk slowly toward his destination.

✠

Why had the bishop ordered him to hear a confession when he had been retired for three years? Monsignor Kaltenbrunner asked himself. He heard the door of the confessional booth open, and the man wasted no time.

"Bless me, Father, for I have sinned. It has been five days since my last confession."

The man sounded hurried or, perhaps, anxious. Kaltenbrunner glimpsed an off-kilter necktie through the shadowy partition screen, and it was odd the man had not removed his hat, being in church as he was.

"I have had . . . troubling thoughts, Father."

"Yes?" Kaltenbrunner replied. The man's voice sounded vaguely familiar.

"Father, if one were to confront a great evil, a Hitler, a Stalin, or even worse, what actions are justified to defend the innocent?"

An odd question. "How do you mean?" Kaltenbrunner asked.

"Hrrh, hrrm," the man coughed then went silent for some seconds. "If there were a person—one in a position of great power—who could harm many, subvert cherished institutions, create misery for the world . . . if there were such a devil personified and a man was able to stop him, should that man not act?"

What sort of confession has the bishop ordered me to hear? Kaltenbrunner asked himself. "Have you harmed anyone, my son? You know the Church does not condone violence."

"Father," the man said with a firmer voice, "is it not true the Church, the clergy, worked in the anti-Nazi resistance? Is it not true that in this very village the clergy once resisted the communists? Did those resistance movements not kill members of those criminal regimes?"

A jolt shifted Kaltenbrunner in his seat. Did this man know of his resistance work against the communists? But that was forty years ago. Who would remember? "My son, it is no sin to resist evil, but those clergymen never took a life, never pulled a trigger. Resistance must derive from individual conscience. A partisan may fight one way, a priest another." There was silence in the other booth. "My son, what is your sin? Was it a sin of commission or—" Kaltenbrunner heard the confessional door open and the sound of hurried steps. He tried to catch the fleeing man, but his arthritic body moved too slowly. The man was gone.

Mannheim placed a call to Rome from the Kaiserdorf airport. When Tormada answered Mannheim said, "See that it's done. May God protect us and save His Holy Church."

CHAPTER XCII

if they will not believe also these two signs . . .
the water which thou takest out of the river
shall become blood upon the dry land.
— Exodus 4:9

The Vatican City

When the engravings were found nailed to the door of Cardinal Mannheim's office, Mannheim had quivered with rage, screaming at Zugli and Avernis for not exposing the evil roaming the corridors of the Vatican.

Teresa spent a week researching the symbols. Much of that time she was in the Vatican archival vaults with Monsignor O'Keefe. He personally helped her wade through her assembled material. At the end of the week, she contacted Roncalli and Avernis, sounding very anxious. "We need to meet as soon as possible," she told them. Within hours Teresa, Avernis, and Roncalli gathered in Roncalli's office.

Teresa explained that she had been working on a theory in light of the new symbols and the collective vision they had experienced with Annalisa.

"If what I suspect is true," Teresa told the two men, "something bad is about to happen." She put the two engravings on the desk for the men to examine again.

Teresa said that her theory was inspired by an ancient document called the Secret Gospel of Mark discovered in Egypt in 1958. The document had been available to the public but had been played down by the Church and largely ignored. "This is a letter written by Clement of Alexandria, a significant bishop in the early Church. He is chronicling the activities of Saint Mark, the alleged author of the biblical gospel by the same name." She showed them copies of the letter and they began to read:

As for Mark, then, during Peter's stay in Rome he wrote an account of the Lord's doings, not, however, declaring all of them, nor yet hinting at the secret ones, but selecting what he thought most useful for increasing the faith of those who were being instructed. But when Peter died a martyr, Mark came over to Alexandria, bringing both his own notes and those of Peter, from which he transferred to his former book the things suitable to whatever makes for progress toward knowledge. Thus he composed a more spiritual Gospel for the use of those who were being perfected. Nevertheless, he yet did not divulge the things not to be uttered, nor did he write down the hierophantic teaching of the Lord . . . but he . . . brought in certain sayings of which he knew . . . would . . . lead the hearers into the innermost sanctuary of that truth hidden by seven veils and, dying, he left his composition to the church in Alexandria, where it even yet is most carefully guarded, being read only to those who are being initiated into the great mysteries.

"This letter," Teresa said, "supports the Gnostic claim that Jesus imparted secret knowledge or *gnosis* to those who were spiritually dedicated or advanced. And this information came to Mark from Saint Peter, who was never even considered to have a good grasp of the Gnostic mysteries."

"Why did they go to such pains to guard the information?" Avernis asked.

"The Gnostic knowledge was passed on but hidden," Teresa said, "because in every age, the forces of darkness and ignorance would suppress, twist, or destroy it. That harsh fate often extended to the prophets and their followers too."

"It wasn't just Christian Gnostics either," Roncalli said. "Jews suppressed the Gnostic Kabbalists and Muslims suppressed their Gnostic Sufis."

Avernis tapped his fingers on the desk. "Okay," he said. "So the high priests and Churches did a number on the Gnostics, but that devilish figure on the left *does* look evil."

"Maybe not. It's called Baphomet, a symbol used by the Knights Templar." Teresa explained that Baphomet had been a hidden symbol of the Knights Templar, the famous Crusader military order. The Templars were probably secret Gnostics. In the fourteenth century, the king of France conspired with the Vatican to destroy the Order. In doing so they had manufactured all kinds of evidence against them.

"So no one ever saw the actual Templar symbol of Baphomet," Teresa said.

"The image was recreated based on descriptions by the Templars' enemies. It's likely this symbol is a perversion of the original or an outright fabrication forced out of Templars under torture."

"Okay, so what are these symbols telling us?" Avernis asked, sounding exasperated.

"The Jewish Gnostics had a secret code in the Kabbalah known as the *atbash* cipher," Teresa said as she picked up the engraving. "Using their code system, the name Baphomet in Hebrew characters yields the name *Sophia—Wisdom.*"

"My God," Roncalli said. "They had to hide their Gnostic beliefs in the symbols."

"Yes. The other symbol is called Tyet," Teresa said. "It dates back to the Egyptians. It represents the Goddess bleeding from the womb."

Avernis ran his fingers through his hair and shook his head. "For God's sake, Teresa. You said you had a theory. Can you get to it?"

Teresa bit her lip and glared at him. "Listen, Robert, I'm groping my way though this on intuition and hard work. I don't know if I'm right, so I'm retracing my thinking for you to make your own judgments. What the hell is your problem?"

Avernis took a deep breath. He looked subdued. "I'm sorry. Mannheim and Zugli are putting the screws on me. Guess they forgot I'm doing them a favor in this. I'm frustrated. If only we could question the one who is placing these things. We finally caught the person on tape but he or she was wearing a black-hooded monk's robe . . . even wore gloves so we couldn't make the hands out as male or female. Clever SOB."

"It's all right, Robert," Roncalli said. "But let Teresa finish things her way."

Avernis nodded.

Roncalli looked at Teresa. She resumed. "Remember in our vision how Jesus talked about '*opening the gates of hell*'? It really bothered us afterward; it sounded so ominous. But I came upon some passages in the Nag Hammadi books and then I realized something—Gnostics thought *the earth* was hell, a place dominated by dark forces suppressing divine awareness and keeping humans bound to the earth plane. From their viewpoint, opening the gates of hell wouldn't mean unleashing evil on earth; it would mean *liberating us from earth,* from the evil forces that keep us from awareness of the higher spiritual planes."

Avernis considered the statements. "Go on," he said.

"Okay," Teresa said. "So *who* is going to liberate us? You know what we saw in our vision. We originated together in a spiritual realm and incarnated on earth. You saw Jesus hold up Magdalene's—Annalisa's—hand and declare that she was Sophia, his other half."

Teresa and Avernis gave a start when Roncalli slapped his hand loudly on the table. "Of course! *The Holy Spirit!*" Teresa had previously explained how the Church erased Sophia's name but couldn't eliminate her importance; so they hid her feminine nature and neutered her. She became the Holy Spirit, a vague, sexless entity that would inspire miracles like those performed by the disciples and saints in the Book of Acts.

"Remember the Bible," Roncalli said. "Jesus promised that God would send a comforter after he was gone. Even the Church believes that comforter was the Holy Spirit. And Gnostics from India to Palestine believed that redeemers came in waves, appearing periodically from the higher realms to rescue trapped souls in the earth plane by imparting divine knowledge. It all adds up."

Teresa leaned back in her chair and exhaled deeply. "Now you see why I'm worried. Jesus was the last savior-redeemer, and look at what happened to him. These symbols depict Sophia bleeding. If Annalisa is Sophia incarnate . . . "

Roncalli held up a hand. "Wait. I know what we saw in our vision, but one thing is missing. The Gnostic wisdom tradition also says that certain events must happen prior to the redeemers' appearances to raise consciousness and prepare humanity for the redeemers' teachings. Jesus' advent was preceded by prophecies of the Messiah, the work of the Essenes, and the teachings of John the Baptist."

"So if Sophia—Divine Wisdom, the Holy Spirit, whatever she's called—is trying to rise again, what events preceded that?" Avernis asked.

They sat in silent thought for a good half-hour until Teresa snapped her fingers. "Of course! Recovery of the Essene Dead Sea Scrolls and the lost Gnostic gospels at Nag Hammadi Egypt—they were found within a year of each other starting in 1945, the year the world lay in ruins after the worst war in human history. It was also the year the first atomic bomb was detonated. Could there be a better time for a new enlightenment to begin reshaping human consciousness?

"Under much criticism, those documents were held the by authorities and not made available to the public until the 1980s, the decade Annalisa was born. If they hadn't discovered those texts, the line of Gnostic wisdom tradition eradicated by the Church would still be lost. Without the texts, we'd have no context to interpret events from a Gnostic viewpoint; we wouldn't be having this conversation. Those discoveries certainly qualify as paving the way for a Gnostic redeemer."

"So then," Roncalli said, "Jesus came to break the cycle of ignorance and evil and he was crucified. If Sophia, his female counterpart, has incarnated and is trying to consolidate what he began, the same forces that crucified Jesus would try and harm her. Hence the bleeding Goddess."

The room grew quiet as they exchanged concerned looks with one another. Then Avernis said, "Teresa, I'm sorry about before. I'll tell Zugli to increase security on the pope immediately." The others nodded in ready agreement.

CHAPTER XCIII

Death is in my sight today
As when a man desires to see home
When he has spent many years in captivity
—Anonymous Egyptian, 1990 BC

Rome

The story of the shootout was all over the Roman newspapers. A black man had been killed after a gunfight in a poor Roman suburb, and the police were looking for the gunmen. Avernis had seen the news reports but didn't think too much about them until he received a call from Teresa asking him to meet in her office.

"I came across something unusual," she said on his arrival. "I thought of you since you're the only policeman of sorts that I know."

"Of sorts," Avernis said, snickering. "So, what've you got?"

"You remember a couple of months back the Nigerian terrorists kidnapped an American oil executive?" she asked.

"I do."

"It made me remember something," Teresa said. She pointed to a screen built into the wall to the left of her desk. "Here, look at the laser clip of the kidnapping that the Nigerian terrorists released."

Avernis looked at the monitor. The clip was a classic terrorist production, with the hapless victim sitting in a chair surrounded by masked, armed men. Teresa manipulated the computer to focus on one of the terrorists. The man was holding a rifle pointing upward with the butt resting on his thigh. The elbow of his rifle arm was propped on his hip and he had short shirtsleeves. The man's arms looked odd. They reflected light unevenly; they looked lumpy, like oatmeal. Teresa rolled the jog wheel and enlarged the digital frame. Avernis stood and walked up close to the screen.

"At first I thought those were those tattoos or tribal scars," Teresa said.

"No, the marks are irregular. Besides, they don't scar arms," Avernis said, looking very interested in what he was seeing. "Those look like wounds of some sort, like nasty cuts."

"Anyway, compare those scarred arms to the ones of the man murdered here in Rome. They look identical to me," she said.

Avernis looked at the two sets of pictures and agreed. "Did you call the Italian police?"

"No," she said. "I figure you're in a better position to deal with the police, and I'm busy preparing for a televised broadcast of the pope's meeting with Nigerian pilgrims tomorrow. The only condition is that if there's a story in this, you tell me so I can jump on it, okay?"

"Sure," he replied.

There was a brief silence, then Teresa said, "Robert, listen, since we've all been getting together to talk about that night in the pope's office and those symbols, I . . . well, I think I'd like to see you again. I was probably hard on you, but I really like you. Enough time has gone by and maybe we can talk this through, that is, if you're still interested."

Avernis smiled. "I know I handled things poorly. I'd like another chance to explain. I can use good company these days too. I'm still having trouble digesting that we may be part of some supernatural story that's been going on since the beginning of time."

Teresa laughed. "Great. So bring me back a scoop on this shooting and you'll score some big brownie points too," she said with a wink.

"With that kind of incentive, I'll try real hard," he said.

Shortly after leaving, Avernis contacted Zugli. They went straight to the Italian police. They related their concerns about a possible Islamic terrorist presence in Rome. The police opened up their files on the case, and Avernis ended up with an all-night homework assignment.

CHAPTER XCIV

Beware the Ides of March.—William Shakespeare

Rome

It was shaping up to be a great morning for Teresa Ferentinos. Annalisa was set to make a "significant announcement" at a gathering of Nigerian pilgrims who were visiting Rome to see their African pope and pray at St. Peter's Basilica. Teresa was also resuming her interrupted relationship with Robert Avernis, and that gave her something to look forward to in her personal life.

This would be the first time she had seen Annalisa since Tehran. She clasped the crucifix hanging about her neck, one of the four Annalisa had miraculously produced out of thin air. Teresa had defined her purpose in life as a witness to the truth, and lo and behold, fate had made her the chronicler of Annalisa's life. That woman had brought more light to the planet than anyone in modern history, and Teresa was proud to have first witnessed Annalisa's truth to the world.

"Get this, Leo. Just in from the Nigerian police to the Vatican," Robert Avernis said to his boss. He had been up all night with Leo Dusayne, cross-checking countless items of intelligence relating to the dead terrorist in Rome. An idea Avernis had yesterday had just paid off this morning.. They had forwarded the Nigerian tabloid papers the story and pictures of the dead man. "A doctor in central Nigeria saw the tabloid pictures and identified the guy," Avernis said. "Seems he treated him for machete wounds some years back. Guess who dragged the guy miles to the hospital on a donkey and made them work on the SOB?"

Dusayne's eyebrows furrowed with questions. "Who?"

"Sister Annalisa Basanjo!" Avernis said.

"The pope!" Dusayne exclaimed. "So, there was a connection between the guy shot here in Rome and the pope. What does it mean?"

Avernis' mind clicked into high gear. "Let's walk through this. The dead guy was a terrorist in good standing, next thing we know he shows up shot full of holes in Rome. Two questions: why was he here and who killed him? A foreign intelligence agency, the Brits maybe? He did scribble that note that said *MI5* before he died."

"No," Dusayne said. "Foreign killings are usually done by MI6, but I checked with MI5 anyway. Talked to Sir Colin Preston himself. I know him personally, and I believe him when he tells me neither section was involved. The Brits had nothing to do with it."

"Listen," Avernis said, "We've been assuming he was here by himself and enemies killed him, right? Well, what if he were here with friends and they did it?"

"How's that?" Dusayne asked.

Avernis squinted in concentration and rolled his fingers around in his hand. "Let's assume for a minute he had some falling out with N-FAC."

"Okay, but why come to Rome?" Dusayne asked.

"I don't know," Avernis said. "It must have to do with the pope though."

The men sat silently for a long time pondering the pieces of information until Avernis suddenly rapped the coffee table with his knuckles. "All right, this theory is all speculation but hear me out." He didn't mention his growing sixth sense or the synchronous occurrences that had increasingly been guiding him from the time of his meeting with Annalisa and the discovery of the Magdalene document. He doubted Dusayne would have appreciated that.

But Dusayne knew Avernis had an astronomical IQ, and they were groping in the dark, so he was not about to discourage his speculations. "Take a shot," he told the younger man.

"Okay," Avernis said. "You remember I pointed out that they started hitting Christian targets after Pope Annalisa was elected?"

"I remember," Dusayne replied.

"We've confirmed numerous times they view her as a threat," Avernis said. "Even rank-and-file Muslims down there like her, and she was gaining converts there as a nun. That runs counter to the anti-Western, anti-Christian world view of N-FAC. Now she's a global hero for stopping the Iranian crisis. The Iranians were N-FAC'S patrons. N-FAC needs to instigate a new war to survive, and what's the best way to do that?"

Dusayne nodded, indicating to Avernis he should continue with his train of thought.

"What if N-FAC wanted to kill the pope and he was here to warn her?"

Dusayne looked at Avernis with both eyebrows raised. "He was a thug, but she did save his life. He'd likely have a problem with killing her, I agree, but he could have jumped ship in Nigeria. Why come to Rome?"

"I can think of two reasons," Avernis said. "He needed to get close enough to warn her because he had no one else he could tell. Or maybe he drew the lot to kill her himself and didn't learn about the real assignment until the last minute, here, in Rome. But I still don't get the MI5 note. Can we go look at that again?"

"We scanned the note," Dusayne said. "We have it down in the lab. Let's go."

After studying the scan, Avernis tapped on the desk. "That note was bloody and scribbled as if it were done in a hurry, at the last minute," he observed.

"You mean while he was wounded, just before he was killed?" Dusayne asked.

"Or even while he was dying," Avernis said.

Dusayne frowned. "In either case, if it were tied to the pope, what would MI5 tell us?"

"If you're dying and desperate to write a message, you need to do it quickly," Avernis said. "Maybe it was shorthand for something."

They had the technician enhance the picture on a digitized computer screen. They were looking at an enlarged view. "Leo, look here, right after the *M.* Does it look like a punctuation mark to you?" Avernis asked. "And the letter *I,* the way it's written, it could be the number one."

Dusayne stared intently at the screen. "It's pretty messed up, but yeah, it could be a period or a comma or just a spot on the paper. And that could be a one."

"Okay," said Avernis. "Let's tick off the possibilities. It could be: M,I5; M.I5; M,15 or M.15. Hmmm, M.15-an abbreviation? For a date maybe? March fifteenth or May fifteenth?"

"Holy shit, Bob. If it's a date, *today is March fifteen!* You don't think— "

Avernis' hand slapped the table. "Oh, God! The Ides of March—Caesar assassinated in Rome! The pope is the heir to Caesar's Rome. Damn, Leo, we need to call the Vatican ASAP and see where the pope is today. It may be nothing, but it's all too coincidental not to check it out."

"I'll make the call myself," Dusayne said.

It took twenty minutes to clear the Vatican bureaucracy and reach a bishop in the pope's office. Dusayne inquired about the pope's schedule. Almost immediately, his face paled and he said, "Get me through to Colonel Zugli, now!" Dusayne put a hand over the phone and said to Avernis, "The pope is meeting with a group of Nigerian pilgrims as we speak. God, I hope to hell we're way off base. These incompetent assholes are trying to find Zugli. Damn, they take so long."

Avernis was frozen in place by the news for a few seconds, then it hit him—Teresa, she was there with the pope! He grabbed another phone and dialed her vid-phone number. *Dear God, he prayed, I hope she hasn't turned it off.*

CHAPTER XCV

Greater love hath no man than this, that a man lay down his life for his friends. —John 15:13

The Vatican City

Teresa was in the Sala Regia, where the pope was greeting a group of her fellow Nigerians. The gathering of about thirty people was spread out in a rough fan shape that widened toward the back of the room, away from where the pope stood. Cardinal Berletti flanked the pope on her right and the papal secretary, Monsignor O'Keefe, was to her left. Cardinal Roncalli stood further off in the wings of the gathering.

Swiss Guards stood to the back and on either side of the pope, and other guards stood toward the rear of the group. No guards were on the right side where Teresa and her cameraman had set up because they abutted a corner wall.

The pope, to the delight of the Nigerians, had spoken to them in several indigenous languages. She now reverted to English, which was the common tongue of her country. The visitors all wore traditional Nigerian garb, which consisted of loose-flowing, brightly colored robes and a variety of head coverings.

Teresa was whispering instructions to the cameraman when she felt a buzzing at her hip. She had switched her vid-phone to its vibration mode since the room tended to produce echoes and she did not want ringing noises to interrupt the occasion.

She was too busy to be bothered, so she would let it vibrate until whoever it was hung up—only they didn't. After several minutes, the phone was still tickling her hip. *Who the hell is calling now?* She thought. She plucked the phone from the clip holder on her waist. She placed her finger on the off button, and there it rested for a few seconds. Some instinct told her not to push it. Maybe London was calling her for some reason. Better take it to be sure.

She tapped the cameraman on the shoulder, pointed to her phone, and with hand signs told him she was moving further back to get the call. He nodded and kept on filming.

She huddled up against the corner of the room and pressed the reception button. A worried looking Avernis popped onto the screen. "Robert?" she said in a raspy whisper. "What's wrong?"

Avernis said, "Teresa, listen to me very carefully and don't talk. We have reason to believe the pope may be in danger. This is no joke. There may be people in that Nigerian group who came to assassinate her. We're trying to reach the Swiss Guards. Go to the nearest guard, tell him to get the pope out of the room, then get yourself the hell out of there. Do you understand?"

"Robert, I—"

"TERESA, JUST DO IT! I'll stay on the line. Go now!"

Teresa looked around the room. The guards who had been standing to the rear across the room from her had moved toward the front. The quickest way to reach any of them was to push through the crowd, which is exactly what she started to do. Her cameraman reflexively started to move forward with her.

Numerous video cameras from several networks were in the room that day, and when investigators later reviewed the incident, this is what they saw in composite slow motion recordings:

Teresa was making her way to the front to alert the guards. Because of Avernis' warning, she was acutely aware of possible assassins in the crowd. Directly ahead of her, she saw something that sent pins and needles shooting through her. A man dressed in a blue robe had sweat pouring down his neck even though it was cold in the unheated room.

Then she noticed his robe bulging out on the right side, and a wave of panic staggered her. *He's got a gun!* she thought. If she were correct, the crowd was cutting her off from warning the guards. Suddenly, gunfire broke out to her left, and people fell to the ground screaming. Teresa, in a half-crouching posture, glanced across the room to the source of the gunshots.

Another man had drawn a gun at that moment, shouted something, and started firing at the pope. Cardinal Berletti, who was in the process of leaning in to whisper something to Annalisa, took a bullet in the side. The frustrated gunman turned to the left to take out a Swiss Guard who was in the process of drawing his gun. He hit the guard in the chest then wheeled back around to target the pope again.

He fired off two more rounds. One struck Berletti, who had slumped over from the first shot and was momentarily propped against the pope's shoulder and chest. Monsignor O'Keefe, upon seeing Berletti leaning against the pope and then falling to the ground, leaned down and across the pope's body to assist the fallen cardinal. The second bullet took O'Keefe in the temple. He dropped over Berletti like a leaden shroud.

The remaining Swiss Guards now concentrated their fire on the first assassin. A split second before he went down, the blue-robed man drew out his weapon and started to fire. Throughout the pandemonium, Teresa had kept him in her peripheral vision. Though she had suspected he carried a gun, Teresa froze in shock when he actually pulled it out and started firing.

The first gunman, who was now dead, had diverted the Swiss Guards. They were not able to protect Annalisa when the blue-robed man loosed two rounds, one striking her in the upper right chest, the second hitting her in the lower solar plexus.

Roncalli, by now realizing what was happening, acted on instinct. Seeing his friends felled, he ran toward Annalisa. He could not secure a stance in front of her because of Berletti and O'Keefe's limp bodies, so he flung himself across the bullet's plane of trajectory as the blue-robed man fired a third round. Roncalli grunted as the bullet tore through his arm, exited, and nicked Annalisa's shoulder.

The remaining killer was readying to fire a fourth shot at the pope who, incredibly, remained standing. Annalisa stood locked in a dance of death, almost appearing to accept the bullets coming her way. At that moment, Teresa recovered her senses. From behind, she bashed the assassin on the side of his face with the heavy microphone she carried.

The man let out a yelp and turned to face his attacker, one hand covering his cheek and the other raising the gun he had lowered, when she struck him. Teresa's body was immobilized in a helpless web of fear. She knew she was going to die, and she was angry, angry at being a helpless victim. She wanted to claw the bastard's eyes out before she went, but there was no time. She felt the bullet hit her, and she collapsed.

"TERESA, TERESA!" She heard Avernis' voice over the phone. He had not hung up; he had stayed with her the entire time. She smiled at that, and then all consciousness went to shadow.

The assassins were dead, the shooting had stopped, and the Swiss Guards were reasserting control over the room. Pietro Roncalli was not even aware of the guards trying to staunch the flow of blood from his arm. He saw dark blood oozing from the wound on O'Keefe's head and realized his friend was dead. The guards were lifting O'Keefe's legs, which were still draped over Berletti's inert body. Roncalli tore away from the guards and crawled toward Annalisa using his good arm.

"The pope?" he gasped as he broke through the circle of kneeling men.

"Your Eminence," one of the guards said. "You're wounded. You should—"

"THE POPE?" Roncalli repeated with single-minded focus.

The guard shook his head. "She has no pulse, Eminenza. She's gone."

As Roncalli absorbed the implication of the statement, there was a new commotion. Vatican emergency medics had flooded the room and were ordering people out of the way. As a team tried to move Roncalli, he said, "No, I stay here," and despite their pleading he remained by the pope's side.

They performed manual CPR on the pope until the doctors came in with cardio-resuscitation equipment. Roncalli winced at each electric arching of her small, limp body.

At this time, Cardinal De Faissy entered the room just as the ominous buzzing of the machine ceased. A doctor announced, "The pope is dead."

All motion ceased, all sound stopped for Roncalli. "NO!" His voice sounded like a clarion trumpet. "NO, THE POPE IS NOT DEAD!"

De Faissy placed a gentle hand on Roncalli's shoulder. "Pietro, she is gone. Please, let them take you now."

Roncalli snapped his eyes to attention, looked at De Faissy, and said, "The pope is not dead!" Then in a barely audible whisper he said, "She only sleeps."

De Faissy looked at Zugli. They knew their friend was in shock. For thirty minutes, they tried to remove him from the carnage, but he clung to the hem of Annalisa's robe with one hand and held her wrist with his other. No one knew what to do. De Faissy instructed they should wait until the cardinal calmed down.

"There is a pulse," Roncalli said in a hoarse, cracked whisper.

De Faissy looked at a doctor, who frowned and shook his head.

"There is a pulse," Roncalli insisted again.

De Faissy motioned to the doctor, who sighed, knelt, and took the wrist from Roncalli's hand. De Faissy turned away to confer with Zugli about clearing the room when a voice halted him in midsentence.

"HOLY MOTHER OF GOD, THERE IS A PULSE!"

De Faissy whipped his head around. It was not Roncalli, but the wide-eyed doctor speaking. "Impossible, impossible! My God, there is a pulse!"

As they were clearing the room of the injured and dead, Cardinal Mannheim entered. "Oh, dear God, what has been done here?" he asked, eyes opened wide. "Is it true, has the pope been killed?"

"Shot, not killed," De Faissy explained. "Berletti and O'Keefe are dead."

"So is one of my guards and three of the Nigerian pilgrims," Zugli added.

Mannheim made the sign of the cross. "May God rest their souls."

Zugli stopped one of his young Swiss Guards on the way out the door with the medics. The shaken young man recounted his ordeal. The pope, he told them, stood upright even after they shot her. It was only after they killed the second assassin that she collapsed in their arms. She did not say a word; she merely closed her eyes like she was going to sleep.

The guard had been standing about ten feet behind the pope. He told Zugli he had seen a woman strike the assassin who had shot Annalisa, and this had given them time to fell the man before he could get off another shot. Zugli asked who the woman was. The guard was unsure, but she had been shot too, and he presumed she was dead. Zugli made further inquiries about the woman, but people were too scattered and confused to give useful information. They must already have removed her while everyone was focusing on the pope.

"Your Eminences, I must clear the room now," Zugli said. "Several investigative jurisdictions will be here and we cannot risk contaminating the scene."

"Of course, Roald," Mannheim said. "I must call a meeting of the College of Cardinals. We will have numerous issues to face while the pope is incapacitated. Does anyone know how badly she is injured?"

Zugli shook his head. "At first they said she was dead. I'm told she is just borderline now. Look, they're moving her."

"You call the College together," De Faissy told Mannheim. "I'm going to the hospital."

Mannheim nodded, and with no further discussion, he left the room with haste.

O'Keefe, Berletti . . . De Faissy knew the Church had lost some of its brightest luminaries today, and the light that stood behind them all was flickering on the edge of extinction. He would pray; he would do anything he could to help keep that flame alive. They had come too far for the darkness to have its way once again.

CHAPTER XCVI

And all the winds go sighing for sweet things dying.
— Christina Rosetti

Athenry, Ireland

They buried Desmond O'Keefe on a knoll overlooking a lush field. The cemetery was in a part of Ireland famous in that country's balladry. Once, in the Vatican, Roncalli had visited O'Keefe, and the monsignor had played the ballad about those fields. Its plaintive, elegiac tones filled the man's humble apartment with music that moved Roncalli to melancholy.

He had asked O'Keefe a jovial man, why he listened to such sad music. The monsignor had told him that pain, sorrow, and loss were part of the Irish people, and so must be held near to the heart. Those feelings inspired them to poetry, to music, to all manner of beauty. It tempered their souls, made them human, and enabled them to touch the pain in others.

The song he had played was about a man who had stolen corn to feed his starving family. He was caught and they were sailing him out on a prison ship for Botany Bay, never to see his wife and child again. It was not so many years ago that they really did this to people, O'Keefe had reminded Roncalli. The monsignor explained how Irish ballads moved people to see the violence they do to one another. By eternally enshrining tragedy and injustice in their music, perhaps in some measure they would deter future travesties by reminding us that other souls suffer for the blind acts we commit.

As they lowered his coffin into the moist earth, the ballad of the fields played its soft farewell to Desmond O'Keefe. An O'Keefe cousin, possessed of a beautiful tenor voice, sang in honor of the departed "pride of the family".

And so, Roncalli's dearest friend, one of the finest men he had ever known, passed from the earth.

The Vatican City

Pietro Roncalli opened his eyes as the sun crept through the window of his

Vatican office, warming his face and melting his recollections of that misty Irish day. Being in Ireland for a few hours to pay final respects to Desmond O'Keefe was the only time he had left Rome since the shootings three days ago. He had already buried Cardinal Berletti, a great man, the man who would have been pope. Now he would return to the hospital to stand vigil.

Annalisa was still alive but her vital signs remained extremely low. He walked to the hospital carefully, for his arm was still in a sling from his bullet wound. He lingered a few minutes, enjoying the warmth of the sun on his face. Perhaps he could take its warmth with him on the lonely walk. He hoped to God that he would not have another funeral to arrange.

CHAPTER XCVII

Jesus said . . . when you see your images that came into being before you and that neither die nor become visible, how much you will have to bear!
—The Gospel of Thomas

Rome

The pope did not die, much to the surprise of her doctors, but she did not regain consciousness either before or after the operation to remove bullet fragments from her body. Her vital signs were steady but her brain wave activity was low. Most perplexing was the fact that she had been clinically dead for forty-five minutes. Astonished physicians were trying to explain her revival with theories that she entered a yogalike meditative state.

Roncalli knew better, though. She *had* died . . . and *returned. I know it,* he thought. The doctor gave Roncalli a report. It was grim. Even if the pope survived, she would likely be brain damaged from the lack of oxygen during her apparent death. Bullet fragments also hit her spine, so she would be paralyzed from the waist down. Roncalli gave the doctor a mechanical nod. He then walked across to another wing of the hospital to visit Teresa. Avernis was there.

Teresa was recovering from her injury, happy to be alive. The terrorist's gun had been a few feet away from her, but it was not his bullet that struck her in the shoulder. A split second before he pulled the trigger, a bullet fired by a Swiss Guard had caught him in the back of the head. Forensics showed that the bullet in Teresa also came from the gun of a Swiss Guard, an errant shot due to the confusion and her proximity to the assassin.

With time and physical therapy she would recover the use of her arm, but her job was secure. The investigators had pieced together all the video footage from the various cameras in the room, and it clearly showed Teresa and Roncalli were heroes. Teresa stopped the terrorist from getting off a point-blank shot at the pope while Roncalli's diving body deflected another bullet that might have struck her head-on.

Their faces were on every television newscast, magazine, and newspaper around the globe. Cardinal Roncalli had already thanked Teresa on behalf of the entire Church. Tonight they talked a while, and he said a prayer by her bedside, held her hand, and blessed her.

Then Roncalli said, "Our vision that night in Annalisa's study proved to me that we're part of a family around Annalisa that is doing God's work. I had a foreshadowing of that vision at my first meeting with her in Africa. Desmond, with his unorthodox views, pushed me along and then, of course, Annalisa gradually revealed herself, but I now know we're connected in a cosmic drama that is still playing out."

Teresa cried at the mention of O'Keefe's name. She could only nod her head and weep as Roncalli drew the unspoken words out of her soul.

"Before Desmond died," Roncalli said, "he entrusted me with a secret that I want to discuss with both of you. I think it explains everything. You see, Desmond had been keeping certain rare texts hidden in the library. The Church considers these texts heretical."

And Cardinal Roncalli read some passages to them. They contained awesome, mystical words that spoke of a great force and movement behind human life. They spoke of the origins, destinies, and purpose of humankind. Then he focused on a particular excerpt:

"Oh, hapless spirit, see what doom thine actions have wrought.
Sweet heaven's light eclips'd from the eyes of men,
captive souls in tombs of flesh forgotten of their home divine,
and all their anguish is but thine."

"This is the final communication from the Vatican's mystery person," Roncalli said. "It was left on my desk the morning just before the shooting along with Desmond's instructions where to find the secret Gnostic texts. I had no time to act on it before the pope's audience that day."

Avernis looked at Roncalli. "Are you saying . . . "

"Yes," Roncalli said. "It was Desmond who placed all the symbols."

"But why?" Avernis asked.

"The answer to that lies in Desmond's hidden books and his journal," Roncalli said. "When he was a young priest assigned to the Vatican Library, Desmond noticed this passage scribbled on a wall in an obscure area of an underground vault. It's called *Sophia's Lament.* He couldn't get it out of his mind. He asked the then prefect of the library, old Valentinus, about it. Valentinus said it was heresy and told him to forget it. He couldn't. He obsessed over it. Finally, Valentinus showed Desmond these lost texts."

"Valentinus was a Gnostic? In the Vatican?" Teresa asked.

"He was the Keeper of the Texts before Desmond," Roncalli said. "And where better to hide them than in the Vatican, the heart of the enemy? *Sophia's Lament* is in *The Book of Remembrance*. It tells of the tragedy and the triumph of the First Souls, their fall, their burden, their fate and their glory. It goes back to the creation, even before Genesis."

"The First Souls," Avernis repeated with eyes closed.

"Yes," Roncalli said, and he read from the book again. "It spoke of God, a Father-Mother God, generating two primal spirits, Logos and Wisdom —Christ and Sophia. It told how Sophia broke the pattern of creation by an act of imbalance. She acted without her male counterpart, thus leading to the creation of the imperfect material world. Sophia regretted her actions. She had to redeem the spirits trapped in the matter of the lower dimensions.

"To do this, Sophia and other spirits evolved the human body to be a vehicle for holding divine consciousness. They used their spiritual power to manipulate the evolution of apelike primates. When the bodies were ready, they projected their consciousness into them. Suddenly, Homo erectus became Homo sapiens, conscious man. That union of spirit and flesh gave birth to the First Souls, the link between body, or matter, and spirit."

"It speaks of the First Souls in the plural," Teresa said. "Who were they?"

"Christ and Sophia were the first spirits generated by God to become souls, but not the only ones," Roncalli said. "They were bonded to a grouping of like-minded spirits named in the books: Justice, Witness, Faith, and Perseverance. They were the archetypes for the higher qualities of humanity. Their names personified the central principle of each soul."

"The theme, the defining principle," Teresa said, looking at Avernis. "Robert and I have spoken about that several times."

Roncalli nodded. "You recognize Christos," he said, "the savior, the first to remember his divine origin and awaken in the person of Jesus of Nazareth. Sophia was the soul who led the exodus to the material plane. Sophia means *wisdom* in Greek. The pope had frequent visions where a voice would call her to find wisdom and find herself. As for the others . . ." Roncalli showed them the journal entries. O'Keefe had scribbled Teresa's name next to Witness, Robert next to Justice, Pietro next to Perseverance, and Desmond next to Faith.

Avernis audibly sucked in a gulp of air; Teresa's head sank into her cupped hands.

"You're surprised after our vision with Annalisa and all that's happened?" Roncalli asked. "Teresa, I know you've given this thought. Describe your life's theme."

Teresa's eyes were wide and she shivered. "To be a witness," she replied.

"And Robert?"

Avernis remained silent. "Tell him, Robert," Teresa said.

Avernis looked at her. "Justice," he said. "But—"

Roncalli held up his hand. "Valentinus chose Desmond to pass on the knowledge because the Gnostic texts and symbols awakened Desmond's latent consciousness. Similarly, Desmond used the symbols and texts, like the Magdalene fragment, to awaken us. The wisdom and power of these signs and writings attract the elect like a flame attracts a moth."

"The elect?" Avernis said.

"The elect," Roncalli explained, "are those born spiritually inclined, perhaps through many incarnations. They're sensitized to people and things that raise spiritual consciousness. Desmond knew Annalisa from the Gnostic prophecies and his own intuition. He also knew her soul grouping would gather around her, so he began placing the symbols to draw us out."

Avernis and Teresa both acknowledged that the symbols did bind everyone together.

"And they awakened us too," Roncalli said. "Remember Teresa's dream and the way you so fluidly deciphered the meaning behind the first symbols, Robert? That was your spirit memory awakening. All the heightened intuition we have been displaying is the result of Desmond exposing us to the Gnostic mysteries."

Teresa said, "I guess with everything we've been through, we can't deny the truth of this. Remember what we saw in our vision that night? We were there in the Holy Land with Jesus and Magdalene. We *are* part of this. But what is the purpose behind it all? Why did God . . . why did Sophia . . . why did *we* enter into this craziness we call life?"

Roncalli smiled. "A question for the ages. Read this passage in the *Gnostikon.* It may help," he said as he opened the book to a marked page.

> *God is endless, all-encompassing, like a sun emitting infinite rays of light. His light streams out filling the dark void, but without anything off which to reflect, it is merely an endless sea of light with no horizon. Just for this reason has God formed us as multiple mirrors to catch the light-streams from each of His rays. He can now 'know' Himself, experience the reflection of his own infinite light playing out in innumerable dramas."*

"We're His reflections." Teresa spoke as if remembering a thought long forgotten. "Our souls are the streams of light, our bodies are the mirrors. All humanity is a part of the same source, the One appearing as many, is that right?"

Roncalli nodded, "Yes, but the forces of this imperfect world are low and dense. They fragment our consciousness like bending light through a prism. We lost remembrance of our origins; our identities became confined to the boundaries of our skin. God projected us into this world for the experience of it, so He let the feminine creative power lead the fall from a higher state. This feminine power will continually reappear to lead us to remembrance of our true nature, but this time working in balance with Christ, her male counterpart. Christ is the Holy Word, the instruction that opens the mind, Sophia is the Holy Spirit, the intuition and feeling that opens the heart. Miracles happen when the two are joined in perfect balance."

"Balancing our male and female sides, just like in my dream," Teresa said.

Roncalli showed them more passages from the book. They recounted how Sophia, and her incarnation of Eve, were blamed for the divine fall. By extension, all women became stigmatized in the racial memory and so came the male dominance that disrupted the balance of nature and colored the character of this world. Even Jesus' teaching of the equality of women was rejected. So it was that early female leaders of the Church like Mary Magdalene were pushed aside, and the records of their truth were altered or expunged.

"But where do we go from here?" Teresa asked. "What do the Gnostics say?"

Roncalli smiled. "Remember the hundred monkeys in Dr. Herron's notations to the Magdalene document? I suspect that when enough people reach a critical mass of consciousness, we'll see a visible transformation of our world. Annalisa was the beginning. She changed the Church mass and the way we pray. She taught people how to heal. She redirected our vision from the material to the spiritual. She helped humanity uncover its true nature. Not since the golden age of Greek philosophy have so many people seriously delved into their spiritual depths whether in Church or in the solitude of their own homes.

"We avoided a holocaust, and we've seen a dramatic rise in clairvoyance, prophetic dreams, and healings — all these miracles are following in her wake. She's moving our collective perceptions toward what Gnostics always desired — the direct experience that we are the One expressed as the many. This is what Jesus really taught — that we are all Christs in potential because we are all of God's spiritual substance. We just have to remember our divinity. Each person who awakens in consciousness literally experiences heaven on earth. That is the real resurrection where the flesh is spiritualized and the spirit is materialized."

Avernis shook his head in confusion. "I know what I saw in our vision, but the reality still hasn't registered. If I'm a part of this story, if I've lived and died before, I don't exactly remember. I certainly don't feel very grand or important."

Roncalli smiled "It may take lifetimes to completely remember. I have no direct memories either, but I have glimpses. The Gnostic gospels revealed that Saint Peter was plagued with doubts. He relied on external reenactments of Jesus' life because he didn't understand his inner teachings. That mirrors my life until now, but think, Robert, how we all came together around Annalisa during these times. We were all destined to play roles in this great transformation. One day we'll all remember who we were . . . who we are."

"Can any one of us really matter that much?" Avernis asked.

"I believe so," Roncalli replied. "If justice is your life's theme, Robert, follow that truth. When we follow the good path, the path of Jesus, of Annalisa, the effect each of us has on this earth becomes thunderous in its own way."

"Yes, but must our redeemers always suffer and die to help humanity?" Avernis asked.

Roncalli sighed. "The forces on this plane trap us so deeply by the illusion of life. It takes suffering, death, and resurrection to shock or inspire us out of our ignorant slumber. Perhaps that's why remembrance of our true selves is only won by the blood of fallen angels."

After a quiet moment, Roncalli said, "One last thing before I leave. Teresa, you know that the Hebrew language had a code where each consonant was assigned a number, right?"

"Yes," Teresa said. "It's called gematria. They added up the numbers to reveal messages."

Roncalli gathered up O'Keefe's books. "Desmond noted that all the letters of Annalisa's name added up to one using the numerical coding system. One is the Hebrew number for God. Now, this could be coincidence. Other names can add up to one. But he observed another characteristic. The letter *A* was the only vowel assigned a number in the Hebrew system, and that number is one." Roncalli showed them O'Keefe's notations. "Look at the letters highlighted with their numerical values below. Annanlisa has three A's in her name, evenly spaced. There are three Alphas, designating God three times . . . "

A N N **A** L I S **A**
1   **1**   **1**

"I get it!" Teresa whispered. "The three aspects of God—Father, Son, and Holy Spirit! Her name not only adds up to the number of God but it also reveals the Trinity!"

Roncalli nodded. "God the Father and Christ the Son are known by all, but only the Gnostics named the Holy Spirit — Sophia — the feminine aspect of God who fell to the earth in order to rise again over many lifetimes and bring materiality into the realm of Spirit."

"Annalisa, the Holy Spirit rising," Avernis said. "It's still so hard to believe."

"Annalisa is the symbol of spirit rising in all of us. We're all one in essence, just separate in appearance," Roncalli said. "Whether or not you believe the story of the First Souls is a literal account of our lives, those books and our lives are still a metaphor for God's truth."

"Your Eminence," Teresa said, "you comforted us today, so let me comfort you. Saint Peter denied Christ three times. You doubted Annalisa, but you never denied her, not once."

"Ah," Roncalli sighed in gratitude. "Perhaps I've atoned for past mistakes. Think of all these wonders that have happened, and we are part of it. It would not have been the same if we had not been part of it. Focus on that fact. The rest we'll learn in time."

"Your Eminence, I love her with all my heart and pray for her every day," Teresa said.

Roncalli kissed her hand. "That is why she will live, I think. Your love and the love of millions will call her back to life. God responds to heartfelt love — and so does the pope."

Midnight arrived marking the end of the third day since the pope had been shot. While fingering his rosary, Roncalli heard Annalisa cry out in a drawling whisper: "Uuuncle!" and her eyes blinked open. "My Uncle Hakim is dead. I saw it."

"Yes," Roncalli said grasping her hand. "The authorities identified the man shot in Rome as your uncle. You saved him once despite what he did to you as a girl. We believe he died trying to save you. But we lost some very dear friends." She nodded her head. She knew. "I waited for you," Roncalli said. "I knew you'd come back today. He too rose on the third day."

Annalisa nodded as his comment transported her to another time. "But now God's foothold in this world must grow stronger, Pietro. The end comes soon, yet events must still unfold."

The end? Once Roncalli might have worried over such words, but now he wanted to see where all these years of mystery and wonder, of pain and of sorrow were leading them. He leaned toward Annalisa, clasped her hand, and said, "I am ready for whatever will come."

CHAPTER XCVIII

Fate doth weave by both the right hand and the left.
—Anonymous

Rome

Robert Avernis was walking through the Borghese Gardens thinking about all that Roncalli had told him when his vid-phone rang. It was his distant cousin, Ubaldo Deci. When Avernis had filled out all the forms and disclosures to get his job with the Company, his relation to Ubaldo Deci was a conspicuous omission. Ubaldo and Avernis' father, Donato, were second cousins.

As a young boy, Avernis had met Ubaldo on a trip to Sicily with his father, the only time Avernis had gone with him to the old country. Ubaldo was considerably older, and Avernis' recollections of his distant relative were not sharp. When Avernis became a teenager, his father mentioned Ubaldo's affiliation with the Sicilian mob. He was neither proud nor ashamed of it; he just spoke of it as a fact.

"What's going on, Ubaldo?" Avernis asked the face looking back at him on the phone.

"That matter you asked me to look into a while back," Deci said. "I have information. We should meet very soon."

When Roncalli had asked him for help on investigating the Church's financial loss, Avernis knew there was nothing he could do directly, but he immediately thought of Ubaldo. Ubaldo was an attorney, a consigliere for the Maniati family in Sicily. The Maniatis had tentacles everywhere, and Ubaldo straddled the line between the legitimate and the not-so-legitimate worlds. That made him well suited to gather information discreetly.

As luck would have it, Ubaldo's boss, Don Ippolito Maniati, had lost money in the Church financial scandal. His bank had pooled an investment with the Vatican to get a better return — what he got was a lot of red ink. When Ubaldo learned that Avernis might lead him to unraveling a fraud, he was only too grateful to help. The Maniatis were still hoping to recover their loss.

"I'm giving you the name of a cardinal we suspect," Avernis had told him. "Just get me information, not the details of how you obtained it, okay? Forgive me, Ubaldo, but you work in circles that would end my career if I were linked with them. No offense, but, to my bosses' way of thinking, if I hung around you, I'd have to arrest you."

"No offense taken," Deci laughed. "Leave it to me."

It now seemed that conversation had paid off. "Meet me in the outdoor cafe at the south end of the Villa Borghese. We can talk there," Avernis told his cousin.

When Deci arrived at the café, they seated themselves at a table where they could speak privately. "Okay, Ubaldo, what've you got?" Avernis asked.

"Tell me, Roberto, how is your Latin these days?"

"You're kidding, right?"

"Actually, I am quite serious." Deci produced a mini-disc player out of his briefcase. "Two men are speaking Latin on this disc. What they are discussing will be of great interest to you. I had the conversation transcribed into English." Deci handed him the transcript. "The speakers are Cardinal Van Kluysen and Bishop Alvaro Maria Delgado, leader of a Catholic secular order called Milites Domini."

"Very efficient," Avernis remarked. He read the translation as the disc played:

> **Van Kluysen:** With Mannheim out, the investigators are targeting me. She was supposed to die, damn it.
>
> **Alvaro:** What did you expect? You were in charge of finances. Just stay calm.
>
> **Van Kluysen:** Mannheim had the power to impede them while Clement was alive. No one ever expected to get this kind of pope. She does not care about bad publicity.
>
> **Alvaro:** Yes, we planned to have a different pope with whom we could deal.
>
> **Van Kluysen:** She has recovered and seems here to stay, but perhaps there is another way. We offer the money to her on the condition she stops the investigation.
>
> **Alvaro:** Not again, not now. It will raise more questions and sound like an admission.
>
> **Van Kluysen:** This pope wants money to support church-sponsored programs. Things have eased somewhat because people are giving again, but the Church is still in serious financial trouble. The price for the money is for her to step down.
>
> **Alvaro:** That will not work with this pope. Give up that idea. What of Mannheim?

Van Kluysen: Mannheim's power has greatly diminished since the woman became pope. He is desperate to have her out, but everything we planned has failed so far.
Alvaro: Be patient for now. You have already profited financially. Let that be your consolation. Do not panic and do something stupid.
Van Kluysen: But if she is not out, the investigation will go on.
Alvaro: Do not get panicky. I told you, it will be impossible to prove . . .

"This is the latest of several discs I've accumulated," Deci said.

"I read several things into this, all bad" Avernis said. "Give me some context here."

For the next forty-five minutes, Deci outlined the history of Milites Domini, the sinister, ultraconservative shadow organization with official Church sanction. He spoke of the many circumstantial links they had to several financial scandals in Europe, during which time they became major players on the world financial markets. He cited numerous mysterious deaths of individuals whose companies had been ruined by affiliation with the group.

With the precision of a lawyer — for despite his notorious client, that is what he was — Deci laid out his theory of how Milites conspired with Van Kluysen to defraud the Church out of hundreds of millions of dollars. It appeared they had been trying to use the Church's own money to buy control of the Vatican, "and my disc collection will prove it," Deci said.

"How did you come by these recordings?" Avernis asked, pointing to the disc player.

Deci shrugged. "We bugged Van Kluysen's office then, eventually, Delgado's phone in Spain."

"You guys have balls, bugging a cardinal's office," Avernis said.

Deci smiled. "You should hear the disc collection I have. They prove Alvaro and Van Kluysen's guilt. It took some time to assemble this information. This Alvaro is crazy. We even have him talking about using nuclear weapons."

That got Avernis' attention. "Listen, Ubaldo, whatever you've got it's not that simple. Your discs were obtained illegally, and all of them are inadmissible in any court. I suppose I should have known you people would go about it like this."

Deci gave him a searching stare. *"You people?"* he said sounding indignant. "Ah, I see. Listen, Roberto, neither I nor my clients was responsible for your father's death."

"Maybe not," Avernis shot back, "but they're cut from the same cloth, working in the shadows, reaching out and killing innocent people if it serves your ends."

Deci smiled and shook his head. "Such an idealist, a crusader. You speak of shadows and killing, yet you join with the CIA. Is that the acceptable way to gain justice for your father?"

Avernis sighed. "There's a difference, Ubaldo. I fight the antisocial, psychopathic scum that victimize people like my father."

Deci grunted. "Relative definitions, but I won't debate morality with you, Roberto. You came to me with a problem, now you criticize my methods . . . my successful methods, by the way."

"Point taken," Avernis said, considering Ubaldo's logic. "Now what about Alvaro and that nuclear bomb business?"

Deci opened his briefcase, pulled out a marked disc, and placed it in the palm playback device. Avernis heard two voices speaking in English. One had a Spanish accent; the other spoke perfect American English. It did not take long for the shock to set in. He swayed in his chair as if he were having a seizure. "Holy Mother of God," he whispered. He recognized the American's voice. It was his commander-in-chief, President John Davidson.

CHAPTER XCIX

That power that erring men call chance. — Milton

Rome

Two days later at 7:00 p.m., Avernis, as instructed by Deci, went to a flat in a rather seedy section of the city. He walked down the stairs to a basement apartment and knocked on the door. A burly, sullen man in a cap answered.

"I'm here to see Ubaldo Deci," Avernis said.

The man looked back into the room over his shoulder, then turned around and gave Avernis a curt nod to come in. As he entered the foyer, a man in a ski mask came down the dark corridor toward him. The man reached up to peel off his mask. It was Ubaldo.

The lawyer raised an index finger to his pursed lips. "I apologize for this," he said in a soft voice, holding the limp mask in his hand. "Our guest must not know my identity so that we may keep our advantage."

I can't believe I'm doing this, Avernis thought. *Having a Catholic cardinal kidnapped.* But what he had heard on Ubaldo's discs forced his hand, and he had to get more proof, more information. Avernis looked at the mask extended in Deci's hand, the same type of mask he had seen the N-FAC terrorists wear.

He inwardly cringed at the implications of accepting it and walking into that room. If he did that, there would be no turning back. Where would that leave him? What would that make him? But if ever he had a role to play in bringing truth and justice to light, this was it. The enormity of what he had heard on the Alvaro-Davidson tape eclipsed even the colossal crime perpetrated against the Church and, perhaps, the pope. There was an incalculable amount at stake, so if he had to bend the rules to get justice, well . . .

Deci chuckled. "Van Kluysen sang like Pavarotti, and you would not believe your ears. He's in such a state of panic he'd turn his own mother in to save himself."

Avernis took the ski mask from Deci's hand. "Okay, let's find a way to make this work."

The two men entered the sparse room, where a very nervous-looking cardinal sat in an old wooden chair. The warped floorboards creaked as they walked. The room's walls were yellowed and shedding wallpaper. The carpet was a musty mass of frayed magenta fibers. Deci sure knew how to pick the right environment for an occasion.

"Who are you?" Van Kluysen asked with a wavering voice as Avernis entered.

"I'm your only chance to get out of this with your skin intact," Avernis said. "If you tell me everything, and if I believe you, I'll help you to obtain the best possible outcome for yourself. If you cross me . . ." Avernis let the words dangle as he guided Van Kluysen's vision to the two masked thugs standing with folded arms in the corner of the room.

For the next hour, Avernis expertly grilled, cajoled, and threatened Van Kluysen into relating a tale that would put fiction to shame. Milites Domini, the cardinal explained, had seen Armageddon on the horizon — an imminent confrontation with Islam, neo-communism, and hordes of Asiatic barbarians. Internally, liberal forces were poisoning the Church and weakening the will of Christ's flock. The Church did not have the proper leadership and backbone to guide the West in the forthcoming struggle.

Bishop Alvaro had approached Van Kluysen with a proposition some years back when Van Kluysen was still prefect for Economic Affairs. If he would work with them on a scheme to divert Church funds into Milites' control, Alvaro promised that millions of dollars would reach the Van Kluysen family business accounts offshore of their native Belgium.

Milites' intention was not to steal from the Church, Van Kluysen self-servingly declared. They only wanted to use the Church's weakness to buy control of the papacy so they could prepare the Church for what needed to be done. Three things had sidetracked their plans. Clement refused their deal, and so did Mannheim, the secretary of state. Mannheim had his own plans for the papacy; he would never let Milites control him.

Did Mannheim know about the scam? No. He suspected Van Kluysen had received kickbacks for making risky investments, nothing more. He blocked investigation into the matter because he wanted no bad publicity while he schemed to become pope.

Their final and biggest setback was the totally unexpected election of Annalisa as pontiff. All indications at the time were that a conservative would be elected, and a conservative would have seen the wisdom of Milites' requests, especially with all that money attached to it. A more conservative pope would have bargained with Milites.

Annalisa was Milites' worst nightmare come true. A reformer of reformers who weakened Church traditions, a doctrinal heretic, a woman, and an African whose mother had been Muslim — it did not get much worse.

Avernis recalled disturbing words from Van Kluysen and Alvaro on the discs—Van Kluysen: "She was supposed to die" Alvaro: "We planned to have a different pope with whom we could deal." Did that mean they expected and hoped for a new pope if Annalisa died, or did it mean they actually planned the assassination? Given Milites' shady past, anything was possible. He took a shot in the dark. "When was the decision made to kill the pope?"

His question had a startling effect on the cardinal. Van Kluysen paled like white-washed canvas and swallowed so hard that the rolling in his throat looked like his tongue had balled up and dropped to his stomach. "What pope?" he sputtered.

What pope? Avernis repeated in his mind. *Oh, my God!* With great effort he kept his composure, mentally shelved his conclusion, and looked at the Belgian. "Who do you think? Pope Annalisa, of course."

"I-ah, wh-what are you talking about?" Van Kluysen stuttered in an effort to recover.

Now was the time to press hard and drive it home. "Come on, Cardinal," Avernis said with cold eyes boring through the skull of the trembling prelate. "I said you had better come clean with me. If you assume we're ignorant, you've made a fatal mistake."

He motioned to Deci, who in turn barked out a short command in Italian to his two henchmen. They both withdrew evilly long stilettos from their pockets.

Avernis clamped his hands on Van Kluysen's shoulders and put his face near the man. He caught a faint whiff of something acrid. It seemed the good cardinal had pissed in his cassock. "You're guilty as sin, Cardinal, and not just of greed. I'll make you a deal. Tell us all you know about the assassination and I'll promise you two things; you get out of here alive"—he jerked the Belgian's head back in the direction of the thugs to keep his meaning clear—"and I'll even try and help you legally, get you off lighter for cooperation."

"Who are you that you could do that?" Van Kluysen rasped out the question.

"Who I am is of no matter," Avernis snapped. "Your only concern is saying the right thing with your next words. Think carefully."

Tears welled up in the cardinal's eyes. His words were too choked to be intelligible.

"Get a grip on it, Cardinal," Avernis said. "Speak up!"

"I didn't do it! It was Mannheim!" the prelate blurted out in the terror of discovery, and then he began sobbing uncontrollably.

Mannheim? Not Milites Domini? Mannheim! Avernis was so taken aback by this revelation that it took all his will to control his facial muscles and hide his incredulity. He needed to maintain his posture as the all-knowing inquisitor. *Mannheim! Christ Almighty.*

"Was Milites Domini connected with the assassination plot in any way?" Avernis asked in an even voice that concealed his excitement.

The sobbing cardinal could not reply, but shook his head no to indicate his answer.

Nothing here is what it seems, Avernis thought. "Get him some water," he said to Deci.

They brought water to the cardinal. "Drink it," Avernis said. "Now pull yourself together and tell me everything. And I mean everything."

Van Kluysen slowly recounted the events leading up to the day of the assassination. Powerful Vatican cardinals had united in their belief that Annalisa was an Antichrist come to destroy the Church from within. They began discussing ways to remove her. They could not poison her because she was too young and healthy to die by seemingly natural causes.

As they labored over how to dispose of her, an answer fell into their laps. A bishop from Lagos, Ogunsanya by name, called Mannheim one day with an unusual story. A Nigerian terrorist had approached Ogunsanya claiming Annalisa as a mutual enemy. He said he would eliminate her if Ogunsanya found a way to get them close to her. Ogunsanya took the bait. He hated the pope for many reasons, but this was over his head. He called Mannheim, leader of the Vatican opposition against her. Mannheim dispatched Cardinal Trevi, who was already in Cairo on Church business, to fly to Lagos.

Trevi and Ogunsanya spoke with the terrorists. Though ostensible enemies, their mutual hatred of Annalisa created a pact made in hell. The cardinals' plan with the terrorists was now sealed. They agreed to arrange access to weapons within the Vatican for an attack on the pope. The terrorists in turn would furnish suicide assassins to do the actual killing. It was a perfect cover for the Vatican conspirators.

Everyone knew the Muslim extremists hated Annalisa's influence in Nigeria, and the assassins would leave no tales to be told. That cleared the cardinals of suspicion. They placed the killers among a group of visiting pilgrims. The cardinals planted weapons at specified locations behind Vatican security checkpoints. Van Kluysen divulged the names of the other conspirators: Mannheim, Tormada, LoPresti, Trevi, and Villendot. Another cardinal, DeGolia, had affiliations with the group but had not participated in the actual plot.

Avernis then wound the clock back to an earlier slip by Van Kluysen. "Now, Cardinal, there's more, isn't there? Tell us what you know of *Pope Clement's* death."

Van Kluysen shuddered. "Cle-Clement? I know nothing."

Avernis nodded, and the stiletto-wielding thugs inched toward the cardinal. "Come on, Cardinal. When I asked earlier if Milites tired to assassinate the pope, you asked, 'what pope?' Clement was the first pope to turn down your offer. You know more. Speak up or our deal is off along with some of your skin." The threats came easier now that Avernis had seen the depth of Van Kluysen's betrayal.

"I know nothing for certain," Van Kluysen blurted back. "Milites needed a pope who would make a deal. Clement died right after he refused them. Knowing what I do of Milites' reputation—people dying of heart attacks, I mean—I had suspicions, only suspicions. I swear that is all I know, all I wanted to know."

After the entire sordid tale had been told, Avernis and Deci retired into another room. Avernis' head was swimming and he felt sick to his stomach. "Jesus, Mary, and Joseph—these people are supposed to work on God's behalf?"

Deci had a smug, triumphant look on his face.

"Don't gloat yet, Ubaldo," Avernis told him. "We obtained all this information illegally. We have a live bomb in our hands, but what do we do with it?"

"That is your job, Roberto," Deci said. "We need a way to get action from legitimate authorities to recover my client's money . . . and the Church's too, of course."

"Yes, but what authorities?" Avernis asked. "The Italians? Interpol? My agency has no jurisdiction. What authorities?"

The two men sat and pondered for a while until Avernis snapped his fingers. "I have an idea. I want you to hold the cardinal here until I contact you. Not a hair on his head is to be touched, you understand?"

Deci readily agreed. "He's our proof and only link to two major scandals. We will guard him with our lives, rest assured."

"Okay. When I call, all I will tell you is where to come with the cardinal, understood?"

Deci nodded. "You did well in there, Roberto. You would have made a good Sicilian."

"I *am* a good Sicilian, Ubaldo, just a different kind. Now, keep the cardinal on ice until I call you," and with that, Avernis turned and left.

CHAPTER C

Justice is conscience, not a personal conscience but the conscience of the whole of humanity. —Alexander Solzhenitsyn

The Vatican City

It was past midnight when Avernis arrived at the Swiss Guard Station at the Porta Della Santa Anna. "Get me Cardinal Roncalli and Colonel Zugli on the phone immediately. This is an urgent matter related to Vatican Security."

The Guards made the call. They escorted Avernis inside the Vatican and ushered him into an office where Colonel Zugli and Cardinal Roncalli awaited him with heavy eyelids.

"Gentlemen," he said, "you'll probably want to be seated when you hear what I have to say," and he proceeded to tell them the entire fantastic tale that had unfolded in the last seventy-two hours. At times, Roncalli shut his eyes and nodded his head in agreement with certain statements as if he already knew the facts.

On several points pertaining to Mannheim in particular, Zugli could not believe what he was hearing, but Roncalli said, "It is true, Roald, do not ask me how I know, but I believe he is telling the truth."

Avernis then further shocked them with his suspicions about Clement's death and Alvaro's discussion of nuclear weapons. "I checked my government's records. The day that conversation occurred, the satellite scramblers went offline, otherwise the conversation between the president and Alvaro would not have come out. It's as if God were watching over us."

Hearing the tapes of Van Kluysen and Alvaro, and of Mannheim's role, Zugli had to give credence to the story. "All the pieces fit the gaps. A den of vipers," Zugli said, looking physically ill. He once took orders from those men.

"The problem," Avernis explained, "is that the information was illegally obtained, and if we turn Van Kluysen over to the regular authorities, he'd deny everything and get off. But there is one jurisdiction where that would not happen—the Vatican City."

Zugli and Roncalli agreed. "We are our own sovereign state, these men are all citizens of the Vatican, and the crime against the pope was committed entirely on Vatican soil," Roncalli said. "We have our own judicial system. The pope herself is technically the final judge." The eyes of all three men caught one another at the irony of that circumstance.

"We have the power to detain and arrest these people," Roncalli said. "Cases involving murder are customarily remanded to Italian authorities, but these are extraordinary circumstances, and we are not compelled to involve them."

"What about Alvaro and Milites Domini?" Zugli asked. "He's in Spain. How will we avoid involving the Spanish authorities?'

"I thought of that. Here's my idea," Avernis said. "Call Alvaro and tell him the Vatican would like to talk to him about arranging a loan. That will get his attention. Tell him the pope herself is requesting his presence. He will have to come here to address the issue. When he puts his foot over the threshold, arrest him. You'll then have all the guilty parties in one place under your control until we can figure out what to do."

The men agreed on Avernis' plan. He then he placed a phone call to Deci. At 3:30 a.m., Deci delivered Van Kluysen to the Vatican. Roncalli and Zugli had to listen a second time to the sordid story, this time from a fellow cardinal who would not look them in the eye as he spoke. If there were any lingering doubts about the truth, Van Kluysen dispelled them after he finished. He dropped to his knees in front of Roncalli to beg for forgiveness.

He was a pitiful figure. Roncalli offered the sobbing man the sacrament of confession, but what was said there and what penance was advised would always remain a secret.

Deci said, "I hope our role in this is not forgotten."

Roncalli said, "Signor Deci, if the Church recovers its money, you will recover yours. You have my word."

Deci looked at Avernis, who nodded. Satisfied, Deci left.

Two days later when Bishop Alvaro entered the Vatican, Roald Zugli personally arrested him. "I hear you are a chess master," he said to Alvaro.

The Spaniard glared at him under dark, baleful brows.

Zugli pulled a chess piece from his coat pocket. He held the black bishop under Alvaro's nose, dropped it to the ground, and stomped it with his boot. Alvaro looked at him quizzically. "Checkmate," Zugli said. "Now take this scum out of my sight," and he motioned for Alvaro to be led away.

All the conspirators in the greatest scandal in the Church history were now in the custody of Vatican security forces except Bishop Ogunsanya with whom they would deal with later. Roncalli, Zugli, and Avernis had conferred with the pope over the forty-eight-hour period. She seemed saddened rather than angered by the whole affair. She said she would make the decisions about the men personally.

When Milites officials in Spain were arrested, Zugli and Spanish security turned them by playing them off against Alvaro. They admitted that after Clement had refused to let Alvaro buy the Church, Alvaro had Clement poisoned to simulate a heart attack and clear the way for election of a more compliant pope.

Avernis participated in the interrogation of Alvaro, but only on matters concerning the American presidential elections. Zugli handled questions about the financial fraud and the death of Clement. When confronted with the incriminating evidence on Deci's recordings of him and Davidson discussing Iran, the admissions of his own subordinates on Clement's death, and Van Kluysen's confession on the Church money scandal, Alvaro knew he was in trouble. Still, he remained uncooperative. At the end of a thirty-six-hour grilling, Avernis asked for five minutes alone with Alvaro. He told him they had decided to turn him over to Don Ippolito Maniati's men for justice.

Hearing that broke Alvaro. In no way did he want to fall into the hands of the Italian Mafia. He made a taped confession of his influence on President Davidson's election and Davidson's premeditated promise to annihilate Iran. He also confessed to defrauding the Church and ordering the poisoning of Clement. The Vatican agreed to hand Alvaro over to the Italian government on condition of a special sealed tribunal.

Days later, Robert Avernis made preparations then flew to Washington, D.C. He met National Security Advisor Rachel Worth and played Ubaldo Deci's discs. He had placed copies of the discs with the Vatican and sympathetic sources inside the CIA. They would go public with the material should any "accidents" befall him. A shaking Ms. Worth then arranged the most important meeting of Avernis' life at a certain house on Pennsylvania Avenue.

After a pointed talk with Avernis, President Davidson said to him, "Of what crime am I accused? Breaking election laws? As a frontline agent, you of all people know terrorism is engulfing us. The only way to fight terror is greater terror. I acted in our defense. They will never stop until we show them we're willing to use the harshest means."

Avernis thought for a minute. "Sir," he said, "there is a better way, and the pope has shown it to us. Don't mistake her for the pacifists and liberals that led us into this mess. Those people are caught up in short-sighted secular ideologies that let them feel good about themselves and their 'humanity' but divorce them from solving the real problems. They're isolated from the usually negative consequences of their misguided actions because they always think they're acting for the betterment of the world."

"Oh? And just how is she different from them?" Davidson asked.

"The pope is acting from a balanced place, a spiritual place," Avernis replied. "She understands our need to defend ourselves, but she showed us that human beings are in transition. We can fight, defend, even kill if necessary, but still hold a spiritual ideal that seeks to abolish wars, fighting, and killing. If we keep that ideal strong, it will be our salvation, but it's a razor's edge not to give in to the hate."

Davidson looked at Avernis with skepticism and perplexity written on his face.

Avernis said, "You are just as blind as the people who got us into this global chaos. Your way, sir, was premeditated murder: death by ideology, not by necessity. You were going to commit indiscriminate murder at the first excuse you had. I suppose that in the end, your crime was dereliction of duty — not finding another way. I think you owe that to the people, sir. The government needs to step back. We have a chance now to build some bridges, people to people. It's a delicate process. I can't sit by and let your way destroy that. I will use the discs if I have to."

Davidson was shocked at how Avernis' words echoed those of his own wife. She once told him she begged God's forgiveness for not seeing another way. He waved Avernis out with his hand, slumped into his chair, and sat there looking like a very solitary figure.

It's in his hands now, Avernis thought.

CHAPTER CI

For those whom God to ruin has design' d, He fits for fate, and first destroys their mind. —John Dryden

The Vatican City

Pietro Roncalli waited with the guards in the anteroom of the great hall where, one by one, the pope passed judgment on the conspirators. The pope refused any security presence in the hall despite strong objections by Zugli. Even more surprising than that were the decisions she handed down to the criminals who had sought to slay her.

She pardoned DeGolia, as he had not actually been part of the assassination conspiracy.

Roncalli wondered what Tormada felt when he saw Annalisa in a wheelchair. He had personally planted the guns that shot her. Tormada was given the same option as LoPresti, Villendot, Van Kluysen, and Trevi — remain with the Church as a monk the remainder of his life or seek a living elsewhere. He chose to leave the Church, recalcitrant as ever.

"Though I can forgive those who sought to harm me, I cannot ignore the accusations surrounding the death of pope Clement," Annalisa said to a closed-mouthed Alvaro.

Annalisa ordered Alvaro held in the Vatican pending his handover to the Italian authorities. By agreement with Avernis, the Italian courts sealed the charges pertaining to Alvaro's dealings with President Davidson. This allowed Avernis to continue handling that situation his own way.

To avoid prosecution, Alvaro's underlings cooperated in turning over all Milites Domini assets to Church control, including the Vatican's defrauded money. Milites Domini leadership would resign, but the organization would continue with a new ethic and new guidance — no more brainwashing of members, dirty tricks, or fraudulent financial schemes. Annalisa promised to repay Maniati's bank. A satisfied Ubaldo Deci would recover his client's money. About Deci's involvement in breaking the case, Annalisa said to Avernis, "You see, in the end, even evil dances to the purpose of God."

Mannheim was the last of the conspirators to see the pope. She sat in her wheelchair looking at him in silence. For what seemed an eternity, they stared at each other. Finally, Mannheim growled between his teeth, "If you expect me to beg for mercy, you're wrong. I know what you are. Only the devil could have cheated me out of my rightful place. I was the one who had the faith, foresight, and steadfastness to preserve the Holy Mother Church, but now you destroy her, sitting on the throne of Saint Peter, masquerading as a beloved provider."

The pope did not reply, but she held his gaze as he ranted.

"The prophecies are right," Mannheim declared. "The Antichrist seeks to destroy the Church from within at the highest pinnacle." He pounded his fist on a nearby table in rage and frustration. "If you think I am afraid of being turned over to the Italian authorities, go ahead, I don't care. If after two thousand years we have not taught the world enough to recognize evil when it looks us in the eye, we don't deserve to survive."

Again, Annalisa waited. Finally, she said, "You think I am Satan," and her statement echoed from the walls. She wheeled toward Mannheim, never taking her eyes off his. When she was a few feet from him she said, "Does it surprise you that what you call God and the devil are one?" she asked.

Mannheim recoiled in horror. "There, the proof of blasphemy from your own mouth!" he said. "You would equate God with the devil?"

"Remember the words of Isaiah about your god," she said. "I am the Eternal, there is nothing else. I make the light and create darkness; I make peace and create evil."

Mannheim clenched his lips, and his body was rigid. He did not respond; she was trying to confuse him with tricks and gibberish.

Annalisa's gaze bore straight into him. "There is one True God, but He is beyond space and time. Everything has arisen from him, and, indeed, he allows light and darkness, but the god you worship is the one steeped in the shadow."

Mannheim sneered. "Judge me now and be done with it," he commanded. "I will listen to no more lies."

"YOU WILL LISTEN!" Annalisa said, "And not for my sake, but yours. God is everything, Heinrich. If our thoughts were always on the True God of love, there would be no evil, but we chose to place our thoughts elsewhere. We strayed so far, so very far. Our 'sin' is forgetfulness and divided attention, nothing more, nothing less. We plunged into a dark dimension and created false, dark gods. Now they create us. They shaped our world and we live in it, forgetting who we are. But we have the chance to bring light to this desolation if we overcome the darkness implanted within us."

Mannheim shook his head. "That is insanity."

"Yes, purposeful insanity," Annalisa said. "And see how it played out in your own life. You created and shaped the Church in your own image and it all went wrong because it was a flawed creation. You stayed blind to the real power above you, the power that leads to perfection. But our evil serves God's ends, you see? Evil brings forth the good in us. Every Caesar will draw forth a Jesus, every epoch of barbarism will give birth to an epoch of light. It all plays out under God's sight until the entirety of creation awakens in light."

"Exalting humanity's sinfulness *would* be one of your deceptions," Mannheim said.

Annalisa sighed. "You see humanity as a weak flower, Heinrich. You see it live a short while and die, so you say it is inferior, it dies because of sin. Yet you forget—a flower lives by its root. The root is hidden so the flower does not die; *it is born again and again.* God is the root; we are the flowers. We are of the same substance as God, and our souls are ever taking new forms until we realize our true nature."

Mannheim broke his silence and pointed the damning finger of his indignation at her. "You are saying that man is *consubstantial* with God? That is blasphemy!"

"God is consciousness and so are we," she replied. "Consciousness is energy directed by intelligence, Heinrich. That is the basis of creation. That is how God creates and how we create through Him. You misuse your creative gifts. You act as if God were a distant abstraction, a dogma or a theory of being. You gave up seeking the True God of all things and so you became a false god relying on your own intellect."

"Where do these blasphemous ideas come from if not the devil?" Mannheim shouted.

"They come from the one you worship as the Son, if you had but understood him," she replied.

"You talk of illusion, hah!" Mannheim snarled. "This world of sin is all too real. There is nothing simple, nothing elegant about it. It is war, a constant war of good and evil."

"No," Annalisa said. "That is the state of *your* mind, not of God's. Listen," Annalisa said in a calm, even voice. "At the heart of heaven, there is no war because there is total awareness and attention on God. The fall from grace was a shift in our consciousness. We chose to express our individuality over our oneness. We projected our awareness into physical bodies but our bodies overwhelmed us. Our 'sin' was getting lost within the confines of our skin. We came to believe that our *materiality* was our *reality.* Our sin was forgetting our oneness, letting our egos, not our higher selves, define our reality."

Mannheim covered his ears and shook his head. "Enough!" he cried, sounding anguished.

Annalisa wheeled toward him, clasped his elbows, and tore his hands from his ears. "I want you to remember! When we were one, we could not war on or hate one another."

Mannheim wrenched his hands from her grasp. "You know nothing of God and you are far from heaven!" he shouted.

Annalisa's expression, a poignant mixture of melancholy and patience, now became animated. "Yes, yes! We are all far from heaven, so far that the false gods of our diminished powers made this world a hell. But one True God rules over all. If we can conquer our illusions we can remember Him and make Him our reality again. He let us go this far for a purpose. We are the fingers of God touching the experience of the material world, giving Him individual expression to the farthest, most dense corners of creation. When we remember what we truly are we will realize that is an exalted state, not a sinful one."

"You wretched creature," Mannheim snarled. "Your day of punishment will come," and for the first time he looked neither proud nor haughty, but fatigued.

Annalisa patted her hand to her breast. "Punishment? Our souls are of God. We dreamed ourselves into these bodies, into this life. God would no more punish us for that than you would punish a child for dreaming, and how do you punish a dream?"

"Enough!" Mannheim said. "Pass your judgment. Why do you waste your words and blasphemies on me?"

"Because you are a great man worth saving," Annalisa said. "You were brave and steadfast, but your labors of courage and sacrifice were always for yourself and the Church, not the people. You loved the Church but forgot the people, and the Church is the people."

"Bah, don't lord your false righteousness over me," Mannheim said.

Annalisa's eyes cast down in sadness. "I have nothing to lord over you. You are a brilliant man, Heinrich, more brilliant than I am. And why am I pope and you are not?" she asked rhetorically, then sighed. "You were blinded by your own brilliance, blinded to higher possibilities above yourself. If there is a difference between you and me, it is that I realized my place, realized my insignificance. I humbled myself and stepped aside, but when I did, something far greater than both of us took hold."

Mannheim stood limp and still. A deep silence ensued before Annalisa said, "I never wanted the papacy, but it came to me, precisely because I did not want it. You wanted it for your pride and glory, and the more you sought it, the more it eluded you."

Mannheim looked puzzled. Annalisa's eyes searched out his soul. "Your attention was on yourself, my attention was on everyone but myself. Perhaps that is the lesson. Perhaps the greatest rewards come when we want them for others."

Mannheim's hands squeezed the cross hanging on his chest. "I should have led the Church through its darkest hour; instead, the one who would do us harm has us firmly in his grasp." His face twisted in anguish. The man realized his time had come and gone.

Then the pope reached out for the last time over the distance that separated her from the one who was once so high, once so promising in the ranks of the Church. She came within inches of the man who thought himself her mortal enemy. She reached out and clasped his hand; he was too startled to withdraw it.

"Be very careful now," she said in a tender voice scarcely above a whisper. "It is not for me to judge you, only to forgive you, and God forgives all of us, you see? But you have not yet judged yourself, and that judgement will be the most formidable one you face, I assure you. Go in peace and use your remaining days to forgive yourself. Take care . . . *Mannemius.*"

Mannheim stood frozen hearing that name, the very name she had called him in his recurring dream. He jerked his hand from her grasp. "Witch! Of all the judges of men, I have no need of forgiveness from *you,*" he said. He then turned his back on her, and as a king still enthroned, he walked the length of the room and through the door, never looking back. That was the last time he ever saw the woman who was once his pope, yet if he had turned but for a second, he would have seen her hands folded in prayer, and that prayer was for him.

On the way out of the hall, Mannheim encountered Roncalli in the anteroom. Still defiant, the German said, "Do not gloat, Cardinal, you of all people, the footservant for the heretic who has destroyed the Church and seeks to rule the world."

Roncalli replied by leaning forward and speaking into Mannheim's ear: "Be careful of the pride that deceives you. You bear the burden of all betrayers before you. The day you tried to kill her she was to announce her abdication."

Mannheim staggered backward. "You . . . you are lying."

"No," Roncalli replied. "You are blind," and he turned his back as the guards led Mannheim away.

CHAPTER CII

But the age of miracles hadn't passed. — Ira Gershwin

The Vatican City

It started in Rome when Pope Annalisa gave a globally televised news conference. When she spoke the words, *"I now lay down the ring of the fisherman and abdicate my office as pontiff of the Roman Church,"* one could almost hear a collective groan issuing from all corners of the earth. Never in memory had any public figure been so loved by so many.

And the pope then rose from her wheelchair and ignited pandemonium in the room. Even Cardinal Roncalli staggered at the sight.

"She walks! Oh, God, she walks!" the people cried. Many crossed themselves and fell to their knees, for they had all seen the pictures of her damaged spine.

"No! Do not bow before me; do not worship me," she said, and she walked forward into the crowd. "If you kneel before me in awe, so I kneel before you," and she did so, going to her knees right in the aisle amidst the gathered people. "Do not tempt me by separating me," she said with tears in her eyes. "As you see God in me, I see God in you.

"If you feel you are in a world you did not create, that has changed. You have evolved. You rose from animals by receiving the consciousness of the Holy Spirit. You lived through the pain of spirit awakening to the entrapment of flesh as the forces of this world oppressed and deluded you, and then you received the Word, the divine knowledge from the Christ and the other messengers of light.

"My legacy to you is this: each one of you must take responsibility for nurturing your spirit. Never rely on any authority to tell you what life is or is not. The knowledge of your divine origin is spreading; the illusion of helplessness is waning. If you approach life with love in your heart, desire to know God in your soul, and gratitude for what you have, you will open the channel to healing, to miracles, and to the secret that you have evolved to be cocreators of a new reality. One by one with God's grace you shall become superhuman.

"You see what I have done and you marvel, yet see what you have done. You have stopped war. You have expressed love and justice, patience and wisdom on a scale never seen before because you chose to think in an uncommon way. You chose to think with your God Mind and see yourselves not as Christian,

Muslim, or Jew but as *human.* We are all the children of God, and this is the time of miracles, for is it not written that 'what I have done ye shall do and greater?' Ye shall do greater! Remember that as you remember me."

And all present swore that at that moment, just as depicted in the icons of a Church, a light appeared around Annalisa's head as each person came forward to embrace her.

The week of the pope's abdication was a week of great events and miracles. If anyone doubted a new force now permeated the earth, they were not alive or had not yet been born.

That week, astounding news arrived from Carcassonne, France. Vatican archaeologists had uncovered the full Magdalene gospel in the exact area Annalisa had predicted. It was apparently written by Magdalene and another female disciple of Jesus named Tezrah. The documents astonished the scholars, for they showed an entirely new picture of an early church led by Magdalene before she was martyred at the hands of a Roman named *Mannemius.*

That week, Annalisa met with Cardinal Roncalli. She had looked sad when she first told him of her final conversation and warning to Mannheim. But now she stood at a window, the sunlight striking a marvelous glow in her eye, and she looked to the horizon with joy and wonder. She motioned Roncalli to come and hold her hand. "A new era has started, Pietro. Humanity is emerging from a cocoon to a new state of being; they are finally moving from blind faith to knowledge of their great power. They are learning to listen to their intuition, to pray and to heal others. It will take time, they will face challenges and backlash from the opposing forces, but each success shows them the true nature and reality of the Power Behind All."

"The true Church restored," Roncalli said. "I asked you of that when we first met."

"And I did not lie," Annalisa replied. "The secret Church was ever in the human heart."

He gazed with her into the distance, and upon a time he turned and asked her, "Who are you? Tell me one last time from your own lips that I may put aside all illusions."

She closed her eyes, and when she spoke her voice changed and the words came in an unknown tongue, but Roncalli understood. *"I remember the ink tide of darkness that covered the cosmos and the fear that distorts all vision and clarity of thought. Where is the light? Where is the Source and the Father of All? All is fallen into the shadow of my ignorance and error.*

"And when I saw the light, I moved toward it, and to my horror found it was a reflection of myself. For time uncounted I was alone, far from heaven, trapped by my ignorance and guilt. But now I see the irony of it all, for I and all who followed me were but the way God becomes conscious of Itself. Who am I, you ask? Why, I am you."

"Holy Sophia," Roncalli whispered in final recognition. "Spirit of my spirit."

"You will now lead them, Pietro, you will be pope," Annalisa said, now her own voice.

Roncalli looked at her with surprise and uncertainty. "You will lead the Church now," she told him. He tried to say something, but she raised her hand. "You are no longer the same person you once were. Any man willing to lay down his life for another has the moral authority to lead. You saved me for a work I was meant to do. You know that, and the world knows it. They will look up to you. You *will* lead. My work is done. Humanity is realizing its true nature, but their next steps must be on their own. Enough light illuminates, too much burns."

That week, as Annalisa predicted, the College of Cardinals elected Pietro Roncalli pope by acclamation, the first such vote in Vatican history. He took the title of Valentinus the First, the first American pope. His name surprised Church scholars. Valentinus was a Gnostic bishop of the second century who came within a hair's breath of becoming pope before the Gnostics were exiled then eradicated from the Church. A few remembered Valentinus was also the name of a former prefect of the Vatican Library, the mentor of the late Monsignor O'Keefe. Pope Valentinus would consolidate the work begun by Annalisa.

That week, President John Davidson announced he would step down from office for personal reasons. He retired from the public eye to his home in Kansas. The world would speculate for years on the cause of his resignation.

That week, Robert Avernis and Teresa Ferentinos announced their engagement.

That week, based on Van Kluysen's confessions, Washington took action against N-FAC. The Nigerians, outraged that the men who shot the pope lived in their country, finally helped. They let American Mobile Counterterror units into Nigeria. They grabbed Moustafa. He led them to his boss, Alhaji. Leo Dusayne and Avernis had the pleasure of watching the commandos take him out on infrared satellite video. They were starting to hit N-FAC field cells too. N-FAC was finished as a terrorist threat.

That week, on the final day, news came to the office of the new pope Valentinus. In a little village outside of Rome, on a small, verdant hillside below the monastery of Santo Stefano where Mannheim had lived a short time as a monk, a worker found the former cardinal's body hanging from a tree. A note pinned to his robe read:

> *Quo vadis, Domine?* Whither goest thou, Lord?
> So I follow, not in the shoes of the Fisherman, but
> in those of the lost Apostle. May God have mercy.

Pope Valentinus, upon hearing of the German's death, could only wonder. Mannheim and others had believed Annalisa to be the destroyer, not the builder, yet in the aftermath of Iran, at the height of her influence, Annalisa rejected all worldly power. Had Mannheim finally seen the light?

When he learned the contents of the German's dolorous death note, he heard the echo of Annalisa's final warning to Mannheim and his own parting words to the German. As for that admonition, perhaps, in the early morning solitude of contemplation, the proud former cardinal had finally faced that formidable judge of whom Annalisa had cautioned him.

CHAPTER CIII

Lord, how shall we be able to prophesy to those who request us . . . ?
— The Apocryphon of James

The Vatican City

Umberto Segri visited pope Valentinus in the papal study one afternoon with a copy of the Breverarium under his arm. "For the benefit of posterity, I have been annotating the prophecies in light of recent events." He set the heavy tome down with a thud on the table. "Many of us, not just the conspirators, worried Annalisa might be the Great Deceiver."

"And you were correct," Valentinus said. "The Great Deceiver, the Great Heretic—the prophecies were correct. She was the one, and the Church as we know it has fallen. What we did not understand was that it was an act of renewal, not evil."

Segri raised an eyebrow as he considered that thought. "Do you remember these passages?"

"THE SHE GOAT UNDER SATURN SHALL BE LED FOR SLAUGHTER BY THE SEVEN SINS.

BEFORE THE RESURRECTION, THE ENDING OF THE LINE SHALL LEAVE THE SHAKING DOME ON THE HILL.

PETRUS ROMANUS, THE BEGINNING OF THE END, SHALL CONFRONT THE BEAST WHO WILL OPEN THE BOX OF PANDORA.

THE DARK ONE WILL TRIUMPH AND LEGION WILL LIE UNDERFOOT; THE CHILDREN OF ABRAHAM REUNITE."

"I remember it quite well," Valentinus replied. "Again, I say the entire prophecy has been fulfilled. The she goat Annalisa, born under Capricorn, the sign of Saturn, was led for slaughter by the seven cardinals. Her resurrection? She was shot, pronounced dead, but lived."

"But the ending of the line and Petrus Romanus," Segri said. "What of that?"

"Petrus Romanus marked the ending of the line," Valentinus replied. "Petrus Romanus was the line of *male* popes and *male* clergy that Annalisa ended. She ended the line of old Church practices. She ended those lines because she was the *new beginning.*"

"Ah, and now the circle is complete," Segri observed. "*Petrus* is Latin for 'Peter,' *Pietro* in Italian. Petrus Romanus was indeed the last but also the first pope of the new line — *Pietro Roncalli.* How fitting! *The first pope, Peter of Rome sits again on a renewed throne!*"

Even Valentinus was awed. That double meaning had never entered his mind. Then, on reflection, he realized that Annalisa's life and the Gnostic prophecies were mirror images of the Breverarium predictions. It was a matter of perspective. Both had been accurate, but the Church prophecies reflected fear and imputed evil at the prospect of change and breaking of traditions. The Gnostic prophecies viewed the events as redemption and restoration of the true knowledge of the Christ spirit.

Segri continued his ruminations. "The Beast was Havenei, and Pandora's box was the release of the biological poison that killed him, those things seem clear," Segri said. "But what of the triumph of the Dark One and the children of Abraham reuniting?"

Valentinus smiled. "The children of Abraham — the Semitic nations of Israel and the Arab states — are now working out agreements to share resources. As for the Dark One, I think she did triumph. Annalisa, the Dark One, the first *black pope.* Her courage trampled the legions of war underfoot. The prophecy was predicting the advent of Pope Annalisa."

A chill raced through Segri's body. A truth inspired by the Almighty a thousand years ago had been staring them in the face, but only now came into focus. Segri folded his hands on the table, took a deep breath, and said, "I believe I am able to complete my annotations now." The two men then said prayers together, both aware that the workings of the Holy Spirit had surely been revealed in their lifetimes.

CHAPTER CIV

When one man dies, one chapter is not torn out of a book, but translated into a better language. —*John Donne*

The Vatican City

On Christmas Day, a phalanx of charcoal gray clouds massed along the outskirts of Rome and then marched forward, rolling over the city, containing her ancient walls, temples, and basilicas in a captivity few foreign conquerors had achieved over the centuries. The army of darkness then loosed its torrents of rain upon the Eternal City, and gusting winds whipped the rain into cutting ribbons of liquid that snaked through the empty streets and plazas. On this day, Pope Valentinus heard a knock at his door as he sat reading his Bible.

"Your Holiness," said the small female priest whose hand was extending a piece of paper. "Your Holiness," she repeated in a fading voice.

"Mother LaTourney? From Vatican Communications, is it not?"

She nodded in response to his question.

"What brings you such a distance to my door, Mother?"

Her eyes began to well up in tears as he took the paper from her hand. "Your Holiness," said the priest, and unable to find words, she bowed her head slightly, gestured to the paper in his hand, and bit down on her lower lip. She then turned and receded down the hall in silence. He closed the door and walked back to sit on his chair. Ripping peels of thunder tore at the sky as he opened the folded paper and read.

The note dropped to the floor from his nerveless hand. *She longs for the sweetness of holy oblivion.* Those words once spoken by his departed friend Desmond O'Keefe rushed back to numb him like a plunge through the ice of a wintry river's torrent—Annalisa was dead.

✠

"A-Amaaziing Grace! Ho-ow sweeet the sounnnd . . ."

That hymn, what a genius of inspiration it was, Valentinus thought. Most verses ended with *M* or *N* consonant sounds so the pauses were drawn out to fill every speck of brick and mortar, every aspect of body and soul, with sonorous, chanting vibrations. The plaintive sounds hummed in the ear and uplifted the spirit.

The music still clung to his soul as it had done for almost every waking minute since the news of her passing. Annalisa had loved the song since an elderly lady in a Harlem church had given a recording of it to her on her trip to America. How odd — a Protestant hymn, but one truly best sung in those old Catholic churches with the music vaulting to the high ceilings of heaven and the devotion reverberating from the enduring walls of stone.

Grieving people overflowed the basilica, spilling back into St. Peter's Square then spilling back again from the square to the streets, until it seemed that all humanity had become flakes of snow floating down here and there, there and here, to cover all the land in a blanket of mourning flesh.

They had filed into the basilica to the sound of the hymn, and it would play continuously until the memorial mass started. Loudspeakers carried the music to those standing outside. It was a beautiful Sunday, and as he listened to the lingering notes of the organ, Valentinus hearkened back to his first Sunday as a new priest. He remembered greeting his flock for mass amid the bells and music of his own small church.

That was another time; now he was the pope, and he would hold mass at the greatest cathedral in all Christendom. From behind specially erected screens, from an inconspicuous area where they could not see him, he had observed them entering earlier: Orthodox patriarchs, Protestant bishops, Jewish rabbis, Muslim imams, and even people from the Far East in saffron robes or white turbans.

And he, Valentinus, now pope, was to eulogize his friend and predecessor — but he had no eulogy prepared. He had been unable to find words to express his grief.

He sat alone, kneeling in a chapel behind the altar. His arms rested on the railing in front of him. His thumb and index finger pressed his eyes shut. A third finger had come to rest on one side of his face so that he could feel each breath of life entering his nostrils. The weight of his head rested on this trinity of fingers as it bowed in contemplation. Then, as if in answer to his need, a verse from the hymn leapt into his awareness:

"T'is grace hath brought me safe thus far, and grace will lead me hommme . . ."

There was his eulogy, right in the words of the music. This hymn she had loved so much was describing the meaning of her life. When we faltered in the darkness, had God through the ages not sent us light-bearers to lead us home?

She had come from Africa, home of the human race, surrounded by nature, unencumbered by the sophisticated barriers the Church had erected between humanity and God. With the thinnest of veils between her and the Supreme Being, she discerned God's motion and God's will; she accepted, she labored, she sacrificed, and she endured.

Annalisa's journey had ended, but she still spoke to him. She spoke of learning, self-mastery, and transcendence—she had been about transformation, and that was the key to her life. Her love and wisdom transmuted everything it touched for the betterment of humanity, and was that not the true hallmark of God's presence? That was why so many had come today from far and sundry places to honor her. She was one of those special souls who reaffirmed that God is with us, is *within* us. She reminded us that God expresses Himself through us with no boundaries but those we create for ourselves.

Roncalli's eyes closed and his body swayed gently, almost imperceptibly, as he reflected on the essence of his friend's life. Perhaps she touched us so because she was not a mere giver of knowledge—we already have all that there is to know sleeping inside us; he believed that now. No, she was, rather, a reminder, one of those loving gatekeepers who unlock the wretched prisons of our self-created ignorance. She helped us see who we really are, she encouraged us to become what we are meant to be; she pointed the way back to where we are meant to return.

Suddenly, Roncalli's dormant senses registered a vibration, and a rumbling took hold of his body until he thought another earthquake was shaking Rome. He was right. Another earthquake was shaking Rome, but not an aftershock of nature's destructive caprice—it was the congregation assembled in the basilica.

The people had started to sing and hum the music of "Amazing Grace," and then the people in the square followed them. Now, even those in the streets beyond picked up the hymn. The power of their collective voices was vibrating the walls of the basilica.

For a time too brief, she had been the heart of their lives. She was the dove that lit upon the shoulder of humanity, sang its song of joy, then flew to heaven to be embraced by the beckoning fingers of a billowing white cloud. Around a world electronically united, people watching the televised service across the globe started to sing the hymn in a reflex expression of pure love. And if it were true that angels hover over this earth, then surely their ethereal voices joined in the song that shook the heavens with a power of spirit not heard for two thousand years—

"A-Amaaziing grace ho-ow sweet the sound
tha-at saved a wretch li-ike me.
I once was lost, bu-ut now am found,
wa-as blind, bu-ut now I seeee . . ."

Now because so many had gathered for her in God's name, the awesome energy was too much. The emotion broke the pope down. It broke him down to the ground in joy and in sorrow, in gratitude and in tears. On his hands and his face, on the cold stone, it broke him down. All these things pushed on his heart, and he wept.

He knew her spirit was present and that death was no barrier. It was just . . . just the remembrance, the remembrance of having been with her in this life and the fact that he missed his friend. She had moved humanity to an unprecedented expression of love this poignant day, and he took comfort that a world once stretched by the power of such love would never regain its original dimensions.

In this world, he would miss her until the end of his days. He would miss her until they were reunited in that world beyond the grave, beyond the veil. He took comfort in the knowledge that she had gone to where she always wanted to be, and that this time, no man had laid killing hands on God's messenger. Then the pope shed his last tear; he said his personal farewell. He now had a multitude to face and a song of triumph to sing.

Valentinus left a single flower at the foot of the chapel, and ending his oblation, he rose to his feet. He turned and walked through the shroud that separated him from the fellowship of gathered souls, and he came around to the altar where the eyes of the world awaited him.

Sounds echoed softly off the massive stone walls of the basilica—people clearing their throats, wooden pews creaking under shifting bodies, and low rumblings of human grief. Valentinus felt himself melting into his audience so that when he spoke, he would speak with their minds and their feelings.

After conducting mass, he delivered his eulogy. At the outset, he paused for a moment in the pulpit, looking into the eyes of each person in the assembly, and just when his pausing bordered on being overlong, he spoke his first words—

"These," he said, "are the days of endless possibilities . . ."

And Valentinus then delivered a spontaneous eulogy for the small woman from Africa as if he had prepared for it all his life. And if the truth be known, he really had.

EPILOGUE

Our birth is but a sleep and a forgetting
The soul that rises with us, our life's star
Hath had elsewhere its setting
And cometh from afar;
Not in entire forgetfulness,
And not in utter nakedness,
But trailing clouds of glory do we come
From God, who is our home.
— William Wordsworth

A Ω

The words spoken by a small African woman were seen by millions, inscribed on a mausoleum below the Vatican, in a place reserved for the popes of two thousand years:

Oh, Intimate Stranger, Thy words I
heard burned deep within my mind,
Thy words of love for humankind:
Go tell my children that I wait,
go tell them they are not alone,
and never will it be too late,
go tell the wanderers, come home.
ANNALISA PONTIFEX MAXIMVS
AD 2028–2032

Many people over the years visited that mausoleum and prayed in the manner taught by the African pope whose body rested in the tomb. Children always asked questions about the woman whose likeness was carved onto the stone frame of the sepulcher. She was the only female depicted in effigy, and she looked so young. The children naturally asked how she died.

The adults often responded with a story that had been passed along, some say as fact, some say as lore, but, in any case, it was told like this:

Annalisa Basanjo, first female pope of the Catholic Church, died one Christmas morning not long after she had returned home from a great travail. A priest, Mother Ansanay, attended her as she rested upon her bed. Mother Ansanay was one of the women Annalisa had trained in the arts of prayer, meditation, and healing. She was also one of the first women to be ordained as a priest.

Ansanay's cherished ambition had been realized thanks to the slumbering woman in front of her. She gently woke Annalisa, who seemed to have been sleeping for days. When she inquired about bringing her food, Annalisa patted Ansanay's hand and said, "It is too early in the morning and too late in my life for that kind of nourishment," and then her eyes blinked shut again in sleep.

Then she said something so softly that Ansanay had to bend over and ask her to repeat it. Annalisa was gazing at some distant point above them. She gave a tired smile and said, *"These are the days of endless possibilities."* Then her eyes blinked shut again in sleep.

Mother Ansanay sat by her bedside wondering what she had meant. She marveled at how vibrant and healthy Annalisa had been looking even though she had not moved from her bed these past days. Despite the mother's protests, Ansanay decided that she would bring some tea to set out for Annalisa whenever she would awaken.

As it was, Ansanay was the last person to hear words from Annalisa's lips. In death, the expression on the pope's face seemed so alive, but the breath had left her body. And Ansanay then heard a heavenly choir she thought to be angelic, and she was not far wrong, for the voices issued from the children of the village. They had gathered outside the window to sing "Silent Night" to their beloved mother. As Ansanay moved the shutters of the window aside, the last words of the carol caressed the now still room: *"Sleep in heavenly peace, sleep in heavenly peace."*

Ansanay fought to contain her tears when the children asked if the pope had heard their song. She looked at the tranquil and radiant figure on the bed, then she turned back toward the eager faces and said, "Mother rests now children, but she has heard. Even in her sleep she heard because you sang from your hearts."

Some said that on her final day in that bed Annalisa performed her last miracle, willingly laying down her life because she had finished her work on this earth; she departed from what she called "this far land" to walk with God and so complete her soul's ambition.

There immediately ensued a massive movement worldwide to have her beatified and canonized as a saint; was anyone more deserving? But this was not to be, for in a note attached to her final epistle to pope Valentinus I, she requested never to be sanctified and asked him to remind people everywhere that each of them were expressions of the living God in equal measure.

It was rumored that she had written a secret epistle for her successor that spoke of mysteries and prophesied things to come. As Annalisa predicted, Roncalli, as the new pope, Valentinus, read her letter. He read it in awe, and he finally understood her admonition that it should not be made public. He complied with her wish that it not be given unto the churches until it had lain sealed for a hundred years.

And many marvelous and wonderful things did she say in that letter, but if all her thoughts were revealed, I suppose the whole world could not contain the beauty and the power therein.

A Ω

AUTHOR'S NOTE

This book, and the trilogy of which it is part, is about the *forces* that shape human experience. If we think of these forces in typical ways, we get very hung up. Differing beliefs about gods and goddesses, monotheism and polytheism, the spiritual and the psychological, the material and the paranormal, will always color our thoughts with ingrained preconceptions. But whether you are a believer or a materialist, a spiritualist or a psychologist, no one can deny there is a pattern of forces that affects our lives.

This world is full of challenges. Life is a story of our desires and the opposition to those desires. Opposition may come from other people or from circumstances and events, but I have never met a person who did not face obstacles, adversity, and suffering in his or her life. In fact, as humans, we are defined by the degree to which we overcome these challenges. At the end of the day, life is really a personal school or boot camp we attend for growth. Our human journey is the stuff of art, the core of religion, and the object of scientific inquiry.

But why isn't earth the easy paradise symbolized by the biblical Eden? Why is the material world different from the heaven so many of our religions envision, a beneficent place where earthly cares are shed? Christianity says original sin is the reason for our misery.

But another tradition exists that directly addresses the questions above. As I pursued spiritual matters throughout my life, it became apparent to me that certain threads interconnected the course of human spiritual history. From India and Asia through Persia and on into the Middle East and Europe, echoes of a universal wisdom appear in multifold traditions from Hinduism to Buddhism, Manichaeism, Greek philosophy, the Mediterranean mystery schools, and ultimately the three Abrahamic religions.

Like the Bible, this tradition, directly or indirectly and to a greater or lesser degree, speaks of a fall. This fall is really a change from a higher to lower state of awareness. But unlike the fall depicted in orthodox Judeo-Christian traditions, the fallen, according to this wisdom, are never really separated or different from that from which they have fallen away. Neither was the concept of sin attached to this event. The fall, though apparently a mistake, was ultimately intentional, because the Source and the fallen were one.

The Source—call it God, the One, the Monad—permeates everything. Therefore, the fall was an act of conscious self-limitation, a dispersing of one

Universal Consciousness into the appearance of many limited points of view. i.e. many human lives. This limitation to gain personal experience had consequences. Limitation means ignorance of the whole, and ignorance is a form of shadow. So, shadow and error were inherent in human experience. This is why offshoots of this tradition often describe the world as an illusion. Illusion means that human consciousness is separated from the reality of its oneness, not in fact but by misperception.

Central in the collective story of this universal tradition is the recognition that the universe, both seen and unseen, was shaped by intelligent forces. In physics, we have gravity, electro-magnetism, and the strong and weak nuclear forces. These unseen forces shape our physical world. But, according to the ancient wisdom, even these energies were controlled by higher forces that affected the human soul (also called the psyche) as well. Natural law had a mathematical precision, but the psychic world of the mind and soul was chaotic. It appeared to be subject to random chance and full of suffering. The order of natural law stood in stark contrast to the chaos of the human mind and soul — it was good and evil dwelling side-by-side. How is this duality possible when both the scientist and the religious believer instinctively sense a unity behind all things? The scientist searches for the holy grail of a grand unified field theory to unite all the natural forces. The religious person seeks God, and if God is everything, how can a loving god be the source of all the evil in the world? What kind of god toys with us by tempting us into evil with the gift of free will?

The Gnostic, or Western, branch of this ancient wisdom answers this question by telling us that God did not create the world — not exactly. There is one God, but God operated through intermediary energies or intelligences in the creation. Most major religions echo this belief in some form, even the ones most zealous about their monotheism. Christianity has the Christ and the Holy Spirit as well as the angels and devils they share in common with their Judaic and Islamic cousins. Islam has jinns. Hinduism and Buddhism have their gods and goddesses, each one differing in their intrinsic blend of light and shadow.

In keeping with the notion of intermediary forces, Gnostics believed the creator of the material world was not the One True God, but an inferior force, generated by the Source, but too far removed from it to create perfection. Think of how videos or CDs degrade in clarity with each successive copy and you have the general idea behind this notion. Thus we have the genesis of the rampant flaws and evil evident on the material plane of existence. The goal of the Gnostic was to attain the spiritual knowledge necessary to overcome these limiting forces that intervened between humanity and the True God at the root of all things.

Far fetched? Much needless conflict has occurred over the nature of God, for even the "monotheistic" religions believe in intermediary creative forces. At their roots, even the "polytheistic" religions believe that one Supreme Being manifested all. These religions may use differing names for the intermediary forces, but like the universal spiritual tradition, they too hold that unseen intelligences play a great role in human life. Also, most religions recognize that the various non-material powers are not entirely beneficial to human development. Thus we have the concepts of devils, jinns, and evil spirits—in other words, retardant forces. Gnostics and their myths accounted for the fact that the further the manifested forces were from the Source, the more "shadow" they contained. Their distinction between the immediate Creator God and the "hidden" True God is a clear explanation for the dichotomy between the flawed material world and the perfection we are always told that God truly represents.

Gnosticism was one of many ways ancients interpreted the Christian experience, but it was not the interpretation accepted by the majority of bishops. Heresy, like history, is defined by the victorious, and so Gnosticism was labeled heresy. Several themes in this book are a combination of certain Gnostic traditions, my own meditations, and other mystical sources. It does not purport to contain "the truth"—how presumptuous would that be? It does seek to present compelling possibilities for consideration that may help others gain a new perspective on their own spiritual growth.

Gnosticism was not monolithic. There were varieties of belief. For those interested, the works of Dr. Elaine Pagels present some of the most accessible scholarly writings on the topic. Despite their differences and the fact that they culturally or religiously identified with differing religious traditions, Gnostics were distinguished by several core beliefs. Their most central conviction was that *spirit, via the human soul, is trapped in a material dimension into which it keeps incarnating until awakened by the acquisition of esoteric knowledge gained from the guarded teachings of divinely inspired beings like Jesus of Nazareth.* This knowledge had to be verified in practice by study, meditation, and contemplation until each person attained a subjective experience—call it a psychic awakening, if you will—that allowed them to overcome the intervening forces of opposition. It showed them the oneness behind all and their place in it. Yes, that Buddhist-sounding orientation is how many Christians thought over two thousand years ago.

An undercurrent of the Gnostic tradition was a variety of *dispensationalism.* This concept recognizes that every revealed instance of enlightenment is eventually overtaken by ignorance. So, God dispenses revelations in waves through different prophets when most needed to keep reminding humanity of their true spiritual nature. Thus in the great Indian epic the *Mahabarata* we have the Hindu deity Krishna saying: "*When Righteousness Declines . . . when Wickedness Is strong, I incarnate from age to age, and take Visible shape, and move among men, Supporting the good, thrusting back evil, And setting Virtue on her seat again.*"

The Gnostics, who were among the very first to embrace Christianity, understood Jesus' teachings as part of that continuity of revelation, the highest and clearest revelation of the ancient tradition. Certainly, the earliest sayings of Jesus, particularly in the gnostically oriented Gospel of Thomas, support this contention. Even the canonical gospels, when read carefully, demonstrate the affinity of Jesus' teachings with the ancient tradition.

How can these obscure revelations from the past help us today? How can one practically apply these teachings in his or her life? *Apperception* is a term that means taking observations and relating them to past experience. In effect, we process our beliefs according to the weight of past sensory and emotional experience, and that is how we see the world. An even less efficient filter of reality is adopting the perceptions, ideas, and dogmas of others and taking these beliefs on faith.

To this the Gnostics would say, "Hold on. Don't take anything on faith until you have tested its truth by your own experience." And by the way, they didn't mean ordinary sensory and emotional experience. They meant experience gathered from deep meditative states where the senses and emotions take a backseat to transcendental perceptions, states similar to those experienced by the prophets when they had their revelations. Yes, you can reach such states to greater or lesser degrees if it's important enough to you. If you seek with your heart and mind you will eventually have a transformative experience. The problem is that most people have too many distractions and too little desire.

The orthodox version of Christianity that prevails unto this day represented a substantive break in the continuity of the ancient universal spiritual tradition. The adherents of the old spirituality in their many forms and permutations were eventually put down by the Church as pagans or heretics. The inherent feminine characteristics of the old spirituality were also casualties of the orthodox domination. These tragic losses underpin much of the thematic content of this book.

It's indicative that in this age of self-advocacy, the thing we least self-advocate is our spiritual life. Most Western societies seem caught between the smug, cynical smog of secular materialism and an equally dulling reliance on old religious dogmas. Neither of these paths provide direct experience or real internalization of extraordinary truths.

Annalisa's way espouses personal spiritual responsibility. She does not believe original sin was incurred by Adam and Eve and passed on to us like a cursed inheritance. She believes each of us creates and perpetuates our own "sin" (the actual meaning of which is "error") and that error is simply ignorance, a forgetting of or disbelief in the original higher state from which the human soul descended. If we were not so fixated on this world of imperfection we would open our eyes to that state of bliss known as heaven. That is our error. We chose to be here, in this state of misperception; we must choose to work our way out by developing more accurate perceptions, in effect, by seeing through new spiritual eyes.

Annalisa feels we all have divine potential within us since we are all projections of the Divine Unity. We are all capable of changing, of healing, of helping others, and all these things are miracles. Spiritual presence is like a 24/7 radio frequency but to find it, you have to spend time tuning the dial, and most of us don't make that time. We are busy with work, family, and the pressures of everyday life. But, unless we dedicate a portion of each day to study, prayer, meditation, and contemplation, we will keep stumbling along in darkness. Spiritual responsibility requires effort, but the rewards are great.

At some point in our meditative practice we build up a critical mass of spiritual energy. Guidance then comes in the form of information gained in dreams, feelings, hunches, and synchronous experiences. New directions become apparent, and miracles start to happen. What are miracles? Hollywood-type miracles do happen, but miracles are really changes of seemingly locked-in patterns. Alcoholics or dope addicts kick their habit. The depressed start to cope without drugs, a long-term illness goes into remission, war and conflict take a detour toward peace—all these events are miracles where habitual patterns that are negative and seem apparent give way to new patterns that are positive despite seeming unlikely.

It's unfortunate that books like this will inevitably be viewed as attacks on their beliefs by the Church and by people who identify themselves as fundamentalists. I can only tell my friends of such beliefs that this is more in their own minds than in my intentions. If Annalisa could step out of these pages to talk to you, she would tell you she takes your spiritual beliefs quite seriously regardless of your religion or spiritual orientation.

Annalisa is a Christian. She accepts the birth, crucifixion, and resurrection of the Christ. Where Annalisa differs from traditional Christianity is that she sees religion not as a static set of beliefs and practices cast in stone, but as a continual process of personal growth. She sees scripture as a point of departure, but does not view it as a four-walled enclosure within which an individual is eternally bound.

The problem here is soul growth being tracked or boxed into a commonly accepted belief system like a loudspeaker drilling away at people in a locked room. Spiritual awareness, like any other form of growth, is born from accepting challenges. Dogmas and doctrines are to be learned, understood, and critically tested in the personal growth process, not to be blindly accepted as the final word.

Some will say this book is meant to confuse or lead Christians or other religionists astray. These are often the people operating the loudspeakers in the "four walls" metaphor above. Please give people more credit. Those who read this book with prejudice will think that it is rubbish and will not be "led astray." But, those who are open to alternate perspectives will take what they need from the book for their own spiritual evolution. Annalisa did not seek to create a new religion. She is a Christian who does not seek to destroy or bash the Church from without, but to renew its vision from within, all with the caveat that the individual is free to make up his or her mind as to what nuances of belief to accept. Many fear such freedom would destroy the Church as it is—Annalisa obviously felt the opposite. If all of us have the divine within us, we are all the same, and ultimately, we all end up in the same place regardless of the different paths we take.

Though the Church and other religions have much of value in their religious and intellectual history, most organized religions stop short in the process of spiritual growth. The key word here is *process.* Organized religions have packaged their doctrines and traditions. They encourage people to adhere to the party line. If that were not true, we wouldn't have so many religious conflicts where each side proclaims the certainty of its righteousness. Though mainstream teachings can be beneficial if used with some judgment, they also tend to fix a person's spiritual growth by insistence on adhering to dogma. Thereby, they deter people from pursuing what might amount to a higher personal vision gained in the contemplation of their own being.

If anything, I hope this book encourages people to take charge of their own spiritual life as much as you take charge of your family or financial life. Don't blindly believe anyone else (author included), but respectfully adopt ideas provisionally until you prove or disprove them in your own spiritual experience. Remember though, your answers will come in symbols, dreams, and actual events in your life, so be alert. No easy-to-identify commands like your grade-school principal telling you what to do next over the PA system. Sorry. That's for the people trapped in the four walls.

A word about this book's source material—all the quoted Gnostic gospels are actual historical documents. O'Keefe's hidden Gnostic texts are fictional, as is the Magdalene Gospel (although there is an actual gospel of Mary Magdalene from the Nag Hammadi find). The fictional gospels in the book are my distillation of compiled Gnostic writings. Again, there was no single organized group called Gnostics. Gnostics held many nuanced shades of belief, but their most prominent common tenet was that personal knowledge of (not faith in) the divine is the path to salvation from a world that traps souls in the slumber of unreality. So, Gnostics might be called the seekers from within, which is where Jesus proclaimed we would find the Kingdom of God.

There are large gaps in both biblical and Gnostic history. Where such ellipses existed, I have tried to make reasonable interpolations to or extrapolations from existing material. In some places information channeled from my own meditations was employed. In doing this I believe I am keeping in a tradition used by all biblical writers, Gnostic or Orthodox, consciously or unconsciously, who, to some extent, tap into archetypical stories and symbols to impart intuited spiritual truths.

If, in any way, this story inspires you to examine your spirituality (whatever that means for you) and you act on that feeling, it will have served its purpose. Please watch for the sequel to *Pope Annalisa,* entitled *The Thirteenth Disciple*, where the origin of the First Souls and the mystical teachings is further revealed in the life of Mary Magdalene and the characters of Roncalli, Teresa, and Robert.

POPE *Annalisa*

BOOK ONE OF THE FIRST SOULS TRILOGY

Visit POPEANNALISA.COM
for background information on the book and
The First Souls Trilogy. Learn what Pope Annalisa has
in common with quantum physics, molecular biology,
and Jungian depth psychology.